THE FRONT

PART 2: ROGUE CASTES

EPISODE 4

REBELLION

RYK BROWN

The Frontiers Saga Part 2: Rogue Castes
Episode #4: Rebellion

Dedicated to Bradley Haddix
February 1955 – February 2017
Without your son's talents, the world shared on these pages would not be as vivid.

CHAPTER ONE

A swell of emotion washed over Nathan as the words echoed in his mind. *Aurora... Arriving.* It seemed like only yesterday that he had left her decks and turned himself over to the Jung.

To Nathan, it had been just over six weeks ago. Six very long weeks, which had, at first, been spent in a Jung medical facility while Jung and Corinairan nanites waged an agonizing war inside of him. Then, in a prison cell, hauled out to be displayed for all the Jung citizens to see as he stood trial for his crimes against their empire. The last thing he remembered was taking his own life, so that Jessica would not have to carry the guilt with her.

Or was it...

In all the excitement, he had not had a chance to think things through... To sort things out, inside his own head. He was Nathan... Nathan Scott, of the planet Earth. But he was also Connor Tuplo, of the planet Rakuen... Which seemed quite odd to him, as he didn't even know where Rakuen was.

But he did. Or Connor did... Which meant Nathan did... It was all very confusing.

"Nathan," Jessica whispered, nudging him gently as she stood beside him at the bottom of the Seiiki's ramp.

Nathan realized he had slipped into his own little world inside his head, tuning out everything around him. As he snapped out of it, he realized that everyone in the massive hangar bay was standing at attention, their right hands up at their temples saluting... *To him.*

It was both a familiar and unfamiliar feeling. But

part of him instinctively knew what to do. He stiffened up, trying his best to stand tall and erect, and raised his hand to return the salute. He imagined he had done so in perfect military fashion. But something in the back of his mind told him otherwise.

"Welcome back, Captain," Cameron said, finishing her salute and stepping forward to give him a hug.

"Thanks," Nathan replied, his voice still hoarse and barely audible. He spotted Vladimir, behind and slightly to the right of Cameron. The big, bushy-haired Russian looked like he might start crying at any moment. Nathan took a careful step forward, the subsiding adrenaline from the morning's events leaving him even more unsteady than when he had first awakened in his new body. He opened his arms for his old friend, who eagerly embraced him.

"I'm so happy to see you," Vladimir said as he wrapped his arms around Nathan.

"Easy, there, big fella," Jessica warned Vladimir. "He's only been alive for about twenty minutes now, so he's a little on the weak side."

"What?" Cameron said, suddenly confused.

Jessica glanced over at one of the med-tech teams standing by and signaled to them. "We need a gurney over here!"

"No, that's okay," Nathan insisted in a scratchy, but confident, voice. "I can walk."

"Are you sure?" Jessica asked, unconvinced.

"I walked out of that lab, didn't I?"

"With our help," Jessica reminded him.

Nathan looked at her, determination in his eyes. "I want to walk."

"The captain requires medical attention," General Telles insisted as he approached from the open transfer airlock on the starboard side of the hangar bay.

"Of course," Cameron agreed, still unsure of what was going on.

"He should be kept in isolation, as well," Michi added, stepping out from behind Jessica.

Cameron looked at Michi curiously.

"It's okay," Jessica told Cameron, noticing her concerned look. "This is Doctor Sato. She's been taking care of him," Jessica explained as she and Marcus remained on either side of Nathan to help him across the bay.

Cameron stepped aside, looking confused, as they walked past her toward the forward end of the bay. "What's going on here?" she asked, looking at General Telles. "What did she mean by 'he's only been alive for twenty minutes?'"

"I will explain everything to you," General Telles assured her. "But, first, you must take measures to ensure that the Dusahn cannot pursue this ship. I cannot allow them to follow us back to the Glendanon."

"The Glendanon?" Cameron asked. "How could they possibly..."

"Do you have jump-pursuit evasion tactics?" the general asked.

"No," Cameron replied. "We've never needed them."

"Uh, we've worked out a few tricks," Josh said, stepping down off the Seiiki's ramp.

"Nice to see you again, Josh," Cameron said, "but I think we can figure it out."

"It might be prudent to allow Mister Hayes and..."

"This isn't the same ship it was seven years ago," Cameron insisted, cutting General Telles off mid-sentence. She wasn't about to let anyone tell her how to run her ship, not even someone with the general's experience and expertise.

"We're not suggesting that we fly her, Captain," Loki added. "But we can give your people some very effective pursuit evasion maneuvers that have already proven effective against the Dusahn."

"The Dusahn are not only adept at tracking jump ships, but they are quite aggressive, as well," General Telles warned. "If you expect me to allow you to rendezvous with the Glendanon, then I must insist that you follow our evasion protocols."

"This is our part of the galaxy, Cap'n," Josh told her. "We know what we're doing."

Cameron looked at General Telles, noting his usual, confident demeanor. She then looked at Loki, whom she had always found to be an honest, well mannered, trustworthy, young man, with solid navigational and piloting skills. Then she looked at Josh, who had the same cocky, smug, little smile on his face, just like on the first day she had met him back in the rings of Haven. "I can't believe I'm agreeing to this," she said with a sigh. She looked at one of the security officers nearby. "Show them to the bridge."

"We know the way," Josh explained. "Unless, of course, you changed that, too," he added, looking around a hangar bay that was considerably different than he originally remembered.

Loki nudged Josh to follow the security officer, and both of them fell in behind the man.

"You've got a lot of explaining to do," Cameron told General Telles as she, Vladimir, and the general followed Josh and Loki to the exit.

"I will explain everything," the general promised, "once we are safely under way."

* * *

Admiral Galiardi stood at the window that overlooked the central plaza of Port Terra. It had taken nearly two years to complete the facility in the southern region of what was once the Karuzara asteroid, the first six months of which had been spent excavating the massive cavern where the complex was later constructed. The trees and gardens at the center of the complex had grown nicely over the years, and with the massive, curved projection dome over the top of the cavern, visitors were hard-pressed to say that they were not on the surface of the world that the facility orbited.

Like all the other facilities bordering Port Terra's central courtyard, Alliance Fleet Command had been built into the sides of the cavern, with her facades sticking out just enough to give the appearance that the cave continued far beyond its view from central plaza. In fact, even from the top floors, where his office resided, it was impossible to see where the buildings on the far side connected with the walls. So complete was the illusion, that the admiral often found himself spending weeks at a time without going back down to the surface.

Commander Macklay entered from the door connecting the admiral's office to the Alliance Command Center next door. "It took some doing, but we finally got confirmation," the commander said, holding up a data pad. "Just as you suspected, there was a message carried on the last jump comm-drone from the Ghatazhak. One not meant for us."

Admiral Galiardi turned away from the window to face his subordinate. "Then?"

"You were right. The message went to Winnipeg," the commander said. "Not directly, of course. It went through about twenty forwarding e-message addresses first, but eventually it ended up at the Department of Land Management."

Admiral Galiardi looked surprised.

"At which point, the comms tech there put the message on a data chip and had it couriered to the office of Miranda Scott-Thornton."

"That was too easy," the admiral decided.

"Not entirely," the commander corrected. "There was no official record of the message being couriered."

"Then how did you learn of it?"

"There was also no record of the message's disposition. It just *disappeared.* One of the techs in that office is a Fleet reservist. We promised not to activate him in exchange for running an audit on the message logs. Then, when a message turned up missing, we pushed him even harder, and got him to find out where the message went. He *really* doesn't want to get activated."

"Perhaps he will be of use later?"

"Maybe, but you'd have to be pretty stupid to route covert messages through the same office more than once or twice. We'll keep him on the hook, regardless."

"Good work," the admiral said. "You *were* careful to ensure that he tells no one of our inquiries."

"It was made quite clear by his handler, Admiral."

Admiral Galiardi sighed as he moved to his desk chair. "Still, it is not evidence that the two events are connected."

"Perhaps not conclusively," the commander agreed as he took a seat across the desk from the admiral. "However, the next day, Miss Scott-Thornton took a personal day. As you know, she is on our watch list. She did not spend that day at home."

"Where did she go?" the admiral asked, curious.

"All we know is that she went to the Winnipeg airport, then returned home about five hours later."

"Was she at the airport the entire time?"

"No way to know," the commander admitted. "There are dozens of private shuttle services at that airport, with hundreds of flights per day. More than fifty small shuttles departed and arrived during that time, and more than half of them were round-trips. And half of those did not file flight plans and were not tracked by IATC."

"So, how does that give us anything?" the admiral wondered.

"The next day, Lieutenant Commander Melei Chen, a medical doctor on reserve status who was due to be activated and assigned as the Chennai's CMO, was reassigned as the *Aurora's* chief medical officer."

"I remember her," the admiral said. "She served with Taylor on the Aurora during their first mission. Maybe Captain Taylor requested her?"

"Nope," the commander replied. "The request was made by the director of fleet personnel, Rear Admiral Kovacic. Who, I might add, was once Captain Taylor's executive officer aboard the Celestia. Turns out, he and Doctor Chen had a little thing going back when the Aurora was helping to rebuild the Celestia, just after the liberation of Earth."

"Maybe he was just doing a favor for an old girlfriend?" the admiral suggested.

"Maybe," Commander Macklay admitted, "but he didn't get any calls from her, and I'm pretty sure he doesn't regularly look at the assignment rosters."

"Did he get *any* calls that day?"

"Plenty, four of which were from civilian comm-exchanges. We've identified two of them, but the other two were bounced all over the place, most likely on purpose. So, the president's daughter gets a covert message from the Ghatazhak and takes the next day off. On that same day, Kovacic reassigns Doctor Chen to the Aurora. Two days later, the Aurora departs for the Pentaurus sector."

"Supposition," the admiral argued. "Coincidence does not prove cause and effect."

"No, but I'll bet if we turn the heat up on him, Kovacic will give up the name of the caller. After all, Dumar gave him both his position and rank. He's one of the few you *didn't* replace when you took command. And we all know what a cushy position it is, what with all the wealthy and powerful wanting favors for their sons and daughters."

"Better that we don't tip anyone off at this point," the admiral decided.

"But without proof..."

"Sometimes speculation is more powerful than proof," the admiral explained.

"But, Admiral, if the President of Earth is undermining the decisions of the Alliance Council and acting counter to your security recommendations, especially when the entire Sol sector is on alert and the Jung threat is at its highest... Those are *treasonous* acts, sir. Surely, you have the right to act on them."

"Even if Kovacic told you that Miss Scott-Thornton called him and requested the transfer, and even if she admitted that she asked Lieutenant Commander Chen to give a message to Captain Taylor requesting that she disobey orders and go to the Pentaurus cluster, the president's daughter would simply fall on her sword to protect her father." Admiral Galiardi thought for a moment. "No, we cannot take action on this, at least not yet. However, there is value in this information. At least, now, I know that I have been right. The Scott administration cannot be trusted to protect the people of Earth."

The seriousness of the admiral's statement struck the commander, although he tried not to show it. "What is our next step?"

"I take it you trust those who have dug up this information for us?" the admiral asked.

"Of course," the commander replied.

"Keep the circle of those you trust as small as possible," the admiral warned him. "There is a chance that we will have to take actions that will be controversial, and we must be sure of the loyalties of those under us."

"What is it you plan to do, Admiral?"

"My job, Commander," Admiral Galiardi replied. "Same as you."

* * *

"Captain on the bridge!" the guard at the Aurora's port entrance announced as Cameron entered. General Telles followed her in, with Josh and Loki two steps behind.

"Report," Cameron requested as she headed for the command chair at the center of the bridge.

"We're currently half a light year out," Commander Kaplan replied, standing from the command chair and stepping aside to make room for her captain, "four point five light hours off the primary shipping route between Darvano and Savoy. The ship is still at general quarters, and all weapons stand ready. The first of our Eagles have just jumped in and are inbound for landing. We are expecting the rest of our birds shortly."

"I've got the conn, Commander."

"Yes, sir. I'll return to combat," Commander Kaplan replied, taking a moment to cast a suspicious eye on each of their visitors. "Gentlemen."

"Holy crap," Josh muttered, possibly a bit louder than he had thought. His eyes widened as he took in the updated Aurora bridge.

"Things have changed," Loki added.

"Like I said," Cameron told them as she led them to the center of the bridge. "It's not the same Aurora you two piloted nine years ago."

"Talk about information overload..."

"That's an understatement," Loki muttered.

"Captain, the sooner we get started..." General Telles reminded her.

"Of course," Cameron replied. "Lieutenant Dinev, Ensign Bickle; Mister Hayes and Mister Sheehan have developed maneuvers designed to prevent the Dusahn from tracking jump ships. At the behest of General Telles, I would like you to use them...for now."

"Yes, sir," the helmsman, Lieutenant Dinev, replied.

"Hi, there," Josh said, stepping up to the lieutenant with a lecherous smile on his face. "Josh Hayes, chief pilot of the Seiiki, and you are?"

"Josh," Cameron warned him.

"What?"

"Loki Sheehan," Loki said, reaching out to shake the navigator's hand.

"Pol Bickle," the young ensign introduced himself. "So, what have you got?"

"It's pretty simple, really," Loki explained. "It's

just an algorithm I developed that pretty much guarantees you never make the same maneuver twice in any series, and maximizes the odds against the Dusahn being able to pick up your old light in time to catch up to you."

"Nice," Ensign Bickle replied, watching Loki key the algorithm into the navigation console for him.

"Is that all you've got?" Lieutenant Dinev quipped at Josh. "A little math?"

"He does the math," Josh replied, nodding toward Loki. "I'm the one doin' the yankin' and crankin'," he added with a wink, "if you know what I mean."

"Why does that not surprise me," Lieutenant Dinev said under her breath. She watched the nav data being drawn out on the see-through glass display in front of her station as Loki typed in the algorithm. "I don't think we can make those turns, Captain," she warned. "Not while staying within our performance envelope."

"Performance envelope?" Josh laughed. "Are you kidding me? This ship can make the turns... trust me. You just have to boost the power to your maneuvering thrusters and kick in a little decel thrust on the inside of your turns. And, if that ain't enough, add your docking thrusters in to the outside at full power."

"Docking thrusters?" the lieutenant questioned in shock, finding his idea laughable. "You're joking, right?"

"Every little bit helps, sweetie. And I never joke about flyin'. It's what I do."

Lieutenant Dinev turned to look at the captain. "Sir, the only way we're going to get the Aurora to make these turns is if we rewrite the thruster safeties."

"How long will that take?" Cameron asked.

"Ten, maybe fifteen minutes?"

"You don't need to rewrite anything," Josh insisted. "Just go manual."

"This isn't a fighter, Hotdog," Lieutenant Dinev reminded him. "You don't just *go manual* unless the flight control computers are down, and *that* doesn't happen."

"And you call yourself a pilot?" Josh accused.

"I call myself a helmsman," the lieutenant corrected him impatiently. "There *is* a difference, you know."

"Pilot, helmsman…same diff. And how'd you know my call sign?"

"Captain," the lieutenant objected.

"You'd better get started rewriting those safeties, Lieutenant," Cameron replied. "And Josh…" Cameron added, gesturing for him to step aside and leave the lieutenant to her work.

"Captain, perhaps you should let Mister Hayes take the helm, just until we get clear."

"The lieutenant will take care of it," Cameron explained. "Besides, we're not going anywhere until we finish recovering our birds."

"And how long will that take?" the general asked.

"About the same amount of time it will take the lieutenant to rewrite the safeties," Cameron replied. "Meanwhile, maybe you should start explaining to me what Jessica meant by 'he's only been alive for twenty minutes.'"

General Telles paused a moment, looking to either side. "Perhaps we should speak in private."

"This crew followed me here, knowing that I was violating orders by leaving the Sol sector. If *they* cannot be trusted, then I don't know who can."

General Telles paused again, looking around the bridge at the men and women busily working at their stations. "Very well, Captain. I suppose they will eventually learn the truth, anyway." The general took a breath. "Nathan Scott committed suicide in a Jung prison cell on the eve of his execution. I was there, as was Lieutenant Nash. However, before doing so, we copied his consciousness and memories to a portable storage unit. The man in your medical department is a physical clone of Nathan Scott...one who *now* carries the consciousness and memories of the original."

Cameron kept staring at General Telles before finally replying, "You're kidding."

* * *

Lieutenant Haddix checked his forward sensor display as his Reaper came out of its jump. "Got her," he announced, sounding slightly relieved. "One four six, twenty down, five hundred kilometers. She's headed away from us, twenty degrees off our course to port."

"Outstanding," Ensign Weston declared from the copilot's seat. "I love it when things go right."

"Looks like both Blue and Red Flights are already back."

"Aurora Flight, Reaper Six, inbound for landing," Ensign Weston called over comms.

"*Reaper Six, Aurora Flight. Welcome home. Enter the port, high approach, high speed. Auto-flight in two.*"

"Port high, speed up, auto-flight in two, for Reaper Six."

"Jump flashes, two four seven, twenty-eight up, about two hundred clicks. Twelve targets."

"That would be Green Flight, no doubt."

"Looks like everyone made it home," the lieutenant said, obvious relief in his voice. "Not bad for our first op in the PC, huh?"

"Any op you make it home from, brother." A new contact appeared on the long-range sensor screen. "Uh... We've got another jump flash."

Lieutenant Haddix looked at the sensor display as his copilot adjusted the sensors to get a more accurate reading. "One of ours?" he asked, a hopeful tone in his voice.

"All the Eagles are in the pattern, and we're the last Reaper in," the ensign replied. "Besides, it's too small to be a..." The ensign's eyes widened in horror. "Oh, fuck. It's paintin' us!" he warned as he started arming the Reaper's weapons systems.

"Is he targeting us?" the lieutenant asked, his hand hovering over the joystick, ready to take manual control of the ship.

"No, he's just scanning the entire area!" the ensign replied as he continued activating his weapons systems. "I think it's a drone. I'm taking it out!"

"Aurora! Aurora! Reaper Six! We've got an unknown target actively scanning the area. Two five seven, forty-one high, five hundred thousand kilometers and closing fast. We are engaging!"

"Launching a tweety!" Ensign Weston announced.

Both men glanced out their forward windows as a small missile streaked past the left side of their cockpit, turned slightly to port, then disappeared in a blue-white flash.

* * *

"This would be an extremely inappropriate time for me to make a joke, Captain," General Telles replied.

"Captain!" Ensign deBanco reported urgently from

the Aurora's comm-station at the back of the bridge. "Reaper Six has engaged an unknown target at two five seven, forty-one high, five hundred thousand kilometers and closing fast!"

"I've got it!" Lieutenant Commander Kono reported from the sensor station. "It just jumped in. Looks like some sort of recon drone."

"Reaper Six has launched a zapper," the comms officer added.

"What the hell's a Reaper?" Josh wondered.

"Any other contacts?" Cameron demanded.

"No, sir!" Lieutenant Commander Kono replied. "Only friendlies. The target is scanning us as... The target is gone, Captain!"

"Did the zapper get them?" Cameron asked.

"No, sir. The target jumped just as the zapper came out of its jump and acquired!" the sensor officer replied.

"What the hell's a zapper?" Josh wondered amidst the chaos.

"The contact is likely to be a Dusahn jump recon drone," General Telles surmised. "They use them to search for jump flashes. The Dusahn likely launched dozens of them along your initial jump route, at various distances. It is how they track jump ships."

"We need to jump the hell outta here," Josh warned.

"Flight Ops, Captain!" Cameron called out over her comm-set. "How much jump left in our Eagles?"

"*Telemetry shows lowest bird has about two light minutes left, Captain.*"

"Jump everyone to tango four two, right now!" Cameron ordered.

"*Aye, sir! Tango four two!*"

"Helm, as soon as those birds get clear, turn us

hard to port, jump twenty light minutes, then turn and jump us to tango four two!"

"That won't do it, Captain," Loki insisted.

"He is correct," General Telles warned. "That drone has already reported to the Dusahn. They will send more drones, followed by ships, and they will do so in seconds."

"Birds are clear!" Lieutenant Commander Kono reported.

"They will see the direction that your fighters jumped, and they will follow them."

"Maybe, but they *might* also follow us," Cameron argued.

"Their *ships*, yes," the general conceded. "But their *fighters* will follow fighters."

"How long until those safeties are rewritten?" Cameron asked Lieutenant Dinev.

"I can't rewrite them and fly at the same time," the lieutenant replied.

"Jumping in three..."

"I can do this," Josh told them, looking at Cameron and, then, the general.

"...Two..."

"Jump flashes," Lieutenant Commander Kono reported.

"...One..."

"...Dusahn fighters..."

"...Jumping..."

"...At least eight of them!"

The blue-white flash filled the bridge for a moment.

"Jump complete!" the navigator announced.

"Cap'n," Josh pleaded.

"More jump flashes!" Lieutenant Commander Kono warned. "Two this time...Dusahn fighters."

"Six followed your fighters," General Telles surmised.

"How?" Cameron asked.

"They probably jumped in half a light minute out and picked up their jump flashes," the general explained.

"We've seen them do it before," Loki added. "They multi-jump their way in, probably picking up old light in between each jump."

"That would work," Lieutenant Commander Kono agreed from the sensor console.

"Evasive pattern Lima Four," Cameron ordered. "Execute when ready."

"Lima Four, in three..." the navigator replied.

"They will track you," the general insisted.

"...Two..."

"They're fighters," Cameron replied. "They're not a threat."

"...One..."

"Perhaps not to you, but to your fighters..."

"...Jumping."

"Hard to starboard, get us on course for the rendezvous point and jump when ready," Cameron commanded without missing a beat. "We'll join up with our fighters and provide cover fire until they land," she added, turning back toward the general. "Then we'll shake the tail."

"Hard to starboard, aye," Lieutenant Dinev acknowledged.

"You're chances of success are low without Mister Sheehan's algorithm," the general told her.

"We'll out jump them," Cameron argued.

"And once you have used up your jump energy and are forced to spend hours recharging?" General Telles challenged.

Cameron looked at him.

"Another jump flash, Captain!" Lieutenant Commander Kono reported. "Another drone!"

"Captain," the general urged, pushing for a decision.

"Drone has jumped away," the lieutenant commander added.

"How long until we finish the turn?" Cameron asked her helmsman.

"Eighty seconds," the lieutenant replied.

"Nothing takes eighty seconds to turn!" Josh protested. "Who taught you how to fly?"

"In forty seconds, a Dusahn warship will appear. They will open fire the moment they do. You will jump to escape, and then they will launch another twenty or thirty jump drones, and within a minute, they will locate you again."

"Screw this," Josh declared, turning to leave. "You all wanna die, that's fine. Just open the door first, so we can get the hell off this ship before it's too late."

"More ships will move into position in an attempt to box you in," the general continued.

"Jump flash!" Lieutenant Commander Kono interrupted. "Dusahn warship!"

"They're launching missiles!" Lieutenant Commander Vidmar reported from the tactical station.

"The missiles are jumping!" Lieutenant Commander Kono warned.

"Execute escape jump!" Cameron ordered.

"Escape jump, aye!" Ensign Bickle replied as the jump flash washed over them.

"Lieutenant Dinev, Ensign Bickle, you're

temporarily relieved," Cameron ordered. "Mister Hayes, Mister Sheehan, you're up."

"Captain," Lieutenant Dinev protested, turning back toward her captain.

"Lieutenant," Cameron snapped, a determined look in her eyes.

"Move it, sweetie," Josh said, pushing Lieutenant Dinev out of the way and taking her seat.

"Sorry about this," Loki told Ensign Bickle as the ensign rose from his seat.

"No problem," the ensign replied, stepping aside so Loki could take his place.

"Another jump flash!" Lieutenant Commander Kono announced.

"Jesus!" Cameron exclaimed.

"They are very good at this," General Telles said as the ship began a hard turn to port. "I suspect they practiced the process at great length prior to invasion."

"What are you doing?" Cameron asked Josh as the ship began to roll quickly to port and nose down sharply.

"Yankin' and crankin'," Josh replied as he pulled the Aurora out of her diving roll to port. "How're you doin' over there, Lok?"

"Just give me a second..." Loki stopped mid-sentence, his jaw dropping open. "Holy crap! It's still here!"

"What's still here?" Josh asked.

"My layout!"

"Jump flash!" Lieutenant Commander Kono reported. "Another drone!"

"My nav layout is still in the memory! After all these years! How is that possible?"

"I used it as the basis for my layout," Ensign

Bickle explained from the side. "It was taught to us at the Academy. It's very efficient..."

"Enough with the history lesson," Cameron urged. "I need you to get us to the rendezvous point."

"Hold your course a few seconds," Loki instructed Josh.

"I'm on it," Josh replied, already knowing what Loki was thinking.

"Drone has jumped away!"

"Turn to one seven four, twenty down!" Loki instructed. "Decel thrusters to full burn!"

"One seven four! Decel at max!" Josh replied, turning the ship toward the new heading and pitching down as he brought the Aurora's deceleration thrusters to full power.

"What are you doing?" Cameron asked, apprehension in her voice.

"Slowin' her down," Josh replied.

"We drop speed and then dial up the jump power," Loki explained as he frantically typed commands into the Aurora's navigation computers. "If we do it quickly enough, the Dusahn will think we've jumped a lot further than we actually did."

"And this works?"

"Hell, yeah!" Josh declared.

"Well, we *think* so," Loki admitted. "I mean, they haven't been able to hold a track on us yet, so..."

"Jump us ahead on one-sixty," Josh instructed.

"One light hour, jumping," Loki announced as the jump flash briefly bathed the interior of the Aurora's bridge in subdued, blue-white light.

"Turning to one-seventy," Josh announced. "Killing the decel, going to full power on the mains."

"Dialing back the jump power," Loki replied.

"One-seventy in five..."

"Jumping in three..."

"You *are* going to get us to the rendezvous point, right?" Cameron asked as Loki counted down to the next jump.

"...Two..."

"Jump flash," the sensor officer announced. "Another drone."

"...One..."

"One-seventy," Josh announced.

"...Jumping."

Again, the jump flash washed over the bridge as Josh brought the Aurora's main engines back down to zero.

"Killing the mains, bringing decels back up," Josh reported.

"Dialing the jump power back up," Loki replied.

"Evens?" Josh asked his partner.

"Sounds good," Loki replied. "Jumping seven light minutes..."

"One seven two," Josh reported.

"Now," Loki replied, the jump flash washing over them again.

Cameron watched, saying nothing and showing no reaction as the two men continued to execute the most unique maneuvers she had seen in a long time. "Is this really necessary?" she wondered.

"The last thing we need is for that warship to follow us to the rendezvous point," the general told her. "That would greatly complicate the recovery of your ships."

Cameron tipped her head slightly in agreement as another jump flash washed over them.

"Turning back to one seven four and accelerating," Josh announced as he brought the Aurora's nose back to the left two degrees.

“Any drones?” Loki asked.

“Negative,” Lieutenant Commander Kono replied.

“Jumping,” he replied. The bridge lit up one more time with the blue-white light of the jump, after which Loki leaned back in his seat to take a breath. “We’re at the rendezvous point,” he announced.

“Not bad,” Cameron nodded.

“Multiple contacts!” Lieutenant Commander Kono reported from the sensor station. “Eagles and Reapers! And they’re fighting off twenty Dusahn fighters, Captain!”

“Interceptors!” Cameron ordered. “Lock on every damned one of those targets and light’em up!”

On the forward, upper side of the Aurora’s outer hull, just inboard of her forward flight deck gateways, two rectangular missile launchers popped up from their positions tucked neatly into the hull. They immediately rotated to starboard, tilted upward slightly, and let loose ten projectiles, each about three meters in length and a meter in diameter. The projectiles, departing in flashes of blue, magnetic energy from their launch tubes, fired their engines to maneuver slightly, then disappeared seconds later as they jumped away.

“Interceptors are away!” Lieutenant Commander Vidmar reported from the Aurora’s tactical station.

“Get us close to those fighters,” Cameron ordered.

“We’re on it, Cap’n,” Josh replied, turning the Aurora toward the battle.

“I’ll jump us in about two kilometers from them,” Loki said.

“Jump flashes!” Lieutenant Commander Kono announced. “Ten interceptor missiles!”

"Interceptors have engaged the targets!" the tactical officer reported.

"Comms! Notify flight ops! Tell them to warn our birds we're jumping in close!" Cameron ordered. "And tell them to be ready to get down on the deck as quick as they can!"

"More jump flashes!" Lieutenant Commander Kono announced. "Targets are jumping away!"

Cameron turned to her left, toward her sensor officer. "Any more drones jump in?"

"Negative," Lieutenant Commander Kono replied.

"Multiple hits!" Lieutenant Commander Vidmar exclaimed.

"I can jump us in any time," Loki reported.

"Wait," Cameron ordered. "Give our birds time to get ready." She turned back to Lieutenant Commander Kono. "How many did we get?"

"Eight of them, sir!" the lieutenant commander replied. "The other twelve jumped ten light seconds. They're turning back to reacquire our ships."

"Jump us in now," Cameron ordered.

"Jumping," Loki replied.

The blue-white jump flash washed over the Aurora's bridge, again, as she jumped in close to her waiting ships.

"Get them on the deck!" Cameron ordered.

"Dusahn fighters are jumping back in!" Lieutenant Commander Kono warned.

"Locking point-defense and plasma cannons on the enemy fighters!" Lieutenant Vidmar announced from the tactical station.

"Their fighters are highly maneuverable and difficult to hit," General Telles warned.

"Eagle One Seven is hit!" Lieutenant Commander Kono reported. "He's breaking up!"

"Did the pilot get out?" Cameron asked urgently.

"Negative, Captain!"

"Damn it!" Cameron exclaimed. "Pipe the battle in!" A split second later, the sound of radio chatter between the Eagle and Reaper pilots was coming through the loudspeakers for all to hear.

"One, Four! Break right! Engage the guy at zero four zero, low!"

"Four! I've got him!"

"Shit! This guy is all over me!"

"Two Five! One Seven! Reverse your turn and hit your decels hard! I'm lining up for a shot!"

"I can't! I've lost my starboard decel thru..."

"Goddamn it! Leader! One Seven! Two Five is down hard! No eject!"

"One Seven! Leader! You've got one at your four high!"

"Red Flight! Red Leader! Get on the deck! Combat landings! Roll your asses in fast to make room for the next guy! Nobody hits an elevator until the Aurora jumps!"

"Somebody get this son of a bitch off of..."

"We just lost another one, sir," Lieutenant Commander Kono reported.

"Can we launch more interceptors?" Cameron asked.

"Negative, Captain," Lieutenant Commander Vidmar replied. "We're too close to the targets!"

"Aurora! Check your fire! Check your fire! Keep our approach lanes clear!"

"Red Five on deck!"

"Red Six on deck!"

"Red Two on deck!"

"Dusahn fighter just jumped in aft of us!" Lieutenant Commander Kono warned. "Starboard side! He's making a run for the starboard landing deck!"

"I've got him!" Lieutenant Commander Vidmar assured them. "Aft plasma cannons!"

"Captain!" Lieutenant Commander Kono exclaimed. "A Dusahn warship just jumped in! Heavy cruiser, at least! They're locking weapons on us!"

"Jump missiles on that cruiser!" Cameron ordered.

"Jump missiles, aye!" the tactical officer acknowledged.

"You got'em, Viddie!" Lieutenant Commander Kono exclaimed.

"What?" Cameron asked.

"The Dusahn fighter headed for the starboard flight deck," Lieutenant Commander Kono explained. "We got him with our plasma cannons."

"Jump missiles away!" Lieutenant Commander Vidmar announced.

"Cruiser has jumped!" Lieutenant Commander Kono reported.

"What?"

"Jump flashes!" the lieutenant commander continued.

"Our missiles!"

"No sir! Theirs! Four of them! Five seconds!"

"Firing point-defenses!" Lieutenant Commander Vidmar reported.

"Brace for impact!" Cameron warned.

The impact-alert alarm echoed throughout the ship, reaching all the way into medical.

"What the hell?" Jessica wondered.

The ship suddenly shook violently, nearly

knocking Jessica off her chair next to Nathan's bed in the medical bay.

"What's happening?" Nathan wondered, trying to get up from his bed.

"You're not going anywhere," Doctor Chen told him sternly, pushing him back down.

"I've got to do something," Nathan protested.

"Like the lady said, you've only been alive for what, *thirty* minutes now?" Doctor Sato said.

"But, my ship," Nathan insisted, his voice still hoarse.

"It's not *your* ship, Nathan," Jessica reminded him. "Not yet, anyway."

Doctor Chen and Doctor Sato continued examining Nathan. As she studied the peculiar readings on her medical scanner, Doctor Chen looked suspiciously at Doctor Sato and Jessica. "You two *are* going to tell me what the hell is going on with this man sometime soon, right?"

"He's a clone," Doctor Sato told her.

"A what?"

"A clone."

Doctor Chen looked down at Nathan as he flashed a small smile to confirm. "Are you sure?"

"I should be," Doctor Sato replied. "I'm the one who cloned him... Five times, I might add."

"Oh, yeah. There's a lot you two are going to have to tell me," she repeated as the ship continued to shake.

"Damage reports!" Cameron barked from her command chair at the center of the Aurora's bridge.

"*Primary jump array is offline!*" the chief of the boat reported from damage control. "*Secondary is still good. Engineering is tying the primary energy banks into the secondary jump system, so we won't lose use of that energy. We've got hull breaches along the port side. Sections four, seven, and eleven. Decks Charlie and Delta."*

"What about wounded?" Cameron asked.

"*Currently at twenty-three, with at least that many unaccounted for. Rescue teams are on their way to the breached decks to look for survivors in safety compartments, but most of the intercoms are out in those areas, so we have no idea if anyone is alive."*

"Target is launching more missiles!" Lieutenant Commander Kono reported from the sensor station.

"How many more birds still need..."

"Flight reports all remaining Eagles are on deck!" Ensign deBanco replied, anticipating his captain's request. "Reapers are still standing off!"

"Their missiles are jumping!" Lieutenant Commander Kono warned them.

Cameron glanced at the navigational charts on the clear display panel directly ahead of her, between Josh and Loki, noting that their jump line was clear. But before she could give the command, the blue-white flash of their jump filled the bridge.

"Escape jump complete!" Loki announced.

"Good anticipation, Mister Hayes," Cameron replied calmly. "Flight, Captain," she called tapping her comm-set.

"Missiles jumped in behind us!" Lieutenant Commander Kono reported. "If we hadn't jumped..."

"Send all Reapers to rally point Hotel Seven. Form up for quick recovery."

"*Hotel Seven. Form up for quick recovery, aye,*" the flight controller replied.

"They're launching missiles again!" Lieutenant Commander Kono told them urgently.

"Skip us ten! Starboard climbing arc, reverse on the threes!" Cameron ordered.

"Skip ten!" Loki replied, their jump flash filling the bridge before the words left his mouth.

"Starboard climbing arc," Josh replied, turning the ship to starboard and pitching up as they came out of the jump. "Reverse on threes."

"As soon as we finish, jump us to Hotel Seven, Mister Sheehan," Cameron added.

"Hotel Seven, aye," Loki replied, his fingers dancing across his console as he set up the next jump in the series and activated it.

"Last sensor reading showed the cruiser turning to intercept," Lieutenant Commander Kono reported from the sensor station. "Suspect the target is trying to anticipate our escape route."

"That's what I'd do," Cameron muttered as the third jump flash in the series of ten washed over them.

"Reversing course and pitching down," Josh reported as he leaned his flight control stick hard to the left and pushed it forward.

"What the..." Lieutenant Dinev exclaimed, watching Josh push her ship through a turn that she didn't think was possible. "How the hell are you getting her to turn so fast?"

"Just use everything you've got," Josh muttered as the fourth jump flash washed over them. "She wants to turn and burn. You've just got to cut her loose and let her."

"We've lost the target," Lieutenant Commander Kono announced from the sensor station as the fifth jump flash lit up the bridge.

Cameron watched silently as Josh manipulated every thruster and propulsion system at his disposal, forcing her ship to fly more like a fighter than a fifteen-hundred-meter long warship- main thrust directors, attitude thrusters, maneuvering thrusters, deceleration thrusters...even the docking thrusters. The man had an uncanny knack for flying, and apparently that knack applied to just about anything that flew.

"Reversing our turn back to starboard and climbing," Josh reported as the sixth jump flash in the series washed over them.

"Are you varying the jump distances?" Cameron asked Loki.

"You bet... Uh...sir," Loki replied as the next jump flash washed over them.

"Reverse your turn again, but hold pitch," Cameron ordered.

"Reversing to port, holding the climb," Josh replied, yanking the stick back to the left and adjusting all the thrusters as well.

"Make the next two short, Mister Hayes," Cameron added.

"Aye, sir," Loki replied as the eighth jump flash washed over them.

"I've got them," Lieutenant Commander Kono declared.

General Telles glanced at the tactical display to Loki's left, between the navigation and sensor stations. "Directly in front of where we would have been after the next jump," the general said as the next jump flash lit up the compartment. "Nicely done, Captain."

"I do have some tricks up my sleeve," Cameron quipped as the tenth jump flash illuminated the bridge.

"Turning to Hotel Seven," Josh reported.

"Jumping in five seconds," Loki added.

"Enemy cruiser is turning toward us," Lieutenant Commander Kono warned. "I'm pretty sure they've spotted us."

"Deploy a standard mine field between the target's estimated intercept course and us," Cameron ordered.

"Three..."

"Launching mine clusters to starboard," Lieutenant Commander Vidmar replied from the tactical station.

"...Two..."

"Hundred-meter spread," Cameron added.

"...One..."

"Hundred-meter, aye."

"...Jumping."

For the eleventh time in the last minute, the bridge of the Aurora was momentarily illuminated by the subdued, blue-white light of her jump fields as the warship finally jumped ahead to the alternate recovery point.

"Multiple contacts!" Lieutenant Commander Kono reported from the sensor station. "Eight Reapers! Dead ahead! Two formations!"

"Slide in under them, Mister Hayes," Cameron instructed. "They should be spaced perfectly to touch down on both forward flight decks."

"Slick," Josh replied approvingly. "Sorry, I mean yes, sir."

"As soon as those Reapers are down, you can start your algorithm, Mister Sheehan," Cameron added.

"Yes, sir," Loki replied. "But it's not going to get us all the way to Big Blue. We're going to have to stop and recharge along the way."

"Pick a spot where we're least likely to be

detected," Cameron said. "Something well away from any shipping lanes. You two are locals, surely you would know."

"I think I can figure something out," Loki replied.

"Jump flash," Lieutenant Commander Kono announced. "Dusahn drone."

"They never give up, do they?" Cameron declared.

"No, they do not," the general replied.

"All Reapers are on deck," Ensign deBanco reported from the comm station.

"Drone has jumped away," the sensor officer added.

"Very well, gentlemen. Show us what you've got," Cameron instructed.

"Jumping in three..." Loki began.

"Maintain alert status until we're sure we've lost them," Cameron ordered.

"...Two..."

"Aye, sir," her tactical officer acknowledged.

"...One..."

"Picking up the cruiser again," Lieutenant Commander Kono reported.

"...Jumping."

"Looks like she passed right through the mines, taking at least a few hits. Looks like some hull damage, and some collapsed shields."

"Executing first turn," Josh announced.

"Hopefully, that'll slow them down a bit," Cameron commented as she turned to face General Telles. "Now, perhaps you'd like to finish telling me what's going on."

"How far back would you like me to begin?" General Telles asked.

"I want everything," Cameron insisted. "So, maybe

you should start right after Nathan surrendered himself to the Jung."

* * *

"*All hands, maintain condition two,*" the voice announced over the loudspeakers and intercoms.

"How do you feel?" Doctor Sato asked Nathan.

Nathan tried to clear his throat. "Like I'm recovering from the worst bender of my life."

Doctor Sato looked at Nathan, a puzzled expression on her face. "Bender?"

"An Earth expression," Jessica explained. "Like he was out drinking all night."

Doctor Sato didn't look any less confused.

"Alcohol intoxication," Doctor Chen added. "Like he's suffering from withdrawals after consuming excessive amounts of alcohol."

"We don't consume alcohol in my culture," Doctor Sato stated. "Although, the Corinairans did so from time to time, but rarely in excess."

"Dehydration, headache, blurred vision, nausea, mild vertigo, feeling rather disconnected from one's senses..." Doctor Chen elaborated.

"Oh, yes. All of that is to be expected, considering the circumstances."

"Do all your people go through this when they change bodies?" Nathan asked, his voice still rasping.

"Oh, no. Not at all. It does take a few days to get complete coordination back, but other than that, we generally feel quite normal after a transfer. Some even feel rejuvenated."

"Not the word I would choose," Nathan whispered, trying to save his voice.

"I believe I can help your throat a bit," Doctor Chen told him. "I'll be right back."

"How is your vision?"

"I'm not seeing double, anymore, so that helps," Nathan replied. "It's still hard to focus from one thing to the next, especially when they're at different distances."

"That will improve within a few hours," Doctor Sato assured him.

"Nathan, do you remember anything about Connor?"

"Yes, I do," Nathan replied. "It's weird, actually. The best way I can describe it is like I was a spy or something, pretending to be Connor Tuplo, except that I didn't *know* I was pretending."

"That actually makes sense," Jessica told him. "It's one of the things they taught us in spec-ops training. That you have to be careful to not actually *become* the person you're *pretending* to be. There are actually documented cases of undercover agents doing just that."

"I even remember the pain of not knowing who I really was, if you can imagine that," Nathan added. "It's all very confusing."

"It will take time to sort out these memories," Doctor Sato told him. "Our people experience similar problems in differentiating which lifetime a memory is from."

Nathan shook his head wearily. "Like I said...very confusing."

"How much do you remember about your life before...you know."

"Before I killed myself?"

"I would have phrased it differently," Jessica said. "More like you *sacrificed* yourself."

"I remember most of it, I think. It's still kind of hard to say. It's all a bit overwhelming." Nathan looked at Jessica. “I don’t suppose anyone has a mirror?”

Jessica picked up the data pad next to the bed and activated its camera, reversing it so that Nathan could see himself.

“I look like him,” Nathan said as he touched his scruffy beard, then reached up and touched his long, unkempt hair. “I look like Connor.”

“Well, that would make sense, since he was your clone,” Jessica quipped.

“I need a shave and a haircut,” Nathan surmised.

“One thing at a time,” Jessica told him.

Doctor Chen returned with a small bottle. “Drink this,” she instructed, handing it to Nathan.

Nathan sniffed it, his face contorting as he recoiled from the odor. “Are you sure? It doesn’t exactly smell good.”

“It smells, but it has no taste whatsoever,” Doctor Chen assured him. “It’s from a root on Sorenson. It has become very popular on Earth. It numbs the throat and relaxes the muscles around the vocal cords a bit. It should help you speak without the discomfort.”

Nathan held the small bottle away from his nose and took a breath, then downed its contents quickly. His apprehension quickly turned to surprise. “You’re right, it doesn’t have any taste.”

“You should feel some relief in a few minutes.”

“So, what’s the verdict, Doc?” Jessica asked Doctor Chen.

“Well,” Doctor Chen said after a sigh, “his body temp is a little high, and he is definitely dehydrated. His electrolytes are all out of whack, and he seems to be throwing a few ectopic beats here and there. I’ll need to do labs and run full spectrum scans, but, right now, I'm not seeing anything that we can't deal with fairly easily."

"Then I can go?" Nathan asked, his voice already becoming clearer.

Both doctors put their hands on him to keep him down.

"Not so fast, Captain," Doctor Chen stopped him. "You just came out of a clone bath, for Christ's sake. Not that I understand what that even means, medically speaking, but I'm sure it means that you should take it easy and let me run a *lot* more tests before you start leading the charge."

Nathan looked at Doctor Sato, hoping for a differing opinion.

"I'm afraid she is correct, Captain," Doctor Sato confirmed. "Even if the transfer process was conducted in a normal fashion, this body is not yet fully compatible with the transfer technology, and it was still scheduled for another year in the growth chamber. There are *many* tests to be run. Not only medical, but also psychological and memory tests. We must determine an accurate baseline condition, against which to measure any future changes."

"Changes?" Nathan asked. "What kind of changes?"

"I do not know," Doctor Sato admitted. "We have been making a lot of this up as we go."

Nathan lay back down, resigning himself to the inevitable. "So, I'm an experiment."

"I'm afraid so," Doctor Sato replied. "But thus far, you are a remarkably successful experiment."

"Why does that not make me feel any better?"

* * *

"You could have just told us the truth from the start," Cameron told the general.

"If we told you that Connor Tuplo was a clone of Nathan Scott, who carried his memories but did not have access to them, would you have been just as inclined to abandon your obligations to your world?"

"Yes," Cameron replied. "And, for the record, we didn't abandon our obligation to our world. We simply upheld our obligation to the members of the Alliance in the Pentaurus sector, who deserve our protection every bit as much as the people of the Sol sector. Besides, I was referring to the rescue of Nathan's consciousness. We would have been willing to help."

"Of that I have no doubt," the general assured her. "But there was nothing more any of you could have contributed to the effort. In addition, the greater the number of people who knew that Nathan's consciousness did not die on Nor-Patri, the greater the risk of discovery. The stakes were simply too high. Besides, the genuine grief of people such as yourself only served to reinforce the mistaken belief that Nathan Scott *was* dead."

Cameron took a deep breath, letting out a long sigh as another jump flash washed over the Aurora's bridge. "Not a conversation I ever thought I would be having, that's for sure."

"Captain," Loki called.

"Yes, Mister Sheehan."

"We're down to about a light year's worth of jump energy. And this is as good a position as any to do a layover. I'm assuming standard practice is still to always arrive with a light year of jump range in reserve."

"Indeed, it is," Cameron replied. "Where are we, exactly?"

"Pretty much equal distance between Borne, Norwitt, and Haydon," Loki reported.

"So, still in Dusahn-controlled space, then."

"Yes, sir."

"You didn't think it would be better to head out of the cluster? Out of Dusahn-controlled space?"

"Isn't that exactly what they'd expect us to do?" Josh remarked. "I mean, you'd have to be crazy not to, right?"

"Precisely what I was thinking," Cameron replied. "Very well. We'll do our layover here. But next time you want to do something crazy, you might want to check with me, first."

"Yes, sir," Loki replied sheepishly. "I've finished programming the ship's jump-nav computers to utilize the evasion algorithm. So, all you have to do is activate it, and it will provide you with a random series of maneuvers and jumps that should shake free any pursuer."

"I've changed the safeties on all thruster systems to be overridden whenever the algorithm is being used," Lieutenant Dinev chimed in. "So, we won't even need to go manual."

"Chicken," Josh joked under his breath.

The lieutenant lightly smacked the back of Josh's head in punishment for his quip.

Josh looked at Loki and mouthed, *I like her.*

"Your crew should be able to handle the evasion without any problems now, Captain," Loki assured her.

"Thank you, gentlemen," Cameron replied, although somewhat begrudgingly. "We likely owe you our lives."

"Hey, it's what we do," Josh bragged as he rose from his seat to turn the helm back over to Lieutenant

Dinev. “Want to get a drink later?” he asked the lieutenant as he stepped aside.

The lieutenant said nothing and rolled her eyes as she sat down at the helm again to resume her duties.

“I see some things have *not* changed,” Cameron said to General Telles.

The general nodded.

“It’s all yours, Ensign,” Loki told Ensign Bickle as he stepped aside.

“Thanks,” the young ensign replied as he took his seat at the navigator’s station. “Nice work, by the way.”

“Thanks.”

“The crew could use a break, sir,” Lieutenant Commander Vidmar reminded the captain.

“You’re probably right,” Cameron agreed. “Let’s go to condition three, though. I want to be ready to fight on a moment’s notice as long as we’re still inside the cluster.”

“Yes, sir,” the lieutenant commander replied.

“Keep the first light year’s worth of jumps in the algorithm loaded and ready, just in case we get an unexpected visitor,” Cameron instructed her navigator. “And don’t wait for someone to give you the order to execute.”

“All hands, set condition three,” Ensign deBanco announced over the Aurora’s loudspeakers.

“Aye, sir,” Ensign Bickle replied.

“Have Commander Kaplan report to the bridge and take the conn,” Cameron instructed as she rose from her commander chair. “I’ll be in medical.”

“Aye, sir,” Lieutenant Commander Vidmar acknowledged.

"Captain, it may be too soon," General Telles warned her, stepping in front to block her path.

Cameron paused, looking the general squarely in the eyes. "One of my *best* friends, whom I thought was *dead* for the last *seven years*, is alive in my sick bay. He is there because *I* disobeyed orders and brought *my* ship, and *my* crew, across a *thousand light years* of space, into *battle* no less. Early or not, I'm going to speak to him."

"As you wish, Captain," the general nodded, stepping aside.

"Mister deBanco," Cameron said as she headed for the exit. "Let Commander Kamenetskiy know that he can join me in medical just as soon as he has the recharge running at maximum rates."

"Aye, sir."

* * *

"This is new," Nathan said as Doctor Chen slowly moved the scanning head over his body.

"Not really," Doctor Chen replied. "It's the same tech, just miniaturized."

"So, no more lying down on a cold, metal table, half naked?" Nathan said, looking at Jessica and smiling.

"I think we can skip the memory tests, for now," Jessica said, grinning back.

"What else has changed while I've been out?" Nathan wondered.

"Plenty," Doctor Chen replied. "Nanite tech has made my job a lot easier. In fact, that big room that used to hold the medical scanner is now a nanite production lab."

"You make them here?" Jessica asked in disbelief.

"Yup. Special fabricators. Crank them out by the millions. And we don't just use them to heal or repair, anymore. We also use them prophylactically, to maintain good health."

"The Ghatazhak have been doing that for a few years now, as well," Jessica said. "Only we don't have the means to manufacture them ourselves. We have to buy them on the black market."

"That should do it," Doctor Chen said, turning the device off. "Now, if you'll excuse me, I have quite a few wounded to deal with, and we are somewhat short-staffed."

"Can I be of assistance?" Doctor Sato wondered. "I am a medical doctor."

"We'll take all the help we can get," Doctor Chen replied, nodding.

Nathan watched as Doctor Sato followed Doctor Chen out of the room. "So, she stuck with me all these years?" he asked after they had both left.

"She and Megel both," Jessica replied. "They left everything they knew behind. Spent their lives trying to resolve the compatibility issues between Nifelmian and Terran genetics and the transfer systems."

"And I'm—or this *body*—is the fifth clone?"

"Yup."

"Why so many?" Nathan wondered.

"As I understand it, the genetic changes in your brain had to be done incrementally. They originally predicted that it would take at least eight cloning cycles, but they somehow managed to get it down to five."

"I hope they didn't cut any corners, so to speak."

"Doubtful. Nifelmians are *very* meticulous," Jessica promised him. "How are you feeling?"

"That stuff the doc gave me helped," Nathan replied. "I may not sound like myself, but at least it doesn't hurt to speak anymore."

"What about the blurred vision and headache?"

"The headache is still there, but the vision is getting better. It was worse in the hangar, where there were objects much further away to focus on. In a small room, it seems to be okay." Nathan held up his hands, looking at his palms and fingers as he flexed them. "I still feel a bit...disconnected, though. It's like when you're using VR training, and you're moving *your* hands to make your *VR* hands move." He looked at her. "Hold up your hand."

Jessica raised her left hand and held it in front of Nathan.

Nathan reached out and touched Jessica's hand with his right index finger. "When I try to touch something, my brain isn't quite sure *when* my finger is going to make contact."

"Is it a depth of field problem?" Jessica wondered.

"No, I feel like my depth perception is fine. I think it's more of a proprioception thing. Like I'm not sure of my body's position in space, in relation to everything around me. Like my brain is slow in processing sensory input. But that's getting better, as well. When I first woke up, it was a *lot* worse... *Believe* me."

The door to the examination room slowly opened, and Cameron peeked inside. "Am I interrupting?" she asked politely.

"Cam," Nathan greeted. "Please, come in."

Jessica stepped up to greet Cameron, giving her a long overdue hug. "It's good to see you, Cam."

"You too," Cameron replied. She turned her attention to Nathan, moving over beside his bed, making room for General Telles to enter the small exam room.

"I'd hug you too, but I'm still kind of slimy," Nathan said, reaching out his right hand to her.

"I can't believe you're really alive," she said with a quiet laugh.

"Neither can I, to be honest."

"Are you alright? How do you feel?" Cameron asked, unsure of what else to say.

"Why does everyone keep asking me that?" Nathan wondered, looking back at Jessica for a moment. "You all act like I was just resuscitated or something. Like I was brought back from the dead."

"To us, you were," Cameron replied.

"To me, it's like I just woke up from a really long nap." Nathan sat up a bit more. "Except that I was dreaming the entire time. Dreaming about being Connor Tuplo."

"Then you retain the memories of both identities," General Telles concluded.

"A general now, huh?" Nathan said, reaching out to shake his hand.

"That is correct. I lead what is left of the Ghatazhak."

"Yeah, I know," Nathan reminded him. "Connor's memories, remember?"

"Do you now have access to all of your original memories, as well?" General Telles inquired.

"It's still pretty fragmented as best I can tell, but new memories are popping into my head all over the place. Some big, some small. Every sight, every sound, every word... They all trigger new memories to appear. And when they do, more pieces begin to fit together. It's a bit overwhelming."

"*New* memories?" Cameron wondered.

"New is probably the wrong word," Nathan admitted. "*Forgotten* might be more appropriate."

"So, you don't remember *everything* just yet?"

"No, I don't," Nathan admitted. "But I suspect I will, in time."

"In time," Cameron said, repeating his words, as if for emphasis.

"What are you getting at, Cam?" Jessica wondered.

"It's alright," Nathan assured Jessica, placing his left hand on her arm. "She's just doing her job, protecting her ship and her crew." Nathan turned back to Cameron. "Look, Cam, I have no desire to take your command from you. The Aurora is *your* ship. Her crew is *your* crew. I'm here to lead the *Karuzari*...and as a *figurehead* more than anything else."

"You just woke up after seven years, and you already know all of that?" Cameron asked, an eyebrow raised.

"I have the memories from my life as Connor Tuplo," Nathan explained. "In fact, I remember *those* details more clearly than I remember details of my *own* life. Like you would remember what happened yesterday more clearly than what happened a year ago." Nathan looked at Jessica. "To be honest, I feel more like Connor Tuplo right now than I do Nathan Scott."

Cameron let out a long sigh. "That's what has me worried," she admitted. "I *trust* Nathan Scott. I don't even *know* Connor Tuplo."

"Well, *I* do," Jessica told her, "and *I* trust him. Not only because Connor and Nathan are just two names for the same person, but because of what Connor did *before* he even had Nathan's memories back."

"You see, Jessica, even you see him as two separate people," Cameron argued.

"It's just a figure of speech, Cam."

"I suspect it will take time for Captain Scott to become himself...to regain *all* of his former abilities," General Telles said, hoping to ease Cameron's concerns. "As well as to integrate his experiences as Connor into them." General Telles turned to speak directly to Cameron. "In the meantime, we should concentrate on working our way safely back to the Glendanon. If, after Captain Scott has recovered from his ordeal, you are still having concerns as to his fitness to lead, we can address them at that time."

"Of course," Cameron agreed. She turned back to Nathan. "Don't misunderstand, Nathan. I just have to be sure. I'm responsible for this ship and her crew."

"You don't need to explain anything, Cam," Nathan assured her, placing his hand on her arm. "I completely agree with you. To be honest, I'd be concerned if you didn't ask these questions."

Cameron smiled. "Thanks." She placed her free hand on top of his. "And I *am* very happy to see you alive again."

The door suddenly swung open, and Vladimir appeared. "*Bozhe moi!* Nathan!" He paused suddenly, looking at the tense expressions on their faces. "You are Nathan, aren't you?"

"It's me, Vlad," Nathan replied, smiling.

Vladimir charged forward, nearly knocking Jessica over as he spread his arms wide to embrace his long-lost friend, nearly lifting him from the bed. "I can't believe it!"

"Easy, Vlad!" Jessica warned.

"You, I am not speaking to," he told her. "In fact, I plan to kill you later, for not telling us he was alive."

CHAPTER TWO

"Man, this place has changed," Josh commented as he and Loki made their way across the main hangar bay toward the Seiiki. "Is it just me, or is this bay bigger?"

"It's definitely bigger," Loki agreed. "The Seiiki never would have fit in here before. To be honest, when they cleared us to land, I was thinking, 'Land where?'"

"Me, too. Then I saw the huge apron around the midship, and the gaping openings on either side, and I figured maybe they knew what they were talking about."

"It was still a tight fit, though," Loki replied.

"Phffft! Nothing tight about it," Josh scoffed.

"Right."

Josh and Loki approached the aft end of the Seiiki. The ship was still sitting where they had left her, on the starboard side of the hangar, tucked nose first to the massive door in the starboard bulkhead that said "S2" in big white characters in the middle. Only the door was no longer there. Instead, there was a big, empty transfer airlock, exactly like the one on the port side, through which they had cycled into the main hangar bay.

"What took you guys so long?" Marcus asked as he came down the Seiiki's cargo ramp to meet them, followed by Dalen and Neli.

"We had to show them how to fly their ship," Josh bragged.

"Right," Dalen replied, knowing Josh's tendency to exaggerate.

"No, seriously."

"You flew the Aurora," Dalen said skeptically, still not buying it.

"We had to show them our anti-pursuit maneuvers and set up the algorithm for them," Loki explained. "Otherwise, Telles wouldn't let them near the Glendanon."

"Not exactly *flyin'* the Aurora," Dalen remarked, feeling satisfied.

"No, I had to actually fly it for them," Josh insisted. "Their helmsman...or should I say, helms-*woman*," he added with a lascivious look, "couldn't pull off the maneuvers manually. So, I had to take over."

"*We* had to take over," Loki corrected, in a futile attempt to put Josh's ego in check. "And I'm pretty sure she *could* have pulled the maneuvers off herself, if she'd had a bit more time to figure it out."

"So, you're saying *we* didn't save the day?" Josh challenged, turning to look at Loki. "Seriously?"

"You two flew the Aurora," Dalen said, this time in disbelief rather than denial.

"Fine, we saved the day," Loki acquiesced. "Are you happy now?"

"No good can come of this," Marcus grumbled, stepping down off the ramp onto the deck, and turning to head forward under the Seiiki's left wing-body.

"Where are you going?" Josh asked.

"I'm gonna watch the left nacelle," Marcus replied. "Dalen, you watch the right."

"What for?" Josh asked.

"The deck chief is griping at us to move the ship into the starboard transfer airlock, so he can keep his deck clear."

"Then why didn't you just move it?" Josh wondered.

"Marcus insisted that we wait for you two."

"Why? He knows how to taxi the ship," Josh said.

"Honestly, I think he just wanted to show the deck chief that he couldn't be bossed around," Neli explained. "For a moment, I thought they were going to call security on him," Neli added, nodding toward the deck chief standing in front of the P2 airlock door on the other side of the hangar bay.

"We'd better move it," Loki said, starting up the ramp.

"Whoa!" Josh exclaimed, noticing several ships parked along the aft wall of the hangar bay. "What are those?" he wondered as he headed for them.

"Josh," Loki said in warning, trying to stop him.

Josh didn't even hear him as he was so enthralled with the ships in front of him. "Hey, Lok!" he called, turning back toward Loki as he walked. "Do you think those are those Reapers they were talking about?"

"Oh, jeez," Loki muttered, turning to follow Josh. "How do I know?"

"Hey," Josh called out to one of the men near the row of ships. "Are those Reapers?"

The technician turned to look at Josh, confused. "Huh?"

"Are you deaf, mate? Are those ships Reapers?" Josh repeated as he moved closer.

"Josh," Loki called out after him.

The technician looked over at his team leader for guidance.

"Who are you?" the technician's senior officer asked, moving in from the right.

On the far side of the hangar, the deck chief noticed Josh and Loki approaching the technician and his senior near the line of ships. He signaled two security officers near the main entrance, then headed across the bay himself.

"I'm Josh, and this is Loki," Josh told the senior technician.

"That supposed to mean something to me?"

"Well, since we're the ones who just saved your ass, then yeah," Josh said irately.

"Man, your timing stinks," Loki muttered as he caught up to his friend.

"I think you've got that backwards, mister," the senior tech responded.

"Stop where you are!" one of the approaching security guards warned as both men raised their weapons while they approached.

Josh and Loki spun around, throwing their hands up, seeing the approaching guards with weapons raised.

"Whoa!" Josh exclaimed. "What the fuck..."

"Stand down!" a booming, heavily accented voice commanded from behind the guards.

The two guards halted their advance. The guard on the left turned to look in the direction of the command, while his partner held his aim fast. "Do as he says," he told the other guard as he realized the order had come from the third in command of the ship.

The two guards lowered their weapons, came to attention, turning to face one another, parting just enough for Josh and Loki to get a clear view of the man who had given the order. There, walking toward them from the main entrance at the forward end of the main hangar bay, was a familiar-looking bear of a man, with a mop of thick, brown hair and heart-warming grin.

"Vlad!" Josh exclaimed excitedly, reaching over and tapping Loki on the chest as if to say, *look who's here.*

Commander Kamenetskiy strolled across the deck, larger than life, the smile on his face growing broader with each approaching step. "My old friends," he said warmly as he neared. He grabbed Josh and gave him a hug, nearly squishing him in the process, then repeated the same with Loki. "I am so glad to see you both." He put his arms around each of them, pulling them in close on either side. "I want to thank you both," he said in low tones. "I understand that Nathan would not be alive without your help."

"It was our pleasure," Josh replied.

Vladimir laughed. "Especially you, Joshua. I understand you have been with him, so to speak, for five years now?"

"Something like that, yes."

"I have decided not to kill you," Vladimir explained graciously. "Nor you," he assured Loki.

"What?" Josh asked, confused.

"For not telling us that Nathan was alive. I know that Jessica forbade you to tell. And I understand that she can be quite intimidating...even to me."

"You don't know the half of it," Josh replied.

"What is the problem?" Vladimir wondered, changing the subject.

"I don't know," Josh insisted. "I just asked these guys if these ships were Reapers, and they got all twisted up about it."

"Josh," Loki began to object.

"Forgive them," Vladimir interrupted. "Everyone is a bit wound up these days. These people, they all agreed to disobey orders and follow Captain Taylor here. And *without* knowing about Nathan, I might add."

"No problem," Loki said. "We understand. And Josh can be a bit, you know...*Josh*."

"What the hell does *that* mean?" Josh demanded.

"These are indeed Reapers," Vladimir started, wanting to avoid the irritating exchange between the two friends that he knew was about to follow. He pushed both of them toward the Reapers, walking along with them. "They were developed to replace the Falcons that you two flew so many years ago."

"That would explain why they look like a cross between a shuttle and Falcon," Loki reasoned.

"Just not as cool-looking as either," Josh added.

"What's their mission profile?" Loki wondered as they got to the front of the nearest Reaper.

"Who cares," Josh interrupted. "How do they fly?"

"More like a Falcon than a shuttle, I'd say," another man replied from behind them.

Josh and Loki turned to see a man in a flight suit approach, carrying a flight helmet in one hand and a life-support pack in the other.

"Commander," the man said to Vladimir, nodding politely.

"Lieutenant," Vladimir replied. "Josh, Loki, this is Lieutenant Haddix, one of our Reaper pilots."

"Lieutenant," Loki replied, reaching out to shake the man's hand.

The lieutenant put down his gear and took Loki's hand in greeting. "Jon. Jon Haddix."

"Josey?" Josh asked, noting the name on the lieutenant's helmet.

"Long story," the lieutenant replied.

"These gentlemen used to fly for the Alliance, back in the day," Vladimir told the lieutenant.

"Hotdog and Stretch," Lieutenant Haddix said, nodding. "Heard all about you two back at the academy."

Josh's head grew two sizes in the blink of an eye. "They still tellin' stories about us?"

"Mostly as examples about what to *not* do, in order to stay out of trouble."

"That makes a little more sense," Loki said, holding back a satisfied grin over Josh's deflating ego.

"So, you fly these things?" Josh asked.

"You bet. Best ship a pilot could ask for."

"I dunno," Josh said, turning back to look over the Reaper. "Looks like a glorified shuttle to me."

"It can be," the lieutenant admitted. "Then again, it can be one deadly-ass ship. Just depends on how she's fitted out."

"What's her mission profile?" Loki asked again.

"Just about anything. Recon, long-range intercept, ground support, troop insertion, SAR... You name it, Reapers can do it."

"How is all *that* possible with *this*?" Josh challenged.

"The middle door there is actually a bay that can be swapped out, depending on your mission. Same with the aft bay between the engines."

"Nice," Loki commented.

"Think I'd rather be in a Falcon," Josh disagreed. "Or even an Eagle, for that matter."

"A Reaper can take on ten Eagles and come out with barely a scratch," the lieutenant boasted. "But if you'd rather die in an Eagle, looking *cool*, that's your choice, I guess."

Josh didn't respond and instead headed aft, dragging his hand along the Reaper's folded back, port wing.

The lieutenant remained silent, waiting until Josh disappeared behind the Reaper before speaking.

"Sorry about that," he said to Loki, keeping his voice down. "I just couldn't help busting your buddy's chops a bit."

"No problem," Loki replied, a slight smile on his face. "His chops could do with an occasional busting."

* * *

"Medical reports six dead, thirty-two wounded. Twenty of them are expected to return to duty within the day."

"What about the missing?" Cameron asked her XO.

"All but three have been accounted for," Commander Kaplan replied. "That's where we lost six, by the way, to sudden decompression. The rest made it to safety zones."

Cameron sighed, studying her data pad as she sat at the desk in her ready room. "Who's missing?"

"Ensign Sara Dorso, crewman Wilson Lang and specialist Ross Pelter. There is still hope, though."

"How so?"

"There is an escape pod missing from that section," the commander explained.

"Do we have a launch confirmation?" Cameron asked.

"No, but that doesn't mean it didn't."

"No beacon picked up?"

"Not at the time, but again..."

"Very well," Cameron said. "We'll consider them MIA until proven otherwise." She looked over the damage report on her data pad again. "Kamenetskiy says he can get the primary array back up during the next recharge layover, but the hull breaches will have to wait until we reach the Glendanon."

"How are we going to fix them there?" Commander Kaplan wondered. "She's a cargo ship, right?"

"The Ghatazhak stashed a few fabricators off-world prior to the Dusahn attack, along with some raw materials to feed them. General Telles says the Glendanon has a number of empty cargo pods that can be disassembled and used to patch up the hull, as well. Between our fabricators and theirs, we should be able to make it work. If not, we'll just have to fly with holes in our side. It wouldn't be the first time."

"I suppose not," the commander agreed.

"How long until we reach full charge again?"

"Secondary banks are already at full charge. Primaries will be ready in a little over an hour. Engineering rigged up a quick and easy manual cross-feed switch so that we can use either bank with the secondary array. So, we'll still get enough to get another twenty-nine light years out of the next jump series. After that, if all goes well, the primary array will be back online."

"Very well," Cameron replied.

"So, did the general give you any idea how much further we'll have to jump to reach the Glendanon?"

"All I know is that the rendezvous point is at least one hundred and fifty light years away. So, I'd count on at least four more recharge layovers."

"So, a full day's travel, then."

"Yup."

Commander Kaplan paused for a minute, thinking. Finally, she spoke. "So, is it really him?"

Cameron sighed again, leaning back in her chair. "I don't really know," she admitted. "He sure *seems* like him. But you heard the story, right?"

"I listened to the bridge recordings... *Twice.* Still find it hard to believe. A clone. Never in a million years would I have come up with that. Which reminds me... Why don't I know about the Nifelmians?"

"They requested that their true nature not be made public, at least as much as was possible," Cameron explained. "They were afraid of getting hit with a rash of requests to do exactly what two of their own did with Nathan."

"I get that. But you'd think they would be willing to help humanity out a bit. I mean, we're talking eternal life, here, right?"

"I'm sure they have their reasons," Cameron said. "And it is certainly their right."

"Still, to be forever twenty-five?"

"It's a little more complicated than that, I think."

"So, are you going to give him command?"

"He's not asking for it," Cameron replied.

"But if he did, would you step down?"

"If I was one hundred percent sure he was Nathan, yes, I would. In a heartbeat. I've never met anyone who was as good at thinking on their feet as Nathan Scott. The problem is, how do I *know* it's him? I mean *really* him. And I don't mean *physically* him, as in the same DNA. I mean, is he *still* the *same man*, with all the same *capabilities* as before?"

"Well, if he's not *asking* to take command, then it doesn't really matter, does it?"

"I don't know that, either," Cameron admitted. "He's going to lead the rebellion. Even if he is only acting as a figurehead, sort of a *poster boy* for recruitment purposes... I really don't know."

"Tough position to be in," the commander admitted. "Sort of makes me glad I'm just the XO," she added as she rose from her seat to depart.

"Thanks a lot."

* * *

Nathan sat on the edge of his bed in the small, private exam room in the Aurora's medical complex, his eyes closed. Images randomly appeared in his mind. One image led to another, and then another. Memories of a life that still seemed not his own flooded into his consciousness, as if the spill gates had been opened. He tried to slow them down, to absorb each and every one of them, but he seemed to have little control over the rate at which they appeared. He had considered asking the doctor for something to knock him out, hoping that when he next awoke, all his memories would simply *be in place*, as usual. But after being essentially *dead* for the last seven years, *sleep* was the last thing he wanted.

But he hadn't really been dead, had he? At least not for the full seven years.

He remembered his life as Connor Tuplo the same as if he had always *been* Connor Tuplo. In fact, he had been telling the truth when he told Cameron that he felt more like Connor than Nathan. At least, he had at the moment. Now, it was becoming a bit more confusing. As more memories of his life as Nathan Scott were revealed to his conscious mind, he felt Connor slipping away.

Surprisingly, this saddened him, which was another emotion he hadn't expected. There were many aspects of Connor's life that Nathan envied. He had his own ship, with no one to answer to. Free to wander the galaxy, to find his fortunes wherever they might hide. His only responsibility was for the well-being of his small, but loyal, crew...his family.

His family.

It was another confusing aspect of his awakening. As Connor, he had no recollection of his real family. Only that which he had read in a file constructed for him by Doctor Sato and Loki. But now, with the memories of his *real* family finding their way into his mind...

It was indeed confusing.

Even more confusing was the clarity with which his memories appeared to him. Each and every one of them seemed as though they had happened only moments ago. Every detail, every nuance, every emotion he had felt at the time. And it wasn't just those of Nathan. It was also those of Connor.

But every now and then, one of Nathan's worst memories would appear, and it would overwhelm him. Such death and destruction he had witnessed. So much suffering. So much loss. His own family. His mother. His sister's husband. His own brother... and at Nathan's own hand.

That last one had nearly crushed him when it had appeared. The only thing that had given him the strength to get past that memory was another memory that followed. One of long talks with his sister Miri, many weeks after Eli's death. She had helped him put his guilt to rest. But he had still carried the bullet that took his brother's life with him to the grave.

My grave.

Yet another thought that brought unexpected emotions to the surface. He had no memories of his memorial service. After all, he had been dead at the time...so to speak. He had considered asking Vladimir to bring him a vid of the service, but decided to wait until he was stronger.

He knew that Miri was aware that he was still alive. She had seen him in the vid message, although she did not know at the time that it was Connor Tuplo who had sent the message, and not him.

Or was it?

Even Nathan found it confusing. The line that separated his experiences and those of Connor Tuplo had been quite clear at first. But, with each passing moment, it was fading away more and more. He wondered if it was supposed to happen that way. If both sets of memories were supposed to just *come together* in such fashion.

And there was something else. Something that surprised him even more.

“How are you feeling?” Doctor Sato asked, poking her head into Nathan’s room.

“Better, I think,” Nathan replied. “You tell me.”

“Well, I have reviewed all of your test results with Doctor Chen, and we both agree that you appear to be in decent health.”

“Decent?”

“Well, your physical body has been suspended in a cloning bath for more than a year, so I expect that you will become easily fatigued. This is a common side effect of the cloning and transfer process.”

“What about this *disconnected* feeling I have?” Nathan asked.

“That, too, is common. It will pass, as well. In fact, the more you use your body, the more quickly your mind will become accustomed to your new body.”

“But it’s *my* body,” Nathan said. “Shouldn’t I already be accustomed to it?”

“This body is several years younger than your original, and without any of the previous injuries that you might have suffered during your original lifetime. Such injuries, especially when not properly treated, often lead to reduced range of motion or other impairments that we tend to ignore over time. It is more pronounced when coming from a much older body to a younger one, but I would expect you to feel it, as well."

"I did get pretty banged up as a kid."

"Really?" Doctor Sato replied, seeming surprised.

"Defenseman. Ice hockey. Broke a few things over the years."

"I'm not familiar with the sport."

Nathan laughed. "Funny, seeing as how you're from an ice world."

"You remember Nifelm?"

"Quite clearly, in fact," Nathan replied. "I've never actually been on the surface, but I remember the data readouts like I read them minutes ago. Two hundred and thirty-three degrees Kelvin. PSI of nineteen point one four. Thirty-eight percent oxygen. Fifty-four percent nitrogen..."

"You remember that level of detail?" she asked, astonished. "From more than seven years ago?"

"Yes, and more. It's weird. I mean, I know it was from a long time ago, but it feels like it *just* happened. And I don't mean that it just happened a few weeks or a few months ago. More like a few *minutes* ago. When the memories hit me, they do so with such clarity and such detail. It's difficult to describe."

"It's not an uncommon phenomenon after a transference," Doctor Sato assured him. "Although I don't remember ever reading about a case where it was with such clarity."

"Great," Nathan said sarcastically. "Leave it to me to be the first."

"I'd like to do some more tests, if you don't mind."

"I was really hoping to get out of here. I've been cooped up in here for hours, now. I want to walk around, see how the ship has changed. This was my home for two years, you know."

Doctor Sato thought for a moment. "Perhaps, but you need to take it slow. The more stimuli you have, the more your memories will come flooding into focus. It is standard practice on Nifelm to keep a newly transferred subject in isolation for several days, to allow them to go through the awakening process at their own pace, without it being rushed."

"I'm not sure we have that kind of time, Doctor," Nathan reminded her.

"Perhaps not."

"What kind of tests were you talking about?" Nathan asked. "More scans? More blood?"

"Nothing like that. I was hoping to test your cognition and recall capabilities. Doctor Chen was kind enough to give me your baselines from your last physical, prior to your original body's untimely demise. I'd like to do a comparison."

"How long will that take?"

"Hours, I'm afraid. But it need not be done all at once."

"Then I *can* leave this room?"

"Yes, I suppose so. But, perhaps, you could limit your activities? Maybe find someplace familiar where you could relax a bit?"

"Like where?"

"Maybe aboard the Seiiki?" Doctor Sato suggested. "That would be a familiar place...one that is more recent."

"Deal," Nathan said, rising to his feet. He felt unsteady at first, grabbing the bed rail for balance.

"Maybe I should get Jessica back in here to help you?"

"Maybe that's a good idea," Nathan agreed. "But do you mind if we take the long way back to the Seiiki?"

* * *

It wasn't uncommon for the captain of an Alliance ship to have time-delayed messages in his personal queue. Often, important orders were sent ahead of time to ensure that those orders would be received at a specific time. A jump-capable ship, especially a warship, was often unreachable by Fleet Command, as they did not know her exact location.

It was unusual, however, to have one that was not from Fleet Command, but from the captain of another Alliance warship.

Captain Robert Nash, commanding officer of the Alliance destroyer named for the ill-fated world of Tanna, sat staring at his message queue, waiting for that one message to count down to its intended time of delivery. He had been waiting for this moment for more than a week. At first, he had thought nothing of the message. But when he had received a top-secret communiqué from command regarding the mysterious 'loss of contact' with the Aurora, he had become suspicious. He had even considered asking his communications officer to try to crack the time-lock on the message, but he decided against it. For whatever reason, Captain Taylor had sent *him* a private message, likely *before* disappearing.

What had truly surprised him was that, for some reason, he had chosen *not* to inform his superiors of the message. Something was going on, and in forty-seven seconds, he expected he would find out exactly what it was.

The timer on the message reached zero, and the color of the message header turned green, indicating that it was unlocked. Robert touched the message header on the screen, and a single sentence appeared in a small box at the center of his data pad.

What was her nickname for you as a child?

No one called Robert anything but Robert, Captain, or Captain Nash. Not Bob, not Bobby, not Robby. Even his mother called him Robert. Only one person was ever allowed to call him by another name.

He keyed in the name *Bobert*, and pressed enter. It wasn't much of a security measure, but it was enough. The entire message appeared next, and Robert nearly dropped the data pad. A minute later, he finished reading and pressed the *secure delete* link to destroy the message.

Captain Nash leaned back in his chair, in a state of shock. He took a deep breath, letting it out slowly as his mind raced. Finally, he leaned forward again and reached for the intercom on his desk. "Tactical, Captain," he called.

"*Tactical, aye,*" the intercom squawked.

"Status of our recon drones?"

"*Four are back, two are still out.*"

"ETA to their return?"

"*Ninety minutes, and two hours, sir.*"

"Drop a redirect buoy for Tau Ceti, patrol sector four seven five mark two, and tell the helm to prepare to jump to same."

"*Aye, sir.*"

"What the hell have you gotten yourself into, Jess?" he muttered, leaning back in his chair again.

* * *

Nathan stepped into the main central corridor leading from the Aurora's medical complex, directly aft, toward her main hangar bay.

"Are you sure you're up for this?" Jessica wondered, standing next to him, ready to grab him if he lost his balance.

"I walked in here, I can walk out," he insisted,

pausing to straighten up. After a moment of concentration, he began to walk down the corridor, headed aft, one careful step after the next.

Jessica walked next to him, matching his pace perfectly, ready to offer support should he need it.

"Stop it," Nathan told her under his breath.

"Stop what?"

"Stop hovering over me like I'm a newborn taking his first steps," Nathan said. "I've got this."

Two technicians came out of a side corridor, turning toward him. They spotted Nathan and immediately stopped and came to attention.

"Captain," the senior of the two technicians greeted, offering salutes.

Nathan raised his hand in a rather lazy salute as he continued slowly down the corridor, concentrating on each step in order to avoid losing his balance. Less than a minute later, another crewman appeared, also stopping to salute.

Again, he returned the salute, and then again when two more of the Aurora's crew appeared.

"Jesus, how does anyone get any work done on this ship, if they're always stopping to salute each other?" Nathan said under his breath.

"That's why the Ghatazhak don't salute," Jessica replied as she walked beside him. "That, and because it makes their officers a target."

"I always wondered why their combat armor didn't have any rank insignia on them," Nathan admitted as he returned yet another salute. "I'll tell you one thing... I'm going to be an expert at returning unnecessary salutes by the time we get to the Seiiki."

"We're going straight there?" Jessica asked. "You don't want to go anywhere else?"

"At this point, I just want to lie down in my own bed and take a nap."

"I didn't realize you were that tired," Jessica replied.

"I didn't tell the docs, for fear they'd keep me in medical. I never could sleep in hospital beds."

"Are you sure you're okay?"

Nathan stopped and looked at her. "Please stop asking me that. In fact, tell Cam to issue a ship-wide order for *everyone* to stop asking me that." Nathan returned another salute from a passerby. "And for everyone to stop saluting me, for Christ's sake."

"Maybe we should take you back to medical," Jessica suggested.

"Don't make me order you to take me to my ship," Nathan replied.

"I don't take orders from you," she retorted with a grin. "I take them from Telles."

"It's nothing physical," Nathan explained. "It's all these memories coming at me. It feels like the pace is accelerating. It's like I'm fast forwarding through a video of my entire life."

"Have you gotten to the part where we first met?" Jessica asked, trying to take his mind off his difficulties.

"I'm well past that part," Nathan replied as they stepped through the entrance to the main hangar bay. "But I'm planning on coming back to it later," he added with a smile.

"Yeah, you're fine."

Jessica escorted Nathan further into the main hangar bay, then to their left, toward the starboard number two transfer airlock. The door was open, and the Seiiki was parked inside. As large as the airlock was, the Seiiki barely fit within the diameter of its rotating center platform.

"This place has really changed," Nathan commented, looking around the main hangar bay as they walked toward the Seiiki. He glanced aft, noticing the row of odd-looking, high-wing combat shuttles. "What the heck are those?"

"Reapers, Cap'n," Marcus replied, coming down the Seiiki's cargo ramp to greet them. "Sort of like a Falcon and a shuttle, all in one."

"Unusual looking."

"Downright goofy-looking, if you ask me. How are you...?"

Jessica held up her hand, cutting him off. "He's good. Just a little tired."

Dalen and Neli were next to appear, coming down the port-side ladder of the cargo bay.

"They're blocking the..." Nathan paused a moment, allowing his eyes to focus on the far, aft end of the massive hangar bay. "There are no transfer airlocks along the back."

"A *lot* has changed on this ship," Marcus said. "I convinced the deck chief to give me a data pad with the ship's deck layout. Of course, he had to check with the chief of the boat, who had to check with the XO, who had to check with Captain Taylor."

"I imagine everyone is going to be overly cautious," Nathan said as he started up the ramp. "At least for a while."

Jessica tried to help him up the ramp, but Nathan pushed her hand away.

"I can make it on my own," he insisted.

Marcus looked at Neli and Dalen as Nathan passed him, nodding for them to help the captain.

"Good to see you again, Captain," Neli greeted.

"Good to see you too, Neli... Dalen."

"What do we call you?" Dalen wondered. "Connor? Nathan? Na-Tan?"

"Definitely *not* Na-Tan," Nathan said. "As to the other two, I'll let you know." Nathan grabbed the port ladder and started a slow climb up to the catwalk. "For now, Captain will do."

"You got it, Cap'n," Dalen replied, positioning himself under Nathan, just in case.

Jessica and Marcus watched silently as Neli and Dalen followed Nathan up the ladder and onto the short catwalk that ran along the side of the Seiiki's cargo bay.

"Where are Josh and Loki?" Jessica asked as she watched them disappear through the port companionway hatch leading to the two cabins on the port side.

"Gettin' the grand tour from some Reaper pilot."

"Why is the Seiiki in a transfer airlock?"

"Deck chief wanted us out of the way," Marcus explained. "Apparently, the Aurora normally carries two transport shuttles, one in each of these big-ass airlocks." Marcus nodded toward the open transfer airlock opposite them, on the port side of the main hangar bay.

Jessica turned and looked at the transport shuttle in the other airlock. "Where's the other one?" she wondered.

"I didn't ask," Marcus admitted. "But it appears that this airlock is our home while we're here. To be honest, I'd just as soon get off this ship...sooner, rather than later. This recharge layover shit stinks. Makes us an easy target."

"We're well outside of the Pentaurus sector by

now," Jessica assured him. "And they're following Loki's algorithm to avoid pursuit."

"Still, I don't much like having our ship locked up inside another."

"Well, we should catch up to the Glendanon in another twelve hours. In the meantime, you'll just have to make the best of it. Doctor Chen and Doctor Sato both want to keep Nathan nearby, until they finish their tests. Besides, I'm sure you can cycle out and launch quickly enough if the Dusahn find us." Jessica looked around the main hangar bay. "Where's Combat One? They didn't leave, did they?"

"Downstairs," Marcus replied. "On the hangar deck. You should see it. Fuckin' huge. They gutted the cargo bays on the sides and opened it up. I'm telling ya... I was this ship's COB once upon a time, and even *I* could get lost on her now."

"Really," Jessica commented. "I should take a look around."

"Don't be surprised if you find a couple security guards following you," Marcus warned. "They've been keeping tabs on all of us since we got here."

"Good to know," Jessica replied, heading forward. "Nathan plans on taking a nap," she called back as she walked away. "Give me a call when he wakes up."

"Where ya goin'?" Marcus asked, calling after her.

"To find Telles."

* * *

For the last seven and a half hours, Sori Gullen had sat on the uncomfortable, grated, metal floor of the massive cargo pod, where the Ghatazhak rescuers had stuffed her and a couple hundred other prisoners.

Had it not been for the promise of one man—one

who appeared to be the leader of her rescue party—she would have been certain that she had simply traded one prison for another. Seven plus hours later, she was starting to wonder if that might not be the case.

I will take you to your father.

Those words continued to sustain her, despite the fear and despair she saw in the faces of everyone around her. Their only accommodations in the dimly lit pod were a bottle of water and two nutrition bars each, and a portable toilet in each corner. It was chilly, and it smelled of sweat and tears. Two med-techs had come down from the hatch at the top of the cargo pod and had cycled throughout the prisoners, checking for injuries or illness. Four Ghatazhak soldiers walked above them on catwalks that lined all four sides of the cargo pod, keeping an eye out for anyone who might cause a disturbance, and thereby jeopardize the safety of everyone.

Despite the breathable atmosphere, minimal amount of heat, and the weak but adequate gravity, one fact remained-they were all stuck in a giant box. One that offered minimal protection against the harsh environment of deep space as they were jumped repeatedly across the galaxy on their way to...*someplace.*

Again, as it had many times over the past seven hours, the cargo pod shook, the rumble of the pod hauler's maneuvering engines vibrating throughout the pod. Every time those engines fired, the people inside braced themselves. Once again, they felt the pod shift from one side to the other, twisting on its axis as the pod hauler that carried them changed course for perhaps the thousandth time.

But this time was different. The engines fired

sporadically, with the rumble changing quickly from one corner of the pod to another, and then back again. This went on for several minutes, to the point where people around her began asking each other questions. *Were they landing? Were they docking somewhere? Was this the end of their long, dismal journey? Would they see freedom when the doors opened, or would they see another captor?*

All four corners of the pod rumbled in unison for a few seconds, after which there was a sharp sound of metal striking metal, shaking the entire pod, and the artificial gravity suddenly increased to what felt like normal gravity for Corinair.

They had landed!

Sori Gullen immediately rose to her feet in anticipation, just like everyone else. They could not have landed on a hospitable world, as their engines had not burned long enough, or at a high enough intensity. And they had not docked with another ship, either, for the metallic *thud* had come from all four of their landing gear, and not from a docking collar on one side.

Sori's heart leapt into her throat. Her pulse raced, and her breath quickened. But nothing happened. As the passengers became restless, a voice came over the loudspeakers.

"*Attention all passengers, this is your captain. We have just landed aboard the Glendanon. Please be patient as the Glendanon's cargo bay is pressurized. We will begin disembarking as soon as possible.*"

Sori couldn't believe it. *The Glendanon.* Her father's ship. Tears began to stream down her face.

A woman next to her noticed her tears and became concerned. "Don't be afraid, dear. We're safe now."

"I'm not afraid," Sori replied, a small laugh

escaping her lips. "I'm happy. The Glendanon is my father's ship."

"Your father's?" the woman asked.

"He's the captain."

The woman reached out and hugged Sori, sharing her joy. Ten minutes later, the door opened, and they all started down the pod's massive cargo ramp.

Sori had been aboard the Glendanon once before, several years earlier, but she had never been inside her massive cargo bay. It was larger than anything she had ever seen. No building on Corinair was anywhere near as cavernous inside. The fact that it was part of an even larger ship seemed impossible to her.

On either side of the cargo ramp were more Ghatazhak troops, there to ensure an orderly transfer of passengers from the cargo pods to whatever location aboard the Glendanon they were to stay. She saw the other boxcar nearby, its passengers also walking down her cargo ramp. To her left was a cargo shuttle, out of which streamed a couple dozen Ghatazhak soldiers. Beyond the cargo shuttle, there were at least a dozen space fighters, their pilots climbing down from their cockpits. These were all the people who had risked their lives to save them from execution at the hands of the Dusahn. She wanted to hug every one of them. She wanted to thank them all, again and again, but she suspected they were not looking for thanks. She knew such men. Her father was such a man. Men who did what was right. Not for thanks, but because it was the right thing to do.

Then she saw him, walking out from between the rows of stacked cargo pods, flanked by two of his men. She could see the anguish on his face. The fear that she would not be among those pouring out of the two newly arrived cargo pods.

Then his eyes met hers, and the fear and anguish on his face turned to joy and overwhelming relief.

The general had kept his promise.

* * *

Nickname of the man who taught him to fly?

After a week of waiting for the message to unlock, it was not what Miri expected to see. She looked around her office for a moment, thinking. She felt she should know the answer, but it wasn't clicking.

"Oh, of course," she exclaimed, furiously typing 'Gampy' into the input field.

It worked.

> *I have taken the Aurora, and those of her crew willing to join me, to the Pentaurus sector to assist Nathan. I will do everything within my power to see to his safety. Until I speak directly to him, I strongly suggest that you continue to keep the fact that he is alive a secret. I suspect you understand the possible repercussions, both interstellar and global. I will contact you when I know more. Thank you for trusting in me. I will do my best not to let you, or Nathan, down.*

Miri stared at the message for several minutes, reading it again and again. Her baby brother was alive. She had learned that more than a week ago.

And he was about to take on a whole new enemy. At least this time, Miri had been able to help.

The question, now, was whether or not to tell their father.

* * *

Nathan rose from his bunk, responding to a knock on his cabin door. His body was still weak, but the long nap had done him a world of good. At least he felt like he could move somewhat normally, although he suspected that he would quickly tire out.

He cracked the cabin door open, spotting Marcus on the other side.

"Someone to see you, Cap'n," Marcus said, stepping aside to reveal Cameron standing behind him.

"Of course," Nathan said, opening the door and stepping back. "Come in."

Cameron nodded at Marcus as she stepped past him and entered Nathan's cabin aboard the Seiiki, closing the door behind her. "I hope I didn't wake you," she said.

"It's alright," Nathan assured her, running his fingers through his long hair as he sat down on the edge of his bunk. "I figure I've slept enough to last me a while."

"You've made a lot of changes to the Mirai, I see."

"Seiiki. She's called the Seiiki."

"Of course."

"A lot of changes to the Aurora, as well, I noticed."

"A few."

"What's on your mind?" Nathan wondered. "And don't ask how I'm feeling."

"I don't know, really," Cameron admitted. "I guess I just felt like I needed to talk to you."

"You're trying to figure out if it's really me, aren't you?"

"How did you know?" Cameron wondered.

"It's what I'd be most worried about, if I were you," Nathan explained.

"How do you do that?" Cameron asked.

"Do what?"

"How do you always have the answer?"

Nathan laughed. "Trust me, I don't."

"That's just it, Nathan," Cameron said. "How *do* I trust you? You're supposed to be dead. And now you show up, as a *clone*?"

"You have to stop thinking of me that way, Cam," Nathan told her. He took a deep breath and sighed. "Look, I've been thinking about this ever since we landed here. Who I am. *What* I am. I know this isn't my original body, but it is still my original consciousness, complete with all my memories and experiences. The Nifelmians see the body as nothing more than a vessel to host one's consciousness. Would the same pilot not fly equally as well in one Eagle or another?"

"It's a hard concept to accept, Nathan. You're asking me to trust the safety of my ship, and my crew, to a clone of you."

"Not of me, of my body. My thoughts are still mine."

"But they're copies, too, aren't they," Cameron pointed out. "You were still *you* when you died, right?"

"I suppose so," Nathan admitted. "Luckily, I was spared that memory."

"And what if you were spared other memories as well? What if you have forgotten something important? Something that could cause you to make a bad decision? How do I know that you're *all* there? And if something *is* missing, how do I know how that will change you?"

"You trusted me enough to steal the Aurora and come halfway across the galaxy," Nathan argued.

"Because I thought it *was* you," Cameron replied. "Turns out, the man who *pretended* to *be* you didn't even have access to your memories."

"Yeah, I feel kind of bad about that one," Nathan admitted, hanging his head down. "Sorry. Telles thought it was best not to take the chance, and in my own defense, I wasn't really myself at the time."

"I still would have come, even if you *had* told me the truth," Cameron said. She leaned back in her chair, sighing. "This is so confusing."

"It's not confusing at all," Nathan disagreed. "I *am* Nathan. The PC *has* been invaded, and the Alliance *isn't* keeping its promise to protect it. The Dusahn are glassing *entire worlds*, just like the Jung glassed Tanna and tried to do the same to Earth... just to scare the shit out of people. *That's* why we're fighting. And *that* is why *you're* here. It's got nothing to do with me. It's because you're the same *as* me. You do what's right."

Cameron didn't have a reply at first. "The difference is, I'm not as sure as you are. I don't normally disobey orders, and I definitely don't normally steal warships and go charging off across the galaxy."

"I understand why you have doubts, Cam. I really do. But isn't it *doubt* that brought you here?" Nathan rose from his bunk and paced to the other end of his small cabin. "Millions have already died on Ybara and Burgess, and God knows how many on all the worlds in the cluster. We just rescued more than three hundred people—all of them innocent—their only crime was being related to the crews of jump ships that had refused to surrender to the Dusahn. Every one of them would have been executed." Nathan paused again, turning to look out the overhead viewport. Normally, he would have seen stars outside or a sky, if they had been parked on the surface of some world. Here, it was just structural beams and overhead lighting panels. He sighed, then turned back to her. "*Corinair* was *there* for us when we needed them. They have every right to expect us to do the same."

"We *did* do the same, nine years ago," Cameron reminded him.

"So, we should ignore them now?"

"I didn't say that."

"Something is going on here, Cam," Nathan argued. "Something much bigger."

"*That* is why *I'm* here," Cameron told him. "Something much bigger *is* going on. For some reason, Galiardi has gone *out of his way* to make sure that the Alliance does *not* send help to the Pentaurus cluster. He wants everyone to believe that war with the Jung is imminent, even though we have no solid evidence that the ships that penetrated Alliance space in the Sol system were operated under Jung authority. He's spent the last seven years pushing for a military buildup, and that's exactly what he's gotten. Now, he'll get even more support."

"Are you saying Galiardi is *behind* the Jung incursions into Alliance space?" Nathan asked in disbelief.

"No, I don't believe he's *that* crazy. But I wouldn't put it past him to use the situation to his advantage."

"And what advantage would that be?" Nathan wondered.

"He's been building his political base since the day you died, Nathan," Cameron explained. "His supporters tried to get him to run against your father in the last election, but he refused, stating that his duty was to protect the people of the Earth and the Alliance. But everyone expects him to run next time, and by then, his support base will be huge. Especially if he gets to fight a war before then."

"Assuming he wins," Nathan reminded her.

"He's got at least thirty more jump KKVs roaming around the sector in fail-safe mode. They check in periodically. If they don't get an all-is-well response, they launch. If he wiped out enough of the Jung's infrastructure, it would only be a matter of time before the Jung fleet would have no choice but to surrender."

"I seem to remember that they had more than a hundred ships," Nathan said.

"The number doesn't matter," Cameron said. "Without a supply chain, they can't continue operating. Considering the way the Jung caste system works, the warrior castes that command those ships would most likely cut and run. Probably head out to try to build their own empires, just like we *believe* the Dusahn did centuries ago."

"*Centuries* ago?" Nathan wondered.

"That's what fleet intel believes," Cameron replied.

"Then the Dusahn may be telling the truth."

Cameron looked at Nathan. "About what?"

"When *Lord Dusahn* addressed the Takaran house of nobles, he told them that the Dusahn are independent of the Jung Empire."

"How did you learn that?" Cameron wondered.

"His little speech was broadcast across Takara's

public networks, as well as every other world in the cluster," Nathan explained.

"How can you be sure it's not a ruse to prevent an all-out attack against the Jung by the Alliance?" Cameron wondered.

"We can't," Nathan admitted. "But to be honest, it doesn't really matter. At least not to us. Not if Galiardi is hanging the PC out to dry in order to further his own agenda."

"It *is* important, though," Cameron insisted. "If the Dusahn are *not* operating in concert with the Jung, then it's likely that the Jung do *not* have jump drives."

"And that Galiardi is going to start a war for no reason," Nathan surmised.

"Not *no* reason," Cameron corrected. "Just not a *good* reason. Unfortunately, we have no way of knowing for sure, one way or another," Cameron admitted.

"Have you thought of telling anyone?" Nathan wondered.

"Other than you and my command staff, only one other person," Cameron said. "Robert Nash."

"Jessica's brother?"

"Yes. I sent him a time-delayed message on our way out of the Sol sector. He is still in command of the Tanna, although it's been converted into a destroyer now."

"What do you think he'll do?"

"I don't know that he'll *do* anything. But I had to tell someone the truth of why I took the Aurora, just in case."

"In case what?"

"In case we never make it back."

Nathan sighed. "I apologize for pulling you into

this, Cam. But without the Aurora, we don't have a chance in hell."

"Even *with* the Aurora, our chances are pretty slim."

"They usually were," Nathan replied, a sly smile forming. "That's what she's good at, after all."

Cameron took a deep breath as she rose. "We'll see," she sighed. "Our last recharge layover will conclude in two hours. Would you like to be on the bridge when we rendezvous with the Glendanon?"

The smile on Nathan's face grew larger. "Indeed, I would."

"Then I'll see you there," she said, turning to exit. "But you need a shave and a haircut, first. And maybe a uniform, as well."

"I'll see what I can do."

CHAPTER THREE

The simple act of shaving had done wonders for Nathan. At first, he had feared he might not be able to handle the scissors without cutting himself, but his concerns had proven unwarranted.

When he queried his mind to determine when he had decided to grow a beard, he realized that Connor had awakened with one and simply never removed it. In fact, he clearly remembered a picture of himself in the dossier about Connor that Doctor Sato had given him to learn about himself. He had a beard in that picture as well, one nearly identical to the one he had just removed. He wondered if they had encouraged him, back then, to keep the beard in order to help hide his true identity. It also occurred to him that fear of recognition might also have been why Marcus had always insisted on keeping a low profile. "*The less people see you, and know about you, the better off you are.*" Staying away from the worlds of the Pentaurus cluster had also been Marcus's idea, now that he thought of it. The realization had brought a smile to Nathan's face, as Marcus was always seeing to Nathan's safety.

One thing was sure, Nathan did not wish to have a beard.

His hair had been a bit more challenging. Shaving was relatively easy. Just keep going until you found skin. But the hair...

He had started by trimming his bangs just enough to get them out of his eyes. He remembered having them shorter when he was Nathan and tried to trim them the same way. The overall length had been even more difficult, and after a few snips, he decided to hold off and let someone else do it. Surely, amongst all those rescued from Burgess, someone would know more about cutting hair than he did.

And so, Nathan stood there, staring at himself in the mirror above the tiny sink in his private head. The man he had seen there more than an hour ago had been both familiar and unfamiliar at the same time. Now that he was clean-shaven and his hair was a bit neater, he felt more like himself. It was as if he had trimmed away the last vestiges of Connor Tuplo, finally releasing his true identity as Nathan Scott, after all these years.

For the first time since he had been awakened, he was starting to believe that the identities of Connor and Nathan would indeed one day combine, instead of clash.

Nathan wiped his face, taking one last look in the mirror. He was still a far sight from the image of Captain Nathan Scott. In fact, he was more like the Nathan Scott who had reported for basic training more than thirteen years ago.

Thirteen years. Has it really been that long?

In the mirror, he saw the face of a twenty-five year-old. But this body had been grown in a single year.

Was that a single Earth year, or a single Corinairan year? How old was he? Was it simple math? The current Earth year minus his birth year? Was his age measured physically? Was he twenty-five, or thirty-seven? Or was it something in between?

Nathan decided he'd make that call later, when and if it became necessary.

He left the head, returning to his cabin. Cameron had offered to send him a uniform, but he opted against it. He was not technically a member of the

Alliance, and as of now, his role was undefined. Better not to confuse anyone, least of all himself.

To that end, he had opted for a hybrid approach to his attire. Alliance uniform boots and pants, but his usual, long-sleeved shirt and long, black overcoat. It gave him the look of a renegade, something that seemed appropriate for the role he was likely expected to play as Na-Tan. It made him look confident, and rebellious. Someone willing to take chances. It was a look he rather liked.

Na-Tan.

A role he had hesitated to play nine years ago, the first time he found himself, and this ship... *his ship...* facing an overwhelming enemy in the Pentaurus cluster. But it had proven invaluable back then, just as it would now. People needed a leader. Someone they could look up to. Someone they could follow. Someone they *believed* could lead them to victory.

The question was, could he do it again?

The first time, their victory had been the result of a superior technology, the jump drive, and a lot of lucky breaks. This time, the enemy had the jump drive as well, which meant they would have to outthink them, instead of simply jumping out of the line of fire.

Nathan hated to think about it, as it seemed an insurmountable problem. But he would take it on the same way that he took on challenges in the past. One step at a time.

The fact that he was already thinking about the problem, instead of wrestling with his own inner confusions, gave him hope.

Nathan donned his overcoat, opened the door, and left his cabin, heading aft down the short corridor along the Seiiki's port cabins. He stepped through the aft hatch onto the catwalk above the cargo deck, stepping onto the ladder and instinctively sliding down the rails to the deck below.

Wow. Nathan stood there a moment, thinking. He had slid down ladders before, but not this *particular* ladder. At least, not as *Nathan.* But he had done so many times as *Connor.*

"Looks like you've got your motor skills back," Jessica commented from the top of the Seiiki's cargo ramp.

Nathan turned to look at her. "Yeah," he replied, looking at his hands in surprise. "Looks like." He glanced back at Jessica. "That's good, right?"

"I would guess so."

Nathan scanned the cargo bay. "Where's everyone at?"

"If by 'everyone' you mean your crew, then most of them are topside, repairing some of the damage your ship took during our escape. Neli's at supply."

"Supply?" Nathan asked as he took a few steps toward her.

"Marcus made out like you were low on food, so Cameron agreed to let her stock up on a few things."

"We're *not* low on food," Nathan said. "The Ghatazhak loaded us up before we left."

"I know. But what's the harm? The Aurora is fully loaded but has only half her crew. She can spare a few things. Besides, better that the Seiiki is as stocked up as she can be. We have no idea what her next mission will be." Jessica gestured down the ramp. "Shall we?"

Nathan followed Jessica down the ramp and out across the main hangar deck.

"Cap'n!" Josh called from on top of the Seiiki.

Nathan turned around, walking backward a few

steps as he looked back at the Seiiki, spotting Josh, Loki, and Marcus working on the top of his ship.

Josh flashed Nathan a thumbs-up for the new look, a broad smile across his face. Nathan smiled back as he turned around and continued on his way.

"It's good to finally have him back," Josh said.

"Maybe now we can stop babysittin' his ass," Marcus grumbled as he returned to his work.

Josh watched Nathan and Jessica disappear around the corner. "I have a feelin' the easy part's over."

* * *

The guard at the port entrance to the Aurora's bridge snapped to attention as Nathan and Jessica entered the short airlock tunnel that led from the command deck corridor to the bridge itself. Nathan felt completely familiar with this part of the Aurora, as he had spent two years of his life aboard this ship, most of it on this very deck.

They came out of the tunnel and onto the bridge, to the left of the communications station aft. The entire bridge was bathed in a blue light. Nathan found his eyes transfixed on the main, semi-spherical view screen that wrapped around and above the forward half of the Aurora's bridge. Although more than half of it was currently adorned with various rectangles containing tactical and navigational data, there was still plenty of real estate displaying the view outside.

Ensign deBanco stood at the comms station, watching as Nathan and Jessica strolled by. As they moved forward toward Cameron, more of the bridge crew began to stare at him, as well.

Cameron rose from her command chair, realizing that Nathan had arrived. "Oh, my God," she said, her words escaping her lips by accident. "You really do look younger."

"Maybe I shouldn't have shaved so closely?" Nathan replied, rubbing his smooth chin.

"Maybe," Cameron commented. "But this is definitely better."

Commander Kaplan came around the starboard side of the tactical station, stepping forward.

"Nathan, Jessica, this is my executive officer, Commander Lara Kaplan. Commander, this is Lieutenant Jessica Nash, of the Ghatazhak, and Captain Nathan Scott."

"Commander," Nathan greeted, shaking her hand.

"It's an honor to meet you both," Commander Kaplan replied, her eyes fixed on Nathan. "She's right. You do look young."

"Story of my life," Nathan replied. He looked around the bridge, then back at the main view screen. "I see you finally put the fishbowl to good use."

"We just expanded on your ideas," Cameron replied.

"Big Blue?" Nathan asked, pointing at the view screen.

"We're just about to our jump point," Cameron said. "Mister Bickle?"

"Two minutes, twenty seconds, sir," the navigator replied.

"I'm a bit surprised," Nathan said. "The flight deck has changed so much, I sort of expected the bridge to have changed, as well."

"Not much to improve upon," Cameron replied. "Not since the last refit under your command."

Nathan turned to his left, spotting a familiar face. "Kono?"

"Yes, sir," the sensor officer replied, standing. "It's good to see you again, Captain."

"You too. You're a lieutenant commander now. Congratulations."

"Thank you, sir."

"This is Ensign Bickle, our navigator, and Lieutenant Dinev, our helmsman," Cameron continued.

"Pleasure to meet you both," Nathan greeted.

"And Lieutenant Commander Vidmar is our tactical officer."

"Lieutenant Commander," Nathan greeted with a nod.

"A pleasure, Captain."

"Well, I suppose I should at least thank you all for rescuing me," Nathan addressed the group. "So, thanks." He looked at Jessica.

"Very smooth," she commented under her breath.

"One minute, Captain," Ensign Bickle warned.

General Telles entered the bridge next, coming up behind them. For the first time in all the years she had known him, Jessica thought she saw surprise on the general's face when Nathan turned to greet him.

"General," Nathan greeted.

"Captain," the general replied, after an awkward pause. "Quite the change."

"For the better, I hope."

"Yes, but next time, I think you should consider not shaving quite as closely. A day's growth might make you look a little less...*youthful*?"

"So I've been told," Nathan replied.

"Thirty seconds to jump point," Mister Bickle warned.

"Would you like to take the conn?" Cameron offered, gesturing toward the command chair.

"Perhaps that's not such a..."

"It would help to make an impression on the fleet upon your arrival," General Telles suggested.

Nathan sighed, unsure. "Very well," he finally agreed, taking a seat. "If you insist."

Nathan sat down in the familiar chair. Although he had memories of the last five years as Connor Tuplo, to the part of him that was Nathan, it felt like just recently that he had sat in this very chair.

There was something special about it. He didn't do much while sitting here. It wasn't like on the Seiiki, where he was actively participating in the flying of the ship. Here, he had a few display controls and some comms controls, and very little else. *This* was a chair where one sat and thought about all that was happening, both within one's ship, and outside. *This* was the position from which one wielded their will...*out there*. This was the position from which one could affect change...*serious* change.

It was an incredible feeling of power, even though, technically, *he* didn't have the power at the moment. That belonged to Cameron. Part of him wanted the seat as his own again, yet part of him did not. He wondered, for a moment, if the part that did *not* was Connor. As Connor, he had wandered the Pentaurus sector and the surrounding sectors. He had interacted directly with locals at nearly every port of call. He had taken missions and turned away missions. His only responsibility had been for his crew of four and his small ship. It had been a good life. Trying, at times, but good, nonetheless. And, for a moment, he wondered why he had left it behind.

"Ten seconds," Mister Bickle warned.

Nathan looked at Cameron, who nodded. "Cleared to jump, Mister Bickle," Nathan instructed. The words rolled off his tongue naturally.

"Cleared to jump, aye... In three..."

There had been a time when he hated the responsibility of commanding this ship. All he had wanted was to get away from Earth, from his family, from all the expectations...

"...Two..."

But it seemed that wherever he went, great responsibility was thrust upon him. He remembered never feeling ready... Never feeling like he was qualified to make decisions that affected billions of lives.

"...One..."

But for some odd reason, he now felt ready.

"...Jumping."

There was no jump flash, as the light spilling through the partially covered view screen from the nearby blue giant was already brighter than the Aurora's jump flash. Instead, the blue light that illuminated the interior simply reverted back to normal levels.

"Jump one complete."

"Continue the series," Nathan instructed, his instincts kicking in.

Cameron looked at Jessica, who was beaming, then at the general, who showed no emotion at all.

"Continuing series," Ensign Bickle acknowledged.

"Adjusting course," Lieutenant Dinev reported as the Aurora began a slight turn to starboard.

"Second jump in three..."

Nathan already knew the final series by heart, having memorized it as Connor, before they had departed for the mission to Corinair. There were a total of eleven jumps in this series, with small course and speed corrections in between each jump that were just enough of a change to make it impossible to determine their final destination prior to their scheduled departure.

"It really is a brilliant little algorithm," Cameron commented as the next jump flash washed over the bridge. "I'm surprised Loki came up with it. I didn't realize he was so adept in such things."

"It was a joint effort between Loki, Josh, and Deliza," Jessica explained. "However, the gist of it *was* Loki's idea."

"That makes a little more sense," Cameron said.

"Its main goal is to make the trace difficult enough to ensure that the fleet has jumped to a new location prior to their discovery," General Telles explained further. "Based on our observations, it should take the Dusahn more than a week to complete the trace, *if* they were devoting every resource available to the effort, which is unlikely. Nevertheless, the fleet executes an evasive pattern on a daily basis, just to be sure."

"Wise precaution," Cameron agreed as another jump flash washed over them.

"How many ships are in this fleet of yours?" Commander Kaplan wondered.

"At present, the Glendanon, the Morsiko-Tavi, and two pod haulers," General Telles replied. "Along with a combat jumper, a cargo jumper, and a handful of Takaran Rakers."

"That's it?"

"And the Aurora, of course," the general added.

"I'm not sure that two cargo ships and a single warship constitute a *fleet*," the commander joked.

"We have plans to expand, once we have taken

care of our more pressing needs," the general told her as another jump flash washed over the bridge.

"What sort of needs?" Cameron wondered.

"Our most pressing need is to find accommodations for more than one thousand persons who were evacuated from Burgess."

"Where are they now?" Commander Kaplan asked.

"Living in makeshift dorms inside class-one cargo pods, stacked within the Glendanon's cargo bay," General Telles explained.

"It's not pretty," Jessica added.

"Is that even safe?" the commander wondered.

"Not very," the general admitted. "Additional shielding is being erected, but it will likely not be sufficient for the long term."

"You couldn't just put them on the surface somewhere?"

"You'd be risking the occupants of that world," Cameron surmised.

"Precisely," the general agreed. "The Dusahn, much like the Jung, employ the strategy of fear, shock, and horror to control the masses. If we wish to garner support from the people, it must be provided covertly. Maintaining a mobile base of operations *is* the only viable alternative at this point."

"Last jump coming up, sir."

"Very well," Cameron replied. "Oops, sorry," she apologized to Nathan.

Nathan just smiled as the last jump flash washed over them. When it cleared, the Glendanon and the much smaller Morsiko-Tavi were directly ahead.

"Sensors?" Nathan asked.

"Only the two contacts, sir," Lieutenant Commander Kono replied.

"Tactical?"

"Threat board is clear," Lieutenant Commander Vidmar answered.

"Mister deBanco," Nathan said. "Contact both ships and bring them up on vid-link, main screen."

"Aye, sir," the ensign answered.

Cameron, Jessica, Commander Kaplan, and General Telles all stepped back from Nathan. Less than a minute later, two screens popped up in the middle of the forward view screen, with the faces of Captain Gullen, of the Glendanon, and Captain Tobas, of the Morsiko-Tavi.

"Gentlemen," Nathan greeted, sounding confident and very much like his old self.

"*Captain Scott?*" Captain Gullen said, noticing not only the lack of a beard, but also the more youthful appearance.

"The one and only," Nathan confirmed.

Captain Tobas said nothing.

"*I... I am so glad that you made it back safely, Captain,*" Captain Gullen said, remembering that he was the only other captain in the fleet who knew the truth about what had happened on Corinair a day ago.

"I trust your daughter made it back to you safely, Captain?" Nathan inquired.

"*Yes,*" Captain Gullen said with a joyful laugh. "*Yes, she is here with me now,*" he added, gesturing for her to come to his side. A moment later, Sori came alongside her father, followed by Deliza Ta'Akar. "*I don't know how I can ever repay you all.*"

"*Nor I,*" Sori said.

"*Is everyone alright?*" Deliza asked.

"Everyone is fine. The crew of the Seiiki is unharmed. They are here, on the Aurora, with me."

"*That is good to hear, Captain,*" Deliza replied. "*I'm sure Lael will be overjoyed. And you? Are you…?*"

"I am fine, Deliza. We will speak further, soon. Requesting permission to dock with the Glendanon, Captain."

"*Permission granted, Captain,*" Captain Gullen replied happily. "*I look forward to speaking with you.*"

"I, as well," Nathan replied. "And thank you all, gentlemen. Aurora, out." Nathan waited for the two vid-link screens to disappear, then let out a sigh of relief. "How'd I do?" he asked, turning to Cameron and Jessica on his left.

Jessica looked at Cameron. "I'd say Nathan is back. How about you?"

Cameron nodded. "It certainly looks that way."

* * *

"Our first priority *must* be resources," General Telles insisted, "beginning with ships. Preferably, ones capable of accommodating all of our people."

"By *our people*, I'm assuming you mean those rescued from Burgess," Nathan commented from the end of the conference table. It was not where he normally sat. This was still Cameron's ship, and it was still her command briefing room. Hence, he felt best that *she* sit at the usual place for the Aurora's captain.

"Many of which either worked for the Ghatazhak, or are related to them," the general added.

"Have you *asked* them if they wish to continue their association with the Ghatazhak, or with this *rebellion*?" Nathan briefly scanned those in attendance. "That is what we're calling this, right? A rebellion?"

"*Resistance* might be a more accurate term," Cameron pointed out.

"*Resistance* is more technically accurate, given that the Dusahn only seized power eighteen days ago," General Telles agreed.

"*Resistance* sounds too much like a small group of people carrying out useless attacks on small targets, and never really getting anywhere," Jessica commented. "*Rebellion,* on the other hand, sounds bigger, more organized."

"Excellent point," General Telles agreed. "And the term 'Karuzari' *does* mean 'rebel warrior'."

"Then *Rebellion* it is," Nathan concluded. "And my question remains. I don't think we can rightfully assume that, just because they worked for you in peace, they are willing to do so in war. We *should* give them the opportunity to choose."

"It was always my intention to do so," General Telles assured him. "However, given that their world was unjustly destroyed *by* the Dusahn..."

"Because of the presence of the Ghatazhak..." Nathan interjected.

"...*Because* of the presence of the Ghatazhak, I suspect they will be so inclined," the general finished.

"Or, they may wish to distance themselves from us all, to avoid future retaliation," Nathan pointed out.

"Captain, I fail to see your point," the general said, becoming annoyed.

"My point is that we will need to be extra careful going forward, to ensure that we do not bring similar fates to everyone who *does* decide to help us."

"Hence the need for a mobile base of operations," General Telles reminded them.

"Every ship that joins this fleet is putting a target on their hulls," Nathan countered. "That is no small matter, especially to owner-captains, whose very livelihoods depend on their vessels."

"All the more reason for the owner-captains of jump-capable ships to want to see the Dusahn driven from the sector," General Telles argued. "The Dusahn are demanding the *surrender* of *all* jump-capable ships. They are not simply asking everyone to *register* their ships with them, and then continue with their operations as normal. And even if they were, I suspect they would demand considerable fees to do so."

"So, as an owner-captain of a cargo ship, my choices are to hand over my ship to the Dusahn and hope for the best, or fight for the right to operate my ship freely?"

"Precisely."

"You left out one more option, General," Nathan said. "To cut and run, just as Connor was going to do."

"What?" Cameron was a bit surprised.

"He came back," Jessica told her.

"We all know there are hundreds, if not thousands, of inhabited systems out there," Nathan pointed out. "An owner-captain could simply work his way further and further out, thus avoiding the Dusahn for the rest of his life."

"Assuming that the Dusahn expansion proceeds at a slower pace," General Telles argued.

"I'm not trying to be argumentative, General," Nathan said, recognizing the admiral's irritation. "I'm just playing devil's advocate. I'm assuming we'll be going out and asking these owner-captains to risk their primary assets, all for the greater good. I'm not sure all of them are going to buy your argument."

"You could show them the statistics," General Telles said.

"What *statistics*?" Cameron asked.

"It is a simple process to run the numbers. Ship production rates, jump travel times, rates of technological advancement, available resources and manpower. The Dusahn did not choose the Pentaurus cluster because they liked the name. They chose it for its potential for rapid growth and expansion. They chose it for its abundant resources and its industrial and technological base. They chose it because of its large number of skilled laborers. Even more importantly, they chose it because of its relatively weak, common political structure. In a nutshell, the Dusahn chose the Pentaurus cluster because it will enable them to rapidly grow and expand their influence. The Dusahn mean to build an empire, and they mean to do so on the backs of the people of the Pentaurus sector, and the surrounding sectors."

"And you came to this conclusion, how?" Cameron asked.

"It is the only logical conclusion that the current facts support," the general explained. "A relatively small number of ships for an invasion force. A target that contains a number of planets within relatively close range, thus being easy to cover with a smaller number of ships. And the fact that they went a considerable distance *beyond* the cluster in order to destroy the only force that posed a threat to them."

"Still not enough to assume they plan to expand their little empire," Cameron argued.

"No, but you are forgetting one important fact," General Telles said. "The Dusahn are Jung, and the Jung are conquerors."

"Good point," Cameron agreed. "And if the Dusahn

are a Jung warrior caste that was once expelled from the Jung Empire..."

"Then they're looking for payback," Jessica interrupted.

"I was going to say that they're looking to build their own empire, but..."

"Is it possible the Dusahn *want* a war between the Jung Empire and the Sol Alliance?" Nathan wondered.

"That *would* guarantee that the Alliance would not interfere with their plans in the Pentaurus cluster," General Telles agreed. "Especially if they *knew* of Admiral Galiardi's desire to rid Earth of the Jung threat, once and for all."

"You're not inferring that Galiardi is in *collusion* with the Dusahn, are you?" Nathan wondered.

"More likely they simply have good intelligence," General Telles replied. "After all, if they have similar jump capabilities, it would not be difficult to insert operatives back on Earth, as well as on Nor-Patri."

"Doesn't the Alliance monitor jump traffic?" Nathan asked.

"We do," Cameron told him. "All jump-capable ships have to be licensed by the governments of the Alliance, and they have to be fitted with appropriate transponders. But the amount of civilian jump traffic has increased exponentially over the years. What was once live-tracking has been reduced to more of a paper trail than anything else."

"Then it was really just a matter of time before the Jung got their hands on a jump drive," Nathan said.

"As far as we know, they still *don't* have jump tech," Cameron pointed out. "At least, there is no evidence one way or the other."

"I think it is more likely that Admiral Galiardi is simply taking advantage of the situation to further his own agenda," General Telles surmised.

"It would make it a lot easier to get rid of him, and get the Sol Alliance involved here, if he *was* in collusion with the Dusahn," Jessica said.

"This is exactly why I think politics and the military should never mix," Cameron muttered bitterly.

"We could debate this all day," Nathan said, hoping to move forward. "We *need* to decide what to do next."

"Wars are fought with people, intelligence, and resources," General Telles stated plainly. "We currently have little of each of these."

"Not exactly," Deliza said, finally arriving to the meeting. "I apologize for my tardiness," she added, taking her seat at the conference table.

"No apologies necessary," Nathan assured her. "It is good to see you again, Deliza."

Deliza stared at him a moment, noticing that he appeared much younger than she remembered. "It is wonderful to see *you* again, Captain."

"You were saying?"

"Yes... Ranni Enterprises has holdings in many markets, spread throughout the Pentaurus sector and beyond. Most of those holdings are not yet under the control of the Dusahn, although many soon will be."

"Why?" Nathan wondered.

"My father recognized the amount of resistance he was getting from the nobles of Takara, regarding his desire to move our society to a truly democratic one. He began moving our family's holdings off-world, just in case. After his execution, I continued the same practice, out of fear that the nobles would find a way to legally seize those assets. In the first few years after the fall of House Ta'Akar, the economies of the entire Pentaurus sector were in turmoil. This created many opportunities, which we took advantage of. The effect began in Takara, and spread outward. We simply stayed one step ahead, taking advantage of the change. We were able to amass a considerable fortune."

"Enough to fund a rebellion?"

"Perhaps not *that* much, but certainly enough to get it off to a good start," Deliza explained. "However, we will need to gain access to those accounts, which will require my presence at each institution."

"The Aurora can help with intelligence," Cameron said. "We carry six jump recon drones and twenty jump comm-drones that can be reconfigured to serve as limited recon drones."

"That will be helpful," General Telles agreed.

"What we need are boots on the ground," Jessica insisted. "Human intelligence. Eyes and ears on the Dusahn-occupied worlds. Preferably ones we can turn into underground resistance movements."

"We have already dropped weapons and leaflets calling people to arms on Corinair," General Telles pointed out. "That would be a logical place to start."

"How are we supposed to communicate with them?" Nathan wondered.

"There are always ways," Jessica assured him.

"You will need operatives on the ground, won't you?" Cameron asked.

"At first, yes," Jessica agreed. "To get them organized, and to set up communications. Once that is done, the operative doesn't necessarily have to remain there."

"How are we going to get the operatives onto Corinair and off again?" Nathan wondered.

Jessica looked at General Telles.

Deliza noticed the exchanged glance. "You still have it, don't you?"

"We do," the general replied.

"Have what?" Cameron wondered.

"The jump sub we used to escape from Nor-Patri with Nathan's consciousness," Jessica explained. "It's been boxed up all these years, but it was working when we packed it up."

"Where is it?"

"We moved it off-world, along with other assets, prior to the Dusahn attack on Burgess. We have yet to retrieve it."

"Assuming it still works, who's going to go?" Cameron asked.

"The only person with the training and experience in such matters," General Telles said.

"Which would be me," Jessica followed, reluctantly raising her hand.

"I should go, as well," Nathan said, not sounding convinced with the idea.

"Perhaps it would be best if you were to remain here, where it is safe," General Telles suggested.

"If I'm going to lead this rebellion, I'm going to do so from the front lines, General," Nathan insisted. "Not from a comfortable chair on a bridge somewhere. Not this time."

"But you have only just awakened," the general argued. "Perhaps it would be best for you to take the time to get accustomed to your new body..."

"It's the same body," Nathan argued. "And the more I *use* it, the more quickly I become *accustomed* to it."

"I'm just suggesting..."

"I know," Nathan said, cutting the general short. "And I appreciate your concern. But I *need* to do this. I *need* to be out there, risking my own ass. Otherwise, I don't have the *right* to ask others to risk *theirs*. Besides, the Corinairans all think I'm long dead and buried. They're not going to believe I'm alive unless they see me, in person."

"And if the *Dusahn* see you?" Cameron asked, also not convinced that Nathan should go.

"I never said it was without risk," Nathan replied. "But we're launching a rebellion here. There will be risk, and plenty of it. Besides, it's not like I'm going to walk down the street waving at everyone."

"But it's a foreign world to you," Cameron reminded him. "Jessica's trained for this type of thing. You're not. How are you going to blend in?"

"I've lived in and around the Pentaurus sector for five years now, as Connor Tuplo," Nathan replied. "I speak Angla like a native, and I even know enough Takaran and Corinairan to get by without raising suspicion. I also speak a little Palean, and enough Volonese to order dinner and get my face slapped. I'm pretty sure I'll get by."

"He makes a good point," General Telles reluctantly agreed. "However, I would strongly suggest that you spend some time engaged in rehabilitation, prior to charging off into battle."

"Are you trying to tell me to spend some time in the gym, General?" Nathan asked, smiling.

"I am trying very hard *not* to tell you just that."

"Do we have the time?" Nathan wondered.

"I imagine it will take some time for our people to get the jump sub ready for use," the general said.

"Very well," Nathan replied. "In the meantime,

we should start looking for another ship. Something that can accommodate a few thousand people. I can take the Seiiki out and visit a few ports I know, and ask around."

"What about your rehabilitation?" General Telles wondered.

"I'll take care of it," Jessica offered. "I can go with him. There's room in the Seiiki's cargo hold. I can give him a few good workouts." She looked at Nathan with a mischievous smile.

"I'm sure you can," Nathan said, grinning back at her.

"If I may?" Captain Gullen said, speaking up for the first time since the meeting had started. "There is a cruise ship; the Mystic Empress. She is of Takaran registry, but her captain is Corinairan. His wife and child were among those you rescued. My daughter spoke with them during the escape journey. The Mystic was on the grand tour when the attack occurred."

"The grand tour?" Cameron wondered.

"A twenty-day tour of the Syllium Orfee clouds," Captain Gullen explained. "It's a luxury cruise that jumps from system to system, offering spectacular views of the clouds, and some of the more interesting ring worlds within the systems of the cloud. The tour ends with an all-day party as they slingshot around the blue giant, Syllium AB, that gives the clouds their beauty."

"I've heard of that ship," Nathan said. "Luxury is an understatement. They cater to the upper crust of Takaran nobility, don't they?"

"Mostly, yes, but there are a few Corinairan families wealthy enough to afford the trip, as well."

"You think they're avoiding returning?" Nathan speculated.

"Possibly," Captain Gullen replied. "But it is also possible that they do not yet know of the invasion."

"How could they *not* know?" Cameron challenged.

"Syllium Orfee is at least three hundred light years from Takara, and at least half that from any other inhabited world. The clouds are highly charged, making long-range communication impossible. Even sensors are unable to penetrate the clouds to a significant depth. It is part of the grand tour's appeal. To be completely disconnected from regular life and explore and witness sights that most people will never see in their lifetimes. *If* the Mystic entered the clouds *before* the Dusahn invaded, and they have not yet exited the cloud, it is highly likely that they are unaware of the Dusahn invasion."

"Did his wife say when the Mystic was due back?"

"Only when he departed, and when he was due home. However, if you assume two days at the beginning and end of the journey, one could reasonably assume that the Mystic is nearing the end of her journey."

"Then we should start looking for her as soon as possible," Jessica concluded.

"In such an environment, she will be difficult to find."

"The Seiiki has pretty good sensors," Nathan said. "If we backtrack her course, we should be able to find her."

"Our Reapers might be better suited for the task," Cameron suggested.

"Perhaps, but I'd rather your vessel concentrate on reconnaissance for the time being."

"Of course," Cameron agreed.

"I can speak with the wife of the Mystic's captain," Captain Gullen offered. "She may have some knowledge of her husband's course."

"Very well," the general replied. "Finding the Mystic Empress shall be your first mission, Captain Scott." He turned to Cameron. "Captain Taylor, how soon can you start sending out recon drones?"

"Immediately."

"Excellent. Let's concentrate on trying to establish how many jump-capable ships the Dusahn actually have and what their performance limits are."

"We're on it," Cameron assured him.

"Very well," General Telles said, about to conclude their meeting.

"There is one other thing," Nathan interrupted. "The Seiiki has taken a bit of a beating over the last few days. It's nothing we can't fix en route, but it's a bit more than Marcus and Dalen can handle on their own. Plus, there are a few problems with the additional reactors that your people installed to power our new weapons."

"What is it you require?" General Telles asked.

"Someone with more skill and experience than my people," Nathan explained. "Someone who is creative when it comes to fixing, and *improving* systems."

"I'm assuming you had someone in mind?" the general replied.

Nathan looked at Cameron. "I was hoping you could spare Vlad for a few days."

"You want to *take* my chief engineer?"

"If you can spare him," Nathan said. "I'm sure he could straighten the Seiiki out. And my guy would learn a few tricks, as well."

Cameron sighed. "We still have a lot of damage to repair."

"Mostly structural though, right?" Nathan replied.

"Yes, but..."

"Your jump systems are all back to normal, right? And all your weapons and sensors are working?"

"Yes," she admitted, knowing Nathan was about to get his way. "I'll check with Commander Kamenetskiy. If *he* feels comfortable leaving his ship in the hands of his junior engineers, then I'll allow it."

Nathan smiled.

"Oh, this is gonna be a fun trip," Jessica commented under her breath.

* * *

"Our intelligence analysts assured us that the Alliance would *not* send ships to the Pentaurus cluster," Lord Dusahn exclaimed angrily, "not while the threat of a Jung attack existed!"

"Their operatives on Earth can only report that which the public has been made aware of, my lord," General Hesson reminded his leader. "Their military leader is still making public statements emphasizing the seriousness of the Jung threat and the need to build up their military and take decisive action."

"Then what is the Aurora doing here?" Lord Dusahn said, thinking out loud rather than asking for a real answer.

"It is possible that the Sol Alliance sent the Aurora without revealing such to the public," the general suggested.

"The man is vocal about every move he makes," Lord Dusahn stated. "He wants everyone on Earth to know that *he* is the one keeping them safe, and not their political leaders."

"I doubt he shares the disposition of *every* ship with the public."

"True enough, I suppose. But the *Aurora*? The most visible and well-known ship in the Alliance? To send her, of all ships. Why not send one of his countless gunships? Or a dozen of them? No one would even notice." Lord Dusahn paced across his office floor, stopping to stare out the window over Answari. "No, that old man is up to something. He sent the Aurora to Corinair for a reason." He turned back to the general. "Did they find anything in the rubble at that facility on Corinair? What was it called?"

"Ranni Enterprises, my lord," General Hesson replied. "Owned by the daughter of the late Prince Casimir Ta'Akar, the man who overthrew his brother to regain the throne of his people and was then assassinated by his own nobles."

Lord Dusahn closed his eyes for a moment, thinking. "Ah, yes. The young woman parlayed her late father's holdings into quite a sum, if I remember correctly."

"Shipping, commodities trading, technological research, and development. They even produced a personal jump shuttle that is in wide use. It was later developed into a larger version that is used as a jump-capable passenger transport. We have already captured a number of them. In fact, we believe that it was her personal shuttle that attempted to land during our initial invasion of Corinair."

"And they came back for something," Lord Dusahn surmised, his left eyebrow rising. "Something important enough to involve the Aurora, no less."

"One would think the rescue of more than two hundred prisoners would be enough of a reason," General Hesson said.

"Perhaps, but did not the reports state that the lower levels of the Ranni building were destroyed?"

"Completely, my lord. And in such a way as to ensure that there would be nothing left to recover."

"They came to retrieve something from that lab," Lord Dusahn said. "Something of great importance to them. Something so important that they had to destroy all evidence of its existence."

"There is the other matter, my lord," General Hesson reminded his leader. "The leaflets announcing the return of Na-Tan."

"Nathan Scott is long dead," Lord Dusahn replied.

"Our people have studied the legend. Nowhere does it say that *one* individual is Na-Tan. Many believe the term refers to one who would lead."

"I have read this legend," Lord Dusahn said dismissively. "They are the ramblings of the poor and downtrodden. We have encountered many such legends in the past. This one is of no more importance than any of the others."

"But the people of Corinair *do* believe in Na-Tan," General Hesson insisted. "Especially since Nathan Scott liberated them from Takaran rule."

"The Corinairans *know* that Nathan Scott is dead. If someone claiming to be him *does* show up, they will brand him an imposter."

"I am not as convinced of this as you, my lord."

"You worry too much about the will of the people and the power of their beliefs, my dear General," Lord Dusahn said, waving his hand.

"Perhaps our concerns should be with finding the Aurora. If we find her, we will likely find the Ghatazhak as well."

"A single ship, even one as infamous as the Aurora, does not pose a significant threat to the

Dusahn Empire," Lord Dusahn stated confidently. "To pay her much mind would only demonstrate our lack of resolve in the eyes of those we mean to rule."

"Of course, my lord," General Hesson replied, nodding his compliance.

* * *

Nathan jogged effortlessly down the country path. The air held the faintest smell of the tall, green grass flowing in the breeze on either side of the trail. He could hear birds chirping away from nearby trees, and at times, he thought he could make out the sound of running water, perhaps from a nearby stream or small river.

A small flash of light appeared, high and to his right, quite distant. A few seconds later, a distant clap of thunder followed. He scanned the sky above and ahead, tracking from side to side, knowing that the ship wouldn't be where he perceived the sound to have come from. A moment later, he located the small, cylindrical object. Ungainly looking, with no wings. A shuttle of some sort. By the size of it, probably a cargo shuttle. No surprise, as according to the moving map display hovering in the upper right corner of his view, there was a spaceport nearby.

The trail forked ahead, and Nathan decided to take the trail leading left, toward the direction of the sound of running water he thought he had heard. After a few more minutes of jogging, his suspicion was confirmed. The trail turned to follow a babbling brook. Just ahead, water was cascading down a series of rocks, the trail along the brook gradually inclining up the hill.

A few birds seemed disturbed by Nathan's presence, becoming quite vocal in their warnings as Nathan started up the hill. *Probably to hide the sound of the incline motor,* he thought. *Clever.*

The path he had been jogging for the last ten minutes was smooth, as if it was purposefully made that way for public safety purposes. But now, as he started up the hill, the path became uneven, with little gullies where water had carved into the dirt during heavy rains. There was also the occasional, buried boulder protruding slightly. Nathan's pace became uneven, his stride lagging as he was forced to choose his steps more carefully.

The intensity of the workout was increasing, as well. Nathan felt his pulse quickening, as well as his breathing. Within a few minutes, he was beginning to sweat. As if on cue, the prevailing breeze picked up, helping to cool him down as the water crashing over the rocks became louder, and the incline became steeper and more varied.

Maybe I should have turned right.

Nathan continued upward, feeling the strain on his legs as well as his lungs. He was amazed at how real the ground beneath him felt, and he made a mental note to watch someone else use this device, so that he could witness the mechanism in action.

Minutes later, he reached the summit, and the trail flattened out. The brook again became calm, its waters smooth. Nathan slowed his pace, continuing on another minute before coming to a stop. He bent over slightly, his hands on his knees to rest, as he caught his breath. He looked from side to side, taking in the oak trees to his left and the winding brook to his right. He looked up and spotted another craft flying overhead, this time on a departure course. He watched it for a moment, until it disappeared behind a flash of blue-white light, followed by another distant clap of thunder.

"Not bad," Jessica called from behind him. "Had enough?"

Nathan stood upright. "End session," he instructed. The view around him disappeared. The trees, the winding brook, the sound of running water behind him, the sky overhead...it was all replaced with the interior of the simulator. Stark, white walls that formed a seamless oval wrapped around him in all directions, except directly behind. Even the smell of the green grass was gone.

"Pretty sweet, isn't it?" Jessica said.

"It sure is," Nathan agreed, turning around to face her. "I'm assuming they have other routes, as well?" he added, stepping down out of the sim and into the Aurora's gymnasium.

"Oh, yeah," Jessica replied enthusiastically. "Beaches, city streets and parks, mountain trails... you name it, it's in there."

"I'm amazed at how the ground *really* feels like it's the shape that you're seeing. I assume the treadmill itself is changing shape beneath my feet?"

"Yup. It's pretty cool to watch from back here, too."

"Hop up and give me a show," Nathan suggested.

"Some other time," Jessica replied. "We're here to work *you* out, not me."

"Right. Where do we start?"

Jessica turned and led him away from the motion simulator, toward an apparatus along the wall next to it. "Here."

"What's this?"

"It's designed to practice blocking and dodging

during a fight," Jessica explained. "They call it a 'fight dummy'."

"How's it work?"

"Step back," Jessica instructed, moving to the side control panel.

Nathan stepped back as Jessica activated the device. One by one, padded fists jutted forth from either side of a central pad that stretched from head height to crotch. Left, then right, then left again. Then a short, padded arm came up from the bottom left, swinging upward like a man's knee coming up. Then a long arm swung around from the right, at head height, followed by one from the left at mid-chest height. The pattern repeated, with blows coming from all angles, heights, and directions, at a rate of one every three seconds.

"Variable patterns and rates," Jessica added, turning up the tempo.

Nathan was taken aback, as the machine suddenly sped up its tempo. He laughed as she turned the device off. "You first," he insisted.

Jessica flashed a confident smile as she punched in her desired settings. Once finished, she moved in front of the machine.

"*Stand ready,*" the recorded voice warned.

Jessica raised her hands, closing them into loose fists, positioning her body at a slight angle to the machine and in a ready crouch. "Ready," she announced.

The machine swung a padded arm around toward her left side, which she immediately countered by raising her left arm. Then a padded fist shot straight out at chest height, and Jessica blocked it by tucking her right elbow in to protect herself, pushing outward to deflect the machine's jab to her right.

Next, another padded arm swung up and inward from the bottom of the machine, headed for her left side. Jessica dropped her left arm down as she shifted her body slightly right, preventing the arm from touching her body. Then her right hand jabbed the machine at the strike pad located at head height. The machine produced its own surprise, sending a short arm directly forward at mid-abdomen height. On the tip of the arm, instead of a padded fist, was a rubber knife. Jessica brought her left arm up under the padded arm jutting toward her abdomen, while she brought her right hand quickly down, trapping the simulated knife hand between them, knocking the rubber knife out of the machine's simulated hand in a way that likely would have broken the wrist of a real assailant.

"Nice moves," Nathan said, watching Jessica defend against the simulated attack.

Jessica stepped back out of the machine's reach as it continued to flail at her. "Increase difficulty, level eight, random pattern."

The machine stopped its simulated attack. "*Level eight, random pattern,*" it confirmed. "*Stand ready.*"

Jessica stepped forward, putting herself within reach of the machine once again, reassuming her combat stance. "Ready."

Again, the machine began its simulated attack, sending padded arms and fists punching out, swinging around from the sides, and thrusting up from below...only, this time, at what seemed ten times the previous rate. Jessica responded with grace and calm, blocking every attempt the machine made to land a hit. Jabs to the face, chest, and abdomen. Swings from the outside to both the head and body. Padded limbs coming up from below, seeking contact with her lower body, both front and sides. She continued to block every attempt, even disarming several edged weapons, all while landing several blows to the machine's padded strike pads, attacks that would've seriously injured a real opponent.

"Increase rate of attack," Jessica instructed as she continued to ward off the machine's attack.

"*Increasing rate of attack,*" the machine replied. The rate of the attack increased noticeably, as did both the speed of Jessica's reactions and the strength of her blows.

With each strike, the machine shook violently. Nathan cringed every time she struck the machine's padded strike pads, fearing it would become disconnected from the wall and crash to the floor.

Finally, after several minutes, Jessica stepped back, removing herself from the machine's reach once again. "End session," she instructed.

The machine stopped its attack, its padded strike arms retracting. "*Session ended.*"

Jessica turned to look at Nathan, a satisfied smile on her face. She was only mildly panting, and she hadn't even broken a sweat, yet.

"Impressive," Nathan said. "I hope you're not expecting me to do that."

"We'll start you out at level one," Jessica assured him. "So you don't get hurt...too badly."

Nathan smiled at her. "I appreciate that," he said as he took her place in front of the machine.

"Level one, slowest speed," Jessica instructed.

"Shouldn't we start out with some resistance training or something?" Nathan asked.

"*Level one, slowest speed,*" the machine confirmed.

"Resistance training is to build muscles," Jessica

replied as she keyed new settings into the machine's control console.

"*Stand ready,*" the machine warned.

"Great physical conditioning requires the use of muscles in real-world motions," Jessica added, stepping back from the machine to watch Nathan defend. "Besides, this will help me to gauge your reaction times and overall muscle control, so that we can see how you're progressing over time."

"Of course." Nathan took a breath, then turned to face the machine, stepping forward and assuming a combat position, just as he had been taught back in the EDF Academy on Earth. "Ready."

Just as it had with Jessica, the machine swung a padded arm around toward Nathan's left side, which he countered in similar, although less graceful, fashion by raising his left arm. He blocked the next four attacks with relative ease, finding that he clearly remembered the sequence of attacks that Jessica had experienced. However, when the machine failed to produce a rubber knife headed toward his midsection, he realized his memorization of the original attack pattern was now useless, and he would have to simply react to each attack without being able to anticipate the machine's attempts to make contact with his body.

He managed to defend himself with relative ease, although there was nothing pretty about it. After a few minutes, Nathan realized the machine was repeating the same pattern, and his ability to block effectively began to improve.

By the time the machine got halfway through its third cycle, Jessica could tell that Nathan had memorized the order. "You want to speed it up a bit?" she asked, taunting him.

"Bring it," Nathan replied as he managed to get a shot into the machine's head-height strike pad.

"Increase rate of attack," Jessica commanded.

"*Increasing rate of attack,*" the machine acknowledged.

The rate at which the machine launched its attacks increased, and Nathan picked up his pace, as well. But now, he had the machine's sequence memorized. He was getting his entire body into action, stepping left, right, forward, and back, using his own body momentum to aid in his defense. And he was managing to get a few more blows in, as well, striking the machine in the head, chest, and abdomen strike pads, although not nearly with the force Jessica had.

"You're doing pretty good for a guy who's been dead for seven years," Jessica teased. "How are you feeling?"

"Good," Nathan replied between blows.

"Think you can handle faster?"

"Hell, yes," Nathan insisted, although he wasn't entirely certain it was a good idea.

"Increase rate of attack," Jessica instructed the machine again.

"*Increasing rate of attack.*"

The rate of attacks on Nathan's body increased, yet again. The blows were now coming at a rate of one per second. A jab to the face, which Nathan leaned back and away from. A right cross, followed by a left uppercut and a left knee jab, then two repeated attempts at the midsection followed by a left cross, all of which Nathan either blocked or avoided. And still, he managed to get in one or two blows in the process.

As he defended himself, Nathan realized

something. He wasn't really looking at the machine any longer. Yet, he was still seeing its padded, mechanical arms, reaching out to strike him from different angles and directions...*in his mind.*

As the machine reached the end of its pattern cycle, Nathan closed his eyes and continued defending himself. Jab to the face, right cross, left uppercut, left knee jab, jabs to the gut...each of them countered perfectly; *with his eyes closed.*

An overwhelming feeling of confidence washed over him as he began sneaking blows into the machine's various strike pads between nearly every attack the machine launched at him...still with both eyes closed.

Jessica noticed Nathan's sudden improvement, as well as his closed eyes, and walked around to the machine's control pad as it continued repeating the attack sequence. Without saying a word, she reached out and touched the control pad, increasing the rate of attack, without warning him.

But Nathan heard the faint beep of the control pad, even though it was masked by the whirring of the machine's servos and hydraulics. He felt the rhythm of the attacks increase in speed, and he matched it. The first cycle, he defended only, still with his eyes closed. But, by the next cycle, he began striking back again, and with more force than before.

Another thing surprised Nathan this time. He was huffing and puffing, as expected. After all, he had only been alive for a little over a day now, so he was expected to be a bit out of shape. But he was calm. In fact, he felt incredibly calm. It was almost a dance to him. Stepping back and forth as his arms moved in rhythmic fashion to counter the mechanical appendages of his attacker.

"Faster!" Nathan demanded, finding an unexpected pleasure in the simulated combat dance that he was engaged in with his mechanical dance partner.

Jessica stepped up to the machine again, increasing its rate of attack once again. Only this time, she added a few more twists.

The mechanical attacks were now coming at a rate of two to three per second, yet Nathan was still able to defend himself, and his eyes were still closed. He wasn't landing any blows himself, but he was still poised and relaxed...until it happened.

The machine suddenly changed its rhythm, firing two lightning-fast blows to the gut, the second of which Nathan failed to block. Without pause, the machine returned to what Nathan thought was the beginning of its sequence again, and he raised his hands to block what he expected to be a jab to the face, followed by a right cross.

But that's not what he got.

The next blow came as an uppercut that caught him in the chin, causing him to stumble backward, out of the machine's attack reach.

"*Pausing session,*" the machine announced, its arms retracting.

Nathan's eyes were open now. He knew it wasn't true, but he almost felt as if the machine had just mocked him with its tone. He looked at Jessica, who was smiling, obviously happy with herself. "So, *that's* how we're playing it?"

"I promised to give you a workout, didn't I?" Jessica replied. "So, do you *want* a workout, or do you want to just keep on dancing with Battling Betty here?"

Nathan didn't respond. He stepped forward,

moving into the machine's range once again. After assuming a combat stance, he called out. "Ready."

Betty launched another attack, this time throwing rapid combinations, never repeating a single sequence. Nathan defended himself admirably, albeit with eyes wide open. After a few minutes of getting pounded, he began to see a pattern to Betty's attack. Every combination came in either two, three, or four blows, but never the same number in a combination twice in a row. And the number of blows in each combination increased with each new round, until reaching four, at which point it would go back to two. The randomness was in what single blows Betty would launch in *between* the combinations, and eventually, he began to see patterns in *that* as well.

Now, he was beginning to land his own blows again, and the number of Betty's successful attempts to make contact with his body began to decrease.

Again, Jessica moved into the control panel and changed the settings. At first, Nathan thought she had just turned up the speed again, but he quickly realized she had changed the settings to make Betty's attacks be completely random. Now, half of the attacks were finding their targets on Nathan's body, while Nathan himself was barely able to get any decent blows in.

In short, Betty was kicking his ass.

After several minutes, Nathan stepped backward, stumbling as he tried to regain his balance. "Enough!" he declared, panting heavily.

"End session," Jessica instructed.

"*Session ended,*" Betty replied, retracting her padded arms to her sides again.

Nathan stared at Betty's faceless form. It barely resembled a human, even with the most active of imaginations. Yet, he could swear he saw a smug look on the machine's blank, red, head-height strike pad. "I'll get you next time, bitch," Nathan panted, before turning away and bending over to catch his breath.

"Don't feel too bad," Jessica said, sounding quite amused. "You're not the first man to get a beatdown by Betty."

"Has she always been on this ship?" Nathan asked, still hunched over and panting.

"Since launch," Jessica assured him. "I used to train with her daily back then. She's too easy to be of use to me now."

Nathan looked at her, shocked. "Seriously?"

"Yup."

"What the hell have the Ghatazhak been feeding you?"

"Just really good training," Jessica replied. "Not only physical, but mental as well. That's why I had Betty use patterns at first. I wanted to see if you'd recognize them...and you did."

"Is that a shock?"

"Many people never find the patterns," Jessica replied. "I expected you to, but I didn't expect you to do it that quickly. And the eyes closed thing...now *that* was impressive."

"Thanks." Nathan finally stood up straight, moving over to pick up his water bottle. He took a long drink. "It was weird. I could see her swinging, in my head. It's like a memorized video I had seen or something."

"Were you always able to do that?"

"I don't think so," Nathan replied. "I mean, I've always had a better-than-average memory, but this was *so clear*."

"Interesting," Jessica replied. She tossed a towel to him. "You ready for more?"

"Of Betty?"

"Nope." Jessica got a mischievous smile on her face. "I've got a few other surprises lined up for you."

"I see," Nathan replied, wiping the sweat from his head and face. "I think you're enjoying this too much."

CHAPTER FOUR

Robert Nash stepped off the shuttle wearing civilian attire for the first time in months. He paused a moment to take in the air of Kohara, breathing in deeply, feeling the sun on his face. The air might not have been fresh, given that he was standing on the tarmac of one of the busiest spaceports in the Tau Ceti system. But it was *real* air, not the purified, sterilized, temperature and humidity-controlled air that he breathed, day in and day out, aboard the Tanna.

Robert envied Gil Roselle, the captain of the captured Jung battleship, *Jar-Benakh,* now known simply as the *Benakh.* Being stationed in the Tau Ceti system meant he had access to the surface on a regular basis. Such visits were rare for Robert Nash. Destroyers spent most of their time on patrol, ready to respond the moment a Cobra gunship reported a contact. The planet-side visits he managed were few, far between, and usually short-lived.

It had taken him three shuttles to get to Kohara, but it was necessary to cover any trace of his visit. Had he flown in directly from the Tanna to the military terminal at the Kohara spaceport, Fleet Command would have known of his visit, and that the Tanna had veered from its assigned patrol route, within a few hours. He had, on occasion, used his command authority to change his routing, but it involved additional reports and explanations, which would bring additional scrutiny. Considering the nature of the message he had received from Captain Taylor, additional scrutiny was the last thing he needed.

After leaving the Koharan spaceport, Robert took

a train around the far side of the lake, to a lakeside resort town named Loressigo. He had arrived just after sunset, and having spent the last few hours traveling, he was ready to eat. Luckily, dinner was the first item on his agenda.

Robert walked along the shore, away from the train station, arriving at the small restaurant overlooking the harbor.

"Good evening, sir," the woman at the counter greeted him cheerfully. "Dining alone?"

"I'm meeting someone," Robert replied. "An old friend. Older gentleman. Shorter, graying hair, angry looking?"

The woman nodded. "Oh, yes. He is on the patio."

"Thank you." Robert made his way through the tiny dining room and out onto the spacious patio. At the furthest table from the door, all the way out along the far rail, he spotted his friend.

"Gil," Robert greeted him, walking up to the table.

Gil Roselle rose from the table, shaking Robert's hand before sitting down again. "Good to see you again, Robert. Though, I gotta say I was surprised that you asked to meet me...especially here."

"I figured, since you have a boat here in Loressigo, you'd know of this place."

"Shari and I eat here all the time," Gil replied. "Great *doray* fish."

"So, she's still putting up with your gruff, old ass?" Robert joked as he picked up the digital menu pad and began scrolling through the selections.

"Barely."

"She still trying to get you to retire and settle down?"

"Yup, but I'm holding my ground. I keep telling her that I'd retire tomorrow if she'll agree to live on the boat with me, but she's standing her ground about living in the city."

"You're going to have to give in, sooner or later, Gil. Shari's too hot for you to pass up, you know that."

"What are you trying to say? You calling me ugly?"

"No, I'm calling you butt-ugly," Robert joked.

"That's better," Gil replied, motioning to the waiter. "Two doray plates, and a couple stouts."

"I'm not so sure I'm in the mood for fish," Robert objected.

"You're sitting on a patio overlooking a lake full of the damned things, Robert. Trust me, you'll love it."

The waiter returned promptly with two tall glasses of beer, placing them on the table.

"I'm technically still on duty, you know," Robert said as he picked up his beer.

"You're on leave, aren't you?" When Robert didn't respond, Gill realized something was different. "What the fuck, Robert. What the hell's going on?"

Robert sighed. "I've known you for a long time, Gil. You and I, we're part of a dying breed in this Alliance."

"You got that right," Gil agreed.

"How well do you know Galiardi?" Robert asked.

"Well enough to know I don't like him much." Gil took another sip of his beer. "Don't get me wrong, the man's a brilliant strategist. The problem is, he knows it, and it tends to go to his head. Typical brass, really. Doesn't believe he can do anything wrong." Gil studied his friend for a moment. "Why do you ask?"

Robert sighed, thinking a moment. "I can trust you, right?"

"What kind of a fucking question is that for *you* to ask *me*?" Gil retorted, annoyed.

"Sorry, but I have to ask."

"Yeah, Robert. You can trust me. Besides, I'm probably going to give in and make Shari an honest woman pretty soon, anyway. So, spit it out."

"I got a message yesterday."

"From who?" Gil wondered.

"Cameron Taylor."

"Why'd she contact you?"

"She wanted me to know the truth, in case something happened."

Gil looked confused. "The truth about what? In case what happens?"

"She split, Gil. She violated orders, took the Aurora, and headed for the Pentaurus cluster."

Gil's eyebrows shot up in surprise. "You're shittin' me."

"God's truth."

"What the hell..." Gil shook his head in disbelief. "Has she lost it?"

"She had a pretty good reason, Gil," Robert said.

"To toss her career down the shitter? Hell, if she makes it back alive, she'll likely spend the rest of her life in prison, assuming she isn't executed for treason."

"How is it treason, Gil?"

"Trust me, Galiardi will find a way. What reason could she possibly have that would justify a bonehead move like that?"

Robert stared at Gil, unsure if he should tell him the truth or not.

"What?"

Truth was, he didn't have much choice. Robert still had no idea what he was going to do, or if he was going to do anything, at all. One thing was for sure, though. He needed someone to talk this through with, and Gil Roselle was the only person he could think of who had the balls to keep such knowledge to himself.

"You're making me nervous, Robert," Gil said, wondering why his friend was staring at him. "Are you going to tell me, or what?"

Robert took a deep breath, then blurted out the truth. "Nathan Scott is alive and is leading the Karuzari against the Dusahn forces in the Pentaurus cluster. Taylor took the Aurora there to help him."

"Scott is alive?"

"Yup."

"No bullshit?"

"No bullshit."

"Fuck."

"Yeah, that's how I felt."

"Fuck."

"You said that, Gil."

"F-u-u-uck." Gil leaned back in his chair. "Man, I have about a million questions."

"You and me, both."

"He's going to take them on by himself?"

"I don't really know. All I *do* know is that my sister and the Ghatazhak are with him, as well as Hayes and Sheehan. And Deliza Ta'Akar is funding them."

"Fuck, fuck, fuck, fuck, fuck."

"You know any other words, there, Gil?"

"Sorry, but this is pretty fucking mind-blowing."

"Tell me about it. Here's the kicker. Taylor thinks Galiardi is up to something. Says he's not telling us everything."

"Like what?"

"Like the Dusahn have said they aren't part of the Jung Empire... That they're acting on their own."

Now, Gil was starting to become concerned. "I had a feeling," he said, shaking his head. "Things just weren't adding up, you know?"

"I know," Robert agreed. "You don't think Galiardi would purposely start a new war with the Jung, do you?"

"I think Galiardi will do whatever he believes is best for Galiardi. That's what I think."

"Even if it means the deaths of millions?"

"It's all numbers when you're at his level, Robert. You know that. Right is what gets you what you're after."

"The question is, what is he after?" Robert wondered.

"No. The question is, what are *you* going to do with this intel?" Gil asked.

Robert sighed. "I don't really know."

"Well, I'll *tell* you what you're going to do," Gil said. "Nothing. That's what you're going to do. At least for now. We need more intel."

"We?"

"Yes, we. You just dragged me into this. Thank you for that, by the way."

"My pleasure."

"Did she say anything else?"

"She is planning on sending a jump comm-drone in about a week. She gave me intercept coordinates. I'm assuming she's planning on updating me once she learns more."

"Good for her," Gil said. "She's thinking. She's keeping the lines of communication open back home. Did she *tell* you to tell me?"

"Nope. That was my call."

"I imagine she's not going to be too happy about that."

"I figure she probably expected it."

"Could be right." Gil took another drink of his beer; this time, it was a long one. "Damn," he said, placing his glass back down on the table. "Nathan Scott...alive. Why am I not more surprised?"

* * *

"Uh-oh," Josh mumbled, looking out the back of the Seiiki into the Aurora's main hangar bay. "Looks like you're about to get schooled, Dalen."

"Why?"

Josh pointed at the tall, broad-shouldered man walking toward the Seiiki.

"Who's that?" Dalen asked.

"The man who's gonna show you how dumb you are," Marcus said.

"Relax," Nathan said as he slid down the forward ladder behind them. "He's just going to help us fix a few things around here." Nathan patted Dalen on the shoulder as he walked past him. "We're not tossing you out the airlock just yet, Dalen."

"Gee, thanks, Cap'n," Dalen replied sarcastically.

"Vlad," Nathan called to his friend as Vladimir ascended the cargo ramp. "I'm glad you agreed to join us," he added as he shook his friend's hand vigorously.

"Nothing could have stopped me," Vladimir replied, a broad smile on his face.

"I was afraid Cameron wasn't going to let you go."

"I have a very competent engineering staff," Vladimir boasted. "They will do fine without me."

"Good to know." Nathan turned to his crew. "You already know Josh and Marcus. This young man, however, is Dalen Voss, the Seiiki's chief mechanic, bottle washer, and all-around good kid. Dalen, this is my old friend, Commander Vladimir Kamenetskiy, the Aurora's chief of engineering, and likely the best engineer and all-around Mister Fix-it I have ever known."

"All true," Vladimir agreed. "But you forgot best-looking." He reached out to shake Dalen's hand. "It is a pleasure to meet you, Mister Voss."

"Likewise, Commander," Dalen replied.

"Please, this is not a military ship. Call me Vladimir."

"Dalen," the young mechanic responded.

Vladimir looked at Nathan, smiling. "It will be good to serve together again. I have missed you."

"Let's not get mushy around the crew," Nathan suggested, joking with his old friend. "Besides, we need to get busy. We're scheduled to depart in a few hours, and there are a few things we'd like to get squared away before departure."

"*Da, da, da.*" Vladimir looked back at Dalen. "Maybe you can show me what your biggest problems are?"

"Starting with ones that can't be serviced en route," Nathan reminded him.

"Sure thing," Dalen agreed. "Follow me," he added, heading down the cargo ramp.

Vladimir looked back at Nathan. "I guess I'll get started, then."

"Thanks, Vlad," Nathan replied as his friend turned to follow Dalen back down the cargo ramp.

Marcus watched them step off the ramp and disappear to starboard. "This is gonna be fun to watch," he said, moving to follow them.

Josh followed Marcus, passing Nathan on his way out.

"Where are you going?" Nathan wondered.

"To help them," Josh said, turning around to walk backwards down the ramp. "Besides, I could use some entertainment, as well."

* * *

Deliza stood on the Glendanon's cargo deck, watching as Burgean technicians removed the white, plastic wrapping from around the mini-jump sub.

The aft half of the ship's massive cargo bay had finally been sealed off and pressurized, thanks to the tireless efforts of Captain Gullen's crew and a handful of refugee volunteers from Burgess. They still needed to build a large transfer airlock at her bow, but that would have to come later, once they found a place for the refugees to live. For now, the entire front half of the ship still needed to be decompressed to allow smaller vessels to come and go, which was a slow process at best.

Two boxcars had gone to the Elsyn system to retrieve the Ghatazhak's stashed cargo pods, one of which contained the small jump sub that General Telles and Jessica had used to escape the Jung homeworld seven years ago. Now, it would be her job to inspect it and determine if it was mission ready and, if not, how to make it so.

The first thing she noticed as they peeled away the plastic, form-fitting cover was that two of the jump sub's six jump emitters appeared damaged. Although it would take further inspection to verify her suspicions, she was fairly certain that they had blown during Jessica's escape jump from Nor-Patri. She had seen similar failures during Ranni Enterprise's development of their corporate jump shuttle, when testing in rainy weather. Water trapped in the cracks of the emitter housings had frozen at the moment of jump, for reasons they had never determined. Because of that, they had developed self-heating emitters to prevent icing.

She tapped her first service note into her data pad. *Install heated emitters.*

A technician popped the hatch and stuck his head inside. A moment later he pulled his head out again, a disgusted look on his face.

Her second note. *Clean inside.*

"Got a bit of damage to the nose, here," a technician called from the front of the jump sub. "Should be able to patch it up."

Repair and reinforce nose was her third note.

Deliza stepped up to the side of the jump sub and plugged a cable from her data pad into a systems port on the side of the sub. Seeing the diagnostic data pour in, she was crestfallen. "We have a lot of work to do," she sighed.

* * *

"These power conduits are all wrong," Vladimir insisted, pointing to the thick lines running from the mini-fusion reactors in the back of what was now referred to as the Seiiki's 'gun deck', to the plasma cannon turrets on either side. "The heat dissipation wrap is completely inadequate. If you fired these weapons at full power for more than a few minutes, both gunners would be cooked. A few more minutes, and the deck would melt."

"What do we do?" Dalen asked, dumbfounded.

"We wrap them with liquid cooling wraps and pump the heated fluid to exchangers on the outside of the hull," Vladimir stated. "Preferably in the ship's slipstream, so they will be cooled if used in the atmosphere, as well."

"That means we have to cut more holes in the hull," Dalen complained.

"Then that's what we do," Nathan said.

"Where are we going to get these wraps you're talking about?" Marcus asked.

"We have plenty of them on board the Aurora," Vladimir replied. "Two per side should be enough."

"What about the heat exchangers?" Nathan wondered.

"We can manufacture them in a few hours using the Aurora's fabricators. The most difficult part will be the hull. How many layers did you say?"

"Four," Dalen replied. "Outer, inner, and two layers of shellite core."

"Shellite core?" Vladimir asked, unfamiliar with the term.

"It's a honeycomb structure made out of nanotube stuff the Takarans came up with a couple decades back," Nathan explained. "Very light, very strong, and good at absorbing kinetic energy. Full of tiny air pockets, as well, so it's a good insulator. You'll find it on just about any ship built in the PC up until about ten years ago."

"What do they use now?" Vladimir wondered.

"Some new stuff." Nathan looked at Marcus. "Dolenite or something?"

"Dolenzite," Marcus corrected. "Expensive stuff. It's used in all the Takaran military spacecraft."

"How are we going to cut through the hull?" Dalen asked.

"What did you use to plug up the windows and make the structure around the turrets?" Vladimir inquired.

"Cargo pod hull skins," Nathan replied.

"Seriously?"

"It's what we had at the time."

"You should keep that hatch closed during flight," Vladimir warned.

"We do," Nathan replied.

"And I'd automate these guns," Vladimir suggested.

"That's a bit trickier," Dalen said. "It would take quite a bit of cable routing to connect them to the ship's sensors."

"Why can't you just install sensors on each gun, and put a targeting computer back here?" Vladimir suggested.

"We thought about that," Dalen replied. "But we were afraid that the heat from the plasma generators would fry it."

"But you weren't worried about the people operating the guns?"

Nathan shrugged.

Vladimir sighed, scratching his head. "Maybe we can install plate shields?"

"Never heard of them," Nathan admitted.

"They are new. They're shields, just like on the Aurora, but much smaller. They were developed for the Reapers, and then adapted for the Eagles. They are small, double-layered shield sections that can be angled and moved."

"How small?" Nathan wondered.

"Three to five meters, I believe," Vladimir replied. "We could mount them to the sides of the turrets, so they would project shields on either side. That would offer some protection to your gunners, and to this entire deck. We would just have to adjust them to prevent the shields of one turret from interfering with the shields of the other."

"How long is all this going to take?"

"A couple days, perhaps?"

"We're scheduled to liftoff in six hours," Nathan told him.

"How long will you be gone?"

"We're not sure. A day or two, at least."

"If we install the shield emitters now, as well as the heat exchangers, and run the cabling and fluid lines through a hole behind each turret, and seal it up, we can do the rest en route," Vladimir suggested.

"Is Cameron going to let you come along?" Nathan wondered.

"She told me I was temporarily attached to your command," Vladimir replied with a smile.

"Very well," Nathan agreed. "Get started on the exterior stuff, and get everything else you need to finish up loaded into the cargo bay. But don't forget to leave room. We're bringing along Jessica and a Ghatazhak squad."

"I'll get a few of my men to start on the exchangers, and a couple hull techs started on the exterior openings," Vladimir promised, heading for the door. "This will be fun!"

Nathan sighed as Vladimir disappeared through the hatch.

"Man's got a funny idea of 'fun'," Marcus grumbled.

Dalen looked at the hull behind the port turret, then down at the power conduits that Vlad had been concerned about.

"Something wrong, Dalen?" Nathan wondered.

"How's he gonna power those shields *and* fire the guns at full power? Surely, that's gonna increase the heat load, right?"

"If Vlad says it'll work, it'll work," Nathan assured him.

"I sure hope you're right," Dalen replied, moving

past Nathan, headed for the hatch. "I'd hate to be a gunner in here if it doesn't."

Nathan looked around and sighed. "Me, too."

* * *

"Sorry I'm late," Nathan said as he entered the Aurora's command briefing room and took a seat at the opposite end of the table from Cameron. "I hope I didn't miss anything."

"We were just getting started," Cameron assured him, turning her attention back to Deliza.

"As I was saying, the jump sub is in poor shape overall. We will have to replace its entire jump drive. Emitters, energy banks, field generator, the works. I'd recommend using the same system as the Eagles, but with a fixed-distance, jump-control computer designed to hold two jumps- insertion and escape. The impeller drive and underwater navigation systems are all in working order, as is the life-support system. I would recommend that we lose the fusion reactor, since it is too easy to detect, especially when it's run above twenty percent."

"We never ran it above ten," Jessica argued.

"Which supports my recommendation," Deliza pointed out. "You're using a power source that is larger, heavier, and more complex than your mission parameters require. It also takes up additional space."

"How are we going to power the systems?" Jessica asked.

"Ranni Enterprises developed a step-down system that allows our jump shuttles to pull power directly from the jump drive's energy banks, as an emergency source of power. It would be a simple matter to adapt the technology to provide primary power to the jump sub's other systems."

"Won't that limit its capabilities?" Jessica worried.

"Not if we add two more energy cells to the jump drive's energy banks. Combined, they will take up one quarter of the space that the fusion reactor does, and will be forty-two percent lighter."

"Will that give us enough room in the sub to carry more passengers or cargo?" General Telles inquired.

"We should be able to increase its passenger capacity back to its original design parameters of one pilot and four passengers."

General Telles looked pleased. "That would make it useful for tactical insertion missions, as well."

"How long will it take to get the jump sub ready to go?" Nathan asked.

"A few days," Deliza replied. "A week, at the most. The hull is still intact, although its nose requires a bit of repair, so it's mostly just replacing systems."

"Probably from our recovery," Jessica commented. "It was a bit rough."

"That explains the dent in the Seiiki's forward cargo deck bulkhead," Nathan said. "We never could get that completely true again."

"I would strongly suggest that we give the jump sub at least a few test runs," Deliza warned them.

"I'm sure we can find someplace that will suffice," General Telles assured her.

"It would help if we could do the rebuild here, on the Aurora," Deliza suggested to Cameron. "Your facilities are much better than those on the Glendanon. And your fabricators are more accessible."

"Ours are busy fulfilling orders for the transfer airlock project on the Glendanon," General Telles explained.

"Very well," Cameron replied. "I'll have you speak

with Commander Kaplan. She'll set you up with a workspace and put your team up in guest quarters."

"Thank you, Captain," Deliza replied.

"How is the Seiiki progressing?" General Telles asked, turning to Nathan.

"Vlad has found a few things wrong, as expected. Thanks for loaning him to us, by the way," Nathan said, looking at Cameron. "The most pressing issue is an overheating and shielding problem with our plasma turrets."

"Can this be corrected prior to your departure?" General Telles wondered, checking the time display on the Aurora's wall.

"They're doing the exterior stuff first, so that they can do the rest en route. Syllium Orfee is just over two hundred light years from our present position, so it will take us a few hours to get there. That should be enough time to get the problem solved."

"What else did he find?" General Telles wondered.

"A few other things. An imbalance in the shield generators that makes a weak spot between the port and starboard dorsal shields. A few power conduits that are too small for the load they're carrying. A leaky air scrubber, low hydraulic pressure in the starboard aft gear assembly, and a bunch of other things. But they're all relatively easy fixes."

"You *do* have a dedicated engineer, don't you?" Cameron asked.

"He's more of a mechanic, really. He's pretty good at fixing things, but he's no Vlad, if you know what I mean."

"Anything else?"

"Well, he's already thinking of how we can install plasma cannons in our wing-bodies. Stubby mark threes, I believe. We'd have to get in close to hit anything, though. But they'd make the Seiiki a fair match for any Dusahn gunboat. Maybe even a frigate, if we got the jump on her."

"I'm afraid the mark threes will have to wait until after we have secured the Mystic Empress," General Telles said. "We cannot keep those people cooped up in cargo pods much longer."

"Can we move some of them onto the Aurora?" Jessica suggested.

"You want to put them on a warship?" Cameron said, shocked. "You really think that's wise? We get shot at, remember?"

"We all get shot at, Cam," Jessica pointed out. "Even the Glendanon. At least the Aurora has a fighting chance."

"No, she's right," Nathan interrupted. "Having them aboard will put additional stress on the ship and would limit Cameron's options while under fire. Besides, the Aurora is already operating shorthanded."

"We're already bringing over people temporarily for medical care," Cameron pointed out. "That's the best we can do, for now."

"The Mystic is the best option," General Telles insisted. "Let's focus on securing her, first."

"What happens if the Mystic's captain doesn't want to join us?" Nathan wondered.

"Let's hope that doesn't happen," General Telles replied.

"But if it does?"

"That is why you are taking a squad of my men with you."

"So, we're going to *take* the Mystic Empress by force?"

"I doubt much force will be necessary," Jessica pointed out. "It's a cruise ship, remember?"

"I'm sure they've got some sort of security on board," Nathan argued. He turned to General Telles. "I'm not so sure I'm comfortable with the idea of taking the Mystic by force, General."

"Then I suggest you do your best to convince her captain to join us willingly, Captain," General Telles replied calmly. "However, if he refuses, we will take her by force. We are fighting a war, after all."

"Maybe we should bring his wife and child along with us?" Jessica said. "She might be helpful in convincing him."

"It would be better if she remained here, with us," General Telles pointed out. "Then, the captain of the Mystic will be forced to come to us."

"Isn't that kind of like taking them hostage?" Nathan wondered.

"I prefer to think of it as strategy," General Telles replied.

Nathan said nothing, mulling over the general's words. He understood the urgency of the situation, and he understood the general's point of view. He just wasn't sure he could *do* what the general was asking. The *Nathan* side of him could, but the part of him that was still Connor Tuplo had serious doubts.

He only hoped that the captain of the Mystic Empress would want to help.

* * *

Nathan stood atop the Seiiki's hull, in between her gun turrets, inspecting the work Vlad and his crew had done. "This will hold?"

"Bonded and welded," Vladimir replied. "Both inside and out. We even added a second layer, just to be safe."

"Good." Nathan looked at the shield emitters they had added to the sides of the turrets. "And these guys will provide additional shielding for this entire area?"

"Think of them like the flat armor plates on either side of rail guns on old naval warships," Vladimir explained. "Except *these* are more of a *dome* shape, and the barrels penetrate the shield. Luckily, the heat exchangers for the plasma generators are aft of the shields, so the heat won't affect the shield emitters."

"So, the gun isn't protected, then," Nathan surmised.

"We could expand their coverage, but that would pull more power from the weapon itself," Vladimir warned Nathan. "Besides, the odds of scoring a direct hit on the barrels is low. The goal of this shield is to protect the gunner, not the gun."

"Speaking as one of the likely gunners, I appreciate that," Dalen said.

The conversation stopped as a distant warning horn sounded, and several red strobes began to flash over the number three port transfer airlock door.

Nathan, Vlad, and the others watched as the transfer airlock door rolled upward, and the Ghatazhak's last surviving combat jump shuttle rolled inside the main hangar bay.

"Jessica is coming," Vladimir said, pointing forward.

Jessica walked over to the arriving shuttle, a gear bag slung over her shoulder. Ghatazhak soldiers began stepping down out of the jump shuttle as it rolled to a stop. Words were exchanged, then Jessica and the group of soldiers headed toward the Seiiki.

"Why are they coming over here?" Dalen wondered.

Nathan sighed. "They're coming with us."

"I thought we were going to *talk* with the captain of the Mystic Empress," Vladimir said.

Nathan turned to look at him. "They're plan B."

"*Bozhe*," Vladimir exclaimed softly.

"You all set here?" Nathan asked, gesturing toward the work that had been done around the gun turrets.

"All sealed up, lines and conduits run through," Vladimir replied. "We just have to hook everything up on the inside."

"Good," Nathan replied. "Get all your gear inside. We're departing shortly."

Vladimir nodded as Nathan turned and headed down the starboard side, toward the aft access ladder along the inside edge of the starboard engine nacelle. "Let's hope plan A works," Vladimir mumbled as he and Dalen began gathering up their tools.

Nathan hopped down onto the deck, then turned and headed out of the transfer airlock and into the Aurora's main hangar bay to meet Jessica and her troops.

"Nathan," Jessica greeted as she and her men approached. "You remember Deno Anwar?"

"I sure do," Nathan replied, reaching out to shake the master sergeant's hand. "I see you got promoted."

"Good to see you again, Captain Scott," Master Sergeant Anwar greeted him warmly.

"Sergeants Morano and Vela; and Corporals Rossi and Rattan," Jessica introduced quickly.

"Gentlemen," Nathan greeted. "Aren't squads usually eight to twelve?"

"General Telles's idea of a low profile," Jessica replied as they continued toward the Seiiki.

"It would be even lower if you lost all the battle armor," Nathan suggested.

"If we *are* needed, we'll likely need our armor, as well," Jessica explained. "Mine's in here," she added, holding up her bag momentarily. "I'll come along in utilities for show, while my men wait on board the Seiiki."

"I hope we don't need them," Nathan said, as if he thought she needed to be reminded of the original plan.

Jessica stopped, taking Nathan's arm to stop him, as well, as the rest of her men continued toward the Seiiki. "Look, Nathan. No one wants to storm in and take the Mystic by force. But we'll do it if we have to. You need to understand that."

"I understand it," Nathan replied. "And I agree that it may become necessary, but that doesn't mean I have to like it."

"Well, the Ghatazhak don't always like what we have to do. We just have to live with it."

"I envy your resolve," Nathan admitted as they continued toward the Seiiki.

"You know, you could use some Ghatazhak training," Jessica suggested as they walked.

"I have enough going on inside my head right now, just trying to sort out Nathan and Connor's memories."

"Our training might help," Jessica insisted.

"How is learning to kick ass going to help me?"

"Our training isn't just about combat," Jessica explained. "There's a lot of physical training involved, yes. But there's also a lot of mental training, and education that goes along with it. We believe that one must have the wisdom and discipline required to correctly use the physical techniques and weapons in a safe manner."

"And they let you in?" Nathan joked.

"Yeah, kind of a shocker, huh," Jessica admitted. "Actually, it's been a lot of help. I still have a long way to go—as Telles *loves* to point out—but I've made a lot of improvements. I had a lot of anger built up inside of me, because of everything we went through back then. It was making me reckless and irresponsible."

"I seem to remember a few episodes, yes," Nathan agreed.

"Don't get me wrong. I still have my moments. And I still pull some crazy stunts once in a while. But, now, I'm actually thinking them through beforehand, instead of just acting impulsively."

"Interesting," Nathan said as they approached the Seiiki's cargo ramp.

"You should give it a try," she urged.

"I'll think about it," Nathan replied as he gestured up the ramp. "Ladies first."

* * *

After moving the jump sub to the Aurora, Deliza once again found herself staring at the sleek, black, hybrid vessel.

"So, that's a jump sub," Yanni said.

"Yes."

"I always imagined it bigger," Yanni added. "I mean, this thing actually jumps, from space, into the water, right?"

"Correct."

Yanni shook his head in disbelief. "Seems like it should be bigger."

"Thanks for agreeing to help with this project,"

Deliza said, turning to face him. “It’s been a while since we got to work together on something.”

“My pleasure,” Yanni replied. “Besides, it’s not like I had much else to do. And, to be honest, it’s starting to stink a bit on the Glendanon.”

“I know, right?” Deliza sympathized.

“What do you want me to do?” Yanni asked, looking back at the jump sub.

“I want you to plug into the environmental control computer and see if we can update the software, or if we just have to scrap the entire thing and replace it.”

“Got it. How many people does it need to support, and for how long?”

“Five, maximum,” Deliza replied. “For a couple hours, tops. I’m going to work on adapting the leaching module to power the sub’s systems directly from the jump drive’s energy banks.”

“What are *they* going to do?” Yanni asked, pointing to the Alliance technicians who were already opening up the sub to get access to the interior.

“They’re going to yank out the old jump drive and replace it with one of the spares for the Super Eagles, but using our heated emitters.”

“Shall we?”

Deliza took a deep breath and started toward the sub. “Alright, people! We’ve got a job to do, and it needs to be done quickly. So, let’s get to it!”

Yanni smiled. Deliza had come a long way from the demure young princess who would suddenly talk your ear off once she found out someone had an interest in science. Now she was funding a rebellion and leading its technical team.

* * *

“Ready to depart?” Nathan asked as he passed

Vladimir and Dalen in the Seiiki's port corridor, headed forward.

"We're ready," Vladimir replied confidently. He waited a moment for Nathan to round the corner and head up the ladder to the cockpit, then whispered to Dalen. "You closed the gun deck hatch, *da*?"

"Uh..."

Vladimir's eyes widened, gesturing urgently for him to go and check, then headed forward after Nathan.

Nathan climbed up into the Seiiki's cockpit, taking a standing position behind and between Josh and Loki.

"We're all closed up and green across the board," Josh reported.

"Transfer airlock depress cycle has already started, Captain," Loki added.

Vladimir climbed up the access ladder, moving into the auxiliary station behind Loki, immediately calling up several systems to monitor.

"Something wrong?" Nathan wondered, noticing Vladimir's sense of urgency.

"*Nyet.* I'm just watching various systems...to get an idea of their performance parameters."

Nathan didn't respond.

"Thirty seconds to full depress," Loki reported.

"That's pretty fast for this big of an airlock," Nathan commented.

"Two minutes to full vacuum," Vladimir boasted. "The pumps for the number two locks are the same ones that used to be for the entire hangar bay, before the flight deck rebuild."

"How long ago was that, anyway?" Nathan wondered as the Seiiki began to rotate to starboard inside the transfer airlock.

"Nearly three years ago," Vladimir replied.

"Depress complete," Loki reported. "Outer door is opening."

"That's when they converted the Aurora to her original design as a combat carrier," Vladimir continued. "We were about to go in for our final refit when the Dusahn attacked the PC, and Jung ships began appearing within Alliance space in the Sol sector."

"What was the final refit supposed to be?" Nathan asked.

"All four antimatter reactors were to be removed and replaced with ZPED reactors."

Nathan looked surprised. "Then they solved the problem with the ZPED's gravity well interfering with the jump drive?"

"Not completely," Vladimir explained. "But with proper shielding, and by running several ZPEDs at lower power instead of one big one at higher power, the effect becomes manageable, much like with smaller ZPED-powered, jump-capable ships. Plus, we would be able to run all six reactors at full power and reduce our recharge time by more than seventy percent."

"*Six* ZPEDs?" Nathan said in disbelief. "They were going to put six of them into the Aurora?"

"The Cape Town has twelve of them."

"Aurora Flight, Seiiki," Loki called over comms. "Ready for rollout."

"The Cape Town?" Nathan asked, unfamiliar with the ship.

"The first Protector-class ship built by the Alliance," Vladimir replied.

"*Seiiki, Aurora Flight. Clear for rollout, starboard side, launch position two.*"

"I'm not familiar with that class," Nathan admitted.

"Roll out starboard side to launch position two," Loki confirmed.

"Based on the Defender-class, only bigger. Fully armored and shielded, and armed to the teeth. Plasma cannons, rail gun cannons, jump torpedoes, jump missiles, jump KKVs. She is a beast. A ship-killer to the core." Vladimir explained.

"How big?" Nathan wondered, looking out the window as the Seiiki began to roll out of the airlock toward the opening at the back of the starboard flight deck.

"A third bigger than the Defender-class," Vladimir replied.

"What's her jump range?"

"Same as the Aurora's- fifteen light years. But she's got four full energy banks, so she can clear sixty light years in five minutes' time, which means she can respond to any place in the Sol sector in minutes."

"How many does the Alliance have?" Nathan wondered.

"Just the one. Five more are in progress, but it takes *five years* just to build one. There are five construction bays carved into the sides of Port Terra dedicated solely to the construction of the Protector-class ships," Vladimir explained.

"Port Terra?" Nathan asked. By now, he was sitting in the jump seat behind Josh, his mind processing the new details that his friend was providing him. Undoubtedly, a lot had happened during his absence. At some point, he would need to catch up, and this seemed as good a place to start as any.

"The Karuzara asteroid," Vladimir continued. "It

was renamed Port Terra after the initial refit. They even carved out a massive cavern to hold the new Alliance headquarters."

"Aurora Flight, Seiiki, ready starboard side, launch position two," Loki reported over comms.

Nathan noticed that Vladimir was staring intently at his console. Curious, Nathan rose to peer over Vladimir's shoulder. "Gun deck is holding pressure?"

"Uh... Of course," Vladimir replied, caught off guard.

"Weren't sure, were you?" Nathan teased.

"I never had any doubts," Vladimir lied.

"*Seiiki, Aurora Flight, cleared for departure. Safe journey.*"

"Seiiki is departing starboard side, launch position two. Thanks."

Nathan stood up, looking out the front of the Seiiki's cockpit windows. It was the first time he was able to see the changes made to the Aurora's aft flight decks since his arrival. "Holy crap," he exclaimed in disbelief. "Look at the size of that apron," he said, looking out the right-side windows. "It wraps all the way around to the port side."

"And the center apron goes all the way back to the drive section," Loki pointed out.

"What about the heat exchangers?" Nathan wondered.

"The center deck is a grate, so no heat builds up underneath it," Vladimir explained, rising up to stand beside Nathan to look out the windows as well. "You see that square in the center? That retracts, and a docking column with a cargo elevator comes up. It's designed to dock with the underside of a standard Alliance cargo ship, or with a tanker."

"Man, you guys have expanded the Aurora's

flight operations capabilities just a bit, haven't you," Nathan commented.

Josh twisted the flight control stick, causing the Seiiki to turn to the left, bringing the ship around and accelerating alongside the Aurora, parallel to her line of flight.

Nathan shifted his gaze to the left windows, taking in the forward, starboard flight deck, where the forward launch tubes had once been. "You've got openings in the front, as well," he realized, turning to look at Vladimir. "So, they turned the fighter alleys into flight decks?"

"*Da.*"

"Can you fly all the way through them? Front to back?" Nathan wondered, looking out the left window again as they passed by the forward flight deck.

"*Nyet,*" Vladimir replied. "They were originally intended for such, but it was decided to install the large transfer airlocks, to support large spacecraft, like our heavy shuttles and the Cobra gunships."

"Cobras?" Nathan asked.

"We can use the large transfer airlocks to bring them inside for repairs, if needed," Vladimir explained. "One of the Aurora's new roles is to support distant operations. We have quite the spacecraft repair facility below decks."

"I see you still have the forward launch catapults."

"For launching jump KKVs," Vladimir replied. "The Aurora carries twelve of them. Theoretically, we could take down three or four battle platforms."

"Seems like overkill, doesn't it?" Nathan said.

"Until the Cape Town was launched, we were the only ship that could carry and launch such weapons, other than the dedicated boxcars that had been adapted to carry the super jump KKVs...the *planet killers.*"

"Damn," Nathan said. "Galiardi isn't gearing up to *defend* Earth. He's gearing up to destroy the Jung *entirely.*"

* * *

Commander Macklay entered Admiral Galiardi's office, data pad in hand. "The Tanna has missed two check-ins, Admiral."

"Was she tracking anything?" the admiral asked. "Maybe she picked up a hot track and went stealth to track it."

"SOPs say to drop a comm-drone on a launch delay, in which case we *should* have heard from her by now."

"There could be plenty of reasons they couldn't launch a comm-drone," the admiral insisted. "Did you send a gunship to investigate?"

"Yes, sir. Three of them, actually. Nothing."

"Who's the Tanna's CO?" Admiral Galiardi asked, trying to remember.

"That's the thing that worries me," Commander Macklay said. "Her skipper is Robert Nash, Jessica Nash's older brother."

"Jessica Nash. Why does that name sound so familiar?" the admiral wondered.

"She served on the Aurora under Nathan Scott."

"The spec-ops? The one who resigned, after Scott's execution, to join the Ghatazhak?"

"Yup. She was close to Scott. She was *also* close to the Aurora's current CO, Captain Taylor, and her chief engineer, Commander Kamenetskiy. That's a lot of coincidences."

"Are you suggesting that the Tanna headed for the PC to join them?"

"It's a possibility," the commander suggested.

Admiral Galiardi thought for a moment. "Unfortunately, there's not much we can do but wait, and hope that she turns up with a good excuse."

"Yes, sir."

"If she *does* turn up, send them a message and have the comm-drone ping her logs," the admiral added.

"Yes, sir," Commander Macklay replied, turning to exit.

"And let's initiate active position tracking on all ships. If they move, I want to know."

"Even our gunships?"

"Negative," the admiral replied. "Destroyers, the Benakh, and the Cape Town."

"Yes, sir."

"Commander, anything else on Scott-Thornton?"

"No, sir," the commander replied. "And we've got eyes and ears on her around the clock. If she goes anywhere, or calls anyone, we'll know it."

Admiral Galiardi took a deep breath and sighed. "We need eyes and ears *inside* Winnipeg, not outside."

Commander Macklay closed the door again. "Admiral, are you suggesting we bug the president's office?"

"Our job is to protect the people of Earth," Admiral Galiardi stated. "If that means we have to bug the President of Earth to do so, then that is exactly what we are going to do."

CHAPTER FIVE

Two young men dressed in nondescript clothing walked casually down the streets of Aitkenna, mindful to not look up at the security cameras on each street corner. Arriving at their destination, they slipped into one of the many markets in the neighborhood, seemingly in no particular hurry.

The two men took a cart and began walking down the aisle, plucking random items from the shelves as they moved from row to row. Eventually, they found themselves standing at the meat counter at the back of the market. One of them turned to watch behind them as the other nervously stepped up to the counter to speak to the young man on the other side.

“Excuse me,” the apprehensive, young man said.

The man behind the meat counter stepped closer. “How may I help you?”

“I was told to ask for Anji,” the nervous, young man said.

“Anji is the store manager,” the man behind the counter replied. “He is a very busy man. Perhaps I can help you.”

The nervous, young man shook his head slightly. “I was told to ask to speak to Anji.”

“Who told you to ask for Anji?” the man behind the counter asked.

“A mutual friend. He said Anji might be interested in some merchandise I have.”

The man behind the counter looked suspiciously at the nervous, young man, as well as the young man’s friend, who was watching behind them, glancing back in their direction periodically. "What sort of merchandise are you speaking of?"

"Not exactly *legal* merchandise, if you know what I mean," the young man replied. His words were strained, as if he was deathly afraid of even saying them out loud.

"I see," the man behind the meat counter said as he slowly slid his hand under the counter to reach for his weapon. Robberies had been on the rise since the Dusahn invasion had upset the regular police presence in Aitkenna. Although their Dusahn occupiers had now banned possession of any type of energy weapon, there were still plenty of projectile weapons that would go undetected by Dusahn sensors if fired. And Timin had no intention of letting his father's market get robbed again. "And how did you come across such, *merchandise*?"

The nervous, young man forced a smile. "It sort of *fell* into our hands...from the sky. Literally."

Timin's hand moved from the weapon to the small button next to it and pressed it firmly. "I see," he nodded as he pulled the weapon slowly from its mount under the counter. "The *bathrooms* are through that door to the left and all the way back, on the back side of the storeroom. Please step carefully. We just had a meat delivery, and the floors may be slick."

"*Bathrooms*?" the nervous, young man wondered.

Timin glanced at the security camera display above his head, tucked behind the wall and out of the nervous man's view. He could see his two brothers moving down the aisles on either side of the two customers. "If you have trouble finding them, someone in the storeroom will be happy to help you," Timin added with a smile as he glanced twice in the direction of the doors to his right, hoping that the young man would take the bait.

Finally, the nervous, young man understood. "To the left?" he said, pointing in the direction of the doors. "And all the way back, you say?"

"That is correct, sir. They are on the back side of the storeroom. Take your time. I will watch your cart while you are away."

"Thank you," the nervous, young man replied, looking slightly relieved. He turned to his partner, gesturing for him to follow, and both men headed around the side of the meat counter.

Timin watched both men carefully, his hand still on his weapon, as they disappeared into the side corridor. Once they were out of his eyesight, he gestured to his brothers to move quickly. He picked up his comm-unit and activated it. "Father, two men are entering the storeroom. They need to use the bathroom, in the *back*."

"*Is anyone available to help them?*" his father wondered.

"Dinar and Morri will be there momentarily."

"*Very well, I will watch for them. Remain where you are.*"

* * *

Nathan entered the Seiiki's gun deck. Much to his surprise, there was a new bulkhead installed just aft of the port and starboard gun turrets, with a hatch in the center directly ahead of him.

Nathan stepped further into the compartment, continuing through the new hatch, finding Vladimir, Marcus, and Dalen in the newly created sub-compartment, inspecting their work.

"What do you think?" Vladimir asked Nathan

as he entered. Vladimir was obviously pleased with himself, beaming from ear to ear.

"How did you manage to do all this in only a few hours?" Nathan asked, noticing that they had installed the cooling wraps around not only the power conduits, but also the plasma generators.

"The difficult part was the pass-through points in the hull," Vladimir replied. "But that was done before departure. All of this was just hooking things up and testing."

"But you created an entire sub-compartment," Nathan exclaimed.

"With its own environmental circuit, as well," Vladimir bragged. "Sensors and all."

"Amazing. Where did you get the material for the bulkhead…and the *hatch* for that matter?"

"We keep spare bulkheads and hatches on board the Aurora for emergency repairs. We have dozens of them. I just borrowed a few. I'm sure Cameron won't mind."

"Is it sound?" Nathan wondered, examining the new bulkhead.

"Pressure and heat-wise, yes," Vladimir replied. "But it is not structural. For that, we will need to add beams and spares all around. Those will need to be custom fabricated when we return. But at least this will keep any unprocessed heat from reaching the gun turrets themselves."

"But the cooling wraps will take care of the heat?"

"Better than before, yes," Vladimir replied.

"I still won't hang around in here during a firefight," Marcus commented. "But at least we won't have to worry about getting cooked in the gunner's chairs."

"This means we can install independent targeting

systems in the turrets when we get back," Dalen added. "Pretty slick, huh, Cap'n?"

"Pretty slick, indeed," Nathan agreed. "You guys go ahead and get cleaned up, and get something to eat. We'll be starting our search for the Mystic soon, and we'll need your eyes up here." Nathan continued inspecting the work, noting that all the cable routing and securing was much neater than he was accustomed to seeing from Dalen and Marcus alone. "This is really nice work," Nathan said, after Marcus and Dalen had left the compartment. "I knew you'd be a good man to have on board," he added, patting his old friend on the back.

"Dalen is very smart," Vladimir assured him. "He just lacks formal training. He can figure out how to fix things, but without the science background, he cannot predict how his solution will affect other systems."

"He also doesn't know how to dress lines this nicely," Nathan added.

"I believe that is Marcus's influence. The man is a very good mechanic, but he takes too many shortcuts."

"Well, he's not *supposed* to be doing the repair work around here, anyway. That's Dalen's job. But Dalen's a kid in Marcus's eyes, and Marcus is a bit overprotective when it comes to this ship."

"He does not *trust* Dalen?" Vladimir asked.

"He *trusts* him as a person. He just doesn't think Dalen knows what he's doing. Which, according to you, he doesn't. That's one of the reasons I wanted to bring you on board. I thought maybe you could take him under your wing, teach him a thing or two, while we convert this ship into a combat vessel...

Assuming, of course, that you're up to the challenge," Nathan added with a wry smile.

"Now you are playing dirty, my friend," Vladimir replied, shaking his finger at Nathan. "But I will accept the challenge. Although I may need to remain on board for some time."

"I'll work on Cameron when we get back," Nathan promised.

"I can always resign again," Vladimir suggested.

"Again?"

"I was about to leave the Aurora for an assignment in research and development, when all this started. I only stayed because my replacement had not yet arrived."

"I don't think you need to go that far," Nathan argued. "Besides, your current *status* in the Alliance is sort of *up in the air* at this point, don't you think?"

"Good point. Very well," Vladimir agreed, handing a wrench over to Nathan. "I will leave *her* to *you*, and *I* will go and eat."

* * *

The storeroom ran along the entire back side of the market. It was poorly lit, with racks of sealed boxes along the wall and at least a dozen large wine barrels stacked in the back corner. At the far, right end, was a large roll-up door that likely led to a loading dock. To the left was a room with a window that looked into the storeroom itself, but there were no lights inside.

"What do we do now?" the second young man whispered.

"You put your hands on your head, and you do not make any sudden moves," a voice instructed from their left.

Both men turned toward the voice, but saw nothing through the darkness.

"That was a sudden move," the voice warned as he stepped out of the shadows. "The next one will be your last."

Both young men's eyes widened, and their hands immediately went up as they spotted a man, in his late forties or early fifties, step out of the darkness pointing a rather large and deadly looking weapon directly at them. "We don't want any trouble, sir," the second young man assured the man holding the weapon.

"Yeah, we just want to use the bathroom," the other young man insisted.

Without warning, two more men stepped up behind them, covering the heads of both young men with black hoods as they pressed devices into their backs and activated them. There was a sudden crackling sound, and the two young men felt as if every square centimeter of their skin was on fire. Their bodies stiffened, their jaws clenched, and both of them suddenly realized they could no longer draw breath.

It was the last thing they remembered.

* * *

Jessica entered the Seiiki's galley, looking for something to drink.

"Any luck?" Neli asked from the table in the corner.

"Nope. Is there any coffee left?"

"That bitter brown stuff the Aurora's mess gave us?" Neli replied. "Plenty. I don't know how you Terrans can drink it."

Jessica paused a moment, a smile coming to her face. It had been a long time since she had been called a Terran. "It's an acquired taste," she agreed as she prepared another pot to brew. "To be honest, I never realized how much I missed it until I had it again. I have to remember to plant some of this shit somewhere, after all this is over. I'll make a fortune."

"I don't think it's going to be as popular as you think," Neli warned. "At least not in the Pentaurus sector."

"Maybe not, but at least I'll have my own supply. Besides, it's better than that crap Marcus is always chewing."

"No disagreement there," Neli agreed. "Try kissing him after he's been chewing that stuff all day long to stay awake."

Jessica laughed. "I'll take your word for it."

"How much longer are we going to search?" Neli wondered.

"Well, since we're backtracking the Mystic's course, in a few hours, if we haven't found her, we'll know she's already jumped back to Takara and is probably in the hands of the Dusahn. Either way, the search will be over."

"And if we don't find her?"

"Then we look for some other ship that fits the bill."

"Likely you won't find one as nice as the Mystic," Neli said.

"You've heard of her, then?"

"Only by reputation. People like us could never afford a trip on the Mystic."

"People like us?" Jessica asked as she poured some coffee for herself.

"You know, people who have to work to live," Neli explained. "People who ride on the Mystic usually have life handed to them."

"That nice, huh?"

"That's what they say." Neli looked at her beverage, thinking a moment. "You knew Marcus back then, right? Back when you all defeated Caius and pushed the Jung back out of the Sol system."

"Sure did."

"What was he like back then?"

"Pretty much the same as he is now, I imagine," Jessica said.

"Overprotective of his ship and captain?" Neli said.

"Okay, maybe not *exactly* the same," Jessica admitted, moving over to sit down across the table from Neli. She took a sip of her coffee. "To be honest, I really didn't like him much, at first. I pretty much wanted to toss him out an airlock."

"That sounds about right," Neli laughed.

"But," Jessica said with a sigh, "eventually he proved to be a pretty good guy. Don't ever tell him I said this, but he turned out to be a pretty good chief of the boat."

Neli smiled again, remembering all the times Marcus had mused proudly of his days aboard the Aurora. "Just between you and me, he's always been quite proud of his service to the Alliance. That's what's always confused me, I guess. Why he left to follow Connor...or Nathan... You know what I mean."

"He never told you?" Jessica wondered.

"He always just says, 'Family are those who take care of you, and who you take care of in return.' But that's about it."

"Pretty deep, for Marcus," Jessica commented. "Oh, sorry, I didn't mean..."

"That's alright," Neli insisted. "You're not far off

the mark." Neli sighed. "What I don't understand is, *why* Nathan?"

"I guess it's because Nathan was his way *off* of Haven. Nathan gave him a chance, despite all of our objections. To Marcus's credit, he ran with it and proved Nathan right."

"That explains it," Neli realized.

"Explains what?"

"Marcus never wants to talk about his past much. I think he's ashamed of who he was, or maybe the things he did. Except for his time on the Aurora. It's like everything before that doesn't matter to him."

"Except for Josh," Jessica corrected.

"Yes, except for Josh."

Jessica noticed the look on Neli's face when she mentioned Josh. "I take it you two don't get along?"

"Oh, we tolerate one another. That's about it."

"Well, Josh can be a handful, that's for sure."

"Just like Marcus," Neli said. "Sometimes, I wonder if that's where he learned it."

Jessica looked at Neli, hoping she wasn't overstepping her boundaries. "If you don't mind me asking, how did you end up on the Seiiki? You don't really seem the type for this."

"I was working in a café on Palee, near the spaceport, when they were putting passenger seats in the Seiiki. They used to come in to eat all the time. I had been seeing Marcus off and on, whenever they were in port, so I already knew them. I suggested that they needed a hostess on board, and Connor offered me the job, so I took it. At the time, it seemed a better job than the cafe. I'm not sure Marcus was too crazy about the idea, at first, but it worked out. Eventually, I ended up doing all the cooking and cleaning, as well. I mean, a ship full of men? The place was a mess. If I hadn't been here, I doubt they would have been in the passenger business for very long."

"You had to *clean up* after them?"

"In the beginning, yes. It was a form of job security. These days, I make them clean up after themselves."

Jessica nodded, taking another sip.

"How did you end up here?" Neli asked.

"I grew up surrounded by brothers. I've been competing with them my entire life. The military seemed like a natural fit."

"And now you're a Ghatazhak. The first *female* Ghatazhak, no less. I guess we have a little bit in common, then. Being the only woman around a bunch of men."

"Until now," Jessica said, raising her cup.

Neli smiled, mimicking the gesture. "Until now."

* * *

"*Wake up!*"

It was like a dream, only with pain...lots of it.

"*Wake up!*"

The voice was unfamiliar and distant. *Or was it muffled?*

Cold water suddenly hit his face, snapping him out of his dream state. Tiny prickles crawled over his skin, like little pins driving into it. His head was swimming, throbbing. He wanted to throw up.

He tried opening his eyes, but a bright light made it impossible.

"*Finally,*" the unfamiliar voice said.

He opened his eyes again, more slowly this time. Two lights, not one. He could hear other voices as well.

"*What is your name?*"

"Uh... Birk."

"Birk what?"

"Gorry. Birk Gorry." *Oh, God. I've been turned over to the Dusahn.*

"Why were you asking for Anji?"

"Where is Cuddy?" Birk wondered, confused.

"We are asking the questions. Why were you asking for Anji?"

"We wanted to sell him something."

"What did you want to sell him?"

"Brandy. Palean brandy. We stole it."

"You told the meat man that what you had to sell 'fell from the sky.' Did your brandy fall from the sky?"

"We stole it...from a cargo shuttle... At the spaceport."

"You do not lie well. You were trying to sell weapons. Weapons dropped by the Karuzari, along with claims that the savior Na-Tan was coming to liberate the people of Corinair."

"No, no, no. It was brandy, I swear," Birk insisted. If the Dusahn knew he had weapons, he would be publicly executed, just like those poor people whose family members commanded jump ships and had not reported in as ordered.

"Do you know what the penalty is for possessing weapons, let alone trying to sell them to others?" the voice threatened.

"Please," Birk begged, "we were just trying to make some money. We are no threat to the Dusahn, I swear it!" Birk was on the verge of tears, fearing that at any moment, he would be executed in some cell, and his parents would never know what had happened to him.

"Admit that you have the weapons, and tell us where they are hidden, and we will spare your life," the voice promised.

"There are no weapons!" Birk cried, hoping to convince them. *Surely the penalty for stealing brandy is something less than death.*

"*TELL US!*"

"Where is Cuddy?"

"*HE IS DEAD! HE WOULD NOT ADMIT HIS CRIMES!*"

"Oh, my God!"

"*TELL US! WHERE ARE THE WEAPONS?*"

"They're buried in my yard, in the back!" Birk finally confessed.

"*DESCRIBE THEM!*"

"Eight of them, in a big, heavy case. Big barrels, about as big around as my fist. Half a meter long, with two handles."

"*Do they work?*"

"I don't know! We never fired them! We were afraid!"

"*How is it that we have not detected these weapons? How did you shield them?*"

"We didn't shield them," Birk insisted. "We just buried them. Maybe the case shielded them. I don't know. I'm just a student. I work part-time as a cashier."

"*Why did you ask for Anji?*"

Birk was now sweating profusely. His head was pounding worse than ever, and he was afraid that he would piss himself. "Someone told me he used to be in the Corinari. I thought... I thought maybe he would want them... Or he would know someone who wanted them." Birk started to sob. "We just wanted some money, that's all. I swear it."

The voice from behind the bright lights said nothing as Birk continued to sob, convinced that his death was imminent.

Finally, the voice behind the lights spoke. "*We have your identification. We will verify your claims. If you have told us the truth, we will spare your life.*"

Birk heard the sound of footsteps, a door closing and locking. The lights went out, and he was in darkness again.

But he *was* alive... for now.

* * *

"The Aurora's sensors would work much better in this," Vladimir grumbled as he punched instructions into the auxiliary console in the Seiiki's cockpit.

"Just do what you can," Nathan said. "We'll find her."

"We're back-flying her course," Josh pointed out. "Even if we don't see her, we're bound to bump into her eventually."

"Let's avoid the bumping into part, shall we?" Loki suggested.

"It's possible that she already finished her trip through the cloud," Nathan reminded them. "We're only guessing about her departure date. For all we know, she could have departed two days earlier than we thought."

"Or the Dusahn could have already tracked her down and captured her," Vladimir offered.

"Let's try to keep a positive attitude, shall we?" Nathan scolded him. "Besides, I don't see the Dusahn sending ships three hundred light years out, just to capture a luxury liner. Especially when they know she's going to come back to them. And they wouldn't consider her a high-value vessel."

"Unless, of course, *Lord Dusahn* wants to make the Mystic his own private yacht," Josh mused.

"I suspect the Dusahn are a bit more practical

than that," Nathan insisted. "That would be more a *Takaran* thing to do."

"If the Mystic departed out of Takaran space, then the Dusahn would have her flight plan," Loki pointed out. "They'd know exactly where to find her at any time."

"So, if they felt she was important enough to go after, then we're wasting our time," Nathan speculated. "Well, let's just hope they do *not* think she's important enough to go after."

"I have a weak reading at our ten o'clock, twenty-three up," Vladimir reported. "Approximately twenty thousand kilometers."

"How weak?" Nathan wondered.

"Very. It could be another sensor echo."

"Josh, steer ten left to split the difference, and give us ten up as well. But don't let us stray more than ten thousand kilometers off our primary course track," Nathan directed them.

"You got it."

"Dalen, keep your eyes eleven high," Nathan said over his comm-set.

"*Checking eleven high,*" Dalen replied.

"Marcus, keep your focus to starboard. We're going to veer left of course for a bit to check out a weak reading."

"*Keepin' my peepers to starboard,*" Marcus replied over Nathan's comm-set.

Josh put the Seiiki into a slight turn to the left, pitching her nose up fractionally in the process.

Nathan waited a full minute. At their current speed, they would close half the distance between them and the sensor target in only four minutes. This area of the cloud was fairly bright, due to the proximity of the blue giant star that marked the

Mystic's exit point for her journey. The Mystic had to be at least half the size of the Aurora and would not be difficult to spot, even from several kilometers away.

Dalen sat in the port gun turret, staring out through the transparent bubble that protruded from the top of the Seiiki's hull above her upper deck. His gun was pointed directly to port, which meant he had to twist his body slightly to his right to scan for the Mystic.

As he had been for the last few hours, he alternated between using a handheld visual scanner, set to its maximum zoom, and his vision. Marcus had taught him the technique, scanning the bigger picture with his eyes, and then using the handheld to zoom in on anything that looked like it might be a ship in the distance.

So far, that technique had turned up nothing. But it was less tiring than constantly looking through the visual scanner, now that he had a *possible* target location.

Using the visual scanner, Dalen swept the area to the Seiiki's left and above, occasionally zooming out to take in a bigger area, just in case he was off the mark.

"I don't know how much longer I can keep this shit up," Dalen complained, lowering the handheld visual scanner to rub his tired eyes.

"*We'll rotate the both of you out of there after the next jump,*" Nathan promised. "*We've got plenty of fresh eyes aboard.*"

"How's that contact looking?" Nathan asked Vladimir.

"Still weak, but firming up a bit," Vladimir replied. "Size seems correct, based on the description her captain's wife gave us. And the contact does have an apparent motion indicating a course track in the expected direction."

"If it's got motion opposite ours, then it can't be an echo, right?" Nathan surmised.

"Yes, and no," Vladimir replied. "But more yes than no...I think. Sensors are *not really* my specialty."

Nathan sighed, staring out the port windows. "If that is the Mystic, she's a bit off course."

"Her captain would probably adjust his distance from the blue giant, depending on the prevailing radiation levels coming from the star," Loki said.

"Good point," Nathan agreed. "But twenty thousand kilometers wouldn't make that much of a difference, would it?"

"Doubtful," Vladimir agreed.

"We also don't know her *filed* course," Loki pointed out.

"Another good point," Nathan agreed with a smile. He was beginning to appreciate having Loki aboard, as it removed the responsibility of thoughtful navigation and operations—something that Josh was not very good at—off of Nathan's shoulders.

"I could go active and ping them," Vladimir suggested.

"And if the target is a Dusahn gunship, also searching for the Mystic?" Nathan asked.

"We are armed, Cap'n," Josh reminded.

"Doesn't mean we need to go looking for a fight," Nathan insisted. "We'll stay passive."

"We're coming up on ten thousand kilometers left of course, Captain," Loki warned.

"Vlad?"

Vladimir's face scrunched up. "The quality of the contact continues to improve, but I still cannot be sure of its reliability."

Nathan sighed. "If we continue drifting left of course, and the Mystic *is* on the course we expected, we could miss her entirely while we're chasing a ghost."

"I am watching for contacts along our original course, as well," Vladimir reminded Nathan.

"Yes, but the Mystic could also be *right* of our original course, which would put her out of range of our sensors." Nathan sighed again. "This damned cloud."

"*I think I may have something,*" Dalen reported over their comm-sets. "*A flash of light, like a reflection.*"

"Where?" Nathan asked immediately.

"*Uh... Twenty-four degrees off our bow, seven degrees high... There it is again... Maybe eight thousand kilometers?*"

"That is precisely where my sensor contact is," Vladimir agreed.

"Josh," Nathan called.

"Turning toward the contact," Josh replied, anticipating his captain's next command.

"Pick up the pace a little, too," Nathan ordered.

"You got it," Josh replied. He glanced at Loki. "Ten percent for five seconds?"

"That should be enough," Loki agreed.

"Ten for five," Josh confirmed, reaching for the main propulsion controls.

There was a low, distant rumble, an audible vibration as Josh fired the Seiiki's main engines for five seconds.

"*Another flash,*" Dalen reported calmly. "*Dead ahead this time.*"

"Contact is definitely firming up, now," Vladimir reported. "Moving across our bow from right to left, approaching rapidly. One thousand kilometers." Vladimir's eyes suddenly widened. "They're painting us! *Oh, Bozhe!* We're being targeted!"

"Hard to starboard! Down fifty and accelerate away!" Nathan ordered.

"Starboard, down and away," Josh replied, firing the Seiiki's engines and rolling into a diving turn to the right.

"Gunners, swing aft and be ready to engage," Nathan instructed.

"*What's going on?*" Jessica called over comm-sets.

"*Swingin' aft, and powering up!*" Marcus replied.

"Negative! Don't power up your guns just yet," Nathan corrected.

"*Copy, keep'em cold,*" Marcus acknowledged.

"*Nathan?*" Jessica called again.

"The contact we were chasing just painted us, Jess," Nathan replied over comms. "We're taking evasive, now."

"Firm contact now," Vladimir reported. "I was able to get a good read when she went active. Much smaller than I originally thought. About the same size as us, actually."

"Do the Dusahn have gunships that small?" Nathan wondered.

"They do," Jessica replied, coming up the ladder to the Seiiki's cockpit. "They're similar to the Aurora's Reapers, except they can't operate in the atmosphere."

"Do you think that's what just painted us?" Nathan asked Vladimir.

"I could not tell," Vladimir replied. "I am sorry,

but this cloud makes getting solid readings nearly impossible while on passive sensors."

"Do you think they're still tracking us?" Jessica asked.

"There was only the single sensor pulse," Vladimir replied. "They may not have gotten a clean read on us. If they pulsed again, and we were quick enough, they would have seen nothing with the second pulse."

"So, they might conclude that we were a sensor ghost, as well," Nathan surmised.

"It is possible," Vladimir agreed.

Nathan thought for a moment. "Josh, take us back to our original course track. Minimal thrust. Let's not give them anything to pick up. Vlad, keep your eyes peeled for any pursuit."

"What are you planning?" Jessica wondered.

"For now, we keep looking along our original course. If someone else is out here looking for the Mystic, that means there's a good chance she's still out here."

* * *

Birk had been tied to the chair, sitting in the cold, pitch-black room for what had to be hours. His wrists and ankles hurt where he was bound with restraint bands. He was hungry and thirsty, and he had been forced to urinate all over himself when he could no longer wait for someone to take him to the bathroom.

At first, he thought his captors had abandoned him. He had even tried to free himself, thinking that he might escape. He tried standing, thinking that if he could knock the chair against the wall, it might break, but the chair was secured to the floor.

The room was *so dark*. He had never known such complete darkness. And it was terribly quiet. For the first few hours, he had not heard a single sound. Only his own breathing.

Occasionally, he could hear a distant rumbling sound, like a large truck driving down the road. When he first thought his captors had abandoned him, he felt a sense of relief. With them gone, he at least had time to try to escape. But over time, he wondered if they had sealed him up in an airtight chamber, leaving him to suffocate.

Birk had wept more than once. He was positive that he was going to be tortured and then executed. And he had done *nothing*. Certainly, nothing to warrant *this*. He had not asked for a crate of weapons to be dropped down on him. Yes, he had hidden the weapons, despite the Dusahn order for all weapons to be surrendered. And yes, he had tried to find someone to sell the weapons to, but he needed the money. The shop where he worked had closed its doors indefinitely, its owner having left Aitkenna, like so many others, to hide in the nearby mountains.

The Dusahn had told them that little would change. That life on Corinair would go on, that her people would continue to prosper, likely more so under Dusahn rule. But that was not turning out to be the case. Everyone in Aitkenna was terrified. Most hid in their homes, fearing arrest, should they be stopped on the street by Dusahn security forces. Word of random arrests and interrogations were rampant, and many of those arrested had never returned.

Birk and Cuddy had laughed at the fears of their neighbors, arguing that the Dusahn gained nothing from a paralyzed, non-functioning world. It was in the Dusahn's best interest for the worlds they seized control of to continue to produce, to continue to thrive. The Dusahn needed their *support*, not their *fear*. They needed the people of Corinair to be *thankful* that they had been chosen for inclusion in the Dusahn Empire.

Their arguments could not have been more wrong. The Dusahn may have wanted the people of Corinair to be happy and productive under their rule, but first, they needed them to *fear*. For *fear* was a far more powerful weapon than any gun or bomb. *Fear* was *always* with you, everywhere you went. It even permeated your dreams.

Birk's mind kept wandering back to his friend. Originally, Cuddy had wanted nothing to do with the guns. It had been Birk's idea to bury them in the yard and wait. As with most of Birk's crazy schemes, Cuddy had agreed to go along after Birk's needling. When Birk had decided to try selling the weapons, Cuddy had wanted nothing to do with the idea. Burying them in the yard was one thing. At least they had plausible deniability, as anyone could have buried them, and they had been careful enough to wipe their fingerprints from the case. But *selling* them presented new risks. *Immense risk*, Cuddy had argued. But Birk had reminded Cuddy that they needed the money. Besides, it was their responsibility to help support any resistance to Dusahn occupation, even if it was indirect. And what was wrong with making a few bucks on the side?

If only he had listened to his friend.

The lights suddenly snapped back on, painfully blinding Birk. He had spent so much time in absolute darkness that his pupils were fully dilated. There was the sound of the door being unlocked, then opened, followed by footsteps, several of them.

Two men grabbed Birk, one of them holding him firmly while the other cut away his restraints.

"Please don't kill me," Birk pleaded.

As if responding to his pleas, the man holding him let go, and both men disappeared behind the bright lights. The door slammed shut and locked again, and Birk was left alone in the room, still blinded by the two white lights.

Or was he alone?

Birk rubbed his sore wrists, wondering what was about to happen. He tried listening for the sound of another person in the room, but his own irregular, panicked breathing made it impossible. He thought of standing, exploring the room he was in, now that the lights had been left on, but was afraid. If there was still someone in the room with him, were they waiting for him to stand, before executing him? Was it some twisted code that demanded they release a prisoner from his restraints prior to execution?

Birk had little choice but to sit quietly and await his fate.

* * *

"Any sign of that first ship?" Nathan asked.

"Nothing," Vladimir replied. "They probably thought we were an echo. They only sent one pulse."

"They could be trying to remain stealthy, trying to sneak up on us," Josh commented.

Nathan stood there in the middle of the Seiiki's cramped cockpit, his arms folded as he thought. "It's possible," he admitted. "But if it's a Dusahn gunship, wouldn't they just sweep the area with active sensors? If the Mystic doesn't even *know* about the Dusahn invasion, they wouldn't be trying to remain hidden, and the Dusahn would likely know that."

"Would they?" Loki wondered.

Nathan looked at Loki, puzzled.

"I mean, would the Dusahn even *know* about the cloud? Would they know that the Mystic would be out of touch?"

"We knew," Josh argued.

"Because you two flew these routes all the time," Loki said. "I *knew* about the Mystic, but I *didn't* know she was normally out of contact during most of her journey."

"Good point," Josh admitted.

"The Dusahn obviously had some intelligence before they invaded," Jessica said as she stood, straddling the access ladder at the back of the cockpit. "However, they may have been concentrating more on military assets, and how many jump ships were in operation in the PC. They might not have paid much attention to routes and such, at least not with the civilian ships."

"I'm getting another weak contact," Vladimir interrupted.

"The same ship?" Nathan asked.

"I do not know," Vladimir replied. "Roughly twenty-eight thousand kilometers, directly ahead. Slightly below our track."

"Which direction is the contact headed?" Nathan asked.

"The contact is still too weak to tell," Vladimir admitted, "but there is no apparent motion."

"Which means the contact is either standing still, or is headed toward us."

"Showing slight drift down and away," Vladimir added. "Still a very weak contact." Vladimir studied the sensor readings further. "Twenty-four thousand kilometers, I believe. Yes, closing. Definitely."

"Stand by to reduce our closure rate," Nathan

instructed. "Keep an eye on the contact's drift," he told Vladimir. "If it stops, or even worse, reverses, let me know."

"Of course," Vladimir replied.

"Give us a nose-low attitude, Josh," Nathan instructed.

"Nose-low, aye," Josh replied.

"Eyes peeled, scan straight ahead," Nathan ordered over his comm-set.

"*If I can still keep them open,*" Dalen complained.

"Contact is firming up," Vladimir reported. "Twenty thousand kilometers, still drifting down and away."

"And you're sure it's not that gunship?" Nathan asked.

"I'm sure. It's much bigger. Eighteen thousand kilometers, now."

"If we can detect them with passive, then they can detect us," Jessica pointed out.

"Decrease our closure rate, and slide us down below the contact's projected course track," Nathan ordered.

"Can we reach them on comms?" Jessica wondered.

"Doubtful," Vladimir replied. "But if they *are* detecting us, they will notice that we are maneuvering, which will tell them that we are a *ship*, and not a chunk of rock or something."

"They'd go active, wouldn't they?" Loki surmised.

"Maybe," Nathan replied. "Or they'll change course to avoid a collision. Either way, they'll know we're out here."

"Isn't that risky?" Loki wondered. "What if it's another Dusahn ship?"

"Then we jump forward a few light minutes," Nathan replied.

"Fifteen thousand kilometers," Vladimir reported. "Definitely a contact. Still weak, but it is *not* an echo."

"Captain, if it is the Mystic, or any other ship for that matter, we are closing in on it awfully fast," Loki warned.

"Five-kilometer separation," Nathan insisted. "I don't want to take a chance of not spotting her."

"Nathan, at that range, I should have positive contact on sensors," Vladimir assured him. "Visual will not be necessary."

"If we miss her, we may not find her again," Nathan reminded him. "And we need that ship."

"Yes, sir."

"I'll remind you of that, if her captain turns us down," Jessica told Nathan under her breath.

Nathan shot a disapproving glare at her over his shoulder.

"Ten thousand kilometers," Vladimir reported.

"We're paralleling the target's course," Loki announced. "Opposite direction, five-kilometer offset."

"We'll start decelerating at five thousand kilometers," Nathan said.

"That's not going to be enough distance to reverse course and match the target's forward speed," Josh warned.

"I just want to slow down enough to get a good look at her as she passes. If it's her, we'll come about and come alongside, assuming her captain grants permission for us to do so."

"What if he does not?" Vladimir wondered.

"Plan C," Jessica mumbled.

Nathan turned to look at her, a cross look on his face. "What happened to plans A and B?"

Jessica shrugged. "Just staying flexible."

"Well, stop it," Nathan insisted. "He'll grant us permission."

"We are an armed ship, remember," Jessica said. "He might just jump away."

"He might, but I'm betting he won't," Nathan replied.

"Maybe it would be better if we had been a *little more covert* in our approach," Vladimir commented.

"You, too?" Nathan said.

"It is just an observation," Vladimir defended. "Five thousand kilometers."

"Begin deceleration," Nathan instructed.

"Got it," Josh replied. "Flipping her over and firing mains."

The Seiiki pitched down quickly as Josh brought the ship into an aft-first attitude. A low rumble began to build as he brought the Seiiki's main engines up to full power.

"If she did not see us before, she will definitely see us now," Vladimir stated.

"That's the idea," Nathan replied. "Just be ready on that escape jump, Loki. The minute that contact targets us..."

"My finger is already on the button, Captain," Loki assured him.

"Three thousand kilometers," Vladimir reported. "Contact is solid, now. They're changing course, veering away from us."

"They're trying to avoid a collision," Nathan said.

"They're definitely not a warship," Jessica concluded. "Otherwise, they'd be targeting us right now."

Nathan smiled. "Correct." Nathan stooped down slightly, reaching forward to the overhead communications panel between Josh and Loki. "Mystic Empress. Mystic Empress. This is the Seiiki. Do you copy?"

"Two thousand kilometers," Vladimir updated.

"If that other ship is in the area..." Jessica began.

"I'm using a directional comm-beam," Nathan told her. "So, unless they're on the far side of her, we're good."

"One thousand kilometers."

"Mystic Empress, Mystic Empress. This is the Seiiki. We are now..."

"Eight hundred," Vladimir said.

"Eight hundred meters and decelerating for rendezvous. We have important information for your captain. Do you copy?"

"Maybe they can't hear us?" Loki suggested.

"They can hear us," Nathan said. "Right?" he asked Vladimir.

"From this range, yes. I am sure of it."

"They're trying to decide if they should answer," Jessica said.

"Can they see our gun turrets?"

"From this distance?" Vladimir replied.

"I meant with sensors," Nathan said.

"If they have optics, yes."

"Roll us over and keep our belly toward them," Nathan instructed. "No need to scare them."

"Rolling over," Josh replied.

"They will see our guns eventually," Vladimir warned.

"Mystic Empress, Mystic Empress. This is the Seiiki. It is imperative that we meet with your captain.

We have information that is vital to the safety of your ship and your passengers. Please respond."

"One hundred kilometers," Vladimir warned.

"How far off are we going to pass?" Nathan asked.

"Still five kilometers," Josh replied. "I adjusted to maintain the range you asked for."

"Good. Keep us at five." Nathan turned to Vladimir. "Are they still maneuvering?"

"Negative," Vladimir replied. "Target is holding course." Vladimir watched his display as the contact finally resolved completely. "I have confirmation on the contact, Nathan. It is the Mystic Empress."

"Mystic Empress. Mystic Empress. This is the Seiiki. For the sake of everyone on board, please respond." Nathan waited, growing frustrated with each passing second of silence. "This is just downright rude," he finally exclaimed. "By the rules of interstellar navigation, they should answer us and at least tell us to veer away and get lost."

"Their communications gear may not be as good as ours," Vladimir pointed out.

"Trust me," Nathan replied. "Our comms gear is not *that* good."

"*Seiiki, Seiiki. This is the Takaran ship, Mystic Empress. Your course is illegally close to a passenger ship. Veer away immediately.*"

"Finally!" Nathan exclaimed. "Mystic Empress, Seiiki. We request permission to speak to your captain, in person. We have important information that affects the safety of your ship and everyone aboard her. You will need this information before you leave the cloud. We are requesting permission to come aboard and speak to your captain directly."

"Fifty kilometers and closing," Vladimir reported.

"Bring up the ventral cameras," Nathan instructed.

"The what?" Josh asked.

Nathan suddenly realized he was thinking of the Aurora. "Deploy the landing gear, and give me the nose gear camera."

"Okay," Josh replied.

A few seconds later, the image came to life on the view screen in the center of the forward console.

"Thirty kilometers."

"*Seiiki, Mystic Empress. Who is your captain?*"

Nathan turned to look at Jessica. "Should I?"

"You're going to have to sooner or later," Jessica replied. "In this case, it just might help."

Nathan tapped his comm-set. "My name is Nathan Scott. *Captain* Nathan Scott."

"*Nice try, mister. Captain Nathan Scott died seven years ago.*"

"You're right, I did, but I'm back. Now grant me permission to come aboard and speak to your captain directly, so I can *prove* it to you."

Again, there was a long pause.

"His captain has got to be standing right there," Nathan commented, annoyed.

"Ten kilometers," Vladimir announced.

"Roll us back over," Nathan decided.

"What?" Josh replied, surprised.

"They'll see our gun turrets," Jessica warned.

"We need them to trust us," Nathan said. "If we don't show them now, they'll see them when we approach to dock, and we'll spook them. Better to be honest with them now." Nathan looked at Josh. "Do it."

"You're the captain," Josh replied, initiating the roll.

Nathan and the rest of them stared out the

windows as the Mystic Empress came into view and passed overhead.

"Nice-looking ship," Loki commented.

"Is that one big window along her side?" Josh wondered in disbelief.

"That is most impressive," Vladimir exclaimed.

"*Seiiki, you are armed! Are you threatening this ship?*"

"Like you're gonna answer 'yes'," Josh laughed. "How dumb is this guy?"

Nathan motioned for Josh to be quiet. "Mystic Empress, Seiiki. We mean you no harm. Our gun turrets are for defensive purposes only. If your captain will agree to meet with us, I'm sure he will understand once I share the information I have for him."

"*Who is us?*" the Mystic Empress's comms officer asked.

"Myself and Lieutenant Jessica Nash, of the Ghatazhak."

"Like that's not going to scare the hell out of them," Josh commented.

"If they knew her, they would be," Vladimir commented dryly.

Jessica reached out and hit Vladimir on the side of his head with a flick of her finger.

"Speed is matched," Josh announced. "Shall I continue the burn?"

"Yes," Nathan replied. "Mystic Empress, Seiiki. I should tell you that your captain's wife and child are safe, and on board the Glendanon, at an undisclosed location."

"Now they think we're kidnappers," Josh said with another laugh.

"If that's what it takes to get aboard that ship

peacefully and talk to her captain face-to-face, then so be it," Nathan insisted.

"We're starting to gain on her again," Josh reported.

"We'll be side by side in a few minutes, Captain," Loki added.

"Come on," Nathan said impatiently.

"*Seiiki, Mystic Empress. Permission to dock, starboard side. Only Captain Scott and Lieutenant Nash will be allowed aboard, and your ship will disengage and remain at least one hundred kilometers distant while your captain is on board. Security will escort you to our captain. No weapons will be allowed on board, and you will keep your guns deactivated while in the vicinity of this ship. Do you understand?*"

"No way!" Jessica protested.

"Mystic Empress, Seiiki. We understand and will comply," Nathan replied, holding up his hand to silence Jessica's complaints. "Take us in, Josh."

* * *

What had likely been minutes felt like hours as Birk sat quietly, rubbing his now-unrestrained hands. He wanted to stand, to walk around the room, if only to get the blood circulating in his legs again, but he feared the presence of another in the room. Finally, he could take no more. "Are you going to kill me?"

"*Should I?*" the voice asked from behind the bright lights.

"I am no threat to the Dusahn," Birk admitted. When he had first opened that case of weapons, he had entertained thoughts of starting a resistance, becoming a leader in the fight against the Dusahn. After all, with Na-Tan on their side, surely they had a chance. If Na-Tan could come back from the dead to fight again, then anything was possible. The idea of becoming a mighty warrior against oppression, like the Corinari legends of the war against the Takaran Empire, had an almost hypnotic appeal to him. Had it not been for Cuddy...

He would never forgive himself for his friend's death.

"*That is a shame,*" the voice replied.

"I... I don't understand."

"*We found the case of weapons,*" the voice said smugly. "*It was buried in your yard, just as you said. Was there only the one case?*"

"Yes, only the one. I swear it," Birk replied earnestly.

"*Also a shame,*" the voice said.

By now, Birk's eyes were becoming accustomed to light again. He squinted, trying to see the man through the bright lights. "Who are you?" he finally summoned the courage to ask.

"*You wanted to speak to Anji,*" the voice said as he stepped into view. "I am Anji."

The bright lights switched off, and a single overhead light came on, illuminating the room at a normal, more comfortable level.

Birk stared as the man stepped forward. "You are the man in the store. The man with the gun." Birk's mind was spinning. "What is going on? Why are you doing this to me?"

"We had to be sure," Anji replied.

"Sure about what?" Birk exclaimed.

"That you were not a Dusahn spy."

"A what?" Birk was appalled. "A spy?"

"One cannot be too careful these days. The same can be said for you, young man. We could have just as easily been Dusahn spies ourselves."

"You killed my friend!" Birk yelled, enraged.

"Your friend is still alive," Anji replied calmly. "He is here, in another room."

"But... Why the hell..."

"Like I said, we had to be sure."

"Oh, my God," Birk exclaimed, holding back his tears.

"Approaching someone you do not know, in order to sell them illegal weapons, during an occupation, no less, is very dangerous," Anji said. "Surely, you considered something like this might happen."

"Of course, I didn't!" Birk cried.

"Then you are even dumber than I thought."

Birk couldn't believe what was happening. "Can I see my friend?"

"In time," Anji replied. "Who told you about me?"

"I don't know."

"You don't know?"

"I mean, I heard it around, in the past."

"What did you hear?" Anji asked.

"That you bought things. Things to sell."

"I have a market. I sell things in that market. No secret there."

"No, I mean you *sell* things. Things that people are not supposed to be able to buy. You know, *black-market* stuff?"

Anji laughed. "People use that term as if they are describing some underground organization when, in fact, it is simply regular people, selling and trading things they own with others. Just because no tax is paid to the government for such transactions, it becomes a vast conspiracy."

"Then you *do* sell things?"

"What else did you hear about me?" Anji wondered.

"Some people say you were once in the Corinari," Birk admitted.

"Don't such men usually display their service credentials proudly on the wall, for all to see?"

"I heard you were a *covert* operative in the Corinari."

"Ah, I see," Anji said, nodding his head in understanding. "That would explain why I had no such display, would it not?" He laughed again. "Young man, had I once been in the Corinari, I would already be in hiding, like all the other ex-Corinari, to avoid arrest. Did you ever think of that?"

Birk suddenly felt embarrassed. "No."

"So, I am to believe that you simply wanted to sell the weapons to make money. Even though *doing* so would put you at risk of execution at the hands of the Dusahn."

Birk said nothing.

"How much did you think you would get for such a dangerous commodity? One hundred? Two hundred? Three? Would that have been worth the life of your friend? Was that truly your *only* reason? *Greed?* Your planet; your people; your entire way of life is threatened, and all you can think about are your own needs?" Anji was shouting by now.

"I thought I could help," Birk admitted meekly.

"What!" he demanded.

"I thought that, maybe, if I found someone who wanted to buy the weapons, that I would be helping the resistance."

"Resistance?" Anji yelled. "What resistance?"

"I thought that surely someone would rise up," Birk said. "I mean, all those guns dropping from the sky. The message from Na-Tan..."

"Na-Tan is dead! We all saw his memorial! His place on the Walk of Heroes!"

"I know! But what if he *is* alive?"

"Then you would follow him?" Anji yelled defiantly, bursting out laughing. "You? A meek, little, college student with delusions of grandeur? What could you do?"

"I could help," Birk argued.

"You're going to fight?" Anji laughed again. "Have you ever even *held* a weapon?"

"No, but I could learn," Birk insisted, feeling insulted.

"You want to learn to fight?" Anji asked, taunting him.

"Maybe," Birk replied, becoming more angry.

"Then stand up and fight!" Anji exclaimed.

"What?"

"You heard me! Stand! You want to fight? Then stand up! Fight me!"

"What?" Birk said, confused.

Anji slapped Birk across the face, catching him off guard.

"What the hell!" Birk exclaimed, his hand instinctively reaching for his reddened cheek.

"You can't fight! I'm an old man, and you won't even fight me!" Anji slapped him again.

"Why are you..."

"You want to kill Dusahn, but you sit here and let an old man slap you like you're a child?" Anji slapped him a third time, then grabbed Birk by the collar of his jacket, pulling him to his feet and shaking him. "Are you going to fight back?" Anji screamed in Birk's face, spittle spewing from his mouth. "Are you a man?"

Anji pulled back one hand to slap Birk again, but

the young man raised his hand to block the blow. Birk pushed Anji away from him, his face now red with anger.

"That's it! Fight me! Fight me, you little bastard!" Anji swung at him again. Birk tried to block the blow, but Anji pulled it short and swung with his other hand, catching Birk in the mouth. Birk stumbled backward, blood and spit flying from his mouth. He screamed in anger, lunging at the old man, grabbing him around the middle. Anji countered, quickly twisting and using the young man's own momentum against him. A split second later, he had the angry young man from behind, his arm around Birk's throat. He spun the man around, pushing him up against the rocky wall, pinning him with ease. "You want to fight?" he asked again.

"Yes," Birk said, pleading.

"Do-you-want-to-kill-Dusahn?" Anji asked in slow, deliberate fashion.

"Yes! I want to kill them all!" Birk screamed.

Anji suddenly released the young man and stepped back. "Welcome to the resistance."

CHAPTER SIX

Nathan, Jessica, and Vladimir all stood behind Josh and Loki in the cramped cockpit of the Seiiki as Josh maneuvered the ship alongside the Mystic Empress.

"This has got to be one of the prettiest ships I have ever seen," Nathan commented.

"Her lines are beautiful, yes," Vladimir agreed, "but it is all for show. All those massive, exposed windows? If their shields failed, they would surely suffer catastrophic decompression."

"I'm sure her designers thought of that, Vlad," Nathan responded.

"Still, it is an unnecessary luxury," Vladimir argued.

"It's a cruise ship, Vlad," Jessica said. "It's all *about* unnecessary luxury."

"There's the docking port," Josh announced, pointing out the left, forward window.

Nathan looked in the direction Josh was pointing, immediately spotting the Mystic's starboard docking arm as it began to extend out from the cruise ship's hull, just behind her starboard hangar bay doors. "Looks like a uni," Nathan noticed.

"A uni?" Vladimir asked.

"Universal docking adapter," Jessica explained. "As jump drives began to increase in the Pentaurus sector, they developed a docking system that could adapt to just about any hull shape, or surface, and maintain a proper seal. Actually, it was Ranni Enterprises that developed it."

"Very clever," Vladimir said, impressed. "She probably made quite a bit of profit off that idea."

"I'm sure she did." Jessica thought for a moment. "Now that I think of it, in a way, the uni probably paid for cloning you, Nathan."

Nathan looked at her in surprise. "Seriously?"

Vladimir nodded. "We should install one of those on the Aurora. Think she will give us a discount?"

Nathan smiled. "I think she might consider it."

"*Seiiki, Mystic Empress. You are cleared for hard dock.*"

"Mystic Empress, Seiiki," Loki replied. "Maneuvering for hard dock."

Nathan, Jessica, and Vladimir watched as Josh and Loki maneuvered the Seiiki carefully up to the Mystic Empress's docking arm, then slowly slid her up against its universal docking adapter. There was a small thud, and the ship rocked slightly.

"Contact," Loki stated.

"You still doin' that?" Josh asked wearily.

"Doing what?"

"Always stating the obvious?"

"That's my job," Loki defended, sounding annoyed.

"We all heard the contact, Loki. The ship shook and everything."

"Just following procedures," Loki said as he began shutting down systems. "Mystic, Seiiki. We have hard dock."

"*Docking adapter is secure. We show a good seal. We will notify you when you are cleared to board.*"

"I guess I better go put on my good clothes, huh?" Nathan joked, turning to exit.

* * *

The door swung open, and Birk stepped out of the small room he had been trapped in for hours. The next room wasn't much better. Two young men he recognized from the market stood in the next room, waiting to escort him.

Birk looked at them both with disdain, assuming that they had been involved in his abduction.

"This way," one of the young men told him, leading him through the room and into the next.

At that moment, Birk realized he was in a stone-walled basement, and that his prison was a cave dug out of one side of the basement.

When Birk entered the next room, a wave of relief washed over him. There, smiling at him, was his friend Cuddy, who looked as miserable and scared as Birk felt. The two friends embraced, relieved to see one another. "They told me you were dead," Birk said as he hugged his friend.

"They told me the same," Cuddy replied.

"We must move you both out of the city," Anji explained, interrupting their reunion.

"What? I thought you were going to set us free?" Birk said. "I thought we could go home."

"It is only a matter of time before the Dusahn come for you both. Surely, someone saw you take the weapons when they fell from the sky. The Dusahn have been combing the city, arresting everyone they even *think* knows something about those weapons. And now, you know about this place."

"We won't say anything about you," Cuddy promised.

Anji scoffed. "The two of you would not last a minute under Dusahn interrogation. You have but two choices, I'm afraid. Join the resistance, or die here and now. I am sorry, but I cannot allow you to reveal us to the Dusahn."

"You would kill us?" Birk said in shock. "Just like that? But we're Corinairan, just like you."

"I'm sorry, but this is much bigger than any of us. Our entire world is at stake. We suffered too long under the reign of Caius. We will not suffer yet another dictator, not again."

"We don't deserve to die," Cuddy argued. "We've done nothing to you."

"You sealed your fate when you came here trying to sell us contraband."

"Why didn't you just ignore us and tell us that we were mistaken?" Birk asked.

"We had to know what *you* knew. We had to know if the Dusahn were on to us."

"Damn it, Birk!" Cuddy exclaimed. "I told you this was a bad idea!"

"You can still join the resistance," Anji suggested.

"We're not soldiers," Birk said.

"You said you wanted to kill Dusahn, did you not?"

"Yes, but that was in the heat of the moment."

"There are many ways to serve in the resistance," Anji said. "What vocation are you studying?"

"Electronics," Birk answered.

"And you?" Anji asked, looking at Cuddy.

"Programming."

"Both useful skills, ones that the resistance will no doubt require."

"But our friends...our families," Birk said.

"Your friends would be the first to sell you to the Dusahn, to protect themselves," Anji said. "I have seen it before. And your family? They will just be happy that you are alive."

"How will they know?"

"We will make sure they know," Anji explained. "And you will be able to communicate with them.

Perhaps, in time, you will even be able to return to visit them briefly."

Birk sighed, and Cuddy scratched his head.

"I don't know," Birk said.

"Would you rather I kill you now?" Anji reminded him.

"Actually, no." Birk looked at Cuddy. "We wanted a little more excitement in our lives, didn't we?"

Cuddy looked at him, mouth open. "Not exactly what I had in mind, Birk."

"So, what do we do?" Birk asked. "Is this where we live? Underground? Do you have some kind of tunnel system or something?"

Anji laughed. "You have been watching too many vid-plays."

* * *

"How did you get all this?" Cameron asked as she looked at the images on the various overhead view screens in the Aurora's intelligence office.

"We've been sending recon drones skipping through the Darvano and Takar systems at frequent intervals," Lieutenant Commander Shinoda explained.

"No cold-coasts?"

"No, sir. On the general's advice, we didn't even try."

"We have already made several such attempts," General Telles explained. "We have never been able to remain in the system for more than an hour. Usually, the Dusahn are intercepting us within minutes."

"I don't want to lose any drones," Cameron warned the lieutenant commander.

"Recon and jump intervals are randomized, as are the distances of each jump. And we always use several drones at once, from varying angles, then stitch the data together here. We also programmed the drones to abort their mission and immediately jump clear of the system at the slightest hint of trouble. If anything gets within striking distance, they're gone. It would be next to impossible for the Dusahn to intercept one of our drones."

General Telles nodded his approval. "A sound tactic, Lieutenant Commander."

"Thank you, sir."

"That's got to be real annoying to the Dusahn," Commander Kaplan said, a smirk on her face. "Having all our drones buzzing around them like flies, and not being able to do anything about it."

"Actually, they probably won't even notice half of them," Lieutenant Commander Shinoda pointed out. "The recon drones use the newer, attenuated jump emitters. Shorter range, but much more difficult to detect on sensors. And visual? Forget it. You'd have to be less than ten kilometers away to see its flash, and even then, you might mistake it for a reflection or something. And in the daylight, it'd be lost against the sky."

"I did not know such technology existed," General Telles said. "Is it available for manned vessels?"

"Our recon drones are pretty compact," Cameron said. "Ranging in size from two to four meters. Manned vessels generally require a considerable amount of power to jump any significant distance, so their jump flashes are much more difficult to attenuate."

General Telles seemed impressed. "I wasn't aware you were so well versed in jump drive technology, Captain."

"I'm not," Cameron admitted. "When they first

came out, Vlad wouldn't shut up about them. I think I learned all I ever wanted to know in the first hour they were on board."

"They do have their limits," Lieutenant Commander Shinoda warned. "Too many successive attenuated jumps and the emitters overheat and burn out. It's all about the timing. We generally program them to jump to the edge of the system, and then execute the first insertion jump without attenuation. Then, we use attenuated jump intervals that prevent overheating. Each jump is designed to be executed before the Dusahn have time to detect and intercept the previous jump flash."

"I see," the general replied.

"So, how many ships are we talking about?" Commander Kaplan wondered.

"So far, we've confirmed eighteen warships and twelve gunships. There are still three other ships that we haven't verified. They look more like troop or cargo ships than warships."

"Type and number?" Cameron wondered.

"Four battleships, six heavy cruisers, and eight missile frigates," the lieutenant commander replied. "Although they are all much older Jung designs, the battleships and heavy cruisers have both energy weapons *and* projectile weapons."

"And they have shields," Commander Kaplan added. "That much we've seen."

"Yes," the lieutenant commander agreed. "And the Jung in our neck of the woods didn't get shields until a few decades ago. So, the Dusahn ships must have picked up the technology along the way, or developed it independently while en route. Same with the energy weapons. Sol Jung don't even *have* them on their warships yet. They still haven't solved the heat issues on the larger energy weapons."

"The Aurora handled that many ships all by herself the last time you guys were out here," Commander Kaplan said. "And you weren't nearly as well equipped."

"The Takaran ships didn't have jump drives," Cameron reminded her executive officer. "That puts an entirely different spin on things. The Alliance hasn't even been training to fight a jump-equipped enemy."

"We did *some*," her XO argued.

"There are fifty-seven basic tactical maneuvers for ship-to-ship combat," Cameron pointed out. "Only ten of them are for use against a jump-enabled ship."

"But when you add in all the variants on those ten, it's a lot more," the commander argued.

"You get my point," Cameron replied.

"The captain is correct," General Telles interjected. "Taking on eighteen jump-capable warships with a single ship is not a sound strategy. At this point, the most the Aurora can hope to do is harass the Dusahn, and to support guerrilla operations on the surface whenever possible. If we are lucky, we may be able to prevent the Dusahn from getting a firm hold on the Pentaurus cluster. If we are *very* lucky, we *may* even be able to prevent them from expanding their empire to include the entire sector."

"To what end?" Lieutenant Commander Shinoda wondered. "We can't keep it up forever. Sooner or later, luck has a nasty habit of running out."

General Telles seemed hesitant to speak.

"What are you thinking?" Cameron asked, noticing the general's expression.

"What if the Jung penetrations into Alliance space *are* a false-flag operation being conducted *by* the Dusahn. If we could *prove* this to the Alliance, they might be able to spare more ships to assist us."

"The problem is, we've already bloodied the Jung's nose with KKV strikes," Commander Kaplan reminded them.

"If we *didn't* have a problem with the Jung before, we sure as hell have one now," Cameron agreed. "Galiardi saw to that."

"You still think he has some evil master plan, don't you?" Lieutenant Commander Shinoda said.

"You're in intelligence, Ken," Cameron said. "Don't tell me the thought hasn't crossed your mind more than once."

"Two, three times at the most."

Cameron sighed, looking at the images again.

"Okay, four times, but that's all, I swear."

A wry smile crept onto Cameron's lips. The lieutenant commander had a knack for breaking the tension at just the right moment. It was one of the reasons she enjoyed having him present during such discussions. "Eighteen ships."

"And twelve gunships," the lieutenant commander added.

"The gunships don't worry me," Cameron replied. "Catch them by surprise with a single jump missile, and they're done. But I sure wouldn't mind having a few gunships ourselves."

"I'd rather have a few destroyers," Commander Kaplan argued.

"Warships have less jump range," Cameron pointed out. "It takes us longer to get into position. That makes it harder to fight a guerrilla-style war, especially if we're always going to be staging a hundred-plus light years away from the enemy."

"Until we learn the true range of the Dusahn jump drive technology, we will be forced to stage further out," General Telles said.

"Cobras can cross a hundred light years in minutes," Commander Kaplan suggested.

"That's exactly what I was thinking," Cameron agreed.

"I don't suppose you know where we can get our hands on a few Cobra gunships?" General Telles asked.

"There's no way we'd get any of them to join us," Commander Kaplan insisted. "We're cranking out gunships so fast, every one of their captains is straight out of the academy. They're about as gung-ho, Galiardi-worshiping as you can get."

"I was thinking of gunships *without* crews," Cameron said.

Commander Kaplan looked at Cameron, a stunned look on her face. "Cameron Taylor, are you thinking about *stealing* a Cobra gunship?"

"Actually, I was thinking about stealing five or six of them." Cameron glanced over at Lieutenant Commander Shinoda. "What are you smiling at?"

"Nothing," he said, suppressing a chuckle. "Just not exactly where I saw my career going." He looked up and to the right, as if gazing at a sign in the air. "Kenichi Shinoda... *Space Pirate.*"

General Telles also seemed surprised. "I am impressed, Captain. I assume you have a plan?"

"Sorry, no. I'm actually surprised I even thought of it. I was hoping that you and Jessica might come up with something."

"How hard can it be?" Commander Kaplan

shrugged. "They're being built on at least three different worlds, now. And each one of them has at least a dozen just sitting there at all times."

"We will need more details on their security," General Telles said. "And there are obviously more pressing tasks at hand. However, it is an idea worth investigating."

"How much do you have on the Cobra plants?" Cameron asked the lieutenant commander.

"One of my guys worked security at the plant on Earth for a few years. He might be helpful."

"I'll check the crew's service records, to see if anyone worked at any of the plants, as well," Commander Kaplan promised.

"There is one other way to get information," Cameron suggested. "Before we left the Sol sector, I sent a time-delayed message to Jessica's brother, Robert. He's still in command of the Tanna."

"The converted Jung frigate?" General Telles asked.

"Same ship, only it's been upgraded to a destroyer."

"Why did you send him a message?" the general asked.

"Well, partly because his sister was involved," Cameron replied. "But mostly, because I wanted *someone* back in the Sol sector to know the truth, in case this all went really wrong."

"You think he can help us?" Lieutenant Commander Shinoda asked.

"Maybe. But I'm willing to bet he told Gil Roselle, the captain of the Benakh, as well. And the Benakh is *stationed* in the Tau Ceti system."

"Where one of the Cobra plants is located," Commander Kaplan realized. "Nice."

"Roselle hates Galiardi. He knows the admiral

will never give him a capital ship. In fact, I heard through the grapevine that Gil was thinking about retiring pretty soon."

"How do we get in contact with him?" General Telles wondered.

"In my message to Captain Nash, I included a time and location for an update message. That's a few days from now. In the meantime, we should keep digging at this end and see what we come up with." Cameron looked at her XO, then at her chief of security. "Why are you both grinning like little kids?"

"Going rogue is *so* much more fun," Commander Kaplan replied.

* * *

Nathan stepped into the Seiiki's port, forward corridor, making his way toward the boarding airlock just forward of the galley. Standing by the airlock door were Jessica and Master Sergeant Anwar.

"How do I look?" Nathan asked, half joking.

"I still say the coat makes you look a bit roguish."

"Good, that's the look I was going for," Nathan replied, pulling his collar up.

"You *want* to look like a pirate?"

"No, I *want* to look like a man willing to do anything for the cause that he is claiming to lead."

"The uniform pants and boots are a nice touch," Jessica decided. "It adds a touch of credibility, which you desperately need with that young face."

"I could go back to my cabin and get my eye patch," Nathan suggested, smiling.

"*We just got word from the Mystic,*" Loki called over Nathan's comm-set. "*You're cleared to board, but no comm-sets.*"

"No way," Jessica protested.

Nathan removed his comm-set, handing it to Marcus, who had just stepped out of the galley.

"You're not serious," Jessica said. "No guns, no comms..."

"I'm with her, Cap'n," Marcus agreed. "How the hell are we supposed to know if you need us?"

"Guys, come on. We're lucky they're even letting us aboard. Would you rather we just send the Ghatazhak in, guns blazing?"

"Actually, I would much prefer that," Master Sergeant Anwar stated.

"We're going," Nathan insisted. "No guns and no comms. Besides, if something goes wrong, I'll just have you kick all their asses," Nathan said to Jessica, with a wink.

"That would be fun to watch," the master sergeant joked.

Jessica pointed a finger of warning at her fellow Ghatazhak, then reached over and activated the inner door. The door slid open, disappearing into the bulkhead, after which she gestured into the open airlock. "After you, Captain."

Nathan stepped into the airlock, followed by Jessica, who pressed the inside controls, causing the inner door to slide shut again. Nathan leaned forward, peering through the small window in the angled outer door. "Nobody in the next airlock," he stated.

Jessica stepped over to the outer door controls. "Pressure is good on the other side."

"Open her up."

Jessica activated the outer door, which slid into the bulkhead. Just outside the ship was another small compartment with a hatch. They stepped inside, then activated the outer door of the Seiiki to close behind them.

"Gravity is light here," Nathan commented. He pushed upward, floating up a few centimeters before settling back down gently onto the deck of the outer compartment. "Very light."

The hatch before them was gear-actuated. Nathan pushed the latch bar up, causing several locking clamps to disengage. He then pushed the door open into the next compartment, Jessica stepping in after him.

The next compartment was stark white, with rounded joints at the bulkheads. The first thing Nathan noticed was that the gravity in this compartment was stronger than it had been in the previous one. It still wasn't a full G, but it was close.

He stepped up to the inner hatch control. "It's locked."

Jessica swung the outer door closed and latched it.

"It's still locked," Nathan said.

Pale blue lights suddenly came on overhead, and a computerized voice made an announcement, first in Takaran, and then in Corinairan.

"What?" Jessica said. "All I heard was 'decontamination'."

"It told us to prepare for decontamination," Nathan confirmed. "Take a few deep breaths. When the lights turn yellow, take a deep breath and hold it."

"Is this normal?" Jessica asked as she started purposefully hyperventilating.

"All big passenger ships do this to anyone coming aboard while en route," Nathan said. "To protect the passengers and crew."

The blue lights overhead suddenly turned yellow. Nathan and Jessica took deep breaths and held them as the lights changed to red.

A thin mist began to fill the compartment, coming from tiny ports evenly spaced on all four walls. Within seconds, a dense fog filled the room around them. Thirty seconds after the fog settled, powerful fans sucked it out of the room, after which they were hit with intense light and fans blowing off any particles that had stuck to their clothing.

The overhead lights turned from red to orange, and Nathan let his breath out and resumed normal respirations.

Jessica breathed out as well. “What now?”

Green beams of light shot out from the walls, sweeping over them both, as more instructions were given through hidden speakers. Nathan raised his hands as he rotated around once.

“We dancing now?” Jessica wondered as she followed suit.

The green light beams disappeared, and the computerized voice called out again as the overhead lights returned to their normal white color.

“That’s it,” Nathan said. “We’re clean.” He looked at the control panel again. “The inner door is unlocked.” He looked at Jessica. “You ready?”

Jessica nodded, and Nathan activated the inner door, causing it to slide into the bulkhead. Before them, at the other end of the long boarding tunnel, were four armed, uniformed security guards, their weapons trained on Nathan and Jessica.

One man, likely an officer, stood in the middle of his men, beyond the far hatch. “Raise your hands, place them on your heads, fingers interlaced, step through the hatch, and walk slowly toward me.”

Nathan glanced at Jessica as he raised his hands, placing them on his head and interlacing his fingers. He stepped into the tunnel and began walking slowly toward the officer.

Jessica did the same, following a step behind and to the right of Nathan. Her first thoughts were to count the number of men facing them. Five in total. Four of them were carrying shipboard energy rifles, designed to wound but not to damage the interior of the ship. The assistive undergarment that all Ghatazhak wore under their uniforms and their battle armor would protect her from that, as long as she didn't receive too many shots in the exact same location in rapid succession. She also noticed that, while the officer was wearing a sidearm, none of his men were. She immediately decided that she *could* take them all out, *if* they allowed her to get in the middle of them.

Nathan also recognized the low-power weapons, but he wasn't trying to decide if he could take them out.

"That's far enough," the officer instructed. He barked a quick order in Takaran, and two of the four men lowered their weapons to their sides, out of view, and entered the tunnel.

Jessica immediately began calculating combat probabilities, just in case.

The two men approached cautiously. Once they reached Nathan and Jessica, they began patting them down.

"Open your jacket," one of the men ordered Nathan.

Nathan complied, holding his jacket open to either side so that the man could check him for weapons.

The young guard stared at Nathan as he patted

him down, as if trying to figure out where he had seen him before. When he finished patting Nathan down and stepped back, his eyes widened. "You're... You're..."

Nathan lowered his hand to his face, putting his index finger in front of his lips as he made a "Ssh" sound.

The young guard's expression turned from surprise to complete disbelief, followed by awe as he stepped back, whispering something in Takaran to his fellow guard.

The second guard did not reply, only glancing at Nathan as he patted down Jessica. "What is this?" the second guard asked, feeling something odd on her sides.

"Attachment points," Jessica explained.

"Raise your shirt," the second man instructed.

Jessica untucked her shirt and raised it as ordered, revealing the assistive undergarment and the attachment points on either flank.

"What is this suit?"

"It's a bio-assist undergarment," Jessica said. "All Ghatazhak wear them at all times. Those attachment points are for life-support systems and body armor."

"Why do you need this?"

"Like I said," Jessica explained. "All Ghatazhak wear them, at all times. I didn't think it would be a problem. I can take it off, if you'd like," she added with a wink and a flirtatious smile.

The second guard turned and shouted something back in Takaran to the officer in charge, receiving instructions in return.

"That will not be necessary," the second guard told her.

"I appreciate that," Jessica said as she tucked her uniform shirt back in.

The first guard reported that Nathan was clean, and both men returned to their group, stepping through the hatch at the far end of the tunnel and disappearing to either side. As they stepped aside, the first guard said something in Takaran to the officer in charge. The officer barked at him, again in Takaran.

"You may return your hands to your sides and continue forward slowly," the officer directed.

Nathan took a deep breath and sighed, letting his hands fall back down to his sides as he continued forward at a leisurely pace.

A few moments later, Nathan and Jessica stepped through the hatch at the far end of the boarding tunnel, into a much larger compartment. The guards had moved, taking up positions in all four corners of the compartment, their weapons still trained on the two guests.

The officer in charge stepped up, eying Nathan and Jessica suspiciously. "First, I should warn you. If either of you harms the captain's family, I will kill you both myself."

"Fair enough," Nathan replied calmly, not wanting to make a scene. His goal was to speak to the captain of the Mystic Empress, not to get into a pissing contest with one of her security officers.

Satisfied with his response, the security officer continued. "I am Lieutenant Oronsi, chief of security for the Mystic Empress. My men and I are to escort you to Captain Rainey. While en route, you are not to speak to any of the passengers or crew. If you try anything, if you make any suspicious moves, my men will not hesitate to fire. And while our weapons may not kill you, they will cause you considerable discomfort... And I emphasize the word *considerable.* Are we clear?"

"We will comply with your directives, Lieutenant," Nathan assured him.

The lieutenant turned his attention to Jessica, looking her over, up and down. "Ghatazhak, huh?"

Jessica detected the disdain and disbelief in his voice, resisting the urge to punch him in his smug little mouth. "That is correct," she replied flatly.

The lieutenant said nothing further, turning and heading for the door. "You will follow me," he instructed.

Nathan looked at Jessica, noticing the controlled anger in her eyes. "Down girl," he whispered, gesturing for her to go before him.

* * *

"Seiiki, Mystic Empress. Your captain and first officer are safely aboard and are being escorted to Captain Rainey. Your docking clamps will be released in one minute, and you are instructed to proceed to a standoff position at least one hundred kilometers distant, or at maximum reliable communications range, whichever is furthest."

Loki looked over his shoulder at Vladimir, who was now in command of the Seiiki.

"Do as he says," Vladimir ordered.

"I'm not sure about this," Josh said as he prepared to take the controls.

"Nathan knows what he is doing," Vladimir assured him. "I hope."

"Thirty seconds to release," Loki warned. "Maneuvering is online, mains are coming up."

"I hope so, too," Josh muttered.

Master Sergeant Anwar ascended the ladder into

the Seiiki's cockpit, coming up behind Vladimir. "Did you get the scans?" he asked.

"As requested," Vladimir said, handing a data card over to the master sergeant. "There are several possible points of entry. However, mooring clamp bay doors would be your best bet. There are four of them. The bays appear to be designed to allow service while in transit, so there will be an inner hatch. The bay doors are not thick, so you should be able to cut your way through them quite easily."

There was a sudden thud, and the Seiiki shifted slightly.

"We're free," Loki announced.

"Thrusting away," Josh followed.

"We would need a way to seal up the inner hatch before opening up the inside airlock hatch," the master sergeant continued. "Otherwise, the entire section will likely seal off automatically. And we do not wish to harm the passengers or the crew, if possible."

"*Konyeshna*," Vladimir agreed, thinking. "We have a few panels left over from the reinforcement work we just completed. One of them should be enough, as long as you don't make too big a hole."

"Are you guys planning on boarding the Mystic?" Josh asked in surprise.

"We're just planning ahead," Vladimir assured him, "just in case."

"Does Nathan know about this?" Josh inquired.

"It was his idea," Vladimir replied. "'Always have a plan B.'"

* * *

Nathan and Jessica followed the lieutenant out of the boarding area and up several levels, before reaching the Mystic Empress's main deck. Once they arrived, everything changed. Gone were the corridors lined with conduit, pipes, and ventilation ducts. Gone were the plain whites and grays of the bulkheads, decks, and overheads. Gone were the glaring warning placards and directional signs.

The main deck was spacious and opulent. Marble decks, wood grain walls, vaulted and lavishly decorated ceilings. And windows surrounding the deck, looking out into space in every direction.

The Mystic's grand foyer was like a park, with gardens and trees, and manicured paths that weaved in and out. And sprawling over the top of the massive area was a clear ceiling that wrapped over onto either side. Decorative lighting illuminated the space, accenting the natural beauty of the landscaping. Long, winding staircases came down from all four corners of the space, spiraling lazily into the park itself. It was truly a breathtaking sight.

Nathan remembered a two-week cruise on the Mediterranean Sea back on Earth. He had been a teenager at the time. The ship had felt much the same as this one, with every amenity and activity that one could imagine, all packed into a luxurious setting at sea. He remembered being resistant to the voyage at first, and had wanted to stay home to hang out with his friends in Vancouver. But his parents had insisted, as it was the last time they would be able to take such a cruise together. A few years later, Nathan would be off to college and, with all but one of his siblings married with their own growing families, scheduling such a trip would've been near impossible.

He did not remember much from that trip. However, he did remember enjoying himself more than expected. As he looked at the Mystic Empress, he was quite sure that her passengers were having an equally good time.

As they headed aft along the starboard side of the grand foyer, they received several long stares from passengers. Jessica in her Ghatazhak uniform, and he in his roguish coat. He could see in the faces of several passengers, that more than a few of them thought they recognized him. It all seemed quite surprising, since he wouldn't have thought that a simple beard could hide his identity so well.

Of course, he had spent the last five years avoiding both the Takar and Darvano systems for that very reason. The fringes of the Pentaurus sector had only become tied in with the other worlds by jump drive technology within the last few years. By then, the legend of Na-Tan had faded considerably. Nathan had been known best on Corinair. He even had a monument on the Walk of Heroes in Corinair's capital city of Aitkenna.

They continued along the starboard side of the foyer, passing the lower-level dining area and lounges. As they left the foyer and headed aft, the passageway narrowed slightly, although it was still at least six meters wide. To their left, the massive windows, that had stretched up high and over the top, gave way to ones that were only three stories tall. To their right were shops and entertainment spaces, and above them were two more decks of guest cabins, with private balconies that faced the massive windows and their spectacular views into space.

Eventually, the grand view disappeared as they entered crew-only spaces. Back were the white walls, the gray floors, and the overheads decorated with mechanicals.

They turned right, headed toward the center of the ship, then turned right again to head up several flights of stairs. As they reached one of the levels, Nathan spotted an elevator nearby. "Why don't they use the elevator?" he whispered to Jessica.

"They're trying to disorient us, and tire us out," Jessica whispered back.

"And why did they take us through the passenger areas, instead of below them?" Nathan wondered. "Did they want to impress us or something?"

"Actually, the captain did not want you passing through the ship's critical areas," the lieutenant called back to them as he turned and headed up another set of stairs. "At least, not until he decides if he can trust you or not."

"We're here to warn you of a grave threat," Nathan explained.

"And yet you hold the captain's family as hostages."

"We *rescued* them," Jessica pointed out.

The lieutenant stopped, turning back to look at them. "From what, might I ask? Their comfortable life on Corinair?"

"I would prefer to discuss this with Captain Rainey," Nathan replied.

The lieutenant studied Nathan carefully. "I know who you *claim* to be, young man, and I, for one, do not believe you. And even if I did, you should know that several of my dearest friends died during your so-called *liberation* of Takara, as did the original owner of this vessel. So, in a way, I would love for *your* claims to be true, so that I might have the opportunity to exact my revenge upon you."

Nathan said nothing, staring into the elder lieutenant's steely eyes.

"Good luck with that," Jessica warned in menacing tones.

"Are you going to take us to Captain Rainey, or do you want to take us on right here in the corridor?" Nathan challenged.

The lieutenant stared at Nathan for several more seconds, trying to size him up. Finally, he spoke. "Second door on your right. The captain is waiting for you. My men and I will be waiting outside, in case we are needed."

"Thank you, Lieutenant," Nathan replied confidently, turning to continue down the corridor unescorted.

Jessica followed Nathan, smiling at the lieutenant as she passed. "See ya later, pops."

* * *

Birk and Cuddy waited in the dark stairwell leading from the market basement to the storeroom above.

"I'm still not sure about this," Cuddy whispered in the darkness.

"You heard what he said," Birk replied in hushed tones. "He won't let us leave alive."

"But it's a resistance. Surely, the Dusahn will kill us if they catch us."

"We're screwed either way," Birk said. "Let's just roll with it for now. After we're clear of the city and get to wherever this resistance camp is located, then we can decide what to do. After all, it's not like they're going to have us locked up there, right?"

"I don't know, are they?"

Birk turned and looked at his friend, barely able to make out his face. "How the hell are you supposed to fight if you're locked up?"

"How the hell do I know?"

"Look," Birk said. "If we don't like it, we sneak away in the night or something. It's either that or get buried under a market."

The door above them opened, and Anji appeared. "Quickly," he urged.

Birk and Cuddy came up the stairs and into the storeroom. As soon as they stepped inside, two of Anji's workers moved several large wine barrels back into position, blocking the entrance to the hidden stairs.

"What now?" Birk asked.

"We will smuggle you out of the city," Anji replied.

"How?"

"In those."

Birk looked in the direction Anji had pointed. "In wine barrels?"

"Yes," Anji replied. "Trucks come in from vineyards in the country to swap full barrels for empties. We have done this many times."

"How many times?" Birk asked, unsure of the plan.

"At least a dozen," Anji assured him. "Many ex-Corinari have needed to escape. You will be joining them."

"How long will we be in there?" Cuddy asked.

"An hour, maybe two. It depends on traffic, and how busy they are at the checkpoints."

"Checkpoints?" Birk liked the plan even less. "We have to go past checkpoints?"

"Quickly," Anji urged. "The truck will be here soon. We must be ready."

Anji and his two workers ushered Birk and Cuddy over to the wine barrels closest to the loading door. The two workers unscrewed the bolts holding down the lids and moved the lids aside.

Birk stepped up to a barrel, looking inside. "Uh, there's wine in this barrel."

"Of course," Anji said. "It's a wine barrel."

"You want me to get into the wine?"

"Yes."

"Can't we just use empty ones?"

"The wine hides your body's heat signature from the Dusahn scanners," Anji explained. "Besides, often the Dusahn drain out some wine for their own use. Feel free to pee in the wine, if you like," he added with a sly smile. "They will not know the difference."

Birk climbed cautiously into the wine barrel. "How are we supposed to breathe?"

"With this," Anji said, handing them each a small air bottle with a mouthpiece.

"You're kidding," Birk replied, taking the device. "How long will it last?"

"At least five hours, which should be more than enough," Anji promised. "And do not drink the wine, as you may get sleepy and drown."

"Great," Birk replied dryly.

"I'm not sure about this," Cuddy said as he settled down into the wine barrel, the liquid swelling around him as it was displaced by his body mass. "What if something goes wrong?" Cuddy asked as he raised the breathing apparatus to his mouth. "How will we get out?"

"You will not," Anji admitted. "But in that case, you should drink the wine. At least you will die happy."

"Wonderful," Birk said as he inserted the mouthpiece and submerged himself.

* * *

Nathan and Jessica walked up to Captain Rainey's cabin door. Behind them were the lieutenant and his men, and at the opposite end were two more guards. Nathan pressed the buzzer next to the door, and a moment later, it opened, revealing a man in a stark white officer's uniform, neatly pressed, with perfect creases and well-shined shoes.

"Captain Rainey?" Nathan asked.

The man did not reply, but stepped aside, pulling the door open for them to enter.

Nathan stepped inside, followed by Jessica. The cabin was larger than that of Captain Gullen's aboard the Glendanon, but smaller than Nathan remembered his own quarters being on the Aurora. It was well decorated, keeping in line with the luxurious surroundings that the Mystic's passengers enjoyed, although understated by comparison.

The man in uniform closed the door behind them, taking a position in front of the door itself.

"Are you Captain Rainey?" Nathan wondered, noticing there was no nametag on the man's uniform.

"I am Captain Rainey," another voice called from the next room.

Nathan and Jessica both turned their heads toward the voice as Captain Rainey entered the main cabin from an open side door. The man was a bit shorter than Nathan and appeared to be in his mid-forties, with a slightly receding hairline that was graying at the temples. Otherwise, he appeared fit, and was similarly dressed in a well-pressed, white uniform.

Captain Rainey walked up to them, saying nothing. He did not reach out to shake their hands, nor did he offer any greeting. Instead, he stood, sizing them up for several moments.

"Is this some kind of test?" Jessica asked.

Captain Rainey just glared at her, then turned

his scrutiny to Nathan. "You do look like him, I'll give you that. But I expected you to be a bit older... A lot older, in fact."

"Sorry to disappoint you," Nathan replied.

"Why are you holding my family?" the captain demanded immediately.

"We are not *holding* them, Captain," Nathan explained. "They were rescued by the Ghatazhak, from a detention facility on Corinair."

"The Ghatazhak, huh?" the captain responded, unconvinced. He looked at Jessica, noting the Ghatazhak insignia on her shoulder. "Is that what you're supposed to be? A Ghatazhak?" The captain laughed. "I may not be from Takara, but I know one thing. There aren't any women in the Ghatazhak."

"I'm the first," Jessica replied.

"You don't really expect me to believe that, do you?"

"I could kick your ass all over the room and prove it, if you'd like," Jessica stated calmly.

"Lieutenant," Nathan scolded, warning Jessica to behave.

"Why the hell would my family be in a detention center?" Captain Rainey demanded.

"How long has your ship been in the cloud?" Nathan asked.

"What the hell does that have to do with anything?" Captain Rainey barked, becoming impatient.

"How long?"

"Twenty days," the captain answered begrudgingly.

"And you've had zero comms with everyone outside the cloud the entire time?" Nathan asked, still finding the concept hard to believe.

"That's what our passengers pay us for. Three weeks of luxury and cosmic wonder, cut off from the rest of society. In fact, you're the first ship we've ever encountered in the cloud in more than sixty-eight passages. So, you can see why I'm a bit suspicious, especially since you're holding my family hostage."

"Your family is free to leave whenever they'd like, Captain," Nathan assured him. "In fact, I'd be more than happy to provide them transportation to wherever they need to go."

Captain Rainey cast a suspicious eye on Nathan. "Then why didn't you bring them with you?"

"Because I didn't know if it would be safe."

"Safe from what?" Captain Rainey exclaimed. "You need to start making some sense, young man!"

"And you need to calm down, Captain," Jessica insisted, putting her hand on his chest and pushing him back. She quickly turned her head slightly sideways, spotting the other officer at the door taking a step forward. "Not a good idea, fancy pants."

"Are you threatening me?" Captain Rainey questioned.

"I'm warning you, that's all," Jessica replied.

"Captain, there is no reason for this," Nathan insisted.

"Then tell me what the hell is going on!"

Nathan sighed. It wasn't going at all how he had hoped. "Captain, you might want to sit down for this."

"I'm fine standing, son. Now start talking."

Nathan sighed again. "As you wish." He took another breath and continued. "Nineteen days ago, the day after you entered the cloud, ships of the Dusahn Empire attacked both the Darvano and Takar systems, simultaneously. Later that same day, they invaded the nearby systems, and now control the entire Pentaurus cluster."

"That's preposterous," the officer at the door exclaimed in disbelief.

"Who the hell are the Dusahn?" Captain Rainey demanded.

"We believe they are a rogue caste of the Jung Empire, exiled centuries ago after a failed coup attempt on the Jung homeworld."

"Impossible," the officer at the door exclaimed.

"The Jung don't have jump drives, mister," Captain Rainey argued. "It would take them more than a century just to get here. Besides, the Takarans aren't exactly defenseless..."

"The Dusahn have jump drives," Nathan explained. "We don't know how, but they have them. They attacked with more than twenty ships. The Takaran fleet didn't last half an hour."

"What about the Avendahl?" Captain Rainey wondered.

Nathan could tell that Captain Rainey was beginning to take him seriously. "She was caught by surprise. She went down just as fast."

"They took out the Avendahl?" Captain Rainey said in shock. "A capital ship?" The captain stared straight ahead, eyes unfocused as he remembered. "I had dinner with Captain Navarro just last month. He talked about a vacation he was planning with his wife." Captain Rainey took a step back and sat down. "They were looking forward to returning home for the first time in nearly *eight years*." Captain Rainey shook his head in disbelief. "Oh, my God." He looked at Nathan with pleading eyes. "My family? They are unharmed?"

"They are safe aboard the Glendanon, far outside the Pentaurus sector, out of reach of the Dusahn."

"You don't really believe all of this, Captain?" the

officer at the door protested, moving toward Captain Rainey to plead his case. "We don't even *know* these people."

"I assure you, we're telling the truth. We have videos from the attacks, and the subsequent actions taken by the Dusahn to control the populations. One of those actions was to round up the families of the captains of all jump-capable ships that were not in port at the time of the attack. They broadcasted a message threatening to execute the hostages if the ships did not return within two weeks. The captain of the Glendanon lost his wife. We rescued his daughter, along with the rest of the families being held on Corinair."

"What about Takara?" the other officer asked.

Nathan looked at the officer. "Who are you, sir?"

"This is my first officer, Mister Sorgey."

"What about Takara?" the officer repeated. "I have family on Takara."

"I don't know," Nathan replied. "I assume they did the same thing there, but it is our understanding they were only rounding up the families of ship captains."

"If that doesn't work, they'll likely go for the families of first officers, next," Captain Rainey surmised.

"You may be right."

"Why didn't you rescue the Takaran families?" Mister Sorgey demanded angrily.

"We were barely able to pull off a rescue on Corinair," Jessica defended. "It's not just Takara and Corinair, you know. They *glassed* our world."

"They what?" Mister Sorgey asked, unable to imagine such an act.

"Ybara, as well," Nathan added. "Just because

the Ybaran minister refused to pay respects to the Dusahn."

"What was your world?" Captain Rainey asked Jessica, his eyes full of empathy.

"Burgess."

"In the Sherma system?" Captain Rainey couldn't believe what he was hearing. "But Burgess is a small, peaceful place. No more than a few hundred thousand people. They're not a threat to anyone. Why would they go all the way to Sherma to destroy Burgess?"

"Because the Ghatazhak were based there," Jessica replied. "We fought them, but there were too many."

"How many did you lose?" the captain asked.

"Several hundred Ghatazhak died defending Burgess. Only a few hundred made it out alive," Jessica replied.

"But we managed to evacuate a few thousand of the Burgeans," Nathan added. "Which is why we're here."

"But there were several hundred thousand people on Burgess."

"And several million on Ybara," Jessica reminded him.

Captain Rainey sat quietly for a minute, rubbing his forehead as he thought. "What do the..."

"Dusahn," Nathan repeated.

"Dusahn. What do they want with the Pentaurus cluster?"

"We believe they wish to use its technology, and its industrial base, as a means to grow their fleet and expand their empire. If they are allowed to do so, the entire sector will be next to fall."

"What about the Alliance?" Mister Sorgey asked. "They will send ships to help, will they not?"

"They have their own problems," Jessica explained. "Jung ships have been showing up deep inside Alliance space in the Sol sector. The Alliance was forced to retaliate with KKV strikes. The entire sector is on the verge of a renewed conflict."

"What do you intend to do?" Captain Rainey wondered.

"We intend to fight them any way we can," Nathan replied with conviction.

"But the Glendanon is a *cargo* ship, not a warship. How can you take on twenty ships?"

A mischievous smile crept onto Nathan's lips. "We have the Aurora."

* * *

"Vlad," Loki called, a worried tone in his voice. "I'm picking up something on sensors."

Vladimir quickly climbed the ladder into the Seiiki's cockpit and moved to the auxiliary station behind Loki.

"Could it be another sensor ghost?" Josh wondered.

"Maybe an echo off a dense region of the cloud?" Loki suggested.

"It's possible," Vladimir replied as he studied the sensor display, making adjustments to the sensors. "It's hard to tell while we're in passive mode."

"Maybe we should go active?" Josh suggested. "Just to be sure?"

"And if it's a Dusahn ship?" Vladimir replied.

"Is it?" Loki asked.

"I do not believe so," Vladimir said. "It is too small to be a frigate, and too big to be a gunship."

"An interceptor?" Josh suggested.

"They would not send a lone interceptor into this cloud," Vladimir insisted. "Their sensors are not powerful enough. They'd be flying completely blind. Our sensors can barely see past twenty thousand kilometers in this cloud."

"Then what is it?" Josh wondered.

Vladimir squinted a moment, studying the screen. "It *may* be the same contact as before... I do not know." Vladimir's eyes widened. "*Oh, bozhe,*" he muttered. "*Nye harasho.*"

"In English, Vlad!" Josh exclaimed. "In English!"

"It is changing course," he said, turning to look at Josh and Loki. "It is headed *directly* for the Mystic Empress."

CHAPTER SEVEN

Captain Rainey looked skeptical. "The Aurora. If the Sol sector is on the verge of another war with the Jung, why would they send their most renowned ship a thousand light years away?"

"They didn't," Nathan replied. "The Aurora is here without authorization."

"You went rogue," Captain Rainey realized, one eyebrow popping up. "You stole the Aurora and went rogue." The captain laughed. "You're more reckless than I heard, Captain Scott...assuming you really *are* Nathan Scott."

"I am."

"More reckless than I heard, or you *are* Nathan Scott?"

"Both, I suppose. And it's a bit more complicated than you might think."

"Of that, I am sure," Captain Rainey agreed. "You still haven't told me why you are here, Captain."

"To warn you," Nathan replied. "If you jump back to Takara, the Dusahn will seize this ship, just as they have seized every other jump ship they can find since their invasion of the cluster nineteen days ago."

"This is a luxury cruise ship, Captain. I doubt the Dusahn will see us as much of a threat."

"True enough," Nathan agreed. "However, the owners of this ship will suffer a substantial financial loss. Furthermore, you and your crew will be out of work, likely imprisoned for failing to adhere to a Dusahn mandate within the required time, and possibly executed...as examples to anyone who might entertain the thought of resisting Dusahn occupation."

"Preposterous," Mister Sorgey exclaimed. "We've done nothing wrong."

"Tell that to the people of Ybara and Burgess," Jessica replied.

"We've been out of communication the entire time!" Mister Sorgey argued. "We couldn't possibly have known!"

"Jump-capable ships are way too important to the Dusahn. They are unlikely to give you the benefit of the doubt. They are better served by making an example of you and your crew, just as they did with the people of Ybara and Burgess. You are all worth more to them dead than alive."

"How could you possibly know that?" Mister Sorgey challenged.

"Because I spent nearly two years of my *life* fighting the Jung!" Nathan exclaimed. "Then another forty-five days as their prisoner, being poked, prodded, tortured, and finally paraded about for all their citizens to see in a circus of a trial! *That's* how I fucking know!"

"What is it you're proposing we do?" Captain Rainey asked quietly. "Hide out in the cloud indefinitely?"

"Join us," Nathan urged. "Help us fight them."

"We're a *luxury liner*," Captain Rainey reminded him. "Not a warship."

"We don't need a warship," Nathan replied. "Well, we do, but that's not why we want your ship. We need a place to house the refugees from Burgess. We need a place for our people to *live*. Right now, they're packed like sardines in cargo pods, stacked inside the Glendanon's cargo bay."

"Sardines?" Mister Sorgey wondered, unfamiliar with the word.

"Why can't you just put them on the surface of some other world?" Captain Rainey asked.

"That would put the residents of that world in jeopardy," Nathan explained. "We can't risk another Burgess."

"Then find one that isn't inhabited."

"There are none within five hundred light years of the cluster. That would create an additional logistical burden. Even if there were an inhabitable planet nearby, it would take weeks, if not months, to settle the refugees and get them to a point where their survival would be guaranteed, let alone to a point where they would become an asset. Besides, if the Dusahn managed to track us back to that world, it would be all over. We have to stay mobile. It's the only way."

"And what are we supposed to do with our passengers?" Captain Rainey asked.

"I'm sure we could arrange transportation of anyone who wishes to return to their homeworld," Nathan assured the captain. "It might take time, but..."

"Our passengers are the upper crust of Takaran and Corinairan society," Captain Rainey reminded Nathan. "They will not take kindly to being packed into military shuttles like...what did you call them? *Sardines*?"

"You have escape pods, don't you?" Nathan said. "Jump-enabled escape pods?"

"Of course," Captain Rainey assured him. "No one would be willing to travel with us if we did not."

"Where do they jump to when ejected?" Nathan asked.

"Back to Takara," Captain Rainey answered. "You're suggesting we order the wealthiest, most powerful and influential families of the Pentaurus cluster into their escape pods, for a perilous jump across three hundred light years of space?" Captain Rainey stared at Nathan. "And if we don't?"

Nathan shook his head. "I don't follow."

"Is that why you rescued my family?" Captain Rainey asked directly. "To get me to kick three thousand and seventy-four passengers off my ship and hand it over to you?"

"We rescued *all* of the hostages on Corinair, Captain," Nathan replied, annoyed by the captain's accusations. "Over two hundred of them, I believe. We didn't even know your family was among them at the time."

"But once you learned that they were, you saw an opportunity."

Nathan took a deep breath, remaining calm as he stared at Captain Rainey. "Regardless of what you decide to do, Captain, your family will be returned to you, unharmed. The question you have to ask yourself is what their and your chances of survival will be, whichever path you choose to take."

A hailing tone sounded. "*Captain, Comms. Incoming message from the Seiiki, sir,*" a voice called over the intercom.

"What's the message?" the captain asked.

"*Seiiki reports two contacts on an intercept course with this ship. ETA one minute.*"

"Security!" Mister Sorgey yelled, stepping out of the way.

"Sound the alert!" Captain Rainey instructed the communications officer. "Level three. All passengers to their cabins. Button up the ship!"

Four armed security officers burst into the room from the doors on either side of the cabin.

Jessica immediately went into a combat stance, ready to attack the onrushing guards.

"Arrest them!" Mister Sorgey ordered.

"*Alert level three, aye!*" the comms officer replied.

Jessica quickly evaluated the approaching guards, who had their weapons drawn. She could see fear and uncertainty in at least two of their faces, and none of their movements indicated advanced training. With her assistive bodysuit, she could withstand at least two, possibly three blasts from their low-power weapons, as long as none of them were directly to her head. In that split second, Jessica calculated that she had an eighty percent chance of taking all four of them out, as long as Nathan could handle Captain Rainey and his first officer.

"Is this part of your plan, Scott?" Captain Rainey accused him. "If that's even who you are."

"Wait," Nathan ordered Jessica, putting his hand on her shoulder as she tensed up to strike.

Four more men burst into the cabin from the front door, moving in behind Nathan and Jessica, surrounding them. Jessica froze, scanning and reevaluating the situation.

It was too late. There were now eight weapons trained on her and Nathan.

"This is *not* of our doing," Nathan assured Captain Rainey.

Captain Rainey headed for the exit, pausing momentarily to look directly into Nathan's eyes, only centimeters away from his face. "If you harm a single hair on either of their heads," he began, his voice seething with anger, "I will kill you myself."

Captain Rainey turned and continued out the door without saying another word.

"Lock them up!" Mister Sorgey ordered.

* * *

"I've got three contacts now!" Loki exclaimed. "Wait! Four!"

"I've got another one! Directly in front of the Mystic!" Vladimir said.

"That makes five," Josh said.

"General quarters!" Vladimir called over his comm-set.

"This isn't a warship," Josh reminded Vladimir. "We don't do general quarters."

"They know what I mean!"

"*What the fuck is going on?*" Marcus called over the comm-sets.

"Man the guns!" Vladimir ordered. "Josh! Set course back to the Mystic!"

Master Sergeant Anwar climbed up the ladder into the Seiiki's cockpit. "What's the situation, Commander?"

"Five contacts. One large, at least twice our size, has moved into position directly ahead of the Mystic. The other four are headed toward her from all sides."

"How big are the smaller contacts?" the master sergeant asked.

"Twelve to fifteen meters, maybe," Vladimir replied. "About the size of a utility shuttle."

"Too big for Dusahn landers," the master sergeant decided, looking over Vladimir's shoulder at the sensor display. "The contact in front of the Mystic; I have seen that profile before, in the Pentaurus sector."

"Who are they?" Vladimir wondered.

"I do not know," the master sergeant admitted. "But I believe the smaller contacts are breach boxes."

All along the Mystic's massive windows, armored panels slid into place, one by one, locking together to form barriers that blocked the panoramic views normally afforded to the paying passengers inside.

As the cruise ship closed itself up, four twelve-meter-long tubes, each roughly octagonal in shape, raced toward the luxury liner. As they closed, they flipped over and fired their engines, decelerating rapidly, continuing on their collision courses with the defenseless vessel.

Long, articulated legs came out of opposing faces of the four tubes, in between each of their engines. The legs reached their fully extended positions just as they made contact with the Mystic Empress's hull, giving just enough to absorb nearly all of the momentum.

One by one, the pods slammed into the Mystic Empress's four docking clamp bay doors, their claws penetrating the doors to anchor the pods in place.

Captain Rainey entered the bridge of the Mystic Empress as reports from all over the ship streamed into the communications station. "Report!" he beckoned as he came to stand behind the helmsman.

"Four objects have made impact with us!" the officer of the deck reported. "Each of them with our docking bay doors! I believe they are some kind of boarding pod, Captain!"

"Security! Captain! All forces to the docking clamp bays! Prepare to repel boarders!"

"*Captain! Security! Aye!*"

"Engineering reports main propulsion, power

generation, and environmental are all locked down, Captain!" the comms officer added.

"How many cabins have been secured?" the captain asked.

"Passengers are at fifty percent lockdown."

"Helm, plot a jump out of the cloud, I want long-range communications and sensors back."

"Aye, sir!" the helmsman replied.

"New contact!" the sensor officer reported. "Large; ten thousand kilometers; moving into our flight path!" The sensor officer turned toward the captain. "I think they mean to block our jump path, sir!"

"Helm, be ready to maneuver once you have a jump plot," the captain ordered.

"Sir, I'll have to recalculate the plot if we change course," the helmsman warned him.

"The captain of that ship likely knows that," Mister Sorgey commented.

"Calculate a blind jump. Just enough to get us out of the cloud," Captain Rainey ordered.

"But captain," the helmsman began to protest.

"Just do it!"

Nathan and Jessica were led down the Mystic's corridors, their hands bound by security ties, as the alert lights flashed and the warning tones blared. In front of them were three armed guards, and behind them three more.

"You sure you've got enough men on us, Skippy?" Jessica taunted.

"I think we'll be alright," the guard replied confidently.

"*All teams, prepare to repel boarders,*" a voice squawked over one of the guard's comm-unit. "*Teams one through four, move to secure docking clamp bays.*"

The guards looked at each other as they continued leading Nathan and Jessica down the corridor.

"How many security officers do you have on this bucket? Ten? Twenty?"

"Enough."

"Do you really think it's a good idea to have six of them here?" Jessica continued provoking them. "I mean, we're unarmed, our hands are bound, and I'm a girl, for crying out loud."

"You know, we can help you," Nathan suggested.

"Right," the guard replied, unconvinced.

Jessica turned to look over her left shoulder at the three men following them. "You'd better hope it isn't the Dusahn boarding you," she warned the men behind them.

"The who?"

"If it is, we're all fuckin' dead."

"Eyes forward, sweetie," the guard behind them growled.

"*Sweetie*?" Jessica laughed. "Oh, yeah, you'll be one of the first to fall."

"You've got to listen to us," Nathan insisted. "We're on your side."

"Right," the guard in front replied.

"Do you know who I am?"

Two of the Mystic's security guards charged down the corridor toward the port, forward docking clamp bay, but as they turned the corner, they were met with energy weapons fire. The first guard fell instantly, taking several shots to the face and chest. The second guard managed to return fire but couldn't get to cover in time, joining his partner on the deck in a sizzling mass as four armed men jumped over them, charging past and continuing deeper into the Mystic.

"*Team three! Report!*" the guard's comm-unit squawked.

Jessica looked at Nathan as the guards continued to lead them to the Mystic's lockup in the lower decks of the ship.

"*Team two is taking fire!*"

"*Dickers! Are you at lockup yet?*"

"Negative, ETA one minute," the lead guard replied over his comm-unit.

"*Hurry it up! I've lost contact with team one! They're supposed to be covering the port, forward docking clamp bay!*"

"Team eight is en route," the guard replied. "We'll be there in thirty seconds." He turned to the guards behind Nathan and Jessica. "You guys got this?"

"Yeah, go!" one of the guards behind them replied.

Jessica exchanged glances with Nathan as two of three guards in front of them took off running, disappearing around the next corner. She suddenly stopped in her tracks and then fell backward, tucking and rolling, bringing both feet straight up as she came over into a handstand. Her feet drove into the hands of the stunned guard, knocking his energy rifle away.

At the same time, Nathan charged into the guard in front of him, just as the guard was turning around to see what the noise behind him was about. Nathan slammed into the guard, knocking him to the ground, following the guard to the floor and landing on top of him.

Still in a handstand, Jessica scissored her calves on either side of the stunned guard's head, twisting him over and down with surprising force as her assistive bodysuit kicked in to supplement her strength. The guard fell to his left, knocking into the guard to his side.

Nathan drove his foot into the guard's face as both of them scrambled to get up. The guard's head snapped backward, slamming into the bulkhead and knocking him unconscious.

Jessica flipped back over, bouncing up to her feet, just as the third guard behind them took aim and fired. She twisted her body to the right, leaning slightly as she did so, allowing the bolt of low-power energy to bounce off her left shoulder, sending searing hot pain through her arm. She continued to spin back and around, using her own momentum to sweep with her leg, knocking the third guard over as he fired again.

Nathan was already up on his feet and charging back toward one of the guards Jessica had taken down, who was scrambling for his dropped rifle. Instead, the guard found Nathan's boot connecting firmly with his chin, knocking him back and twisting him around.

Nathan picked up the man's energy rifle and tried to fire at one of the other guards, but the weapon would not fire. The guard spotted Nathan and charged for him. Nathan swung the rifle hard, aiming for the charging guard's face, but the guard swung his arm upward, knocking the weapon up and away from his face. The guard drove his shoulder into Nathan's torso, knocking him back against the bulkhead.

Slammed against the wall, Nathan brought his still-cuffed hands down onto the guard's back as hard as he could, but the man had him trapped against the bulkhead and would not let go.

There was a sudden thud, and the man suddenly fell to the floor, releasing Nathan from his grasp. Nathan looked down at the guard, who was now unconscious. He then glanced over at Jessica, who was pulling a knife from one of the guard's belt pouches.

"Hold up your hands," she ordered as she approached.

Nathan held up his cuffed hands, and Jessica quickly cut his plastic restraints, freeing him.

Nathan took the knife from her and cut her restraints. "We need to get out of here."

"Grab their weapons," Jessica said.

"No good. They must be bio-locked."

Jessica picked up a rifle and tried to fire it, but to no avail. Tossing the weapon aside, she picked up another one, but found it also would not fire for her. "Damn it!"

"Let's go!" Nathan ordered, heading down the corridor.

Jessica searched the next guard, taking his comm-unit and his security badge.

"Come on!" Nathan urged, pausing at the corner to wait for her.

"I'm coming! I'm coming!" she replied, running after him.

"*We've lost contact with teams one and two, and teams seven, eight, and nine!*" the security chief reported over the intercom on the Mystic's bridge. "*Both forward docking clamp bays have been breached, and the intruders are inside the ship. I believe they are headed for the shuttle bays!*"

"Two more contacts!" the sensor officer reported. "They're coming from that ship in front of us!"

"Jump plot calculated," the helmsman reported.

"Hard to starboard; ten degrees down! Get me a clear jump line!" Captain Rainey ordered.

"Hard to starboard, ten down, aye!" the helmsman complied smartly.

"*Captain!*" the Mystic's chief of security called over the intercom. "*The Seiiki's captain and first officer have escaped! I have contact with teams seven, eight, and nine, again. Recommend teams seven and eight to the hangar bay!*"

"Make it happen!" the captain replied.

"Sir, if we lose the shuttle bays..." the first officer started.

"Their men will come pouring in," the captain finished for him. Captain Rainey sighed. "Chief of the Watch, break out the sidearms and seal the bridge. No one enters without my express permission."

Eight men, dressed in various, unmatched pieces of military uniforms and body armor, and carrying heavy assault rifles, converged on the Mystic Empress's port shuttle bay. The six Mystic security guards who had taken positions to defend the bay had been waiting for them, and reduced the attacker's forces by half in the first few seconds of battle. But their low-energy stunners were no match for the high-powered plasma weapons carried by the intruders. The weapons of the security guards were designed to dissipate on contact with anything other than human tissue. With little of the intruders' bodies exposed, it took several direct hits for the stunners to have any significant effect.

The reverse was true for the plasma weapons. They blasted through, or melted, just about everything they struck, and the men wielding them cared little about the destruction they caused.

In less than a minute, six of the Mystic's men lay dead in the corridors, and the intruders controlled the port hangar bay.

Jessica and Nathan ran down the corridor, traversing the bowels of the Mystic as they sought safe refuge. Weapons fire echoed in the distance, Jessica coming to an abrupt halt.

"What is it?" Nathan asked, stopping beside her.

Jessica listened, trying to determine the direction of the sounds. "Those are plasma rifles. Heavy assault type. Either Palean or Takaran issue."

"How can you tell?"

"That screech as they fire. The older ones don't redirect the heat from the muzzle, so the air around the discharge is superheated."

"So?"

"So, these guys are either crazy, or they're being paid *really* well. Those guns will blow the shit out of this ship. The Mystic's security forces won't stand a chance against that kind of firepower. This battle will be over shortly."

"Who the fuck are these guys?" Nathan wondered.

Jessica paced back and forth, thinking frantically. "Why do you hijack a cruise ship? To loot it? To kidnap someone for ransom?"

"To turn it over to the Dusahn for a reward?"

"Have the Dusahn offered a reward?" Jessica wondered. "We didn't hear anything about that."

"Doesn't mean it hasn't happened," Nathan replied. "We've got to do something, Jess."

"We're not armed, Nathan," Jessica replied. "And this suit of mine isn't going to stop a blast from one of those plasma rifles. They'll go for the hangar bays first, so they can get reinforcements on board at will. They'll also go for the bridge and engineering."

"Maybe we can get to engineering before them," Nathan suggested.

"Doubtful, and even if we did, what then?"

"We need to buy time until help arrives. Vlad will see what's going on."

"I've only got five men on the Seiiki," Jessica reminded him. "To take a ship this size, you'd need at least thirty or forty men."

"We have to disable their jump drive," Nathan said. "If the captain thinks he is losing the ship, protocols dictate he jumps the ship back to Takara."

"How do you know?"

"I'm a licensed ship captain," Nathan reminded her. "Or at least, I was. I know the rules Captain Rainey is expected to follow. If he jumps the ship, it'll be crawling with Dusahn troops minutes after arrival."

"But if they take engineering, which they most certainly will try to do..."

"Jump field generators aren't in engineering, Jess. Not on passenger ships. People are afraid of the damned things. On ships like this, they're installed as far away from the passenger spaces as possible. Probably in her outboard nacelles, just like on the Seiiki." Nathan thought for a moment. "We need to find a terminal, something where I can look up the schematics of the ship."

The interior door to the port shuttle bay opened, and twenty men dressed in a mixture of quasi-military clothing, carrying a variety of weapons, entered the corridor. Following them was an older and more nicely dressed man, a rather ornate-looking weapon slung on his hip. The man paused after stepping through the door, as a member of the boarding team came up to him.

“We have secured both bays, and teams are headed for the bridge and engineering. We should be in position shortly.”

“Excellent,” the older man replied. “Tell them to wait until their reinforcements join them. The other shuttle will be landing shortly. What about the passengers?”

“They have retreated to their cabins, as expected.”

“We must disable their escape pod systems,” the older man told them. “If the Dusahn are not willing to pay for this ship, there are many noble houses that *will* pay for the return of their loved ones.”

“Have you decided what to do about the Seiiki?”

“Once we have complete control of this ship, we will deal with the Seiiki.”

“That ship is armed now,” the man reminded his boss.

“I don’t care. I have a score to settle with Tuplo and his band of idiots. That man cost me a small fortune, and I intend to get my revenge.”

“Wait!” Nathan yelled, stopping as he noticed something at the end of a cross-corridor. “Down there!”

“What?” Jessica asked.

“A schematic display!”

Jessica quickly walked the few steps back to Nathan, looking down the corridor in the direction he was pointing. “Where?”

“That door, at the end of the corridor.”

Jessica squinted. “You can read that?”

"You can't?"

"No one can!"

"I'm telling you, that's what it is," Nathan insisted, heading down the corridor toward the door in question. Nathan ran down the side corridor, with Jessica hot on his heels. "You see!" He touched the display and began scrolling through the pages, zooming in on occasion, and then scrolling out even further.

Jessica watched, trying to take in everything as the pages whizzed past their eyes. "Jesus, Nathan, slow down."

"I've got it."

"You've got what?" Jessica wondered.

"The jump drive field generators. I know how to get to them."

"From that?" Jessica looked at the screen. "It's all in Takaran!"

"They're in the nacelles, just as I thought. But we'll have to get into the crawl spaces to get to them."

"And how do we do that?"

"Deck eight, section twenty-seven. Junction one one seven."

"What?"

"Trust me," Nathan said, turning and heading off.

"Why not?" she said, following him.

Captain Rainey watched from the Mystic's bridge as his helmsman tried in vain to maneuver around the ship that was blocking their jump line.

"Captain!" the communications officer called. "I've lost contact with engineering!"

"Security, Captain! Status of engineering?"

"*None of the teams defending engineering are answering, sir!*" the security chief answered over the intercom. "*Myself, and my last eight men, are trying to hold the command deck!*"

Captain Rainey looked at his first officer. "Chief Markum, can you hold?"

"Negative, sir. It's only a matter of time."

"Mister Sorgey, sound the alert. All passengers to the escape pods."

Mister Sorgey said nothing at first, his mouth agape. No Takaran ship had ever fallen to pirates, at least not in the last three hundred years.

"Mister Sorgey," the captain repeated.

"Aye, sir. All passengers to the escape pods."

Terig Espan ran down the empty corridor, coming to a stop outside his cabin door, quickly placing his palm on the scanner pad beside the door. "Come on, come on!" he complained frantically, looking up and down the corridor as he waited for the device to unlock the door. Finally, the indicator light on the pad turned green, and the door unlocked.

Terig pushed the door open and ran inside, letting the door close behind him.

"Oh, my God!" his wife exclaimed, running and throwing her arms around him. "I was so worried! What's going on out there?"

"I don't know," Terig replied, kissing her quickly. "There were shots fired. Lots of them. People were running around like crazy."

"Why didn't you come straight here?"

"I tried," he said defensively. "I had to take a detour to stay away from the fighting."

"What fighting?"

"I think the ship has been boarded...by...by *pirates*."

"What?"

The yellow warning light flashing over the door suddenly turned red, and an alert tone sounded. *"Attention! Attention! All passengers report to your designated escape pods! Repeat! All passengers report to your designated escape pods!"*

"Oh, God," his wife gasped, her hands coming up to cover her mouth in fear. She looked at her husband.

"Honey, we'll be fine," he assured her. "The escape pod will jump us back to Takara, and they'll pick us up, safe and sound."

"Are you sure?"

"I'm sure," he lied, hoping to put her at ease. He put his arm around her and led her toward the door.

"I should grab my things..." his wife began.

"There is no time," Terig insisted. "We have to go...now."

"There's another shuttle headed for the Mystic's starboard side," Loki reported.

"Those shuttles are big enough to hold at least twenty men," Josh told Vladimir. He turned to look over his shoulder. "We gotta do something."

Vladimir hesitated for a moment.

"He's right, Vlad. There's no way the Mystic can defend against that many intruders."

"Maneuver us around to starboard to intercept that shuttle," Vladimir ordered.

"That's what I'm talking about," Josh replied happily, turning around and grabbing his flight controls.

Vladimir tapped his comm-set. "Marcus, Dalen, we're coming around to the Mystic's starboard side to intercept a shuttle. Try to disable it, but do *not* hit the Mystic."

"Disable?" Marcus laughed. *"Are you fucking kidding me?"*

"Okay, okay!" Vladimir conceded. "Destroy it. Just don't hit the Mystic. Things are already complicated enough right now."

"Attention! Attention! All passengers report to your designated escape pods!" the announcement blared over the loudspeakers in the corridors of the Mystic Empress. *"Repeat! All passengers report to your designated escape pods!"*

"That can't be good!" Jessica yelled as she chased Nathan down the corridor and around the next corner.

"There!" Nathan shouted, running up to a small hatch in the bulkhead at the end of the corridor. "Open it!"

Jessica raced up and stuck the security badge into the slot on the hatch control panel. The hatch slid open, and she looked inside.

The tunnel on the other side of the hatch was narrow, with no discernible floor or ceiling. It was poorly lit, and there were conduits, ducting, and pipes running on all sides. Even worse, it appeared to stretch on forever.

Jessica sighed. "Zero-G. Of course."

"At least it's pressurized," Nathan said, climbing through the hatch. He grabbed the first in an endless series of handholds ahead of him, pulling himself into the weightless environment of the starboard engineering crawl spaces.

Jessica was next, leaning into the space and jumping in headfirst, pursuing Nathan. She pulled herself along, rung by rung, staying a few meters behind him just to be safe. "How far do you think it is?" she called ahead.

"At least a few hundred meters," he replied, pulling himself along ahead of her.

"Great," she said flatly. "At least there won't be anyone shooting at us."

"*We're being overrun!*" the security chief warned over the intercom, the sound of weapons fire echoing in the background.

Captain Rainey could hear the weapons fire from inside the bridge, as well. It had seemed so distant at first, but it was growing louder with each passing moment. At that moment, he realized he had no options left.

"Give the order!" Captain Rainey barked. "Launch all escape pods. We are abandoning the ship!"

"Comms!" Mister Sorgey ordered. "Issue the alert! Launch all escape pods! Abandon ship! Launch the automated distress comm-drone!"

"Abandon the ship, launch the distress drone, aye!" the comms officer replied.

"Contact is coming up fast on the Mystic's starboard side!" Loki warned them.

"Marcus! Do you see it?" Vladimir called over his comm-set.

"*I got it!*" Marcus replied.

"Don't let it reach that hangar bay!" Vladimir ordered.

"*No problem!*" Marcus replied.

The sound of plasma cannons firing reverberated throughout the Seiiki and into her cockpit.

"*Bozhe,*" Vladimir exclaimed. "Those things are louder than I thought!"

"*They've got shields!*" Marcus reported as he continued to fire on the shuttle.

"Oh, shit!" Loki exclaimed. "And missiles! Two inbound! Impact in five seconds!"

"Evasive!" Vladimir ordered as the Seiiki went into a spiraling dive to starboard.

"Three..."

"No shit!" Josh exclaimed as he twisted his flight controls to evade the incoming missiles.

"Marcus!"

"Two..."

"*I know! I know!*"

"One down!" Loki exclaimed as one of the incoming missiles disappeared from his sensor screen. "Two down!"

"*I fucking love these guns!*" Marcus declared over their comm-sets.

"*Bozhe!*" Vladimir exclaimed again. "Who ever heard of shuttles with missiles!"

"I don't think they came from the shuttle!" Loki warned.

"Josh! Move us back in behind the Mystic!" Vladimir ordered, realizing what Loki was saying.

"What good is that going to do?" Josh replied as he maneuvered the Seiiki back in behind the Mystic.

"Those missiles were unguided," Loki explained. "Line-of-sight targeting."

"As long as we keep the Mystic between us and that ship, they can't fire more missiles at us."

"What's to stop *them* from moving into a *better* firing position?"

"They're blocking the Mystic from jumping," Vladimir explained. "They've been matching her turns, keeping her blocked, so she cannot jump back to Takara."

"Why the fuck would they want to do that?" Josh wondered. "The Dusahn are there!"

"They don't know that!" Loki reminded him.

"Oh, yeah," Josh replied, embarrassed. "I guess, in all the excitement, I forgot."

"Oh, *bozhe*," Vladimir said to himself.

"What is it?" Master Sergeant Anwar asked.

"Escape pods," Vladimir replied. "Dozens of them."

Escape pods began launching from all along the port side of the Mystic Empress. From the top and sides of her forward section, her midsection, and from the three rows of cabins aft of her command deck. As the pods launched, they burned their tiny engines, arcing away from the doomed luxury liner. Once clear of the Mystic, the pods began disappearing behind tiny, blue-white jump flashes.

"If the Mystic's captain decided to launch the escape pods, that means he expects his ship to fall to the intruders," Master Sergeant Anwar decided. He tapped his comm-set. "Ghatazhak, prepare for immediate deployment. Level three, interior attack."

Vladimir looked at the master sergeant. "What are you doing?"

"Maneuver in behind the Mystic," Master Sergeant Anwar instructed Josh. "Directly astern and above her, about one hundred meters. Match her course and speed, and then spin us around to point your stern at her."

"What are you going to do?" Vladimir asked again.

"Plan C," the master sergeant replied as he turned to climb back down the ladder.

"What is Plan C?" Vladimir asked.

"Let me figure that one out," the master sergeant replied as he moved to the top of the ladder. "Just get me on that ship."

"*Oh, bozhe,*" Vladimir exclaimed as the master sergeant dropped down the ladder. He turned to look at Josh and Loki, both of whom were staring over their shoulders at Vladimir. "You heard him!"

Master Sergeant Anwar raised his suit collar, attaching it to the underside of his tactical combat helmet. His visor display lit up, and his suit status showed that he had pressure.

"*One minute!*" Loki called over their helmet comms.

Anwar turned to his men. "Ready?"

One by one, all four of his men nodded that they were ready to go.

The master sergeant went to the cargo bay door controls at the back of the Seiiki's cargo bay. "Depress the bay," he instructed.

"*Rapid depress, in progress,*" Loki replied.

Red warning lights began to flash in the cargo bay, warning that the bay was in the depressurization process.

"*Thirty seconds!*" Loki updated.

"*Pitching over,*" Josh announced.

"Ghatazhak! Stand ready!" Anwar ordered.

"*Depress complete!*"

Anwar punched the door control, and the rear cargo door lowered from the top down.

"*Fifteen seconds!*"

Master Sergeant Anwar moved to the back of the cargo bay, lining up with his men, as the cargo bay door lowered into a position level with the cargo bay's deck.

"*Five seconds!*" Loki warned.

Anwar crouched, ready to run.

"*Three......two......one......GO!*"

Master Sergeant Anwar was first, running across the cargo bay, out across the ramp, and jumping off into space toward the massive luxury liner only three hundred meters ahead of them.

The other four Ghatazhak were close behind, also running out and jumping into space in smooth, fluid motions. The group of five soldiers, clad in matte black battle armor, sailed through the vacuum of space toward the Mystic Empress. Behind them, the Seiiki fired her thrusters, reducing their speed in relation to the Mystic, to ensure they did not interfere with the Ghatazhak as they traversed the distance to the Mystic.

"We need to get into clear space!" Captain Rainey insisted. "Helm! Jump us out of the cloud, now!"

"Our jump line isn't clear!" the helmsman warned.

"They'll move!" Captain Rainey insisted. "Jump us... NOW!"

"Jumping!"

Jessica nearly crashed into Nathan as he grabbed an overhead railing and held tight, his legs swinging forward under him.

"What the hell?" she blurted out, grabbing onto him to stop her forward drift, as well.

"The sign," Nathan said, pointing.

"I don't read Takaran."

"Seven years in the Pentaurus sector, and you don't read the language of the dominant culture?"

"I can speak it enough to get by, but I never learned to *read it*." Jessica grabbed a side rail to steady herself. “Besides, most of my work has been *outside* the Pentaurus sector.” She looked at the sign. “Gravity?”

“Yup.” Nathan pulled himself along, taking care to keep his feet under him. Just as the sign indicated, as soon as there was a normal deck beneath him, he began to feel the pull of its artificial gravity. Another meter, and he was in about the same gravity as the rest of the ship, which was similar to the Seiiki.

Jessica pulled herself in behind him, her feet also settling onto the deck so she could walk normally.

“Energy banks to the right and left,” Nathan pointed out. “And we already passed her starboard ZPEDs.” Nathan spotted a door at the end of the catwalk. “That’s got to be it,” he said, picking up his pace.

Another minute and they found themselves at the entrance to another compartment. On the hatch was a sign that read ‘Starboard Jump Field Generators’. “Try your card.”

Jessica stepped up and inserted the security badge she had taken from one of the guards during their escape only minutes ago. Like before, the light on the control mechanism turned green, and the hatch unlocked.

Nathan pulled the hatch open and stepped inside. Overhead lighting panels flickered to life automatically as he entered the compartment.

Compared to the maze of mechanicals they had spent the last few minutes floating through, this room was completely different. It was all white and quite clean. There were four jump field generators, each of them at least five meters square. The odd thing was, there was enough empty space in the room to accommodate at least a few more.

Nathan walked up to the nearest field generator, activating the status display screen over its keypad.

"Why is there so much room in here?" Jessica wondered.

"The Mystic used to be an interplanetary luxury liner, used solely within the Takar system. When they added the jump drive, they gutted most of her propellant storage. This entire room used to be a propellant tank. My guess is they decided it was easier to use it as a room to hold the field generators. They probably felt the extra room might be utilized for future upgrades."

"How do you know all this?" Jessica wondered.

"Josh," Nathan said as he cycled through various status screens on the jump field generator. "He loves to read to pass the time. Especially about the history of ships in the Pentaurus sector."

"I always thought of him more as a vid-play type," Jessica commented.

"I think he picked up the habit during all those long, cold-coast recons back in the day."

"Can you shut it down?" Jessica wondered.

"I think..." Nathan suddenly stopped. "Uh-oh."

"What?"

"This thing is about to fire."

"What? What do you mean?"

"We're about to jump."

"Can you stop it?"

Nathan began frantically searching for the control page. "There's got to be a way."

The jump field generator began to spin up, its humming becoming more intense with each passing second.

"Nathan, if this ships jumps back to Takara..."

"I know! I know!" Nathan looked at her. "I can't

stop it," he admitted, stepping back. He looked at the next jump field generator over, noting that it was spinning up to fire, as well.

"Is it safe for us to be in here?"

"I don't know," Nathan replied as he tensed up his body and closed his eyes.

"Oh, fuck," Jessica exclaimed as she did the same.

"The Mystic is powering up her jump drive!" Vladimir warned urgently. "Pull back!"

"What?" Loki exclaimed.

Josh, not wasting any time, immediately lit up the Seiiki's main engines, as she was already traveling stern first, slowly closing on the luxury liner after deploying the Ghatazhak. He jammed the ship's main throttle all the way forward, and the ship began to rumble as both main propulsion nacelles began to generate maximum thrust.

Vladimir watched his sensor display in horror. Non-military ships did not have the quick-jump execution systems that were common in military vessels and in smaller vessels that did not require energy banks to supplement their instant energy source. It took nearly ten seconds for the Mystic to bring her reactors to full power to execute her jump.

"Are they going to make it?" Loki asked.

Vladimir quickly did the math in his head. The Ghatazhak did not show up on his sensors. Their suits were fairly stealthy to begin with, and the cloud made it nearly impossible to track them once they were more than a few hundred meters away. "I don't know," he finally admitted.

Vladimir stood, looking out the back window of

the Seiiki's cramped cockpit, just as the blue-white light from the Mystic's jump flash spilled through.

The Mystic Empress's helmsman opened his eyes, a full second after pressing the button to initiate the jump. He had expected to see his ship coming apart, having struck the vessel blocking their jump line. But they were still intact. "Jump complete!" he exclaimed in joyous disbelief. "Oh, my God, we're still in one piece!" He laughed again. "They must've moved to save their own ass!"

"Lock out the jump drive!" Captain Rainey ordered, not taking a moment to celebrate. "Command authorization only!"

"Locking out the jump drive," the helmsman replied, snapping back to reality to carry out the captain's order.

The sound of weapons fire grew louder, and several thuds could be heard against the locked entrance to the Mystic's bridge as plasma bolts slammed into the hatch itself.

"Gentlemen!" the captain bellowed. "Prepare to defend yourselves!"

Captain Rainey rose from his seat, drawing his sidearm as the entrance to the bridge suddenly blew open with a tremendous explosion. His communications officer was immediately killed, decapitated by a red-hot piece of metal that sliced through him and drove itself into the comm-panel, sending sparks everywhere.

Bolts of red-orange plasma energy, dialed down to avoid damaging the critical control systems on the bridge, spilled into the compartment from the entrance as the invaders blasted in.

"Lock out the jump drive!" Captain Rainey barked as he opened fire on the charging intruders.

"Aye..." The officer of the deck never finished his reply, cut short as a bolt of plasma energy slammed into his back, burning a massive hole through his chest.

Captain Rainey continued to return fire, along with three of his bridge crew, as he tried to make his way to his first officer. But a lesser blast glanced off his left shoulder, sending him spinning to the deck.

Two more bolts slammed into his officers, killing one and wounding the other. A few more weapons blasts and it was over.

Captain Rainey lay on his back, staring at the overhead. Smoke wafted through the air, and the smell of blown circuits and burning flesh filled his nostrils as he struggled to take a full breath through the searing pain in his shoulder. Someone grabbed the weapon from his hand and then kicked him several times in the side. Another man drove the butt of his rifle into the captain's face, sending two of his teeth flying.

"Enough!" a voice called. An older voice. The captain could hear footfalls as someone walked toward him. "Pick him up."

Captain Rainey felt himself being roughly pulled to his feet by two men. He could barely hold his head up, as his neck and shoulder were both screaming with pain. A hand grabbed his hair and pulled his head back, bringing the captain's eyes onto the older man standing in front of him.

"You must be Captain Rainey," the older man said. "Allow me to introduce myself. My name is Sigmund Daschew," the old man said, smiling. "My friends call me 'Siggy'. But you? You must call me 'sir'."

CHAPTER EIGHT

It took every iota of Master Sergeant Deno Anwar's Ghatazhak training to keep his pulse rate and breathing under control as he coasted through space on his approach to the Mystic Empress's hull. Less than a minute ago, as he and his four men slid in between the port and center cabin wings that protruded aft from the upper superstructure of the cruise ship, the Mystic's jump field emitters had engulfed the ship in blue-white light. They passed through the field of light only a second or two before the Mystic's jump drive dumped the additional energy into the fields that were needed to initiate the jump. Two seconds later and they would not have survived.

As the master sergeant coasted toward his target, tiny squirts of thrust fired from ports on his forearms and calves, adjusting his body's attitude in relation to the rapidly approaching hull of the Mystic Empress. Once his body was in the proper position for contact, another thruster in his chest fired, along with all four of his attitude thrusters on his limbs. A few seconds of thrust was all that was left in the system, but it was enough.

Master Sergeant Anwar tensed his body, causing the assistive body suit under his Ghatazhak body armor to mimic his movement. Millions of fluid-filled cells within the fabric squeezed to pressurize themselves, the effect designed to strengthen and protect the wearer's joints from the jolt of kinetic energy they were about to receive.

The master sergeant's hands and feet contacted the hull at the same time, resulting in an abrupt, yet solid, landing. He immediately stood upright against the vertical hull surface, testing the electromagnets in his boot soles, to ensure that they would hold properly. Satisfied with their performance, he turned to see the rest of his men landing around him. Once they were safely down, he pressed a button on his chest, and his chest-mounted thruster pack, and the thruster packs on his limbs, all disengaged, floating freely in the microgravity of space.

The master sergeant scanned his men, waiting for the 'okay' sign from each of them before continuing. He looked up and from side to side. They were standing in a valley formed by two vertical fin-like structures. Along the vertical walls were two rows of windows, the lower row at his eye level. He made his way to the nearest window, peeking inside. On the other side was a modest passenger cabin. Two beds with nightstands, a dresser, a desk and chair, and a sofa with a coffee table. In the left corner were three doors-one to the bathroom, one to a closet, and one that presumably opened into a common corridor.

The master sergeant was about to reach for the explosive charge in one of his belt pouches, when the door from the corridor opened, and a man and a woman came running into the room, hastily closing and locking the door behind them.

The master sergeant leaned to the side, out of view of the passengers who had just entered the room. He turned to look at his men, and signaled them to check the other windows.

The nearest man to him, Corporal Rossi, peeked in his window. He immediately leaned back out of view, signaling the room was a 'no-go'.

The same signals came from the next two men,

Sergeant Vela and Corporal Rattan. Sergeant Morano, however, gave the 'go' sign.

Master Sergeant Anwar and his men all moved toward Sergeant Morano as he placed an explosive charge on the window.

All five Ghatazhak leaned up against the wall on either side of the window. A moment later, there was a flash of light, and the window broke apart, spraying pieces of transparent aluminum out into space, and allowing the atmosphere within the room to escape.

Sergeant Morano stepped up and peeked inside the room. Satisfied that it was clear, he grabbed the upper edge of the window, disengaged his mag boots, and pushed off gently. As his body floated upward, he tucked his feet up and inserted them through the blasted-out window frame, catapulting himself smoothly through the opening and into the cabin.

As he passed through inside, the ship's gravity pulled the sergeant downward. He twisted his body and landed neatly, in a well-practiced fashion. Once inside, he immediately ran to the bathroom to check that the room was clear as the next Ghatazhak catapulted himself through the open window and into the room.

Less than a minute later, all five Ghatazhak soldiers were inside the Mystic Empress.

* * *

Sigmund Daschew glared at the bleeding captain of the Mystic Empress, lying on the floor before him. "Do you understand me, Captain?"

Captain Rainey spit the blood from his mouth onto the floor, looking disdainfully at the leader of the men who had just taken his ship and killed all of his security officers.

"Do you understand me?" Sigmund asked again, sounding impatient.

"Yes, I understand."

Sigmund looked away for a moment, taking a deep breath and sighing. Then he turned suddenly, drew his weapon and pointed it at the captain's face at point-blank range. "You forgot the 'sir'," he said, his voice full of menace. A moment later, he abruptly removed the barrel of his weapon from the captain, pointing it toward the ceiling. "We'll let it go, this time." Sigmund leaned down a bit more, getting closer to the captain's face. "But do not test me further, Captain. I'm not the most stable man around." He smiled cruelly. "Ask anyone."

Captain Rainey watched as Sigmund rose from his squatting position, a satisfied smirk on his face.

"Siggy!" one of his men called. "The Antilla!"

"What about her?" Siggy asked as he holstered his weapon.

"She's gone!"

"What?" Siggy stepped over to the helm station to join his subordinate. "Maybe she just maneuvered out of the way?"

"She is not on the scope. Maybe she jumped?"

Siggy looked at the bank of windows stretching from one side of the bridge to the other. "Open the shutters," he instructed. "NOW!"

One of his other men complied, and the protective shutters covering each of the windows began to lower in unison. Siggy's eyes widened as the view outside the Mystic was revealed. "Bloody hell!" he yelled, turning back toward Captain Rainey. "You jumped the fucking ship!" he swore, punctuating it with an angry kick to the captain's face. "Do you have our previous position?" he asked the man at the helm.

"Yes."

"Then turn us around and jump us back, but take care not to jump in too close to the Antilla," Siggy instructed.

"Yes, of course."

Siggy turned around and squatted back down next to Captain Rainey, pulling out his weapon and grabbing the captain's collar. He yanked the captain up off the deck, once again putting his weapon up to the captain's head. "While there may indeed be a reward for you, in comparison to the one for your ship, it is but a pittance. Therefore, you are not worth keeping alive." Siggy put the weapon into the captain's mouth, and moved his finger to the trigger. "Make peace with whatever god you worship, Corinairan."

"Siggy! Wait!" the man at the helm warned.

"What is it?" Siggy exclaimed, annoyed at the interruption.

"The jump drive is locked out."

Siggy's head slumped as he sighed. He cocked his head slightly to the left, nodding several times, before opening his eyes and looking at the captain again. "Do not think your god has prevented your death," he said, pulling the barrel of his weapon back out of the captain's mouth. "If anything, he has made it more painful."

* * *

"I'm not finding them," Vladimir said as he studied his sensor display.

"Do you think they made it?" Loki asked.

"Stop asking me that," Vladimir snapped. "I do not know."

"Are you picking up any bodies? Pieces of armor..."

"The only thing I can see in this cloud is that

other ship, and it is turning toward us," Vladimir warned him.

"I'm on it," Josh replied, starting his first evasive maneuver.

"We have to go find them," Loki said.

"We can't see more than twenty thousand kilometers in this cloud," Vladimir reminded Loki. "If they jumped to another location in the cloud before jumping clear of the cloud, then we will not see their jump flashes."

"They would've jumped out of the cloud," Loki insisted.

"How do you know?" Vladimir asked.

"Uh, guys?" Josh said.

"Why would they stay inside the cloud?" Loki argued. "They can't see anything; help won't be able to find them..."

"Assuming it was the captain of the Mystic who executed the jump, and not the hijackers," Vladimir countered.

"Guys?" Josh repeated.

"If the hijackers jumped the ship, wouldn't that other ship jump with them to follow?" Loki challenged. "I mean, why did they move out of the Mystic's way and allow her to jump?"

"Maybe to save themselves?"

"GUYS!" Josh yelled.

"What?" Vladimir exclaimed.

"That ship is closing fast. Do you want to gamble on outrunning her, or do you want me to jump?"

"The fact that the other ship is chasing us means the hijackers did *not* initiate the jump," Loki surmised.

"Unless they want to prevent us from following the Mystic," Vladimir argued.

"Fuck this," Josh said. "I'm setting a course back to the Aurora, via Big Blue."

"Wait," Loki began to protest.

"No, he's right," Vladimir interrupted. "If we are going to find the Mystic, we need help. Help with real weapons."

Josh turned and looked at Loki, then back at Vladimir. "We have about ninety seconds before that ship is in missile range."

"Get us out of here," Vladimir decided. "Take us back to the Aurora, via your evasion algorithm."

"Do we need the whole algorithm?" Loki wondered. "It's not the Dusahn chasing us."

"We still don't know that for sure," Vladimir reminded him. "Better to be safe."

"But it will take us nearly twenty hours if we do," Loki pointed out. "Do they have that kind of time?"

Vladimir thought for a moment, torn between wanting to help his friends and wanting to protect the few ships the Karuzari had left. "I cannot risk exposing the fleet's position to the Dusahn," he decided, though it pained him greatly to do so.

"The fleet can move to a new location," Loki urged. "Let *them* spend the time executing the algorithm, *after* they send help to find the Mystic."

"*Gospadee!*" Vladimir exclaimed. "I was just supposed to be here to fix the ship!"

"The captain left you in command, Vlad," Josh reminded him.

"It's your call," Loki added.

"*Da.*" Vladimir sighed.

"No rush, big guy," Josh said. "But that ship's gonna have range on us in twenty seconds."

"Jump us back to the Aurora," Vladimir ordered. "But take us directly to the blue giant first, *then* directly to the Aurora. If we are followed, at least *that* may buy them some time to get under way before being discovered."

* * *

"I was sure we were going to get fried," Nathan admitted as he stood there looking at Jessica.

"Why would you think that?" Jessica wondered.

"Hey, you tensed up, too," he reminded her.

"Only because you did."

"These things put out a considerable amount of radiological and electromagnetic energy when they fire. Especially if they're not shielded adequately. That's why they're required to be installed a certain distance away from passengers."

"Seriously?"

"When we decided to start carrying passengers, we had to move ours half a meter further outboard just to meet regs. It took us a week to move each of them... *half a meter.*"

"And here I thought you were some kind of rogue, outlaw, smuggler captain."

"Oh, we bent a few rules," Nathan admitted as he worked. "Some of them quite regularly. But I tried to run my ship legit whenever possible... For all the good it did me." Nathan stopped shuffling through pages on the display screen, studying the contents of one. "This is it. This is the shutdown screen, but it's locked."

"Can't we just unplug the damned thing?"

"It's tied directly into the ship's reactors," Nathan explained. "If we just pull the plug, we'll likely short the entire thing out."

"So what?"

"So, we were hoping to use this ship, remember? It's not worth much to us if it can't jump."

"And it won't be worth much to the Dusahn, either," Jessica pointed out.

"Assuming the Dusahn get their hands on it."

"Isn't that where we just jumped?" Jessica reminded him.

"We don't know that," Nathan said. "And until we do, we should act as if there is still a chance to get out of this *alive,* and *with* this ship."

"Good point," Jessica agreed. She turned away, and began pacing around the clean, white compartment, looking around for ideas. "These are backups, right?" she asked, pointing to the other two jump field generators.

"Yes."

"They don't look like they're powered up to me."

Nathan stopped what he was doing and turned around to look at the other two jump field generators. Curious, he walked toward the nearest one. He tapped the display screen. "You're right."

"Does that help?"

"It does," Nathan said. "We can disable the active field generators by pulling their control cards, but doing so will damage them. We can disable *these* two *without* damaging them."

"Which means, if we manage to get control of the ship, we'll still be able to jump it."

"Precisely," Nathan replied. "Now all we have to do is figure out how to open these things up so we can *get* to the control cards."

* * *

"Pick him up," Siggy instructed his men.

Two men grabbed Captain Rainey by the arms and yanked him to his feet.

"Over there," Siggy ordered, pointing at the helm.

The two men shoved the captain toward the helm station, nearly knocking him over in the process.

Captain Rainey fell against the helm station, grabbing hold of it to keep from falling.

"Don't make me ask," Siggy warned in disgust.

"What do you intend to do with my ship?" Captain Rainey barely sputtered through the blood and spittle that filled his mouth.

"It is not *your* ship," Siggy corrected. "It belongs to a bunch of rich Takaran bastards...or at least, it did. Now, it belongs to me."

"What do you intend to do with it?" Captain Rainey asked again.

"What I intend to do with *my* ship is none of *your* concern. In fact, *your* only concern should be how to keep yourself alive. Now unlock the jump drive."

Captain Rainey took a deep breath, straightening up as best he could, despite the pain from his beating. "I will not."

One of Siggy's men roughly punched the Captain in his right flank, causing the Captain to keel over and fall to the deck again.

"Not until you guarantee the safety of my crew," the captain groaned from the deck.

"The only thing I will guarantee is that you will witness the slow and painful death of each of them, if you do not unlock the jump drive."

"You wouldn't," Captain Rainey challenged him.

Siggy just looked irritated. He looked at his man who had first identified that the Mystic's jump drive was locked. "Are you sure you can fly this ship?"

"Yes," his man replied.

Without another word, Siggy drew his weapon and shot the Mystic's helmsman standing next to Mister Sorgey, the only other surviving member of the Mystic's bridge crew. The energy blast struck the helmsman square in the face, instantly burning through tissue and bone, dropping him into a smoldering heap next to the Mystic's horrified first officer.

"You bastard!" Captain Rainey screamed, lunging up from the floor at Siggy, going for the man's throat.

Siggy's men grabbed Captain Rainey, pulling him off and beating him mercilessly.

Siggy shook himself off, rubbing his throat where Captain Rainey's hands had grasped him. He straightened his jacket, then finally turned toward the two men who were continuously beating on the Mystic's defenseless captain. "That's enough," Siggy said. He watched for a few more moments as his men beat the captain, then realized the captain had gone limp. "That's enough!" he repeated, louder this time.

The two men let go of Captain Rainey's limp body, letting him drop to the deck.

"Please tell me he is not dead," Siggy said, sounding annoyed again.

One of them bent down to check. "He is still breathing, but he is unconscious."

"Wonderful." Siggy turned to look at Mister Sorgey. "I don't suppose you have the codes to unlock the jump drive."

"No," Mister Sorgey replied. "Only the captain has them."

Siggy stared at him for several moments. "I'm not sure I believe you, but it matters not. Once your captain awakes, *your* torture will begin."

Mister Sorgey glanced at the guard on his right as Siggy turned away. In a quick motion, the first officer grabbed the barrel of the guard's energy rifle, pushing it upward as he drove his fist into the man's throat. He spun the man around in front of him, reaching around and grabbing the handle of the man's weapon as he did so.

Siggy's other men reacted immediately, turning to fire on the first officer. Their shots found the body of their cohort instead, killing the man instantly.

Mister Sorgey managed to squeeze off a series of shots from the dead man's weapon before he could no longer support the man's body weight. Unfortunately, he was unable to wrangle the weapon from his death grip, and he was left without a shield, defenseless.

The next four shots found Mister Sorgey- two in the chest, one in the shoulder, and the last in the head. What had been a valiant attempt to overpower his captors and save his captain and his ship had ended in defeat, leaving the brave first officer smoldering atop the fallen guard.

Siggy sighed. "How many of his crew have we captured?"

"I do not know," the nearest of his men admitted.

"What about the passengers? Did we capture any of them?"

"I do not know."

"Well, find out!" Siggy closed his eyes, taking a deep breath as he tried to control his frustration. "Colin, Siggy," he said, speaking into his comm-unit. "Launch a shuttle, have them get a fix on our position, and then jump back to the Antilla and have her join us."

"*You got it.*"

Siggy looked at his man at the helm station. "What are you looking at?" he scowled. "Figure out how to unlock the damned thing."

* * *

Master Sergeant Anwar glanced back and forth between the makeshift patch they had constructed out of a desktop and several cans of construction adhesive, and the pressure level shown on Corporal Rossi's data pad. It had taken them several minutes to create the patch, and several more minutes for the adhesive to take hold. That didn't include the time it took for the corporal to open up the control panel and bypass the controls so that they could force the compartment to repressurize. Normally, the Ghatazhak would have simply blasted their way through each compartment, not caring about who might die when the next compartment suffered sudden decompression. But this time, it was different. They had no idea where Captain Scott and Lieutenant Nash were located, and although taking the Mystic Empress intact was their primary objective, saving Nathan and Jessica was a very close second.

The patch they had constructed looked a mess, and the master sergeant was quite sure that it would not hold for long. He hoped it would hold long enough for them to get into the corridor and seal the door behind them. The pressure inside would help keep the patch in place, but if that pressure could not be maintained, the automatic safeties in the door control would lock it.

It's a hell of a way to build a ship, the master sergeant thought as they waited for the interior pressure to climb to a normal level. *Having sleeping quarters against an outside bulkhead, and with a window, no less.* However, they were lucky these economy cabins existed on what was considered a luxury for the elite of the Pentaurus cluster, otherwise, he and his men might not have made it this far.

Finally, the interior pressure reached its normal level, and the corporal gave a thumbs-up. They had been comm-silent since leaving the Seiiki, not wanting to alert anyone aboard the Mystic to their presence.

Master Sergeant Anwar went over to the two men standing on either side of the makeshift patch and tapped them both on the shoulders, indicating they should move to the hatch.

Once all five men were gathered around the hatch, Corporal Rossi bypassed the hatch controls, and the pressure locks sprang open. Sergeant Morano pulled the hatch open and quickly stepped through into the corridor, his weapon held ready against his shoulder as he took aim.

Corporal Rattan was a split second behind him, stepping through and taking up a firing position aiming down the corridor in the opposite direction. Master Sergeant Anwar and Sergeant Vela were next, each of them backing up the two previous men. Finally, Corporal Rossi disconnected his data pad and stepped into the corridor through the hatch, pulling it closed behind him. The corporal quickly broke open the control pad on the bulkhead next to the door and attached his data pad to the controls. A few taps on his data pad display, and the door was sealed again, thus preventing anyone from inadvertently opening the door, should the pressure in the cabin fall below normal and the automatic safeties fail to operate. The last thing they needed was for a sudden decompression to catch *them* or any other friendlies off guard. Once his work was completed, the corporal tapped the master sergeant on the shoulder.

Master Sergeant Anwar deactivated the seals on

the neck collar connecting the bottom edge of his tactical combat helmet to his chest piece. The collar automatically sank down into the chest piece, freeing his head to move normally. He then tapped Corporal Rattan on the shoulder, taking up his firing position as the Corporal deactivated his collar seal.

A minute later, all five men were breathing the Mystic's air, rather than what was circulated within their own suits, enabling them to communicate without using their suit comms.

"Everyone good?" Master Sergeant Anwar asked. No one replied. "Morano and Rossi, recon starboard all the way forward. Vela and Rattan, take port. I'm going aft and down, to check engineering. Ghost ops, stealth takedowns only. We rendezvous on the bow observation deck in fifteen minutes. If you find Captain Scott or Lieutenant Nash, do whatever it takes to free them and bring them with. Understood?"

All four men nodded.

"Let's get to work, gentlemen."

* * *

"I found tools," Jessica announced, standing in front of an open cabinet with drawers of tools and test equipment.

"If I'm reading these schematics correctly, the control cards are accessible through panel seven C," Nathan said. He looked around the exterior of the jump field generator in front of him. "Here," he announced, pointing at a panel on the side. "Give me a nut driver."

Jessica pulled a small, handheld, adjustable nut driver from the cabinet and brought it over to Nathan.

Nathan took the nut driver and placed it onto the first recessed nut. The driver adjusted its socket size, gripping the nut firmly. Nathan gave it a twist to loosen it, then squeezed the trigger to slowly rotate it off. "Remind me to steal a couple of these for the Seiiki," he said as he worked his way through all six nuts.

"You don't have them?" Jessica said, surprised.

"Dalen's been begging for them for years now, but these auto-adjust ones are too damned expensive for our budget. It figures they'd have them lying around everywhere. Nothing but the best for the nobles."

Jessica sensed the disdain in his voice, which struck her as odd. Ever since he had awakened with his memories as Nathan intact, she had seen him only as Nathan Scott, and not as Connor Tuplo. But the fact was, he was both men. "But Corinairans travel on this ship as well, right?"

"A few, yes. But only those who have elevated themselves to the same status and regularly rub elbows with their Takaran counterparts. The idea of 'noble houses' has spread beyond the Takar system, starting with Corinair and Ancot, since they're the worlds that have the most interaction with Takara."

"You don't like them much, do you?"

"No, I don't." Nathan paused a moment, thinking. "You know, I'm not sure which part of me *doesn't* like the idea of societal 'classes'. Nathan or Connor." Nathan continued undoing the last of the nuts. "Both, I suppose. Although, I suspect it is more *me* than Connor."

"You talk of Connor as if he is *not* you."

"Yeah. I like to think of Connor as someone I was pretending to be, but I was so good at it that I forgot who I really was. It makes it easier to deal with, *psychologically*."

"Makes sense."

"That's the last one," Nathan said, placing the nut driver on the deck. He carefully removed the panel, revealing a row of at least a dozen palm-sized control cards. Each of their host slots was lit from behind, indicating they were active, and there was a low hum coming from the entire system, now more prominent with the service panel removed. Nathan could almost *feel* the energy flowing through the device, even though it was idle at the moment.

Nathan sighed.

"What is it?" Jessica wondered.

"When I pull these cards, some alarm is going to go off somewhere. The bridge, engineering, jump control, someplace. And someone is going to come to investigate. Maybe we should pull the cards from the backup units first and hide them somewhere, *before* we pull this one. Otherwise, they'll likely just activate the backups and be up and running again."

"Sounds good to me," Jessica agreed.

"Grab another nut driver. We'll take the service panels off the other three field generators, too," Nathan instructed.

* * *

Sigmund Daschew anxiously paced back and forth across the deck of the Mystic Empress's bridge, his gaze shifting between the ship's unconscious captain, his henchman trying to unlock the jump drive, and the view across the forward half of the luxury liner's bow, afforded by the row of windows across the front of the bridge. This job was his once-in-a-lifetime opportunity. Taking the Mystic Empress by force, even outside of the Pentaurus sector, would normally have brought the long reach of the owner's consortium of security forces down upon them in short order. He had seen it before, but with lesser value vessels. Such security operatives were ruthless, stopping short of the savage execution for those involved. Just like Sigmund and his ilk, such men operated outside the law, doing whatever was necessary to accomplish their assignments... which was precisely what Sigmund was planning. *Whatever it took.*

It had taken him nearly a week to put this job together. Seeking financial backers, negotiating payment terms, securing ships and crew, and hiring mercenaries to do the dirty work. It was the most complex job he had ever planned, and during most of it he had felt as if he were in over his head...*and considerably so.*

He and his men now controlled the Mystic Empress, the finest passenger vessel in five sectors. And with that control, Siggy felt incredibly powerful. Until ten minutes ago.

But he was getting impatient. "Have you made *any* progress?" he demanded of his henchman at the helm.

"I'm sorry, no."

"What the hell am I paying you for?" Siggy exclaimed in frustration.

"You're paying me to fly this ship," the man reminded his irritable employer. "I'm a *pilot*, not a hacker!"

Siggy said nothing, only growling and returning to his pacing. "When is that idiot going to wake up?"

"Gorston has medical training," one of Siggy's henchmen suggested. "You want me to call him to the bridge?"

Siggy turned, glaring at the man. "You're just now thinking of that?"

The man raised his comm-unit to his mouth,

discretely calling for his cohort. "Uh, Gortie, you need to double-time it up to the bridge."

"*On my way,*" his comm-unit squawked.

"*Siggy, Estellen,*" a voice called over Siggy's comm-unit.

"What is it?"

"*We found ten prisoners still in their escape pods on the port side, aft end, economy section. They didn't manage to eject before we jumped. They're refusing to come out of their pods.*"

"*Access their control panels next to the hatches,*" another voice called. "*Plug in a data pad and override their environmental controls. If you suck the air out of their pods, they'll come out.*"

After a slight pause, the first man called, "*Siggy?*"

"I'm still here," Siggy replied, annoyed.

"*You want me to do that?*"

"What do you think?"

"*I'm on it.*"

"Thank you," Siggy responded, shaking his head and looking upward. "Do any of you people think for yourselves?"

* * *

Master Sergeant Deno Anwar moved swiftly from corridor to corridor, checking the tactical display on the inside of his helmet visor as he moved. If confronted with approaching targets, he immediately took up a hiding position. He knew that eventually he would need to kill all of the intruders, but until he had a better understanding of what they were up against, it was to their advantage to go undetected.

Luckily, Commander Kamenetskiy had gotten decent scans of the luxury liner, which had very little protection against interior scanning designed into her hull. Therefore, he had a fairly detailed interior layout loaded into his tactical computer. Without it, he would have been wandering blindly, limited only by the short distance that his helmet's sensors could penetrate through the interior structure of the ship.

A small, red icon suddenly appeared on the far edge of his sensor range. A single person, moving toward him in a parallel corridor. The contact was moving at a fast walk, indicating that the person was confident that they were not in danger. It *had* to be one of the intruders.

Deno saw an opportunity. A single man, caught off guard. A chance at an easy takedown, possibly alive, so that he could be interrogated.

The Ghatazhak master sergeant moved quickly forward, turning right at the next corridor and moving to the next intersection. He safed his assault weapon and swung it around to his right flank, where it automatically secured itself. He watched his tactical display, ensuring that the target had not changed course. He turned and put his back against the wall, waiting until the target was near him, then swung his arm out, stiffening it as he struck the man in the face, knocking him backward off his feet.

Deno spun around, punching the man in the face as he tried to get up from the deck. He quickly stripped the man of his weapon, then pulled him into the side corridor while he was still too dazed to fight back.

By the time the surprised man regained his senses, Ghatazhak Master Sergeant Deno Anwar was squatting confidently in front of him, his tactical visor up, staring boldly into the man's eyes. "Do you know what I am?"

"What the fuck?" the man sputtered.

"Do you know what I am?" Deno repeated.

"You work for the nobles?" the man assumed, unsure of his answer.

"Hardly," Deno replied. "I am Ghatazhak. Do you know what that means?"

"That you're a member of a Takaran military force that was put into stasis years ago?"

The master sergeant did not like the disrespectful tone the man had taken and punched him again, although not as hard as before.

"Okay! Okay!" the man agreed, grabbing his nose. "You're Ghatazhak! What the fuck do you want?"

"What are your numbers?"

"What?"

"How many of you are aboard this ship?"

"You're joking, right?" the man laughed. "Siggy would kill me."

"I will do far worse, believe me," Deno promised. He cocked his head to one side. "What is your name?"

"Uh... Gorston. Gennar Gorston."

Deno drew his combat knife from its sheath on his thigh armor as he spoke. "Your only chance at leaving this ship alive, Gennar, is to tell me what I wish to know."

Gennar looked at the knife, then back at the master sergeant. He had never seen eyes that cold and confident, and Gennar had known some very dangerous men in his time. "If you kill me, you will learn nothing," he replied, trying to show the Ghatazhak that he was not afraid.

"At the very least, I will learn your tolerance for pain," Deno replied calmly. "You see, your death will take some time. Admittedly, it will hardly be worth the effort, but it will tell me something about the character of your cadre. That, in itself, will also be of value."

"You don't really think I'm going to just sit here and let you carve me up, do you?" Gennar said.

"Oh, I am quite sure you will try to resist, but that will only increase your level of suffering, and the end result will be the same."

Gennar lashed out at the master sergeant, punching at him as he tried to get up, but the Ghatazhak blocked both attacks, returning with one of his own, followed by a quick lunge of his blade into Gennar's left lower abdomen.

Gennar cried out in pain as his left side opened. He grabbed at his opponent's left hand, which was now clutching Gennar's throat, making it difficult for him to breathe and impossible to move. But the Ghatazhak's grip was like steel, and his arm was unmovable.

"Next, I will make an incision into your right lung, causing it to deflate," Deno explained as he held his prisoner immobile. "With any luck, a tension pneumothorax will develop, which will make you feel as if you are suffocating."

Gennar continued to struggle for several more seconds, eventually giving in to his captor. "You will let me live?"

"Tell me what I wish to know," Deno replied, moving the tip of his blade up to Gennar's right side.

"Okay, okay, okay!" Gennar begged. "Thirty of us came aboard. Twelve in the breach boxes, the rest in the shuttles."

"And the ship? The larger one that was blocking the Mystic from jumping?" the master sergeant asked.

"It carries anti-ship missiles, rail guns, and twenty more men."

"Their level of training?"

"What?" Gennar said, confused by the question and distracted by the searing pain in his left abdomen.

"What level of training does your team have?"

"Only the twelve who came in the breach boxes have training. Palee militia, mostly. The rest are just common hoods for hire."

"If you are lying to me..."

"I swear, I'm not," Gennar insisted.

"And you?" Deno wondered. "What level of training do you possess?"

"I'm just a medic," Gennar promised.

Deno stared at the man.

"I swear it."

Deno placed his knife back into its sheath, purposefully appearing to divert his attention from his prisoner, as he simultaneously loosened his hold on the man's neck.

Gennar fell for the trick, revealing that his level of training, and likely that of his comrades, was greater than he had led Deno to believe. He shoved his left hand up to the Ghatazhak master sergeant's hand on his neck, knocking it aside, then swung his hand back at the Ghatazhak's face.

Deno feigned being taken off guard, falling backward as Gennar tried again to get to his feet. But it was only an act. The master sergeant rolled back onto his upper shoulders, both hands planted on the floor at his sides. In one fluid motion, the Ghatazhak arched upward, his body stiffening as he launched feet first toward the man. He wrapped his legs around Gennar's neck, sitting upright and driving both his fists into the man's ears, stunning him. He then leaned back hard, pulling Gennar forward and down to the deck, twisting his head around and snapping the man's neck as they both hit the floor.

A split second later, the master sergeant was standing over Gennar as the man took his last breaths. "If it makes you feel any better, I would have killed you either way. At least this way, you died with honor."

* * *

Nathan removed the last nut from the service panel on the second active jump drive field generator and removed the panel to look inside. Just like the first one, he could almost feel the energy flowing through the device, and worried what would happen when they pulled the control cards without shutting it down first. "How are you doing over there?" he asked Jessica.

"Four more nuts and I'll have my last panel removed," she answered as she held the trigger on the nut driver, its motor whirring softly as it unscrewed the nut from its threaded post.

Nathan rose from his work and headed over to the backup jump drive field generator with the cover already removed by Jessica. "We have to pull the cards from the two backups and hide them before we can pull the cards from the actives."

"Why can't we pull them all at once and get out quickly?"

"The backups are offline at the moment. So, I doubt anyone will be alerted that their control cards have been pulled."

"Are you sure about that?"

"No, I'm not," Nathan admitted. "But it's a pretty good bet."

"How good a bet?" she asked, removing the last nut from her service panel.

"Fifty-fifty?" Nathan said as he started pulling cards from one of the offline field generators.

Jessica glanced over at him. "Just like that...you start pulling them?"

"The entire system is probably locked out," Nathan explained. "But it's only a matter of time before whoever we're dealing with figures out a way to get past the lockout and regain control of the jump drive."

"I don't understand," Jessica said, taking the control cards out of her unit. "We already jumped. If we jumped back to the PC..."

"This ship can't jump that far in a single jump," Nathan reminded her. "No ship can...at least none that I know of. And we don't even know *who* jumped the ship. It could have been the captain."

"Why would he jump the ship? Isn't he safer in the cloud where no one can find him?"

"Assuming he doesn't *want* to be found. If Captain Rainey didn't believe us, which is likely the case, then he launched a jump comm-drone with a distress call back to Takara. He'd want to jump clear of the cloud, probably along his filed course, so that company security could find him."

"But company security isn't coming," Jessica said.

"He doesn't care one way or the other," Nathan explained. "If company security comes, he's got a chance; if the Dusahn come, he's still got a chance, just not a very good one."

"How does he have a chance with the Dusahn?" Jessica challenged.

"He was comm-blind," Nathan argued. "That's a pretty good excuse."

"Like the Dusahn would care," Jessica insisted.

"They're more likely to just make another example out of him."

"If they're smart, they'd spare him to show that they are not unreasonable."

"I think you're giving them more credit than they deserve," Jessica said, walking over with all the control cards from her unit in her hands. "Where are we going to hide these?" she asked.

"We'll find someplace on the way out."

"Where are we going?"

"Port side, to do the same thing."

"Why? They can't jump with only half the field generators."

"Unless they use the cards from the port backups in these."

"Don't they need four working field generators to jump the ship?"

"Not if they're set up to rechannel all the emitters to two, or even a single, jump field generator," Nathan said.

"They can do that?"

"The Seiiki can. It cuts our single jump range by about sixty percent, but it works. If we're going to disable this ship's ability to jump, we have to take all four field generators offline."

Jessica sighed. "Right. If alarms go off on the bridge when we take the active ones down, there's a good chance we won't make it back into the ship. You know that."

"Yeah, I know." Nathan pulled the last of his control cards out and stood up. He set the cards down on top of the jump field generator, then walked quickly over to the tool cabinet, grabbing a toolbox and dumping the contents on the deck. "This should work," he said, returning to the jump field generator and putting his control cards inside the toolbox.

Jessica put her cards in, as well.

"Shall we?" Nathan said, setting the toolbox aside and going over to one of the active jump field generators. "I'll take this one, you take that one. We'll pull the first cards at the same time. In pairs, as fast as we can, until all the cards are out."

"And if the damned things explode?"

"They're not going to explode," Nathan insisted. "Spark, smoke, catch fire...maybe."

"I feel so much better," Jessica said sarcastically, moving over to the other, active jump field generator.

Nathan stepped up to the open service panel, looking at the glowing row of control cards. He put his hands close to the outside edges of the row of cards, half expecting either an incredible amount of heat, or a sudden spark of electricity to jump to his hands. But neither happened.

"You ready?" he asked, not looking at her.

"No, but that never stopped me before," Jessica answered.

Nathan glanced over at her, checking that she was in position. He took a deep breath, positioned his hands over the first two cards, and counted, "One......two......three......PULL!"

Nathan yanked the first two cards out, tossing them aside as he reached for the next two. As he pulled them out, a few sparks went off deep inside the jump field generator. He repeated the process two more times, each time more sparks firing. By the time he got to the fifth and sixth control cards, sparks were starting to shoot into his face, and smoke was beginning to pour out from the generator.

"Shouldn't these things shut down automatically

by now!" Jessica yelled as she fought through the sparks to continue pulling cards from her jump field generator.

Finally, as Nathan pulled the ninth and tenth control cards, the jump field generator began to shut down. The sparks stopped, and the glow inside the device began to fade as the humming from the unit decreased. He pulled out the last two cards and stood up, triumphant. He turned and looked at Jessica, a victorious smile on his face. "Wait until I tell *Vlad* about *that*!"

* * *

Master Sergeant Anwar moved quietly down the corridor above the main engineering section of the Mystic Empress. The tactical display on the inside of his helmet visor indicated that one deck below, and inboard of him, were six of the Mystic's crew, presumably all members of the ship's engineering department. He also detected four armed men inside the same compartment, and four more guarding various entrances outside the compartment. With eight men securing that section, there was no way that he and his men could retake that department without sacrificing the prisoners. Although he knew that neither General Telles nor Lieutenant Nash would have a problem with losing the six innocent men, he was quite certain that Captain Scott would insist on finding a way to take the compartment without needlessly sacrificing the Mystic's engineers. It was a sound argument, considering that they needed the ship intact and fully functional, which would be easier with the skills of the six men currently being held hostage.

The Ghatazhak master sergeant was already formulating a plan to do just that, but he would need more men; more than just the other four who had come aboard with him.

* * *

The hatch from the starboard engineering crawl spaces cracked slightly, then slowly opened a few centimeters. Ten seconds passed, then the hatch opened a bit more and stopped. Finally, after another pause, the hatch opened fully, and Jessica swung through it, feet first, landing in the artificial gravity of the corridor.

Jessica moved quickly down the corridor to the nearest intersection, checking around the corner to see if anyone was nearby.

Nathan was next, coming through the hatch in similar fashion. Once his feet were back on the deck, he turned and pushed the hatch closed, securing it once again.

"We need to go up a few levels and then across to the port side," Jessica said as she walked back toward Nathan.

"Straight across on the same deck would be quicker," Nathan suggested.

"If they've taken the ship, then they've taken engineering by now," Jessica surmised. "If we try to cut across on the same deck, we're likely to run into them."

"Maybe we can take a few of them out," Nathan suggested. "Maybe even get our hands on some of their weapons."

"And if the ship is crawling with Dusahn already?" she replied. "Jump drive first," Jessica insisted. "Your idea, remember? Besides, our chances of getting the other jump drives taken offline are better while they still don't know we're here."

"Lead the way," Nathan agreed.

* * *

"Siggy!" one of his men called. "I just heard from Torel. They have found more passengers. Some in their escape pods, some still in their cabins. And we have rounded up all of the Mystic's crew. In total, more than three hundred people."

The man's voice sounded justifiably nervous. That many people could easily rush a handful of armed men and succeed in overpowering them. "Assemble them all in the garden deck, in the center courtyard," Siggy ordered. "Post guards on the walkways above, as well as on the garden deck itself. Kill anyone who resists."

"Yes," the man replied.

"*Siggy,*" a voice called over his comm-unit. "*This is Ellis. I'm just forward of engineering. I found Gortie. He's dead.*"

"How?" Siggy asked over his comm-unit.

"*Stab wound to the gut, and his neck has been snapped.*"

"The man was ex-militia, special ops!" Siggy barked. "How the hell did some security guard on a luxury liner do that?"

"*I do not believe it was a security guard,*" Ellis replied. "*Gortie was good. Damned good.*"

"I want every square meter of this ship searched," Siggy demanded. "Find the son of a bitch and kill him."

"*We will need to pull people from guarding the prisoners,*" Ellis warned.

"I don't care. Stop that fucker before he takes someone else out."

CHAPTER NINE

"Jump complete," Loki announced as the Seiiki's cockpit windows cycled back from opaque to clear. "Sensors are picking up the Aurora and the Glendanon."

"Patch me into the Aurora's comm-channel," Vladimir instructed.

"You've got it," Loki replied after a few taps on his console.

"Aurora, Aurora. This is the Seiiki, Commander Kamenetskiy. Put me through to Captain Taylor, immediately."

"*Seiiki, Aurora. Stand by one, Commander.*"

"I've got a clear-to-land signal from Aurora flight ops," Loki reported.

"Take us in," Vladimir replied. "Warn the crew that this will be a quick turnaround. I want to be ready to launch as quickly as possible."

"Got it."

"*Seiiki, Aurora. Actual is ready for you, sir,*" the Aurora's comms officer announced.

"Aurora Actual, Kamenetskiy."

"*Go for Actual,*" Cameron replied.

"Cameron, I need you to launch a pair of Reapers configured for pursuit recon. We'll send you the coordinates."

"*Why? What are they looking for?*" Cameron asked.

"The Mystic Empress. She jumped away after being boarded by pirates...while Nathan and Jessica were on board. You should have General Telles prepare boarding teams, as well," Vladimir added. "And Cam, we came direct. There was no time to fly the entire algorithm."

"Understood."

Cameron switched off her comm-channel, then pressed the button for her comms officer. "Comms, Captain. Notify the Glendanon that we need to move to the next position early. Contact General Telles and tell him we need boarding teams, and have the general meet me in the hangar bay."

"Aye, sir."

"Tactical, Captain," Cameron continued, pressing another comm-button. "Put the ship on alert condition one." Cameron did not wait for confirmation, instead switching to yet another comm-channel. "Flight, Captain. Recall all patrol birds. Fit two Reapers with recon pods and scramble them ASAP; coordinates and mission details will be ready by the time they launch. Fit two more Reapers with anti-ship missiles, and fit the last two for boarding ops with breach boxes."

"Aye, sir."

Cameron switched off her intercom, grabbing her comm-set from the desk as she rose to exit. She passed through the ready room hatch into the bridge as she donned her comm-set. "Call the XO to the bridge. I'll contact her from the hangar deck as soon as I know more," she said, turning to exit the bridge.

* * *

"Shit," Jessica said, ducking back around the corner of the corridor, against the wall. "Back the other way," she motioned to Nathan, moving back the way they had come.

"What is it?" Nathan asked, changing direction with her.

"Two goons just turned the corner and are coming our way. Quick, around the next corner to the left."

"That'll take us all the way aft," Nathan warned. "We'll have to double back along the port side."

"No choice," Jessica insisted, picking up the pace. She pulled ahead of Nathan, feeling compelled to take the lead due to her Ghatazhak training, despite the fact that she had no weapon.

As she rounded the next corner to the left, she paused just enough to translate the corridor markings, in both Takaran and Corinairan. Confident that they were now headed directly aft, she picked up her pace again, turning to the right at the next corridor, heading over to the furthest point along the ship's starboard side.

"Where are you going?" Nathan called from a few steps behind her. "We need to go to port."

"We need to go starboard, then up one deck, then aft, otherwise we'll run right into engineering, which will probably be crawling with bad guys," Jessica explained as she continued jogging down the corridor.

Realizing she was correct, Nathan continued following her as he recalled the images of the ship's deck plan he had studied earlier. It was odd that he remembered them so clearly. He had studied them for less than a minute, and even then, only to find the access hatch to the starboard engineering crawl spaces. He realized now that every single page he had scrolled through was retained in his memory, as if he had thoroughly scrutinized each one. His memory was always good, but never this precise.

Nathan made a mental note to ask Doctor Sato about it when they got back to the Aurora.

That's when another thought occurred to him. *He had not used the word 'if'*. Considering their current circumstances, it would have been natural. Yet the idea that they might *not* make it through this current situation, or any situation in the future, didn't seem to be a question. Rather, to him, survival seemed an absolute certainty, as did victory.

As they continued down the corridor, Nathan wondered if something about the transfer into the new, cloned body, one that Doctor Sato had genetically altered over the course of four clones, had anything to do with his newfound confidence. He was certain it explained his improved memory and his surprising dexterity in the gym the other day. He only hoped it wasn't the start of one of the potential personality disorders the Nifelmian doctor had warned him about.

Nathan came to a stop at the ladder well, waiting a moment as Jessica began her ascent. Once she was a few meters up, he began his climb up the ladder. It was a long climb, as the engineering level was at least twice, if not three times, the height of the average deck. Much of the climb was up through closed tubes. As they climbed, the thought struck him that, if anyone suddenly appeared at the top or bottom of the ladder while they were still climbing, they were pretty much done for. Yet again, he had no doubt in his mind that they would survive.

Nathan worried that this abnormal confidence would make him reckless, but there was nothing he could do about it now. His best bet was to follow Jessica's lead. After all, she had superior training, and he had only been 'awake' for three days.

They continued their climb, passing by a few tiny landings provided for various crawl space hatches. After a minute, Jessica reached the next level and stopped to peek over the deck for any sign of the enemy, before ascending the last few rungs and stepping out onto the landing.

Nathan continued up the ladder to join her, but stopped when he felt her boot on his head. He looked up, confused. "What the..."

"Ssh!" she hissed, peeking around the corner of the landing cutout.

Nathan continued looking up at her as she held out two fingers, then pointed behind her back to her right.

Jessica turned back toward Nathan, squatting to move closer to him. "There are two heavily armed goons guarding the intersection on this side," she whispered. "There are probably two more on the other side, as well. I'm going to lure these guys after me. I'll cut to port further forward. Hopefully, they'll send the other two forward to cut me off. Once these two pass by, you go aft and cut across, and then back up the port side to the access hatch."

"No," Nathan objected, shaking his head. "We stick together."

"Won't work," she disagreed. "The minute we step out of here, they're going to be after us. Better that they're only after me."

"And if you get caught?"

"Trust me," Jessica said, "it will hurt them more than it does me."

Before he could argue further, Jessica rose and purposefully leaned out a bit too far.

"*Hey!*" one of the men yelled in Angla.

Jessica took off running in the opposite direction.

"*Stop!*" the man ordered.

Several energy weapons shots rang out, echoing in the metallic corridor. Nathan could hear the men running, yelling warnings over their comm-units as they approached. He swung over to the side on the ladder, making sure that he was out of sight as the men ran past him, pursuing Jessica.

"Damn it," he cursed to himself as he climbed up the ladder and stepped onto the landing. There was nothing Nathan could do for Jessica now, except to get to that access hatch.

* * *

Master Sergeant Anwar reached the entrance to the Mystic's forward observation deck. He paused momentarily, tilting his head and peeking inside the three-level-high compartment.

The compartment appeared empty. Massive windows, each of them now covered with blast shields, stretched from the deck and wrapped all the way around the compartment. In the middle of the compartment was a garden, complete with trees, grass, and perfectly groomed flower beds. At the back of the compartment were tables and chairs, and along the back wall, a bar.

Anwar checked the tactical display on the inside of his visor. The only contacts he showed were that of his men; two of them were to port, and two to starboard. After peeking one last time, he stepped out through the entrance, passing between the port and starboard sides of the bar and out into the open, sweeping his weapon from point to point, to check that no undetected intruders were present.

Anwar lowered his weapon slightly, noting that the contacts in his tactical display indicated his men were also moving out into the open. He looked around, spotting all four of them as they too scanned the area with their weapons.

"We spotted four on the move," Sergeant Morano reported as he approached.

"Four, as well," Sergeant Vela added. "Traveling in pairs. And another six guarding prisoners in the center courtyard."

"Same here," Sergeant Morano agreed. "I believe the pairs were conducting a search of the ship, perhaps searching for more prisoners."

"That adds up. I saw eight guarding engineering, and the six guarding prisoners you spoke of. That leaves five or six more likely guarding the bridge."

"How did you come up with that number?" Corporal Rossi wondered.

"I took one down near engineering. I believe he was on his way to the bridge. He said there were thirty on board, with another twenty reinforcements waiting on their main ship."

"Any indication of their level of training?" Sergeant Morano wondered. "We couldn't get a good read, but they seemed confident that they had control of the ship."

"He tried to tell me that most of them were common criminals," Master Sergeant Anwar replied. "He even claimed that he was just a medic, but he revealed his level of training when he attempted to prevent his own execution."

"I'm assuming he failed?" Sergeant Vela joked.

Master Sergeant Anwar did not respond, only gave the sergeant a knowing smirk.

* * *

Vladimir came bounding down the Seiiki's cargo ramp before it was completely deployed, jumping off the side of the ramp toward Cameron and General Telles as they approached. "They hit with four breaching pods, big enough to hold four, maybe six, men each," he began as his feet touched the deck.

"Were they Dusahn?" General Telles asked.

"No, not military at all. They looked like they were cobbled together. They had a main ship, as well. It was three times the size of the Seiiki, at least. It had two small shuttles that ferried more men to the Mystic."

"The original boarding parties likely secured the hangar bays first," the general surmised.

"The bigger ship, it was armed?" Cameron inquired.

"*Da*," Vladimir replied. "Short-range, anti-ship missiles and rail guns. Small ones, like for point-defenses."

"No energy weapons?"

"On the main ship, *nyet*," Vladimir replied. "None that we saw."

General Telles held up his data pad. "Did their main ship look like this?"

Vladimir studied the image for a moment. "No, the profile is wrong. It was longer, and wider in the middle. With guns along the sides, top and bottom."

General Telles scrolled through several more images, before showing Vladimir the data pad again.

"*Da!*" Vladimir exclaimed. "That is it! Or very close to that. It was difficult to get clear readings in the cloud."

"What is it?" Cameron asked the general.

"Palean assault ship," the general explained. "Used to put troops on the surface. Fat in the middle because of landing thrusters. They were normally equipped with missiles and rail guns for defense. Most of them were turned into interplanetary cargo ships after the war, then into jump cargo ships after the fall of Caius."

"How many boarders do you think they could carry?" Cameron wondered.

"Fifty, at least," the general replied. "More than enough to overpower the security forces normally carried by a cruise ship."

"I didn't realize piracy was a problem around here," Cameron said.

"Normally, it is not," the general explained, "but now that the Dusahn have removed the threat of retaliation from the owner's security forces, it will likely *become* a problem." General Telles looked at Vladimir. "What of Master Sergeant Anwar and his men?"

"He insisted that they deploy to the Mystic," Vladimir replied.

"Did they make it aboard?"

"I do not know," Vladimir admitted. "The ship jumped before they landed. They were close enough to be included in the jump field, if their fields are the same distance from the hull as ours." Vladimir shook his head. "There is no way to be sure. I am sorry."

"But Nathan and Jessica *are* on board the Mystic?" Cameron confirmed.

"*Da.* We docked with the Mystic, and they were allowed to come aboard, but with no weapons."

"Lieutenant Nash agreed to this?" General Telles asked, somewhat surprised.

"Trust me, she objected."

"How many men can your Reapers carry?" General Telles asked Cameron.

"Twelve troops," she replied. "Probably more like eight fully outfitted Ghatazhak."

"And you have six total?"

"Yes," Cameron replied. "I've already taken the liberty of having two of them configured to carry your men, the other two with anti-ship missiles. The last two are carrying recon pods and are already on their way to find the Mystic."

"Change one of the missile Reapers to troop-carrying," the general instructed. "Do the same with the recon Reaper when it returns to relay the Mystic's position to us. That will give us the ability to put at least thirty-two men onto that ship."

"Will that be enough?" Vladimir wondered.

"It should suffice," the general assured him.

"What if we cannot find her?" Cameron said. "What if she took evasive action...to elude pursuit?"

"Let us hope not," General Telles said, "or our people will be on their own."

* * *

"When the bloody hell is the Antilla going to get here?" Siggy exclaimed in frustration.

"It's only been ten minutes, Siggy," his helmsman said calmly.

"Ten minutes? That's right, it *has* been ten minutes, hasn't it? Ten minutes that you've been *failing* at unlocking that damned jump drive. Isn't that right, Donnel?"

"Maybe the Antilla's jump drive is acting up again," the other man suggested.

"Did I ask you, Hamon?" Siggy closed his eyes, clenching his teeth as he tried to maintain his composure. Things were not going the way he had planned. "I should have spent the money and repaired that damned thing, instead of buying more men," he muttered.

"*Siggy, it's Rikka!*" one of his men yelled over Sigmund's comm-unit. "*We're pursuing a woman in uniform,*" he said between ragged breaths. "*We spotted her coming up an access ladder, starboard side, aft of engineering.*"

"One of the crew?" Siggy asked over his comm-unit.

"I don't think so! The uniform was wrong! And she doesn't move... Like someone who works... On a cruise ship!"

"Then, who the hell is she?" Siggy demanded. He keyed his comm-unit again. "Catch her and bring her to me! Understood?"

"I've got Xander and Eaves... Moving to cut her off... On the port side! We'll catch her!"

"You damned well better!" Siggy warned. He turned to his other man. "That bitch probably took out Gortie."

"No way."

A faint voice squawked from Master Sergeant Anwar's utility pouch on his right thigh armor. He quickly pulled a small, civilian-type comm-unit out.

"We spotted her coming up an access ladder, starboard side, aft of engineering."

"Where did you get that?" Sergeant Morano asked.

"I don't think so! The uniform was wrong! And she doesn't move... Like someone who works... On a cruise ship!" the comm-unit in Anwar's hand blared.

"They must be talking about Nash," Sergeant Vela surmised.

"Why didn't they say anything about Scott?" Corporal Rossi wondered.

"I've got Xander and Eaves... Moving to cut her off... On the port side! We'll catch her!" the comm-unit continued.

"I don't know," Anwar replied. "But I intend to find out," he added. "Morano, Rossi, you two take up positions forward of the bandits guarding the prisoners. Vela and Rattan, you're with me."

"What are you going to do?" Sergeant Morano asked.

"I'm going to find Nash and Scott, then we're going to free the prisoners and get them off this ship, before these assholes get reinforcements," Anwar explained.

"Then what?" Corporal Rattan asked.

"Then we kill these idiots," the master sergeant replied, turning to head toward the exit.

"There's a dog run along the bottom of the ship," Sergeant Morano told Anwar. "Stem to stern, straight shot. It's secured, so it'll be empty. That's how we got past them coming here."

"How'd you get in?" Anwar wondered, pausing for an answer, and turning back toward them.

"Rossi hacked it," the sergeant replied.

"Two eight four six seven," Corporal Rossi stated, obviously pleased with himself.

"Down three decks, can't miss it," Sergeant Morano added.

"Good work," Master Sergeant Anwar said. "Everyone go comms active and secure. If all they have are these cheap-ass comm-units, they'll never hear us."

* * *

"Captain, flight ops reports all Reapers are loaded and ready for departure," the Aurora's comms officer reported. "The Seiiki is also ready to launch."

"Very well," Cameron replied from her command chair in the middle of the bridge. "Launch the strike team."

"Launching strike team, aye."

"Notify the Glendanon and the Morsiko-Tavi. Tell them we start the relocation algorithm as soon as the strike team is safely away."

"Not all of the Glendanon's boxcars have returned, Captain," the Aurora's tactical officer reminded Cameron.

"We'll drop a comm-buoy before we go," Cameron replied. "They'll be able to get the starting code from that. We've already taken a hell of a risk staying put this long."

* * *

"Wake him," Siggy instructed.

"How?" Hamon asked.

"How do I know?" Siggy snapped impatiently. "Throw some water on him or something!"

"What water?"

"We're on a cruise ship, for..." Siggy gave up, moving over to the unconscious captain lying on the deck of the Mystic's bridge. He grabbed him by the collar of his uniform with both hands and began to shake him vigorously. "Wake the hell up!" he yelled.

Captain Rainey began to open his eyes. Slowly at first, then they snapped open. He instinctively grabbed at his attacker's hands, trying to break the grip, but he was too weak.

Siggy let him go and stepped away. "Get him to his feet!" he barked at his two subordinates.

The two men stepped over and grabbed Captain Rainey by his arms, yanking him to his feet. The captain was unsteady, needing a bit of assistance from Hamon to stay upright.

"I'm beginning to lose patience," Siggy told Captain Rainey. "I don't much like being stranded in the middle of nowhere, especially without the cover of that cloud you jumped us out of." Siggy stepped closer to the captain. "Unlock the jump drive, or I will start executing your crew, one by one."

Captain Rainey did not respond at first. Instead,

he stared at his captor, locking eyes with him. Finally, he spoke. "I will not release control of the jump drive to you or anyone else. I have taken an oath, and I mean to honor it."

"Is that right?" Siggy replied. He raised his comm-unit and keyed it. "Jortan, you there?"

Nathan ran along the port side of the engineering level, through the outboard corridor that ran between the Mystic's main hull and her outboard sections. He could hear the occasional sound of distant weapons fire reverberating through the corridors. It made him cringe, wondering every time if the shot had found Jessica and struck her down.

But again, something inside of him told him that would not be the case.

He skidded to a stop before nearly charging past the port engineering crawlspace access hatch. He quickly inserted the security badge that Jessica had given him, unlocked the hatch, and swung it open. He dove headfirst through the hatch, floating freely as he passed from the artificial gravity of the Mystic's interior, to the weightless environment of her crawl spaces.

Pausing just long enough to close and lock the access hatch behind him, Nathan pushed off the inside of the hatch with both feet, propelling himself down the transit path, passing between a myriad of pipes, conduits, and ducting. He grabbed at well-positioned handholds along the way, guiding himself along, avoiding collisions with the tangled web of mechanical and electrical runs all about him. Ahead, he could see the hatch to the port jump field generator compartment, but it was still a distance away.

"Let me guess," Siggy said in measured tones. "Something about protecting your ship, your crew, your passengers... Am I right?" Siggy keyed his comm-unit again, growing impatient. "Jortan!"

"*Yes! I am here, Siggy!*" the man finally answered.

"Select a member of the crew and execute them, immediately," Siggy instructed over his comm-unit.

"*Uh... Are you sure you want to do that?*"

"Of course, I am sure." Siggy was becoming more annoyed.

"*Uh... That might not be a good idea, just yet,*" Jortan replied hesitantly.

Siggy stood, turning away from Captain Rainey. "I did not ask you if it was a good idea, you idiot."

"*I've only got six guys, here, Siggy. And there's got to be at least a hundred prisoners, maybe two. If they were all to rush us at once...*"

"Then you'd cut them down!" Siggy replied, barely able to hold back his rage. "Your weapons do have an auto-fire mode, you know!"

"*I know, I know. But maybe it would be better if we waited for the Antilla to arrive with our reinforcements,*" Jortan suggested over the comm-unit.

"I don't believe this," Siggy said to himself, the hand holding his comm-unit dropping to his side. He looked at Hamon. "You get what you pay for, right?"

Hamon was afraid to respond.

Siggy raised his comm-unit to his mouth again and keyed the mic. "Select a member of the crew, take him into a separate room, where the others cannot see him, and *then* execute him."

After a brief pause, Jortan responded. "*How do you want me to kill him?*"

"If you cannot figure that out on your own, then

you're not worth paying," Siggy retorted. "Get it done!"

"*Yes, sir.*"

Siggy turned to look at Captain Rainey, who was now standing without assistance. "Better take two members of the crew," he said into his comm-unit. "One of them as a witness."

"*Understood.*"

"It will do you no good," Captain Rainey warned. "They took the same oath as I did."

"We will see about that," Siggy replied confidently.

Nathan drifted carefully through the hatch, into the port jump field generator compartment, his feet settling on the deck and taking his weight as he passed into the artificial gravity field produced in the compartment. Without bothering to close the hatch behind him, he ran across the large, white compartment and opened the tool cabinet, removed the nut driver, and headed straight for the nearest offline jump field generator.

As he removed the nuts on the first control card access panel, his mind raced through all the possible scenarios. He was certain they were not back in Takaran space; no ship that he knew of had that much single-jump range. It was possible that the Mystic used only a single jump field generator per side to execute a jump, and that they had actually made two back-to-back jumps, but that still would put them a long way from the Pentaurus cluster.

One thing he *was* sure of was that the clouds of Syllium Orfee no longer obscured their location, and if they had jumped clear of them along their filed route, the Dusahn would arrive shortly.

"*We have two crewmen,*" Jortan announced over Siggy's comm-unit. "*We have them isolated from the others, in one of the galleys.*"

"What are their names?" Siggy asked.

After a pause, Jortan answered. "*Assistant Purser Dallon Archette, and sous chef Vance Shelty.*"

"You realize what will happen if you harm anyone on this ship," Captain Rainey warned.

"I already have, Captain," Siggy replied. "And the answer is, nothing." Siggy stepped up to the captain again, looking him in the eye. "Are you going to unlock the jump drive?"

Captain Rainey did not respond.

Siggy keyed his comm-unit again. "Kill one of them."

Captain Rainey tried to break free of the two men holding him, in order to get to Siggy. "You bastard!"

"Oh, I've been called much worse, Captain." Siggy keyed his comm-unit again. "Is it done?"

"*Yes.*"

Siggy looked at Captain Rainey, pleased with himself. "Shall I kill another?"

"How do I even know you killed anyone?" Captain Rainey challenged.

"You don't believe me?" He keyed his comm-unit again, holding it up to the Captain. "Ask him yourself."

Captain Rainey looked suspiciously at Siggy.

"Go on."

"This is Captain Rainey," the captain finally said into Siggy's comm-unit.

A moment later, a nervous voice responded over the comm-unit. "*This is Assistant Purser Archette. They killed the cook, Captain. They slit his thr...*" There was a sudden gurgling sound over the comm-unit, followed by a gasping of air, like someone trying desperately to breathe.

Siggy looked surprised. “What’s going on there?” he asked over his comm-unit.

“I killed the other one, as well,” Jortan replied.

“Why?” Siggy asked, slightly annoyed.

“I didn’t like the way he was looking at me.”

Siggy smiled. “Well, that will certainly teach him, won’t it?” He looked at his other two men holding onto the captain’s arms. “That’s what you call, ‘taking the initiative’.” He raised his comm-unit back up and keyed the mic. “Grab two more. This time, make them passengers. A man and a woman.” Siggy looked at the captain, noting his defiant gaze. “And bring them here.”

“Right away.”

Siggy smiled cruelly. “We will see how defiant you are, when you are forced to personally witness the execution of your passengers.”

Captain Rainey was fuming. “You will pay for this...”

Master Sergeant Anwar finished climbing the starboard access ladder and stepped onto the Mystic’s engineering deck. He peeked out around the edge of the ladder cutout, checking up and down the corridor. Now that he was on a new level, he checked the tactical display on the inside of his helmet visor. Five icons- four red and one blue. Two of the red icons were in the next corridor over, moving away from them, and the other two were on the port side, also moving forward. But the blue icon was moving aft, in *between* the corridors.

Sergeant Vela stepped onto the deck behind Anwar, checking his own visor. “What the fuck?”

"She must be in the overhead," Anwar surmised. "There's at least a meter and a half between overhead and the next deck, more when you get further aft by main engineering."

"Packed full of shit," Vela replied.

"These ships always have crawl spaces all over the damned place. And she's small enough to get through most of them."

"I guess there's something to be said for all Ghatazhak *not* being the same size after all," Sergeant Vela joked.

"I'll be sure and tell her you said that," Anwar replied with a grin.

"My ass, you will."

"Is she..." Corporal Rattan started to ask as he stepped off the ladder and onto the deck to join them.

"Yup," Anwar replied, cutting him off. "Vela, starboard corridor. Rattan, port. If those fuckers double back, cut them down."

"No more ghost?" Corporal Rattan asked.

"No more ghost."

"Fuck, yeah," the corporal replied.

"Only if you have to," the master sergeant added. "Once one of us lights them up, we lose the advantage of surprise."

"Pretty much lost that when you took out the first guy, Deno," Sergeant Vela commented.

"They still think she did him," Anwar reminded him as he started down the corridor.

"Where are you going?" Sergeant Vela asked.

"I'll get Nash. You two take your positions and hold. As soon as I get her, we'll fall back to here and get back down in the dog run."

"And after that?"

"Beats the hell outta me," Master Sergeant Anwar

said as he headed down the corridor. "I'm making this shit up as I go."

Nathan yanked the last of the control cards from the second offline backup jump field generator, tossing them into the toolbox on the deck next to him. After pulling the last card, he grabbed the toolbox and the nut driver and made his way over to the nearest active jump field generator, and got to work on its control card access panel.

Master Sergeant Anwar swung the hatch to pump room four open and stepped inside. As he entered, the lights snapped on, illuminating the myriad of pumps along either side of the compartment.

He closed the hatch, then checked the tactical display on the inside of his helmet visor. The blue icon representing Lieutenant Nash was growing closer and was just outside the compartment. The icon's progress stopped for a moment, then continued its approach.

He looked up. Above him were dozens of pipes, most of them at least a half meter in diameter. Somewhere above them, the lieutenant was crawling her way across the compartment.

The icon stopped again, this time not more than five meters away. He looked up again and spotted the lieutenant peeking out from behind a row of three pipes. "Lieutenant," he greeted her casually.

"Master Sergeant," Jessica replied. She swung off the pipes and dropped the four meters to the deck, landing a few meters in front of Master Sergeant Anwar.

"Out for a stroll?" Deno asked.

"Just a little diversionary tactic. You?"

"Thought you might be lost."

"Nope. I'm good. You alone?"

"Negative," the master sergeant replied as he handed his sidearm to Jessica. "Vela and Rattan are with me. Morano and Rossi are just forward of the main garden deck."

"Planning on smelling the flowers, are they?" she commented as she checked the weapon.

"Bandits are holding the crew and some of the passengers there. We were thinking about freeing them once we found you and Captain Scott. I take it you were running a diversion for him?"

"Affirmed. He's disabling the jump drives. Any idea where we're at?"

"Not a clue," he replied, pulling a spare comm-set out of his left utility pouch.

"How many are we talking about?" Jessica asked, taking the comm-set from him.

"About thirty, with twenty more possibly on their way."

"Type and arms?"

"Probably ex-military, a mixture of arms. Scatter guns, burners, boomers... Some body armor as well. Crappy comms, though," he added, holding up the comm-unit he took off the man he had killed earlier.

"You picking pockets again, Deno?" Jessica said as she donned her comm-set.

"He didn't need it any longer," the master sergeant replied with a smile.

"Test-test," she called over her comm-set.

Master Sergeant Anwar flashed her a thumbs-up sign.

"*I guess you found her,*" Sergeant Vela commented over comms.

"Affirmative," Anwar replied. "Back to the ladder, boys."

"We need to get Nathan, first," Jessica said. "Where is he?"

"Port side engineering crawl spaces. Section two-fourteen, level D. Just before the main propulsion firewalls."

"No can do, sir," Master Sergeant Anwar told her. "Not directly. We'll have to go down to the dog run, forward, and then back up. Otherwise we'll run right into them. They're conducting a full-on search for you, now. The dog run is our only way to move fore and aft quickly, since they can't get into it."

"How'd you get into it?" Jessica wondered.

"Rossi."

Jessica laughed. "I should've guessed."

The hatch to the Mystic's bridge opened, and a young man and woman stepped inside, followed by an armed guard. Both of them looked at the others in the compartment, their faces full of fear.

"Go back and pick out two more, and wait for my signal," Siggy told the armed escort.

"You got it," the man replied, turning and exiting, closing the hatch behind him.

"Welcome!" Siggy greeted, turning to the nervous young couple. "Are you two...*together*?"

Neither of them answered...they were too nervous to speak.

"Come on, speak up," Siggy instructed, putting his arm around the young woman's shoulders. "Is this your fella?"

"Leave her alone," the young man warned.

"I guess that answers my question, doesn't it?"

Siggy laughed. He stepped back a moment, checking the couple out. "Newlyweds, perhaps?"

Again, neither of them answered.

Siggy looked at Captain Rainey. "A good choice, really. Neither one looks like nobility, so I probably couldn't get much for their ransom. A shame that you're making me kill them. I could've at least sold the young lady to one of those fat, rich bastards on Terrindor. Likely would've gotten a good price, by the looks of her."

"Company security will hunt you all down, and they will kill you and everyone you care about," Captain Rainey seethed.

"Doubtful, considering that the Dusahn control the entire cluster," Siggy laughed. "Oh, that's right. I almost forgot. You've been in the cloud for the last couple weeks. You probably don't know."

"What are you talking about?" Captain Rainey asked.

"Who do you think is offering the reward for jump ships?" Siggy said.

"Then he wasn't lying?" Captain Rainey mused to himself.

"Who wasn't lying?" Siggy wondered, overhearing the captain's mutterings.

"Your cohorts," Captain Rainey replied quickly, speaking up. "The man and woman who came aboard before you. From the Seiiki."

"The *Seiiki*?" Siggy suddenly changed his expression. "That little bastard Tuplo was here? What did he say to you?"

"He tried to warn me about these... *Dusahn,*" Captain Rainey said. "But he said his name was Nathan Scott."

A laugh leapt from Siggy's throat. "*Nathan Scott*?

Na-Tan? The guy has been dead, what, ten years or something? Oh, I have to give it to Connor. That's a pretty original approach, that is." He turned to one of his men. "Can you believe Tuplo?" Siggy suddenly pulled his weapon, turned, and pressed the weapon's muzzle against the young woman's right cheek, forcing her to tip her head to her left, a tiny scream of terror escaping her lips.

"What is your name?" Siggy asked the young man next to her.

"Terig," he replied fearfully. "Terig Espan. Please don't hurt her. We haven't done anything to you."

"Perhaps you should ask the good captain over there. The man who took an oath to keep you all safe."

Terig looked at Captain Rainey, his eyes pleading for help. "Captain..."

"Unlock the jump drive, now!" Siggy ordered.

"I can't," Captain Rainey replied, shaking his head.

"Please..." Terig begged.

"Unlock it, or I swear I will burn a hole right through her head!"

"I CAN'T!" Captain Rainey repeated.

"Captain, please!"

"I SWEAR! I'LL FUCKING WASTE HER!"

"PLEASE!" Terig screamed in desperation as his wife sobbed. "I'LL DO ANYTHING YOU ASK!"

"This is my last warning, Captain!" Siggy announced. "On the count of three, the lady dies!"

"PLEASE!" Terig pleaded with Captain Rainey.

"One!"

"CAPTAIN!" Terig repeated.

"TWO!"

"I'm sorry," Captain Rainey told Terig.

"Oh, God," Terig said, realizing his wife was about to be executed before his eyes.

"THREE!" Siggy yelled, his arm tensing up as he prepared to fire.

"STOP!" Captain Rainey yelled at the top of his lungs.

"UNLOCK IT!"

"I WILL! JUST DON'T HURT THEM!"

"GIVE ME THE CODES!" Siggy shouted.

"Not until you promise me you won't hurt anyone else!" Captain Rainey insisted.

"Give me the codes, and no one else has to die!"

"Alright! Seven seven two, five alpha echo, eight two two, tango one eight." Captain Rainey hung his head low, ashamed that he had given in. But he could not let his passengers be harmed.

"Did you get that?" Siggy asked his helmsman.

"Entering the codes now," he replied.

Jessica dropped the last meter down the ladder into the dog run, following Sergeant Vela and Corporal Rattan. After landing, she stepped aside, then turned to the hatch controls. As soon as Master Sergeant Anwar dropped to the deck, she activated the overhead hatch and secured it, cutting off anyone who didn't have the access codes or a security badge.

"You know the bad guys probably have the crew's security cards, right?"

"Maybe, maybe not," Jessica replied as she turned to head forward. "Better safe than sorry."

"Another Terran witticism," Anwar noted.

"We'll come up behind the garden deck galleys, just aft of the storage lockers," Jessica said as she started down the long corridor. "That should keep us aft of the search parties. Since the passengers don't have access to secured areas, the search parties won't be concentrating on them."

"Unless the search parties are looking for you," Master Sergeant Anwar said.

"Why would they be looking for me?" Jessica wondered. "As far as they know, I'm just some chick in a uniform, running away from scary guys with guns."

"They may think you killed one of their men," Master Sergeant Anwar said, "in rather expert fashion, I might add."

"What happened to ghost ops?" Jessica asked as they continued jogging down the corridor.

"He left me little choice. Besides, we needed the intel."

"Yeah, I'll bet."

"Siggy! I'm picking up the Antilla!" Hamon reported.

"Finally!" Siggy said, relieved. "Tell them to dock on the starboard side and unload the extra men. And send someone to the starboard docking port to let them in!"

"I'm on it."

"I've got control of the jump drive," the helmsman reported.

"Now, we're getting somewhere," Siggy remarked with delight. "I can see the credits piling up now. I'm not sure which is better; turning the ship over to the Dusahn for the reward, or selling it to someone outside the sector."

"Wait..." the helmsman said, double-checking his displays. "Something's wrong..."

"What is it?" Siggy asked.

"The jump drive is down."

"What do you mean, down? He just used it!" Siggy spun around and put his gun to Captain Rainey's face. "What did you do?" he screamed. "Some bogus code that disabled the system?"

"No, no!" Captain Rainey assured him. "We don't even have such a code!"

"Siggy, no!" the helmsman corrected. "He didn't do it. The primaries on the starboard side are shorted out. Somebody pulled the control cards, *while* it was running!"

"What?" Siggy lowered his gun, turning back to look over the helmsman's shoulder at the display. "What about the backups? These ships always have backups."

"They are down, as well. Their control cards are also missing!"

"What about the port jump drives?"

"They are still online, but..."

"Can you use them to jump the ship?"

"Yes, but it will take some time, and our jump range will be greatly reduced."

"Do it!" Siggy raised his comm-unit and keyed his mic. "Someone get to the port engineering crawl spaces and protect the port jump drive!"

"*Right away!*" his comm-unit squawked.

Siggy turned to Captain Rainey, pointing his gun at his face again. "You said Tuplo was on board. What did you do with him?"

Captain Rainey looked confused. "If you mean the man claiming to be Nathan Scott, I had him and his cohort arrested."

"Where are they?" Siggy demanded.

"They escaped during *your* siege of *my* ship," Captain Rainey replied defiantly.

"Watch your tone, Captain," Siggy warned. "Now

that I have full control of your ship, your value is limited."

"Siggy!" the helmsman yelled in despair. "We just lost the port jump drive as well!"

"Well, get it back!" Siggy demanded.

"I can't!" the helmsman replied. "It's completely shorted out, and all the control cards from the backup jump field generators are missing! I can't even power them up!"

"Goddamn it!" Siggy cursed. He paced back and forth a moment. "It's got to be Tuplo! That little son of a bitch! I should've killed him back on Haven!" Siggy raised his comm-unit to his mouth and keyed the mic, yelling into the device. "Find Connor Tuplo and bring him to me! *ALIVE*!"

Nathan stepped back from the smoking jump field generators as they shut down. Occasional sparks erupted from inside the control card bays on both primary jump drives. He dropped the last two control cards into the toolbox, picked it up, and headed toward the exit. His next order of business was to hide it. His second order was to find Jessica.

* * *

"Jump complete," Loki announced as the Seiiki's cockpit windows cycled back to clear. "I've got a Reaper at one four seven, twenty-one down relative at two thousand kilometers."

"*Seiiki, Seiiki. This is Reaper Two,*" the voice called over comms.

"Go for Seiiki," Vladimir replied, standing behind Josh and Loki.

"*Reaper One is running stealth, tracking the Mystic. Prepare to receive coordinates.*"

"I've got multiple jump flashes," Loki reported. "Four more Reapers and a cargo shuttle."

"Seiiki to strike team. Prepare to receive final jump coordinates," Vladimir announced. "Reaper Two, Seiiki. Transmit to all units when ready."

"*Roger that,*" Reaper One replied.

"Seiiki will jump in first, as planned," Vladimir said.

"Why is it the guys with only two guns go in first?" Josh wondered.

"Hey, you're the one who always craves excitement," Loki quipped. "Getting soft in your old age?"

"Look who's talking about *old age*, family man."

"We're receiving coordinates," Vladimir noted.

"Calculating jump plot," Loki replied.

"Guns ready?" Vladimir asked over his comm-set.

"*Starboard gun, ready,*" Marcus reported.

"*Port gun, ready,*" Dalen added.

"Boarding party, ready?"

"*Boarding party, ready,*" Sergeant Torken replied.

"Jump plotted and ready," Loki announced.

"Turning to jump course," Josh added.

Vladimir took in a deep breath, letting it out slowly. *So, this is what it's like to take a ship into battle,* he thought in amazement.

* * *

"Siggy! I've got a contact... It just jumped in. Off our port side, about two hundred kilometers and closing fast," Donnel announced from the Mystic's helm station.

"Can you confirm that?" Siggy asked, turning toward Hamon.

Hamon looked confused. "How, exactly?"

"The sensor station," Siggy urged him, pointing.

"One hundred kilometers, decelerating," Donnel reported.

Hamon stared at the sensor display on the side of the bridge as he tried to figure out the controls. "This is all in Takaran," Hamon said.

"You don't read Takaran?" Siggy asked in surprise.

"It's been a while," Hamon replied. "Give me a minute."

"Fifty kilometers."

"Is the Antilla docked?" Siggy asked over his comm-unit.

"She just made hard dock," one of his men answered. "We're cycling the airlock now."

"Hurry it up," Siggy instructed. "We've got company."

* * *

"Ten kilometers!" Loki reported.

"That ship is still hard docked," Vladimir said. "Can you guys hit it without hitting the Mystic?"

"Just tell Itchy and Twitchy to hold'er steady, and I'll let ya know," Marcus replied.

"Five kilometers," Loki reported.

"You might wanna have Dalen take the shot," Josh teased. "The old man's eyes ain't what they used to be."

"Slow us down, so he has *time* to shoot," Vladimir suggested.

"Increasing deceleration thrust."

"They're bringing their rail guns onto us," Loki warned.

"Forward shields are at full power," Vladimir assured them.

"Those shields are for dust and small rocks," Josh reminded him. "If those rounds are charged..."

"Do you have another idea, Joshua?" Vladimir asked impatiently.

"I dunno... Maybe let the guys with *real* guns and shields do the attacking? Silly, I know, but..."

"Deception is the idea, here, Josh," Loki reminded him.

"I know," Josh insisted. "Doesn't mean I have to like it."

"Two kilometers," Loki announced.

"I should have stayed on the Aurora," Vladimir muttered to himself.

"They're firing rail guns," Loki warned. A second later, dozens of tiny flashes of light appeared in front of them as rail gun slugs slammed into their forward shields. Another second after that, those same slugs, with ninety percent of their kinetic energy removed, bounced harmlessly off the Seiiki's hull.

"Holy shit!" Josh exclaimed. He turned to look over his shoulder at Vladimir. "Those fuckers *were* charged! How the hell did you do that?"

"It's all about cycling the polarity," Vladimir explained proudly. "Really quickly." He tapped his comm-set. "Fire away, guys."

"*Firing!*" Marcus replied.

"Transmitting burst message," Vladimir announced as bolts of plasma energy streaked past the cockpit on either side from the gun turrets mounted aft of them. He glanced out the forward window as the plasma bolts collided harmlessly against the enemy ship's shields.

"*Direct hits!*" Marcus bragged.

"Not that it did any good," Josh added.

"Target is breaking dock with the Mystic," Loki reported as the Seiiki streaked over the top of the enemy ship and the Mystic Empress.

"Dumping energy from the starboard jump field generator," Vladimir reported. "Hopefully, that will fool them."

"Or doom us," Josh added.

"Just don't accelerate," Vladimir reminded him. "And it would help if you flew a little, *sloppy*."

"I don't know how," Josh quipped. "Maybe you should have Loki do it."

"Funny," Loki replied.

* * *

"Sensors confirm, it's the Seiiki," Hamon announced from the Mystic's sensor station.

"No shit," Siggy said as he watched the Seiiki streak above them from starboard to port. "How the bloody hell did they find us? I'm bettin' that little bastard heard about our plans and decided he'd try to get hold of this ship before we did. Well, that's not gonna happen!"

"*The Antilla has completed her offloading,*" one of his men reported over Siggy's comm-unit.

"And tell her to take out the Seiiki!" Siggy ordered. "I want that damned ship destroyed!"

Nathan grabbed an overhead handhold and held on tightly, causing his legs to swing under him in the weightless environment of the Mystic's port engineering crawl spaces. Once he had stopped his forward momentum, he pulled himself upward between two large ducts, and wedged the toolbox containing the control cards above one of the ducts, out of sight. Once he was convinced it was secure, he pushed himself back down into the passage space and continued inboard, toward the distant hatch that would return him to the Mystic's main decks.

Jessica led the group of five Ghatazhak down the corridor, coming to a stop at the intersection. She took a quick peek around the corner, pulling back almost immediately. "Fuck," she whispered.

Master Sergeant Anwar looked quizzically at her.

"That *other* ship you were talking about? I think they are already here. I just saw at least twenty men heading aft."

"Fuck." The master sergeant touched his comm-control on the side of his helmet. "Morano, Anwar. You and Rossi become invisible and stay that way until you hear from me. You've got twenty more bad guys coming up from behind you."

"*Copy that.*"

"Maybe we can still make it past them?" the master sergeant suggested. "They may outnumber us, but..."

"We'll win the battle, but lose the fight," Jessica argued. "The moment we open up, they'll come from all over the ship. Our only hope is to go back down and use the dog run. Half of us go aft, the other half stay forward. Make them split forces, then we both fall back into the dog run and head to the middle and pop up and help Morano and Rossi free the prisoners. With all of them running around, it might give us just enough chaos to get the upper hand on these goons."

"You're going to lose a lot of noncombatants that way, Lieutenant."

"It's a fucking war, Deno," Jessica reminded him.

"Yeah, I know. I'm just making sure you're okay with that. You Terrans are all warm and cuddly that way, you know."

"Fuck you," she replied, noticing the master sergeant's grin.

"I'm getting a burst transmission," Sergeant Vela announced.

Jessica and the master sergeant turned to look at the sergeant. "From who?" Jessica asked.

"The Seiiki."

"Wait, I'm getting it too," the master sergeant said.

"They're here?"

"Apparently," Sergeant Vela said. "And they have a plan."

* * *

"Sloppy, Josh, sloppy!" Vladimir reminded him.

"I'm trying!"

"They're thrusting away and turning to follow us," Loki reported.

"Keep firing," Vladimir urged. "We have to lure them away from the Mystic!"

"They're turning toward us," Loki warned. "If they get their missile tubes on us, our only defense will be to jump."

"Not until they are clear of the Mystic!" Vladimir insisted. "Josh, dive us down, so they have to pass over the top of the Mystic and turn down to get us in their sights. And Loki, be ready to jump."

"You bet," Loki replied as Josh pitched the ship downward.

* * *

Jessica peeked from below the deck, just enough to be able to see the guards at the far end of the corridor. She lowered herself back down the ladder, just enough to remain out of sight, as Master Sergeant Anwar handed her a small grenade. She took the grenade and held it in her hand, her finger hovering over the activation button, while she watched the master sergeant for her cue.

"Ready, Vela?"

"*Ready.*"

"Three......two......one......execute."

Jessica depressed the button on top of the small, round grenade, then tossed it into the deck above, so that it rolled quickly toward the guards at the end of the corridor. A second after she tossed it, she heard the guards yelling. Their cries of alert were cut short by a sudden, shrill noise and a flash of blinding, white light.

Jessica ran the rest of the way up the ladder, stepping onto the deck and firing in the direction of the stunned guards as she moved to the side wall to make room for the master sergeant.

Master Sergeant Anwar leapt up to the deck, with the help of his assistive body suit, and opened fire immediately, sweeping from side to side. A few bolts of energy came from the direction of the guards, but all were wide of their targets. The initial attack was over in five seconds, and five seconds after that, Jessica and Master Sergeant Anwar found themselves standing over the bodies of the dead men who had been guarding the forward entrance to the port shuttle bay.

"Clear forward," Master Sergeant Anwar reported.

"*Clear aft,*" Sergeant Vela replied. "*Taking up defensive positions.*"

Master Sergeant Anwar tapped the comm-panel on the side of his helmet. "Seiiki, Anwar. Port door is open."

* * *

"They've got a clear shot!" Loki warned.

"Can I stop flying sloppy now?" Josh exclaimed.

"Two missiles inbound!" Loki warned. "Ten seconds!"

"Evasive!" Vladimir ordered.

"Finally!" Josh said as he twisted his flight control stick and put the Seiiki into a spiraling, climbing turn to the left.

"Five seconds!"

"Seven jump flashes!" Vladimir reported. "Jump!"

"Jumping!" Loki replied, pressing the jump button.

The Seiiki's windows turned opaque, clearing a moment later.

"Jump complete," Loki reported. "Twenty light seconds!"

"Turning hard!" Josh added.

"Reapers are engaging," Vladimir reported. "The missiles and the target!"

"Hell, yeah!" Josh yelled as he continued to maneuver to prevent the missiles from getting a new lock on them.

"Missiles are down!" Vladimir reported. "Turn us back toward the Mystic and prepare to jump again."

"Turning around!" Josh replied.

"Loading the next jump," Loki added.

"*Seiiki, Reaper One. Target destroyed. You're in the clear.*"

"Seiiki copies." Vladimir reported. "Take us in above her bridge."

"Jumping in five seconds," Loki reported.

* * *

Nathan unlocked the access hatch that led from the Mystic's port side engineering crawl spaces back into her main engineering decks. A sudden feeling of doom swept through him, but before he could react, the hatch swung open wide, and two men with large-bore energy rifles pointed directly at him appeared.

Nathan looked at the two men. "Well, at least you're not Dusahn."

* * *

An Alliance cargo shuttle jumped in five hundred meters away from the Mystic's port side, slightly below her. It moved in swiftly, rotating around to aim its aft end toward the luxury liner's port shuttle bay.

The shuttle continued to move closer while its cargo ramp lowered. As it closed within fifty meters, the shuttle bay doors began to open, and the shuttle fired its docking thrusters to further slow down its rate of closure on the much larger ship.

The shuttle's cargo ramp, now level with its interior decks and the doors to the Mystic's shuttle bay, fully opened. Thirty Ghatazhak soldiers in fully pressurized battle gear ran out onto the cargo shuttle's ramp in two lines, jumping off the end of the ramp out into space, putting themselves on a course toward the cruise ship fewer than one hundred meters away.

Once the last man had stepped off the cargo shuttle's aft ramp, the shuttle fired its docking thrusters again, ending their drift toward the Mystic, ensuring that they maintained a safe distance from the group of drifting Ghatazhak soldiers.

"Siggy!" Donnel called from the helm. "The Antilla has been destroyed!"

"What?"

"And I'm picking up six ships. I've never seen anything like them!"

"Make that seven," Hamon added from the sensor station.

"Who are they?" Siggy demanded.

"I have no idea," Hamon replied.

"One of them is bigger and maneuvering more slowly," Donnel reported. "Probably some kind of shuttle. I'd guess a cargo shuttle by her size."

"The other six are moving fast. Two of them are coming right for us!" Hamon added.

"Hell, they're all coming toward us!" Donnel corrected.

"Who the fuck is this?" Siggy demanded to know.

"They're probably company security, coming to kill you all," Captain Rainey gloated.

"How the bloody, fucking hell did they find out so fast?"

"I launched a distress buoy when you first attacked," Captain Rainey admitted.

"You son of a bitch!" Siggy punched the captain in the face, knocking him to the deck, then started kicking him repeatedly in the face and torso.

Captain Rainey didn't care. If he died now, at least he would die knowing that the man who killed him would soon fall.

Two Reapers jumped in fewer than five hundred meters from the Mystic Empress, above and to either side. They swooped in quickly, expertly placing breach boxes on both sides of the command deck, before disconnecting and thrusting away.

The breach box shuddered violently as it made contact with the Mystic's hull, shaking the six Ghatazhak soldiers inside.

The Ghatazhak squad leader seated next to the control panel waited for the display to indicate that the breach box was securely attached to the hull before activating the automated device that placed a shaped explosive charge against it. "Fire in the hole," he announced over his helmet comms.

The breach box shook again as the shaped charge blasted a tunnel through the Mystic's multi-layered hull beneath them. The squad leader pressed another button, and the telescoping boarding tunnel extended through the breach and into the deck inside.

One more green light, and they had a way in. "Here we go," the squad leader announced. He pressed the hatch button, and the meter-wide, round hatch beneath them split down the middle, the halves sliding into the floor below.

The squad leader watched as each man stepped into the center and pushed himself down through the boarding tunnel with just enough force for the artificial gravity of the deck below to pull them the rest of the way down.

As each man landed, he entered into a crouch, weapon held up and ready to fire, then moved off in a different direction to clear the way for the next man.

Finally, the squad leader landed in the middle of his perfectly deployed squad. "Move out," he ordered.

The entire process of breaching the hull and putting six men on board had taken less than a minute.

Two by two, the drifting Ghatazhak soldiers passed the shuttle bay threshold, and the bay's steadily increasing gravity pulled them to the deck. Each man landed in a run, continuing inward across the deck to make room for the men behind them.

As the last man touched down, the doors began to close. The soldiers moved quickly to the main interior door, which opened as if on cue, revealing a depressurized entry foyer. The men entered, their weapons held up and ready. Once all thirty were inside, the door behind them closed, and the repressurization cycle began.

The platoon leader watched the environmental display, waiting until the compartment was fifty percent pressurized before he unsealed his helmet and discarded the maneuvering jets on his calves and forearms, finally unslinging his life support pack and dropping it on the deck.

At seventy-five percent pressure, the Ghatazhak sergeant on the other side of the door overrode the safeties and caused the interior hatch to open early, allowing the thirty men to enter the Mystic Empress.

Nathan was pushed roughly out of the port elevator by his armed captors as they entered the Mystic's command deck. They continued inward toward the main entrance to the bridge, but were taken by surprise by six men in flat black body armor, carrying military, assault-style plasma rifles.

One man fell immediately, taking a burst of plasma to both his head and chest. The man next to him also crumpled to the ground, taking a single shot to his abdomen. The second man returned fire as he fell, as did the third man next to him, while the fourth man grabbed Nathan and shoved him forcefully down the corridor, causing Nathan to stumble and fall to the deck.

"Get up!" the fourth man ordered, grabbing Nathan by the collar and yanking him to his feet. Another shove sent Nathan stumbling into the arms of two more men running around the corner.

"Get him to Siggy!" the fourth man ordered. "We'll deal with these assholes!"

He couldn't have been more mistaken.

The main garden deck burst into chaos as energy weapons fire rang out from all directions. Red-orange bolts of plasma streaked from every corner of the massive, open space, striking down many of the unsuspecting guards before they could react. But there were now at least twenty men positioned all around the prisoners, and they were on all three levels.

Ghatazhak soldiers ran out into the middle of the gardens, dodging and weaving in impossibly random patterns to avoid being easily targeted. Bolts of energy, both large and small, peppered the garden around them, slamming into the deck, the grass, the trees... Everything organic that the bolts of energy touched either melted or burst into flames. Burning branches fell from the trees, landing around the Ghatazhak as they moved quickly and chaotically across the gardens, charging toward the opposite side, despite the barrage of weapons fire raining down upon them.

Three Ghatazhak fell to enemy fire, but for every man that fell, three more gathered around him, returning the attack as they protected him with their own armor, and dragged their fallen comrade to safety.

The Ghatazhak moved like a wave across the garden. Passengers and crew alike ran in all directions, fleeing for their lives as death came from all directions. Five, ten, twenty fell as bolts of energy slammed into their heads, torsos, and appendages.

The air quickly filled with the smell of burning wood, melted flesh, and burnt hair. Within seconds, the Ghatazhak reached the far side of the garden and engaged the retreating pirates face-to-face. Fists struck, and combat knives flashed, as Ghatazhak soldiers brutally cut their opponents down.

The battle lasted only two minutes.

Nathan fell to his hands and knees, after being tossed through the hatch onto the Mystic's bridge. Two booted feet stepped up to him.

"Well, well, well. Who do we have here?" a familiar voice said.

Nathan looked up. "Siggy." He shook his head in disgust as he looked back down at the deck. "Why am I not surprised?"

Being the only Ghatazhak without any armor, Jessica was the last person to enter the garden deck. "All passengers and crew, get to your escape pods and await orders to launch!" she barked at the top of her lungs. She walked up to Master Sergeant Anwar, who was standing in the middle of the garden deck, watching his men treat the wounded. "Deno, get the wounded to the starboard docking port, and get them ready to load onto the cargo shuttle."

"Right away, sir," Master Sergeant Anwar replied.

"How many of our men are down?"

"Two dead, eight wounded," the master sergeant replied. "We've taken six prisoners, as well."

"Inject them with paralytics and get them on the cargo shuttle. I'm sure the general will want to interrogate them later."

"Understood."

"*Nash, Todd,*" the master sergeant called over Jessica's comm-set. "*Teams One and Two are in position outside the bridge. It's locked down.*"

"Breach it and kill everyone with a gun," Jessica ordered.

"*Sir, they've got Captain Scott.*"

"Understood," Jessica replied. "Hold position. I'm on my way."

"*Understood.*"

"Seiiki squad!" Jessica barked. "With me! Let's move!"

"Seems to me the last time we spoke, you were threatening me. Something about 'feeling the heat of your guys' guns.'" Siggy turned to Hamon. "Wasn't it something like that?"

"I believe it was, Siggy," Hamon agreed.

"So, tell me, Connor. Where are your *boys* and their *guns* now, huh?" Siggy drove his boot into Nathan's gut as hard as he could. "Hiding just outside the door, are they?" He kicked him again. "Where is that old fart, Marcus, and that stupid little twit, Dalen?" Another kick, this time to Nathan's face, sending blood and spit flying from his mouth. "Maybe you even brought that whore, Neli!" Siggy turned to Hamon. "She's not bad on the eyes, though. Maybe she could provide us with a brief respite, eh?" Siggy laughed, spinning around on one heel and giving Nathan another kick to the torso.

Jessica ran up behind the Ghatazhak positioned in the corridor outside the Mystic's bridge. "Sit rep?" she asked as she approached.

"Seven bodies inside," Master Sergeant Todd replied. "One front and center at the helm. One to the starboard side, at the sensor station, two standing in the aft, starboard corner, and one in the middle walking around erratically. *That* one is most likely the leader."

"The other two?"

"Both on the floor. One near the helm, and one further back, closer to the door. The leader has been kicking the guy on the deck closer to the entrance for the last minute or so."

"What about the two in the corner?" Jessica wondered. "Who are they?"

"I'm guessing hostages. Probably bridge staff."

"You got ears?"

"We're working on it," the master sergeant replied. "Thick bulkheads, and only the single hatch to get in. I got a man working on rewiring the intercom to turn it into a listening device."

"No auxiliary hatch? No vents?" Jessica asked.

"Totally sealed. Self-supporting. Power and life support. We can't even gas them."

"What about the hatch?"

"Easy enough to blow with a shaped charge, but getting in without killing Scott is going to be tricky." Master Sergeant Todd looked at Jessica. "What about engineering?"

"They're ready to take it as soon as I give the order," Jessica explained. "I figure we'll take both at the same time, so as not to spook either. Better to let them think they have the upper hand for as long as possible."

"Where the hell did *you* of all people get your hands on so many jump ships?" Siggy demanded. "You know how long it took me to secure the Antilla?" Siggy looked up in frustration. "Do you realize how much it's going to cost me to pay off her owner for her loss?"

"You could always kill him," Nathan sputtered as he tried to catch his breath.

"Did you just make a joke, Tuplo?" Siggy laughed. "I didn't think you had it in you. I can't remember ever seeing you even crack a smile."

"I don't smile much when assholes are around."

Siggy grabbed Nathan by the hair and pulled him up to his knees. "Do you really think it's wise to be insulting the very man who holds your pitiful life in his hands, Connor?"

"My name's not Connor," Nathan growled.

"Oh, that's right. It's Nathan Scott, isn't it?" Siggy laughed, standing again. "Or at least that's the scam you were trying to pull on the captain over there." Siggy looked at Captain Rainey. "You still with us, Captain?" He looked back at Nathan. "Yes, he's still with us. What exactly do you think you're doing here, Connor? How did you hear about my plans, huh? Who tipped you off?"

"I didn't know about your plans, Siggy," Nathan replied. "And my name's not Connor. It's Scott. Captain Nathan Scott."

"*We've got ears,*" Corporal Shapira reported over comms. "*Piping it through now.*"

"*I didn't know about your plans, Siggy. And my name's not Connor. It's Scott. Captain Nathan Scott.*"

"What the hell is he doing?" Master Sergeant Anwar wondered.

"*I have to admit, you do kind of look like him...*" another voice said over the intercom.

"He's buying us time," Jessica realized. "He knows we're out here. I don't know how he knows, but he knows, trust me. He probably knows we're listening to him as well."

"...Only younger. Probably because you shaved the beard off."

"Charges are set," Master Sergeant Todd reported. "And our strike teams are ready to take engineering on your order, Lieutenant."

"I'm telling you, Siggy, I'm him. I'm Na-Tan."

"Tell everyone to be ready. I'll call the go as soon as Nathan gives us the cue."

"The savior of us all?" the man laughed.

"Yes, sir," Master Sergeant Todd replied, turning away to pass the word.

"I totally misjudged you, Tuplo. You not only have a sense of humor, you're a fucking riot, you are!"

"How can you be sure?" Master Sergeant Anwar asked Jessica, keeping his voice low.

"I know Nathan. He always finds a way. We just have to wait for him to do it."

"...And I have to admit, it's a pretty clever, little plan. Not as good as mine, of course, but it does have the advantage of simplicity. Who knows? It even might have worked, if *I* hadn't come along."

Nathan scanned the room as Siggy gloated, noting that there were only two other, armed men in the room besides Siggy, and both of them seemed preoccupied with other tasks. He also noticed a red light on the intercom on the bulkhead next to the entry hatch.

There was still one problem. Although the man and woman standing in the corner were well out of the line of fire, Captain Rainey was on his knees, directly to the left of Siggy. If any of the Ghatazhak shots missed Siggy, they would likely hit the captain. Even if they didn't miss, the Ghatazhak weapons were powerful and would likely burn through Siggy's skinny body in a flash.

Nathan rolled onto his hands and knees. "You've got no way out, Siggy." He sat back on his knees, looking at him. "My ships have you surrounded, your jump drives are offline, and I'm the only one who can restore them. To make matters worse, my men are outside that hatch, waiting to cut you all down on my command."

"Anyone comes through that hatch, and the first shot goes through your head, Tuplo," Siggy threatened.

"There is another way," Nathan told him. "Surrender now, and I'll let you and your men go free. I'll give you an escape pod, and you can program it to take you anywhere you want to go."

"No way," Siggy refused. "I'm in this too deep. Too many people are expecting their cut."

"I'm sorry to hear that, Siggy," Nathan said. "But you should have thought about this possibility. Program the pod to take you to another sector. One that doesn't have a jump drive yet. You can sell them the one from the pod. That should give you enough seed money to start over somewhere else, right?"

"What are you, daft?" Siggy laughed mockingly. "I'm not going to another sector. I'm taking the bloody ship back to the Dusahn and collecting my reward, and I'll likely get a bonus for turning you over, as well."

"It's not going to happen," Nathan insisted. "This ship isn't going anywhere unless I say so."

"Then you'd better start talking, Tuplo!" Siggy threatened, grabbing Nathan by the neck and moving behind to use him as cover in case someone did burst through the door. "Anyone comes through that hatch, and I'll burn a hole through his fucking brain!" Siggy yelled to anyone listening in the corridor.

Nathan reached up and grabbed Siggy's jacket, pulling him forward and bending at the waist. "NOW!" Nathan shouted as Siggy came tumbling forward over him.

There was a sudden explosion, and the hatch flew inward, striking Siggy as he tried to get back up, knocking him to one side. A split second later, two bright flashes of light, and a terrible high-pitched squeal.

Captain Rainey summoned what little strength he had left, to throw himself into the man at the helm as the man pulled his weapon to shoot Nathan in the back.

Several energy blasts rang out, ricocheting across the room. Several more came from the direction of the hatch as men dressed in flat black combat armor came charging in, weapons firing with precision. Screams came from the corner of the room, likely from the hostages.

Siggy rolled over and raised his weapon to fire at Captain Rainey, who was going for the gun of Siggy's helmsman, but Nathan managed to stumble into the line of fire, taking the energy blast in the shoulder, causing him to spin around.

Nathan twisted, letting the momentum from the energy blast in his shoulder carry him full circle, coming to land with his elbow in Siggy's face. He rolled over Siggy, grabbing his gun from the deck as he came up onto his knees, the gun now trained on Siggy.

The Ghatazhak filled the room. Nathan looked at Captain Rainey. "Are you alright, Captain?"

"No, not at all," the captain replied weakly, rolling onto his back to rest. "But I'll survive."

Nathan looked back at Siggy. "I should have fucking killed you back on Haven when I had the chance. Then, none of this would have happened."

Siggy's eyes widened as Nathan pointed the weapon at his face and pulled the trigger.

Blood and tissue spewed in all directions from the point-blank blast from Nathan's energy pistol.

"Are you alright?" Jessica asked Nathan, stepping up beside him.

"No..." Nathan replied, turning to look at her.

He flashed that same old smile, the one that Jessica imagined always got him out of trouble when Nathan was a child.

"...But I'll survive," he added, dropping the weapon to his side.

CHAPTER TEN

Nathan sat on the deck of the Mystic's bridge, enjoying the view out her forward windows and across her bow, while one of the Ghatazhak's combat medics treated the wound on his left shoulder. He felt a sudden, sharp pain as the medic pulled away the burnt fabric of his overcoat and shirt, trying to separate the layers of fabric from the charred skin beneath.

"The anesthetic will take effect shortly," the medic promised. "But I have to separate this fabric from your wound as soon as possible, to prevent complications later."

"Do what you have to do," Nathan replied, preparing himself for the worst. He turned his gaze back outside, trying to ignore the pain by distracting himself with the Mystic Empress's beautiful lines. As Connor Tuplo, he had heard many stories about the famed luxury liner. He had even entered a contest once to win free passage for two. Never in his wildest dreams had he imagined that he would even set foot on this ship, let alone be sitting on her bridge after fighting off pirate boarding parties.

Once again, he was faced with the strange dichotomy that was his life. Both as Nathan Scott and as Connor Tuplo, he had sought to become an obscure unknown...someone operating day in and day out, without being noticed by the public at large. Yet, as either man, he had failed miserably in that goal. He was beginning to realize that fate had never intended for him to have a life of ease and anonymity, and it seemed determined to hand him the opposite at every turn.

Perhaps it was time for him to face up to that fact, and to embrace it.

"How's the shoulder?" Jessica asked, sitting down next to him.

"I suppose it looks a lot worse than it really is," Nathan replied, watching the medic working on him.

"No, it's as bad as it looks," the medic corrected. "But it will heal. I'll give you a general nanite booster to get the process started. They'll clean the wound up surgically when you get back to the Aurora."

"At least I'll get a week off," Nathan said wryly.

"Don't count on it," Jessica warned him.

"Everything secure?" Nathan asked her.

"First sweep of the ship is complete, and we've got about thirty Ghatazhak on board now."

"How many casualties did we have?" Nathan wondered.

"Two dead, eleven wounded. Fifteen dead among the passengers and crew, and another twenty or so wounded. Some of them are being treated by the Mystic's medical staff. The rest are being evac'd back to the Aurora. I've got Rainey's family on their way here."

"Good thinking," Nathan replied.

"I told the Mystic's cheng where to find the control cards. He says he can have the backup jump field generators up within the hour."

"Is that going to be fast enough?" Nathan wondered. "Captain Rainey launched a distress jump comm-drone as soon as he was boarded, so the Dusahn are probably on their way."

"Yeah, but as far as we know, they can't jump any further per jump than we can, so it would take them nearly a day to get here."

"They can send smaller ships more quickly," Nathan reminded her.

"That's why the Avendahl's fighters are here," Jessica replied. "Between them, the Reapers, and the sixteen Super Eagles that the Morsiko-Tavi ferried over, we should be okay."

"Nice work," Nathan commented.

"What are we going to do with the remaining passengers?" Jessica wondered.

"How many of them are there?"

"Just over two hundred of them, plus another one hundred and sixty crew," Jessica told him. "We got them all out of their escape pods and had them gather in the forward observation deck, away from the mayhem of the garden deck, so that we could get a count and see to any of their needs. But we're going to have to tell them what's going on. They don't even know about the Dusahn, yet."

"I'll tell them," Nathan said firmly.

"Are you up to it?"

Nathan looked at the medic. "Are we done here?"

"I just need to apply a sling and restraint, to keep you from moving your arm and shoulder while the wound-assist sets up," the medic explained. "A couple more minutes and you'll be on your way."

"Can I get you anything while you wait?" Jessica asked.

"A bottle of water would be nice," Nathan replied.

* * *

Nathan and Jessica entered Captain Rainey's office, stepping to one side, quietly waiting while one of the medics treated his wounds.

After a few minutes, the medic finished applying ointments and covering the minor lacerations on the captain's head and face.

Captain Rainey opened his eyes, taking notice of Nathan and Jessica standing in the corner, as the medic rose to depart.

"How's he doing?" Nathan asked the medic.

"Lacerations, contusions, a few broken ribs. He'll be sore for a few days, and he'll have to stay off his feet, but he'll be fine," the medic replied. "If you'll excuse me, sirs, I have more people to treat."

Nathan nodded to the medic as the man departed.

"Told you I'd survive," Captain Rainey said, closing his eyes again.

"That you did," Nathan replied.

Captain Rainey sighed. "Then, it's all true."

"I'm afraid it is," Nathan replied.

"And my family?"

"On their way here," Jessica promised. "They should be arriving shortly."

Captain Rainey opened his eyes again. His expression was a mixture of relief and doubt. "I haven't agreed to anything, yet."

"We were never holding your family hostage, Captain," Nathan said. "I told you that from the beginning."

"That you did."

"I am far from perfect," Nathan admitted, "but I am a man of my word, which, according to my father, is the true measure of a man."

The captain closed his eyes again, his head throbbing. "Then you really are Na-Tan."

"I don't know about that, but I *am* Nathan Scott. If that makes me Na-Tan, then so be it. All I know is that I intend to lead the rebellion against the Dusahn."

Captain Rainey thought for a moment. "And what

do you intend to do with my ship, should I agree to join you?"

"It will be used primarily as a residential area, for the families of those serving on our ships. We will use your kitchens to help feed our people, and your medical facilities to help our wounded recuperate. There is a lot we can do with your ship, Captain."

"And you'll protect it?"

"Of course."

"Will it be put in harm's way?"

"Not intentionally, no, but I'm not going to lie to you. The Dusahn will be actively hunting us, and they will not stop until they find and destroy us."

"If all you say is true, Captain, we are already a hunted ship," Captain Rainey pointed out.

"That is true," Jessica agreed. "But at least with us, the owners of your vessel have a *chance* to someday get their property back. If you turn this ship over to the Dusahn, her owners will *never* get their investment back."

"So, in a roundabout way, you'd be protecting the owner's property."

Captain Rainey looked doubtful. "In a *very* roundabout way," he replied. "What about my crew? What about the passengers still on board?"

"They will all get to make their own choices," Nathan promised. "Anyone who wishes to return to their homes will be allowed to do so, without prejudice."

"And what will you do if the entire crew decides to leave?"

"We can always train a new crew," Nathan said. "But, it would be helpful if at least some of your officers stayed behind."

Captain Rainey looked at the picture of his wife

and son on his desk. "Can you do it?" he wondered. His gaze returned to Captain Scott. "Can you defeat these *Dusahn*?"

"They have no more ships than Caius did," Nathan replied. "And we have far more firepower than we did back then."

"But they have jump drives, do they not?"

"That they do," Nathan admitted. "But that doesn't make them invincible."

"But *can* you do it?"

"I cannot promise that we can," Nathan told him. "All I can promise is that I will either *succeed*, or I will *die* in the effort."

"I don't suppose anyone can ask more than that of you," Captain Rainey agreed, his eyes shifting back to the photo. "But how do I choose?"

"Ask yourself this one question, Captain. What world do you wish your son to grow up in?"

Jessica turned away a moment, her hand to her comm-set as she listened to an incoming message. "Your family is on their way up, Captain."

Nathan could see the tears forming in Captain Rainey's eyes. He had nearly lost his family and not even known it. He had nearly made his wife a widow and his son fatherless. The captain must've been overwhelmed.

Captain Rainey rose, slowly at first, wincing from the pain as he stood. "Help me with my jacket," he asked.

Jessica stepped over and picked up Captain Rainey's uniform jacket, carefully helping him put it on as he prepared to receive his family. Once the jacket was on, she helped him button it, then brushed it smooth.

As she stepped back, the door opened, and Captain

Rainey's wife and son ran into the room, throwing their arms around him. The captain grimaced from the pain as he embraced the people most important to him. And as tears of happiness flowed down his cheeks, he made his decision.

Captain Rainey looked at Nathan as he held his family close. "The Mystic Empress will join your fleet, just as soon as we are able to jump."

"Thank you, Captain," Nathan replied, nodding.

"Will you speak to the crew and passengers for me?"

"It would be my honor, sir."

* * *

Birk could no longer feel his hands or feet. Had his respirator not been strapped to his face, he would have drowned in the spiced wine long ago. He wasn't even sure he had remained conscious the entire time. The minutes had become hours, all eventually running together. He knew that his breather had a limited duration, and it must be approaching its limit. But what would he do when those limits were reached? What would he do when he tried to draw his next breath, and nothing came? He was completely submerged in the purple liquid, and it was pitch black inside the barrel where he was imprisoned.

Was this merely an alternate form of execution, thought up by some sick and twisted Dusahn mind? Were he and Cuddy sitting in a vast collection of barrels in some warehouse, all of them loaded with hapless victims who thought they were becoming freedom fighters?

Birk had tested his container on several occasions over the past few hours, but nothing budged. Not the lid, not the walls, and certainly not the floor. Of course, he had never really given it all his strength, for fear that if he really were being smuggled out of the city to safety, he might be discovered and *really* executed.

And so, he continued to rock in his cramped chamber, submerged in the pungent, purple liquid that had always been so popular at parties with his college friends. He was confident in one thing; they *were* moving. He could hear the drone of the truck's engine and felt every bump in the road.

At first, their journey had been stop-and-go, with long waits at the various checkpoints as they made their way through the city of Aitkenna. But for the longest time, their travel had been at a fairly constant rate, with only an occasional stop lasting less than a minute or two.

Recently, Birk was sure they were traveling up a mountainous road. He had clearly felt the constant turning back and forth, as well as the uphill angle. More than once, he feared he would vomit into his own mouthpiece, but each time, he managed to force the nausea back down.

Lately, he had been so thirsty that he had taken to pulling tiny sips of the spice wine surrounding him in through the corners of his mouth. Were they to travel much longer, he would be too inebriated to stand.

Birk felt himself nodding off. He struggled to stay awake, wondering how much of his overwhelming fatigue was chemically induced.

The motion of the vehicle came to another stop. Birk waited, expecting the vehicle to begin moving again at any moment, just as it always did. Instead, he felt a *thump*. He waited, and then there was another thump, but this one was closer, and more distinct. And he thought he heard something...

Voices!

Birk was suddenly wide awake. Were they finally at their destination? Or was this just another checkpoint?

Birk felt the wave of hope quickly fade, and then surge back. They had been on the road for hours. Surely, they were no longer in Aitkenna.

More thumps, then his barrel began to move, but not in the same way as before. Someone was tipping the barrel slightly to one side, and rolling it. He heard a vibration in the water, and in the walls of the barrel. Something mechanical, like a small electric motor. It repeated over and over, in short bursts. Then it happened. The lid was removed.

Two hands grabbed his soaking wet shirt and pulled him to his feet. Men held him from either side, helping him stay upright after spending hours stuffed inside the barrel, submerged in spiced wine.

Another man stepped up and pulled the mouthpiece out, allowing Birk to take in his first breath of fresh air in what seemed like forever. It was dark outside, with very little illumination provided by the headlights of several vehicles.

Birk coughed and sputtered, clearing the wine from his mouth and throat. "Oh, God," he begged, "please don't put me back in there."

"Don't worry," the man in front of him said. "No one will put you back in there. Your journey is over."

"Where's my friend?" Birk asked, looking around.

"He's right behind you."

Birk tried to turn his head, but could not see behind him. "Cuddy?"

"*I'm here!*"

"Are you alright?"

"*I'm okay!*"

"Oh, thank God!"

"Look at me," the man instructed him. "I need you to focus for a moment."

Birk turned back to look at the man standing in front of him.

"We're going to take you inside, remove your clothing, and get you a hot shower. After that, we'll feed you and let you rest. Do you understand?"

"Yes, I think so," Birk replied. "Who are you?"

"What is your name?" the man asked.

Birk had to think for a moment. "Uh...Birk."

"Nice to meet you, Birk. My name is Michael. Michael Willard. Welcome to the resistance."

* * *

The passengers still aboard the Mystic were gathered on the forward observation deck. The blast doors had been opened, and the one-hundred-and-eighty-degree vista of outer space was once again available to all those present.

Along with the remaining passengers were the members of the Mystic's crew who were not busy preparing the ship for her journey to join the Aurora and Glendanon at their new location. The members of the Mystic's crew who were unable to attend, as well as the wounded still being cared for in the ship's sick bay, would hear what was said via the intercoms and public announcement speakers located throughout the ship.

Around the perimeter of the observation deck stood at least two dozen Ghatazhak, their weapons slung behind them so as not to appear too intimidating, despite their aggressive-looking body armor and tactical helmets. Their presence insured not only the security of the people gathered, but also reminded them of the level of training and commitment the Ghatazhak brought to Nathan's cause.

As if to further impress those in attendance, two Reapers, eight Super Eagles, and eight Takaran fighters flew in formation on either side and slightly ahead of the Mystic, in plain view from the forward observation deck.

Nathan stood at the starboard entrance, thinking about what he would say. It had been years since he had given such a speech. Asking someone to put their life at risk, even for their home, or for the homes of others, was always a difficult thing to do.

"Captain?" Corporal Rossi said.

Nathan turned to look at the Ghatazhak corporal. "I've patched this comm-set into the ship's intercoms and public address system. You'll be heard throughout the ship." He told Nathan.

"Thank you, Corporal," Nathan said, taking the device from the soldier. He studied the comm-set for a moment, then put it on his head and adjusted the tiny wire that ran down from the earpiece to pick up his voice.

"Do you have any idea what you're going to say?" Vladimir asked, walking up from behind Nathan.

"Vlad," Nathan said with relief, happy to see his friend again. "Thanks for taking care of my ship," he said, shaking his friend's hand. "And for bringing the cavalry."

"My pleasure," Vladimir replied. "But let's not make a habit of it."

"I'll try."

"So, have you?"

"Thought about what to say? Not really."

"Do not worry," Vladimir told him. "Just wing it. It's what you do best, my friend."

Nathan smiled, patting his friend on the shoulder before turning and heading out onto the observation deck.

"Officer on deck!" the nearest Ghatazhak barked as Nathan entered the massive compartment. All around the observation deck, the Ghatazhak snapped to attention in unison, armor slapping together in their distinct sound.

The sound instantly attracted the attention of everyone on the observation deck. They turned and watched as the young man dressed in a long, slightly damaged, black coat, with brown hair that desperately needed proper trimming, and a sling and restraint around his left arm, walked out into the middle of the group of people.

Nathan worked his way through the crowd, moving to the front of the observation deck, turning to stand dead center in the massive forward windows.

As he took his position in front of the observation deck, it occurred to him that he could not have selected a more impressive backdrop. He climbed up onto a small ledge intended to keep passengers at a safe distance from the windows themselves, elevating himself to be seen by all.

Nathan took a deep breath, and began. "Twenty days ago, forces of what we believe to be a rogue caste of the Jung Empire, known as the Dusahn, attacked and seized control of all the systems within the Pentaurus cluster, including the Darvano and Takar systems. The entire Takaran fleet, as well as the Avendahl, were completely destroyed."

Nathan paused as the audience gasped in disbelief at the news. Before the murmurs had a chance to build, he continued, raising his voice to be heard over them. "In the days that followed, the Dusahn seized numerous jump-capable ships and rounded up the families of the captains of ships that had not reported in, including the family of Captain Rainey, the captain of this very ship. The Dusahn have killed hundreds of thousands of people on both Takara and Corinair, have glassed the entire surface of Ybara for failing to pay respect to the Dusahn leader, and have destroyed the entire population of the planet Burgess, in the Sherma system, simply because the men you see here today were living on that world."

The people had quieted down, allowing Nathan to lower his voice once again. "Some of you may recognize the uniforms of the men here with me. For those who do not, they are the Ghatazhak. There are only a few hundred of them left, yet they have pledged their lives, just as I have, to defeating the Dusahn, and liberating the people of the Pentaurus sector. We are a small force, with only a handful of ships, but we will grow. We will put word out to all the worlds of the Pentaurus sector, and to the worlds of all the sectors that surround her. Ships will join us. Men and women will join us. I know not how long the battle will take, nor how many lives it will cost, but I promise you this... These men, and their brethren, the crews of our ships, and myself, will fight to our last breath. We will defeat the Dusahn, or we will die trying."

Nathan paced over to the left as he spoke. "The Dusahn will try to convince you that life under their rule will be prosperous, and that all who serve them will be rewarded. But the Dusahn exist for one reason, and one reason only... To conquer all that they see. They are merciless in their desire for power, and they make Caius look like a saint. Believe me, I know. Because my name is Nathan Scott."

The murmuring grew louder as people began to examine the young man more closely, noticing the resemblance to the videos they had seen years ago. But that man had died at the hands of the Jung, after surrendering himself so that countless other worlds might live.

"Together, we defeated Caius, and together, we shall defeat the Dusahn. But to do so, we must build a fleet, not just of warships, but of ships to support them. To support the men and women who serve on them, and the families whom they dare not leave behind on worlds that might be 'cleansed' by the Dusahn as punishment for sins never committed. Ships like the Mystic Empress, who *these* men just rescued from pirates who would turn her over to the Dusahn for the reward."

Nathan began walking back in the opposite direction as he continued to talk. The mutterings of disbelief about his identity had seemingly vanished, and all eyes were transfixed on the one they knew as Na-Tan.

"Captain Rainey has met the challenge, and has pledged this ship to our cause. But he has done so on the condition that every person serving aboard her must choose whether or not to follow him. And I am to give each of you that choice, as well. Join us, and we will make use of your skills. If not, we will send you back to your homeworlds, and we will wish you the best of luck under Dusahn rule."

"*How do we know you're telling the truth?*" someone shouted.

"You don't. I can show you vids of the attacks, and of the glassing of Ybara. Vids by the news agencies of your own worlds, in fact. But such vids are easily forged and would prove nothing. The only way you can know for sure, is to return to your homeworld and see for yourself. But if you do, you will be giving up your one chance to make a difference, your one chance to stand up and fight, and quite possibly, your one chance to be free."

Nathan stood there a moment, looking down at all their faces. Men, women, young and old alike, stared back at him and at each other, no doubt wondering who would stay, and who would run away.

"This ship will depart shortly, to rendezvous with the Aurora and the fleet."

More murmurs rose from the crowd at the name of the Aurora.

"Those who wish to join us, report to your cabins, and you will be contacted en route. Those who wish to return to your homeworlds, report to the midship escape pods."

Nathan felt like there was more to say. He felt as if he should offer them something more inspirational, or say a blessing by whatever god they worshiped. But the truth was, he had little else to say. The facts, such as they were, had been laid out in enough detail for anyone to decide for themselves what they wanted to do with their lives from this point forward.

He only hoped that enough of them would choose to stay.

* * *

"You asked to see me?" Nathan said to Jessica as he entered the Mystic's security office. When he stepped inside, he noticed a young man sitting in the corner of the office.

"Nathan Scott, this is Terig Espan," Jessica introduced him. "He and his wife were the ones on the bridge during the takedown. Sigmund threatened to kill them if Captain Rainey didn't unlock the jump drive."

"I had no idea," Nathan replied. "Are you alright? How is your wife?"

"I am fine, thank you. We are both fine. She is sleeping in our cabin," Terig explained. "The doctor gave her a sedative. She will be asleep for hours."

"What can I do for you?" Nathan asked in as sincere a tone as he could manage.

"Actually, I thought I might be able to do something for you," Terig said.

Nathan took a seat on the edge of the desk, listening.

"I work for House Mahtize, on Takara. I am a communications security specialist, for their residence in Answari, the capital city."

"Yes, I'm familiar with Answari," Nathan replied.

"Yes, I'm sure you are."

"How might you be of help to us?"

"Lord Mahtize is the chair of the Council of Nobles. If the Dusahn have taken control of Takara, they will need the nobles to keep the economies and industries of the Pentaurus cluster running smoothly. They will *need* Lord Mahtize."

Nathan looked at Jessica.

"He would hear every communication that took place," Jessica said.

"Part of my job is to maintain the digital recordings of all communications, even those that are face-to-face. Lord Mahtize records *everything*, even private conversations, then has them transcribed as well. It *all* goes through my department."

"He *could* be a great source of intel," Jessica surmised.

Nathan looked at Terig. "Do you realize the risk you'd be taking?"

"I believe so, yes."

"I'm not sure you do. The man who threatened to kill you? Siggy? He's a puppy compared to the Dusahn."

"A puppy?" Terig wondered, unfamiliar with the word.

"If they discover that you're a spy, they will torture you, and extract information from your mind using nanites. And then, when they are certain you have nothing left to give, they will either kill you outright, or send you somewhere to live out what's left of your life as slave labor. And your wife? She will likely become someone's *personal* slave, if you get my drift."

"Nathan, don't you think you're pouring it on a bit thick?" Jessica objected.

"No, I don't," Nathan argued. "If anything, I'm holding back." He looked at Terig again. "I appreciate what you are offering, Mister Espan, and I agree with Lieutenant Nash here. You would certainly be a valuable source of information. I just want you to be well aware of the risks you are taking. Such activity is highly dangerous for *trained* special operatives. For someone like you, it is practically suicide."

"I *want* to help," Terig pleaded. "I am not a soldier. I've never even *held* a gun. But I know these systems. I know how to hide data, and how to conceal that the data has been copied or transmitted. I believe I am what your people call, 'a hacker?'"

"Actually, we call them digi-spooks," Jessica corrected.

"Yes, yes. That's me. A digi-spook."

"How does your wife feel about this?"

"I have not told her."

"Well, at least you got that part right," Jessica commented.

"Are you okay with *not* telling her?" Nathan asked. "I mean, *never* telling her; not even if we win. The three of us would be the only ones who would ever know what you were doing... *Ever.*"

"I'm okay with that. Believe me, I can do this," Terig insisted. "Please, let me. I really *want* to help."

Nathan looked at Jessica. "What do you think?"

"Well, it sounds like he has the smarts for it," Jessica said. "And since this ship left before the invasion, it's highly unlikely that he's a Dusahn spy."

"But not certain," Nathan commented.

"How could I possibly be a Dusahn spy?" Terig protested. "I had never even heard of them until your speech."

"There will be little time to train you," Nathan warned. "We're jumping in less than an hour."

"All he really needs to know at this point is what kind of info we're looking for, and how to relay the data to us," Jessica explained. "I can teach him that in less than an hour."

"I am a fast learner," Terig assured them.

Nathan sighed, still looking at the young man. "Why do you want to do this, Terig?"

"Like I said, I want to help. This is how I can help the best."

"Very well," Nathan said. "We'll see how it goes." Nathan reached out to shake the young man's hand. "It's a brave thing you're volunteering to do, Mister Espan. Brave and stupid, but that's usually how it works."

"Thank you," Terig replied, shaking Nathan's hand. "I think."

* * *

Nathan climbed up the ladder into the Seiiki's cockpit. As expected, Vladimir was sitting at the auxiliary station, and Josh and Loki were in the pilot and copilot stations. "We ready to break hard dock?" he asked as he stepped up behind them.

"The Mystic has already given us the green light," Loki reported. "Captain Rainey is on the line for you now."

Nathan tapped his comm-set. "Captain Rainey, Captain Scott. How are you doing?"

"*Our jump drive is up and ready, Captain.*"

"I trust you won't have any trouble with Mister Sheehan's algorithm?" Nathan asked.

"*I don't expect so,*" Captain Rainey replied over the comms. "*He explained it quite well to our pilots. We should catch up to the fleet in just under thirty-two Takaran hours.*"

"I wish I could ride home with you, Captain," Nathan said. "But I'm afraid I have another assignment waiting for me."

"*I understand,*" Captain Rainey replied. "*I'll keep a seat open at my table for you, whenever you've got the time.*"

"Thank you, Captain. I look forward to it."

"*Thank you,*" Captain Rainey said emphatically. "*For everything...especially the escorts.*"

"My pleasure."

"*Oh, and Captain Scott, I thought you might like to know that none of my crew chose to depart, and only fifteen of the passengers opted to return home.*"

"That's good to hear, Captain. Safe travels. Seiiki, out." Nathan turned to see Jessica coming up the ladder behind him and stepped to the side to make room for her in the cramped confines of the Seiiki's cockpit.

"We may need a bigger cockpit," Vladimir said as Jessica squeezed in between him and Nathan.

"Or a bigger ship," Jessica suggested.

"Take us back to the Aurora, Josh," Nathan instructed, smiling. "We've got a lot more work to do."

Thank you for reading this story.
(*A review would be greatly appreciated!*)

COMING SOON

Episode 5
of
The Frontiers Saga:
Rogue Castes

Visit us online at
frontierssaga.com
or on Facebook

Want to be notified when
new episodes are published?
Join our mailing list!
frontierssaga.com/mailinglist